CHAIN ME

THE ELLIE GRAY CHRONICLES BOOK 2

LANA SKY

Chain Me

Chain Me By Lana Sky

Copyright © 2019 by Lana Sky
All rights reserved.
No part of this publication may be reproduced, distributed, or transmitted
in any form or by any means, including photocopying, recording, or other
electronic or mechanical methods, without the prior written permission of
the author.
This is a work of fiction. Names, characters, businesses, places, events and
incidents are either the products of the author's imagination or used in a
fictitious manner. Any resemblance to actual persons, living or dead, or
actual events is purely coincidental.

Cover design by Sarah Hansen, Okay Creations
Edited by Mickey Reed
Proofread by Charity Chimni
Formatting by Charity Chimni

ISBN: 978-1-956608-02-1

*To my very patient fans. Thank you so much for believing in
this story and allowing me the time to write it.*

"And at all at once, I was consumed; a darkness borne of blood and torment, laid bare at the feet of the Storm."

—A.R. Simone

D.H.

I may have been the heir to one of the richest families in the country, but alas, our vast fortune couldn't buy me *everything*.

Love was beyond the reach of my checkbook—though affection had never been synonymous with the Gray name anyway. Sanity was another elusive trophy, and the past year had served as a biting testament to how little I had left.

But my millions couldn't procure *answers*. Especially the ones pertaining to the brooding vampire who had destroyed my life on a whim and then disappeared.

What else did a bored heiress with too much time and money on her hands have to do with her days besides track him down?

Nothing—*apart* from blatantly lying to the doctor standing in my way, of course.

"Do you think you can help me?" I meekly asked the woman seated across from me. A polished oak desk separated us, the most eye-catching fixture of her rather plain office.

"Good news! I don't think you're dying, Eleanor," Dr. Goodfellow declared. A severe bun kept the graying brown hair back from her round face, enhancing her stern "trust me" expression. If I squinted, her concern almost seemed genuine. "However, I'm glad you dropped by, because I do have some mild concerns. I think another round of tests would help to put us both at ease."

"More tests? Are you sure? I think I'm feeling a lot better, actually—" A cough ripped from my throat, and I attempted to smother it within the sleeve of my sweater. "I feel fine."

"Th-That may be so, dear," Goodfellow stammered. Her gaze settled over my chest, her blue eyes suspiciously narrowed. "But I'm concerned. Your lab results have been… puzzling, to say the least. For instance, your hormone levels seem to be spiking, but since you wrote"—she shuffled a stack of documents before her and scanned the topmost page—"*never* in answer to *could you currently be pregnant?*, well… I must admit that I'm flummoxed. I've even consulted some outside experts for insight. I wish I could get my hands on your old records, but it seems there was a mishap because your file for last year appears to be incomplete…"

She paused as if waiting for me to clarify. Where oh where could a year of my medical history have gone? I knew the answer of course. Into a vampire's coat pocket.

It wasn't an explanation Goodfellow could comprehend, however. When I said nothing, she cleared her throat. "Well, it's only been a month since you were last cleared by your last provider, Dr. Wallis, hasn't it?"

I shrugged. The last time I'd seen Dr. Wallis had been a mere month after the vampire pulling his puppet strings disappeared. He had eyed me the way one might a ghost before promptly refunding my health insurance for every penny spent on the treatment for my supposed illness.

Then he too vanished.

"Is he still in Tahiti?" I wondered, parroting the reason his office secretary gave for his absence.

"Tahiti?" Dr. Goodfellow blinked and adjusted her wire-rimmed glasses. "I'm not sure, dear. But you can rest assured that, even with the gaps in your history, I can address your concerns—"

"I'm fine." I even flashed a charming grin for emphasis. "I don't think more tests are necessary."

"Oh? Over the phone, you said you've been feeling poorly for weeks. Isn't that why you made the appointment? Frankly, I wish you had been more specific, and I would have booked you an emergency consult." She wrinkled her delicate nose in distaste. "That sort of cough is no minor symptom, my dear—"

"It's nothing." I shrugged as my fingers toyed with the silver cross hanging from my throat. Little did the good doctor know that, as long as I wore it, I supposedly was the picture of health. Or so a deceitful vampire claimed. Batting the talisman aside, I tried to look as un-sickly as possible. Another unforced cough didn't help much in that regard. "Do you have a diagnosis yet?"

"It could be fatigue," she said. "But your case has puzzled me. Your symptoms don't seem to fit into any logical diagnostic criteria—"

"So you're saying I'm fatigued?" I sighed to hide my skepticism. Compared to my last life-shattering diagnosis, what a boring ailment.

Thankfully, Goodfellow was right; my health wasn't the real reason for this visit anyway.

"This is quite the premier establishment," I blurted out, eyeing the diploma framed in gold, hanging on the white wall behind her head. "I'm sure you have people of high esteem on the board?"

I knew firsthand that it *did*. Stationed right in the heart of downtown, St. Mary's was one of the leading medical facilities in the country, prestigious enough to attract backing from a variety of benefactors.

The undead kind in search of a power trip, for instance. The kind of man who liked to disappear without so much as a word or a *"Thanks for your virginity, Eleanor. Oh, and your blood, too. Have a nice life!"*

Such a creature would relish the influence this hospital could provide—it was the perfect place to hide in plain sight.

"Ms. Gray?" Dr. Goodfellow had an eyebrow raised, her tone delicate in that annoying way when someone tended to stare off into space for uncomfortable periods of time. A tone I had grown accustomed to.

"R-Right." I snapped out of my daze and cleared my throat. "As you well know, my family has a long history of providing donations to hospitals and charities alike. I would love to do my part to contribute, by any means necessary. Perhaps I could be introduced to the board?"

"Of course!" Dr. Goodfellow couldn't even disguise the greedy twitch of her lips. Suddenly, all concern for my welfare vanished. "We welcome any form of donation. I would be happy to connect you to our Community Outreach Department—"

"Actually, I've already done my research. Here." I fished a brochure from my purse. Its dog-eared pages betrayed how many times I'd peered through them in anticipation of this meeting. One in particular sported a tear right down the middle, suspiciously close to a mysterious name.

"I found a roster of your most recent benefactors, and I'd love to ask them some further questions before I invest. I'm familiar with most, but this person…" I pointed a trembling finger to one entry in particular. Initials, really.

Squinting, Dr. Goodfellow read them out loud. "D.H.?" She seemed oblivious to the shudder that racked my spine. I had to clench my hands into fists to keep them from shaking, crumpling the brochure further. "I'm not familiar with that person, to be honest, Eleanor. But we really should discuss your treatment options. I'll be blunter: Going off your recent results, I found some of your labs a tad alarming. We should schedule an immediate follow-up."

"I don't think that's necessary." Another cough rattled from my chest as I pushed the brochure into my purse. Disappointment was surprisingly hard to swallow down.

My gagging prompted Dr. Goodfellow to shove a napkin into my hands. This time, my coughing fit succeeded in bringing up liquid, which I spit into a nearby wastebasket. Snot, perhaps.

Red, vibrant snot.

"Eleanor…" The doctor's gaze was fixated on whatever substance clung to the tissue. "I really do think we should run a few more tests—"

"So, you don't know that name?" I pressed, impatiently wringing my hands. "What a shame. I thought he might provide a unique perspective on the establishment."

"He?" Goodfellow cocked her head. "Do you know this person? I was under the impression that you didn't."

"Um…" I blinked and coughed again. "I'm sorry, what?"

"You said *he* might provide a unique perspective—"

"Did I? Um, anyway, as you were saying… My symptoms. Are you sure you'll be able to find a diagnosis soon?"

"Of course." She nodded emphatically. "As you yourself mentioned, we are a state-of-the-art facility, Ms. Gray. You can rest easy under our care. I'm glad that you came in when you did."

For all the good it had done. The poor woman didn't even have enough sense to transfer my case to a psychiatrist. Or perhaps a priest would have been more fitting in this instance?

Someone used to dealing with the damned and hopeless.

Still, I attempted to return her smile with a thin grin of my own. "Let's hope it's nothing serious."

"Oh, let's not jump to the worst just yet. However…" She snatched up my hand without warning, lifting it to display the quivering fingertips. "This tremor. It's more pronounced than when you first entered my office, and I see from your preliminaries that you've lost more weight. That cough is concerning as well, considering the color the sputum—"

"Color?" I echoed innocently.

"It looked like blood, Eleanor." Her gentle smile slipped, revealing something far more unnerving underneath. Alarm. "I'm beginning to think that Dr. Wallis may have been a bit hasty in clearing you so soon. It's only been a month since your diagnosis was reversed, after all. I would like to order another blood test—"

"More?" I eyed my forearm where the sleeve of my sweater was rolled up to reveal a bandage—my souvenir from the last round of tests done earlier that morning. "I feel fine, honestly. I would hate to waste your time." I gingerly untangled my hand from hers and started to rise from the leather armchair facing her desk. "Thank you."

"Of course, my dear. We can use your sample from this morning for the new tests. I'll make sure to call you with the results." She folded her hands together. "Now, you should go home and get some rest. I'm sure we'll have an answer for you by the end of the week. In the meantime, keep your chin up."

Her smile widened.

But I merely stooped for my bag and scrambled from her office before she could suggest another battery of tests to suffer through.

My disappointment loomed, inescapable. Even the sky visible beyond the windows of the corridor seemed to reflect it: dark, churning clouds and a smattering of raindrops.

What a fuss for nothing. Though the poking and prodding should have been a small price to pay if my hunch turned out to be correct. *Small,* I insisted as my hands shook over the handle of my bag. Though Goodfellow didn't need to try so hard to feign concern. Apart from my brain, nothing else was wrong with me.

Physically, at least.

For the first time in years, I theoretically had a clean bill of health.

No life-threatening illness to worry about.

No vampire lurking in the corridor to smuggle me his magic blood.

No crippling, fearful uncertainty, no siree…

I was *fine*.

"Are you all right, hun?" someone asked as I made my way to the nearest elevator. A woman, her gaze on my shaking fingertips. A tiny figure clung to her hip, clutching a ratty doll that had seen better days. Paces away a man eyed a wristwatch and sighed impatiently, but as his gaze shifted to the woman before me, all traces of impatience faded from his expression.

"Do you need to sit down?" the woman asked.

For someone so nosy, she should have been older. A gnarled biddy with nothing better to do than butt her nose into other's affairs. But she was young—my age, if I wanted to be generous. A healthy woman who didn't sport blood dripping down her chin and wasn't trembling on her feet. Someone who possessed a family, and security, and all of those pesky things my money couldn't afford.

Someone who seemed conjured by the universe as if to spite me with an eternal truth: *you're alone, Eleanor. You're probably dying, Eleanor. Stop pining over him, Eleanor.*

"I'm fine," I replied with a smile, though the small family didn't seem convinced. The child stuck her head out from around her mother to gape at me, her tiny eyebrow raised.

Who cared? I was past letting strangers comment on my health.

Once I had made it to the front of the hospital and climbed into the back seat of my family's Rolls-Royce, I closed my eyes—only to be thwarted again in my quest for peace.

"How did it go, miss?" my driver inquired.

I peeled one eye open, observing him with a frown. He was a new hire who had come highly recommended. To most, he probably ticked all of the right boxes—overly friendly, sufficiently charming. He was even pretty for a man, with dark, curly hair and eyes the color of chocolate.

I only *slightly* hated him—he wasn't Harper, my long-time confidant and friend. But Harper was probably dead, so this man would have to do.

"It went fine," I replied, closing my eyes again. "I'd like to rest, if that's all right."

As requested, the rest of the journey to the house passed in silence, broken only by the crunch of gravel as the vehicle turned onto the driveway. I startled to awareness, taking in the desolate landscape awaiting me beyond the window with a strange sense of guilt.

I had some damn nerve peddling my money and my resources to hospitals rather than spending it on the only thing my parents had ever deemed important: our supposed legacy. After months of neglect, Gray Manor had certainly seen better days. The house itself loomed above acres of untouched fields and overgrown weeds, as imposing as ever.

Spring had blossomed over the rest of the city, but my familiar home was a landscape clinging to winter. Perhaps it hadn't been a prudent decision to fire most of the gardening staff on a whim?

Make that *all* of the gardening staff.

At least the lack of salaries kept the family fortune intact; Mother would certainly thank me for that.

"Have a nice day, miss," the driver encouraged as I slipped from the car.

Even though he'd been under my employ for nearly a month, I had yet to learn his name—though it didn't matter.

I would fire him eventually. Once I got over my fear of driving, that is. I'd fired everyone else.

There was no butler to greet me as I hastened up the front walkway and mounted the topmost step of the front stoop. I had to fish a key from the depths of my handbag and fit it into the lock myself—a fact that would have scandalized my poor parents. To get the solid oak door to budge, I had to basically throw myself against it.

Maybe firing the handyman hadn't been too smart an idea, either?

A minor inconvenience. One couldn't put a price tag on silence—and I had the lion's share as I wandered the deserted foyer. Cold, drafty desolation lingered between the wooden floors and the cavernous ceiling despite the sweltering heat outside.

Home sweet home.

My breath painted the air white, but there was no one around to adjust the heating system, and I didn't know how. Perhaps Georgie—my estranged sister who belonged to a secret society of vampire hunters—did, though it wasn't like I could ask her.

Screaming *Get the hell out!* at everyone around you tended to have that desired effect. They scattered, no arguments. No desperate pleas to stay.

It was like magic, screaming—and I refused to regret the action one damn bit. Why, when I could strip my coat and leave it right there at the foot of the staircase with no one to stare?

No one to judge, or nag, or patronize.

When I crept into my room, there was no maid to snipe about my rumpled bedsheets or to sigh in pity as I crawled onto the mattress and buried my head beneath the covers. There was no one to witness the shiver that ran down my spine as my stomach contracted. There was no doting chef to care that I hadn't eaten a solid meal in nearly two weeks, despite a ravenous hunger that plagued me almost as violently as a near-persistent bout of nausea.

Nothing was wrong with me.

Nothing but the invisible creature ripping my insides apart, contorting my body in agony.

I barely managed to clear my head from the mattress before copious amounts of liquid expelled from my throat and pooled on the floor. Then I turned into the safety of my pillow, but squeezing my eyes shut didn't erase the image of it. Thick. *Red.*

No bother. I already knew the CliffsNotes version of what was transpiring. I was *maybe* dying again. My body was collapsing upon itself, *yada yada yada*. The doctor's diagnosis would soon confirm it, and then I could commence with the drafting of a will and whatnot.

I'd done it all before, so no harm no foul. Only something told me that a mysterious benefactor wouldn't step from the shadows to offer a solution this time. He had every reason to want me dead, after all, considering I owned ten years' worth of his soul…

I was on my own—a fact that didn't make much of a damn difference in the grand scheme.

I was Eleanor Gray. The only thing on Earth I excelled at was being alone.

At least there was one person who wouldn't leave me just because I demanded it. Well, a *creature*, but he's no less valid. Mr. Tinkles, my dearest Siamese rescue cat, served as the second-to-last living creature dwelling within Gray Manor.

The fact that he only had three limbs might have contributed to why he remained behind at all, but that was beside the point.

The moment I opened the door to his suite, he lunged from the shadows, claws drawn in his typical greeting. A bell hanging from his collar—a custom light-blue velvet one with sterling-silver hardware—jiggled manically, tracking his advance. He lunged toward me, his eyes flashing with murderous intent. By sheer luck, the back wheels of his makeshift wheelchair caught on a bump in the carpet, and I jerked out of range unscathed.

Until the room began spinning.

My stomach crawled up my throat as the wallpaper bled into the carpet. White on red, like fresh blood on pale flesh. Gagging, I slumped forward, and I had only enough time to aim opposite the direction of my cat before I ruined a priceless antique carpet with a stream of vomit. Quite the feat, considering I had nothing left in my stomach to bring up. Just more of that unsettling liquid. Red and vibrant, the puddle resisted cleaning no matter how hard I tried to mop up the mess with the end of my skirt.

It wasn't like I needed a maid. I didn't…

Luckily, I didn't need to guard from Tinkles, either. The blatant destruction of his private suite startled the poor darling into ceasing his attack. Eyes wide, he slunk toward his favorite corner. A haughty meow came a heartbeat later, demanding more food instead of my flesh for once. After I'd fulfilled his request, he watched me, swishing his tail through the air. Then he approached.

So much for his brief ceasefire. I tensed, throwing my hands out before me—but he didn't lunge. In fact, his hackles weren't even raised.

The moment he finally reached my side and curled up against my leg—*without* attacking—I knew then and there that something was horribly, terribly wrong.

Fear so raw that it packed a punch rendered me spineless. I sank to my knees, curling up against the invaluable carpet. And my devious, hateful feline didn't hiss at me once. In fact, I swore I felt the silken brush of his fur settling right against my abdomen.

Hours later, I escaped into the bath and made a game out of ignoring the multitude of changes I hadn't reported to the good doctor Goodfellow.

Because they didn't matter.

Like how pale my skin had become: tissue paper over the bluish veins snaking underneath, carrying my newly "healed" blood. Brittle bones stood out like exposed scaffolding, propping up my gaunt features.

One symptom, however, triggered the most alarm. It was a feeling lurking beneath the water's surface and infecting my skin. Itching. In my muscles. In my bones. Food didn't soothe the irritation. Water, either. It felt deeper.

Perhaps the manifestation of some festering tumor?

Oh joy.

Looking on the bright side, I toweled off and hunched beneath a terrycloth robe. Why all the worry? I had no terminal diagnosis.

In fact, I was supposedly cured, thanks to a vampire who gave me his magic necklace. I eyed the jewelry in question, holding it up for inspection. Some women might have cherished the expertly crafted silver cross. If I squinted, I could have called it beautiful.

Or hideous. It didn't suit me, standing out gaudily as I approached the mirror and tried to salvage my appearance.

If my health continued to decline, at least I already looked the part: dead. My frown was the liveliest thing about me. It remained as I ran a brush through my hair and dressed in an old skirt and a sweater. In the end, I put the sweater on backward and only had enough energy to sweep the worst tangles back from my face before my stomach roiled again.

The Eleanor from yesterday would have written the symptom off. *At least it wasn't hemorrhaging to death, no bother.*

But now… The little detail of my vomit seemed harder to ignore. Remnants of it still speckled the corner of my mouth. Red. Salty. When I swiped at a smear with my thumb, the liquid spread, painting my cheek.

Dr. Goodfellow had noticed it too—a fact that suggested I *wasn't* making it up out of paranoia. Perhaps another scenario, other than a psychotic break, could explain the past few weeks?

Like the prospect that, despite his sudden disappearance, Dublin Helos wasn't done with me yet.

Had he stooped to poisoning me again?

Or perhaps a more nefarious ailment to drive me insane for good?

Anything to retrieve the one thing of value I had that might interest him: his contract. He was most likely stalking me from some unseen hiding place, waiting for the chance to pounce. In the meantime, he settled for gloating from afar. *Ignoring* me.

Well, I would give him something to ignore.

Upon returning to my room, I collapsed onto the chair before my desk. Countless brochures littered the surface, and they fell to the floor as I swiped them aside. Some contained the donor lists of city-owned buildings. Others were political donation rosters. Some pertained to the boards of other area hospitals.

I had scoured them all for even a hint of one name. One mysterious benefactor with a fetish for the dramatic.

Again, my fingers caressed the cross hanging from my throat. The moment he'd given it to me replayed in my mind almost daily.

"Wear it," he'd insisted. *"Take it off and you'll die."*

Despite the warning, I had considered doing just that. I'd even *tried* to in the days after he'd left. But something always held me back. Stupidity, most likely. Or maybe pride?

Resisting him was what the pathetic, old Eleanor had done, and look where that had gotten her.

Though look what the opposite had gotten me, current-day Eleanor.

The same damn thing—loneliness.

Dejected, I watched my hand fall onto my lap. Then I wrenched a drawer open and fished out a page of stationery and a pen from inside it. The moment I pressed the nib to the paper, an odd flash of déjà vu made my hand tremble, which made ink splatter onto the page.

I envisioned a painfully handsome man with the face of an angel, his voice cruel as he dished out his trademark proposal.

"Live or die, Eleanor?"

How naïve I'd been back then. After all, there'd never been a choice. Just a game, but this time, I vowed to make my own rules—even if I had to scribble them hastily in black ink.

I never fell for it, you know. I never believed that you could actually want me. I never did…

When I finished writing, I folded the page and attempted to stick it into an envelope. I would never send it, of course.

I had *some* damn sense of modesty. It was the mere thought of it that mattered: shoving all of my pathetic fears regarding him into a small space and sealing it with a flick of a finger.

"Damn!" Faint heat prickled the pad of my thumb and I popped the digit into my mouth, though I barely felt the sting. Just…

Hunger.

My teeth bored down on their own accord, extending the bitter flavor coating my tongue. I must have grazed my hand over something without realizing it. Something that didn't make my stomach rebel in disgust. Instead, it triggered a thought that blotted out all others.

I need more.

I scanned the surface of the desk as I sucked, hunting for whatever substance I might be tasting. Solid oak. Paper. Black ink.

Red droplets on white parchment.

Light flickered over the domed surfaces while my brain finally connected the taste with sight.

Oh god! I wrenched my thumb from my mouth and lurched from the chair. Too fast. My hand flew out, grasping for the edge of the desk, but I missed. Both legs gave way, pitching me onto my knees. My stomach lurched at the pain. Demanding, sharp, pinching cramps…

Food. That would fix it. All I needed was a meal.

I considered bread, or a salad, or whatever might be lurking in the pantry down below, and I'd barely made it onto my hands and knees before my stomach roiled again. There was no hiding from what came up this time. Crimson painted my fingertips, caught beneath the spray, tainting my touch. Still gagging, I snatched the finished letter from my desk, hauled myself upright, and staggered toward the door.

Modesty was for healthy people.

Sane people.

And I was well beyond both states of being.

My new driver asked way too many damn questions. *"Did you cut yourself, miss? You know this place is deserted, right? Are you sure this is the right address?"*

To compound my irritation, I didn't even know his name. As he opened the door on my end, I asked him purely out of spite.

"François," he blurted after a moment's pause. His wide-eyed expression probably had something to do with the red liquid drying over the corner of my mouth. And my hands.

Rather than explain myself, I shoved the door open farther and pushed past him to mount the curb. A scorching sun cast the property in an uncharacteristically bright light. Spring was waning and warm weather had rudely invaded. Those who passed by were wearing vibrant sundresses and short-sleeved ensembles in pastel pinks and dreamy hues.

On the other hand, *I* was wearing a thick skirt. And a sweater. And an overcoat.

The layers were in vain—I was shivering anyway.

Perhaps my inner emotions were projecting outside? Though, in that case, I should have felt nothing. Numb was the word *du jour* as I pondered the hollowed-out shell of a building before me.

It had been a bustling cathedral only a few short weeks ago. Now, a sign nailed to the grand entrance claimed it *closed for renovations*. How subtle.

If only its worshippers knew what had taken place within this supposedly holy space, just beyond the beautiful façade of stained-glass windows.

God didn't live here alone—that was for sure. Or at least, that used to be the case. Even now, the back of my neck prickled, but a paranoid glance over my shoulder revealed no one in sight. After a moment's hesitation, I crouched and finally slid my bloodied letter beneath the door.

There. Whether anyone actually read it or not didn't matter. I'd made an attempt to have the last word.

The last laugh.

Nonetheless, I returned to the car knowing that it was a fool's errand—but how else did you reach someone who didn't want to be found?

You shouted into the void, of course.

And only silence answered back.

FORTUNE FAVORS THE GRAY

No mysterious visitor appeared to darken my doorstep the next morning. No parcel arrived, stuffed into the mailbox. Either I was losing my touch when it came to dramatic gestures or blood-soaked letters didn't pack the same punch of urgency they used to. Almost as if…

Well, almost as if Dublin Helos *wasn't* lurking in the shadows, watching me.

At least one person did seem interested in my welfare, considering they called almost daily, leaving a message each time.

"Ms. Gray, this is doctor Goodfellow. I am still waiting to hear from some experts in the field about your case. I hope to have an answer soon…"

"Ms. Gray, I've received the results of your last blood test. We should schedule another appointment immediately…"

"Ms. Gray, doctor Goodfellow again. I must ask if you are a government official or in possession of some kind of high-level security clearance, because accessing an opinion on your case at all seems to involve an unusual number of hurdles..."

Dublin Helos had left a void in my life that even one of the best doctors in the country couldn't fill—and he refused to offer any explanation as to why. But I didn't scream, or cry, or fall into hysterics at the possibility of being ignored. Instead, as any uncaring socialite would, I simply wrote him three more letters, each one colder than the last. Four more. What they said didn't matter, just what they symbolized. Nagging. Desperation. Taunting.

I never needed you.

I never wanted you.

I don't dream of you. Every night. I don't imagine slapping you. Punching you. Hating you.

I don't think of you.

Meaningless words. No matter what, he wouldn't have the last say. I would drown him in parchment if I had to. Anything to prove I had already caught on to his little game.

Because I'd come to the conclusion that he was trying to kill me again. How dreadfully uninspired.

I barely had the energy to care. Oh, no, Dublin didn't consume my sole attention. I was much too busy tending my household. There were sheets to change. Puddles to mop. Floors to wear down by pacing circles over them. Most of the time I spent pacing in Mr. Tinkle's room, muttering to him as he watched from his corner.

"It doesn't matter," I insisted, my hands clenched at my sides as I stormed across the Persian carpet. "It doesn't. I mean, even if he is that stupid D.H. donor, I don't care if he ever shows up at all. All he'd want is that stupid book, anyway. Right?"

My cat flicked his tail lazily through the air and blinked.

"Exactly!" Groaning, I paced faster, swaying as my stomach roiled with every erratic movement. "I mean it's not like… It's not like we were a real…" I gritted my teeth rather than hiss the word *couple*. "It was a transaction. I knew that… I *know* that."

My future husband—should the universe decide not to make me a spinster—would be a creature far different from Dublin Helos. Some smug rich aristocrat who would fall hopelessly in love with my wallet. Together, we would suffer a bitter, stiff existence within Gray manor until the day he slipped too many sleeping pills into his nightly brandy.

It was the wholesome, ideal partnership my parents had modeled.

"It wasn't like I even liked him," I added, slowing to a stop. What woman would? Who would consider a man who looked like a pale Adonis attractive? Especially when he ran hot and cold. One minute he claimed to be only interested in money. The next, he had you pinned to a wall, demanding you submit yourself to him fully.

The memory stole into my thoughts, so potent it tore the breath from my lungs. His mouth on mine. His hands, ruthlessly grasping at parts of my body. Him inside me…

Shaking my head, I banished the images. "Who would want that?" I croaked, turning to Tinkles. He extended his tiny forelimbs into a laborious stretch and promptly darted deeper into his corner.

"I wouldn't," I whispered, watching him go. "I don't need anyone. I need… I need to get out of this house."

Every second spent within the ancient dwelling heightened a growing sense of paranoia. That I was being watched, followed and haunted, despite all evidence to the contrary. The walls themselves seemed to be hissing to me, a million admonishments. Secrets and lies.

This was all some elaborate trick, obviously. I wasn't *really* sick. These symptoms were designed to make me seek him out on my own, placing myself right in his trap. Because that's all he really wanted: revenge. Or, more specifically, payback of something more vital than money.

And he would never, ever find it—his precious contract secretly in my possession.

In retaliation, he wanted me panicked and desperate. Paranoia was his goal. Just like before he'd waltz right in with all the answers.

And I would be ready for him.

~

The following day, the phone in the old servant's alcove rang, breaking the monotony. I took my time answering it. Dr. Goodfellow was probably desperate to deliver another vague update as to my health status.

Sighing, I held the receiver to my ear, prepared to humor her. "I hope the test results came back conclusive this time—"

"Hello?" someone replied and I nearly dropped the handset in response. He was… Well, he was *male*. "May I speak to Ms. Gray?"

I held my breath, my fingers tightening over the rim of a nearby table as a single thought set in. *Not him.* I was still sane enough to know that much.

This caller wasn't an ageless figure with a musical baritone and a laugh like the devil. Considering I wasn't the type to get phone calls from strange men, there was only one explanation for this occurrence.

"I'm sorry," I stammered. "Georgie isn't here. However, I could take a message if you'd like." Though only God knew when she might receive it.

"I beg your pardon," the man replied. "But I'm looking for *Eleanor* Gray."

My eyes narrowed. "Why?" Rudeness, aside, it was a valid question. No one ever asked for me. Certainly not by name. Unless, of course, they had souls to buy and sell.

Or money for whoring themselves to an heiress.

"My name is Gabriel Lanic." His suave tone betrayed him as someone used to schmoozing with the upper class. "I'm the chairman of the board of directors at St. Mary's—"

"Oh, y-yes," I croaked, fighting to stamp the suspicion from my tone. "How can I help you?"

"I heard from one of our doctors that you were interested in becoming a core donor?"

Color me impressed; despite such a bold assumption, Mr. Gabriel Lanic managed to sound more charming than money hungry.

"Um, I was," I admitted. "To be honest, I was more interested in learning more about the board members—"

"I'm afraid that I wouldn't be able to divulge much out of respect for privacy."

"Oh, I see—"

"To the typical donor, anyway," he added, before my disappointment could solidify. "Frankly, Ms. Gray, your family name carries a prestige I cannot deny. While I may not be able to divulge much, no one could blame me if a few details managed to slip over dinner. How does eight o'clock sound?"

"D-Dinner?" I gagged at the thought of food, smelling it, seeing it. However, the promise of answers was more than enough to combat the nausea. For now. As long as Mr. Lanic proved my hunch once and for all, he could set a meeting wherever he damn well pleased. "That sounds fine. I mean, y-yes. I mean…"

"I hope you are partial to Italian. The Maria is excellent," he said.

Thick red sauce came to mind and I cringed at the imagery. Still, I managed to choke out, "Wonderful. See you there."

Four hours later, I left the house looking somewhat presentable. For the first time in days, I'd brushed my hair. I even put on a dress, a demure black one my mother had picked out, complete with a modest neckline. When I joined François in the Rolls, I almost felt…at ease?

My stomach was in knots during the quick trip into the city, but for an entirely different reason than usual. Excitement? Hope? Who knew. The only thing I was sure of, as the car pulled up before an exclusive restaurant downtown, was that if Mr. Lanic could give me the answer I wanted, then he could slap his name on Gray Manor for all I cared.

Two words. That's all he had to say. A name. Validation of my paranoid delusion. Evidence to out the man so proud of his own damn mystery that he'd never see me coming.

My blood hummed as I stepped from the car and approached the restaurant's gleaming front. A tendril of unease raced down my spine though I couldn't explain why. It was beyond breathtaking as far as venues went. Glass doors revealed a posh interior, but a man appeared to block my path before I could even make it inside. A professional black suit and tie separated him from the wealthy patrons mingling within the establishment behind him. Given how he cocked his head toward the earpiece tucked inconspicuously behind his ear, I suspected he had been sent to escort me personally.

"Ms. Gray, I presume?" he asked, proving my suspicion correct. "Your companion is waiting. May I show you to your table?"

I nodded, following him inside. A spacious lobby opened onto an intimate space beyond the main dining room with bold burgundy walls and polished floors. Such an obscene display of wealth. My mother would faint at the sight.

Mr. Lanic had gone all out in the hopes of impressing his prey—only one table had been set, strategically placed in the center of the room. No other patrons were dining nearby.

We were alone.

My chest tightened as I spotted the lone creature waiting for me in the center of the room. His back was to me, his build impressive. His hair…black? Not golden.

Disappointment fluttered through my chest as his voice reached back to me.

"Ms. Gray." He turned in a display of poise, flashing a gallant smile no vampire would ever be able to imitate. "I am Gabriel Lanic. Pleasure to meet you."

"Likewise," I croaked, regaining control of my senses.

So, he wasn't Dublin Helos, mysterious benefactor extraordinaire, though he rivaled him in charm. A warm smile offset his handsome Roman features. Dressed to the nines in a tailored gray suit, he didn't seem like the type who'd sold his soul for money and prestige, either. I sensed no air of ice, and the hand he extended for me to shake was warm.

As far as my past year was concerned, he was a rare entity—a handsome, rich *human*.

"Care to join me?" He nodded toward the table.

Silently, I took the seat across from him, and he offered me a business card laden with his personal information.

"Shall we begin?" He'd come prepared, apparently, armed with enough history on the hospital and its various charity enterprises to charm a room full of donors into emptying their pockets. Never once did he mention trading in souls or the like. Instead, he listed target figures and waxed ad nauseam as to the reputation of my family.

So generous we were.

So honorable.

Lies, but delivered so expertly I almost believed them.

"I would be more than honored to receive your investment, Ms. Gray," he concluded. "I would hate to seem forward, but have I managed to woo you?"

He winked, and like a good wealthy checkbook, I reached into my purse on command. It was only as my fingers ran over a brittle piece of parchment that I remembered the question that had brought me here in the first place.

"Your donor list," I blurted, brandishing my brochure opened to the right page. "There's one figure listed by only his initials. Can you tell me his name?"

He leaned forward and brushed his hand over mine while he read. "Why, I believe that is Donald Hildrand," he said with a pleasant laugh, sitting back. "He tends to be too mysterious for his own good. I could arrange for you to meet him if that would put you at ease, though I would be loath to share your company—"

"No." I shook my head and swallowed down the lump that had risen in my throat. "That's not necessary."

Somehow, I had known, even before he'd delivered his answer, that it wouldn't be what I wanted to hear. No, perhaps wanted was too strong a word. What I *needed* to hear. That was how paranoid delusions tended to work out, didn't they?

One healthy dose of reality could make it all fall apart.

"Have I disappointed you, Ms. Gray?" Mr. Lanic wondered. He reached out, his fingertips sweeping upward to bat a loose strand of hair from my face. He must have misjudged the distance, because the tip of his thumb grazed my throat instead.

I flinched back, shaking my head. "No. In fact—" I withdrew my checkbook and scribbled a one in the farthest corner of the amount line. Meeting Mr. Lanic's inquiring gaze, I pushed the check toward him. "Forget I asked. All that matters now is…how many zeros should I add onto this figure?"

Once the poor man returned his eyes back to his skull, I wrote the amount he requested without a second thought. After all, if I were dying, at least my family's name might grace some bench or fountain at St. Mary's to commemorate our benevolent nature. I choked out a laugh, picturing it. It was the only legacy my family could hope I'd pass on. No children or heirs to carry on the name, but an inscription: *From the gracious Gray Family to the whole of the city…*

"Ms. Gray? Are you all right?"

"Huh?" I looked up to find Mr. Lanic staring at the pristine tablecloth in front of me.

Or, at least it *had* been pristine. Three ruby drops now decorated the space beside my plate.

"I'm f-fine." I scrambled to my feet, snatching my checkbook from the table. "I should go—"

"What on Earth?" Lanic frowned, his gaze on something behind me. "I apologize. I insisted upon privacy."

"What?" I turned, catching a glimpse of an intruder, who was already storming out through the doorway, their posture more confident than the average server. Bolder. Not to mention that they allowed the door to slam in their wake, which rattled the wooden frame. Perhaps the restaurant owner coming to bill me for the damage?

No. What little of his features I saw were too impressive for the average man. A luxury suit. Golden hair. Skin like ivory. And a spicy, wintry scent that lingered in the air, tainting my every breath. Either tall, blond men in Armani were becoming a regular occurrence or…

God, it was too dangerous a word to process at the moment. *Or.*

"I was assured this was a premier venue," Lanic groused. "I can have the manager move us to a more private—"

"I-I have to go." I lunged for the door, aware of movement behind me.

"Ms. Gray?" From the corner of my eye, I saw Gabriel start to stand. "Wait!"

I was already in the lobby within seconds, gasping for air. My rib cage had a vise grip on my lungs. My legs were jelly. I almost turned back in search of a chair before I made a fool of myself and fainted.

Obviously, I'd hallucinated.

As if to challenge that thought, the sound of a slamming car door brought my attention to the valet out front. A man was climbing into a car: black, sleek, imported, and most definitely expensive. I couldn't see the owner's face through the tinted windows as I staggered from The Maria's entrance. He drove off, and I had only enough sense to race toward my own vehicle, parked paces away.

"Ms. Gray?" François gaped as I clambered into the front seat.

Then I spit out the most words I'd spoken to him since the day he'd been hired. "Follow that damn car or I will drive this thing myself!"

Already, our quarry had pulled off and woven through traffic nearly a block ahead.

"Okay." François wrenched on the wheel, launching into a pursuit. For all his politeness, my new driver must have driven more than spoiled heiresses in his day. People who valued reckless speed. He tore through alleys and side streets, easily narrowing the distance between us and our prey.

But even he wasn't fast enough.

"Damn!" He slapped the wheel as the other car sped off through an intersection before we could follow. "I'm sorry, miss. Let me try to——"

"Let me out." I tugged on the door handle only to find it locked. "Let me out!"

I slapped the window until he finally unlocked the doors. Even as my heart raced, my strength failed me. It took everything I had to shoulder the door open and climb out. While I staggered down the deserted block, François resisted the flow of traffic to keep pace.

"Where are you going?" he asked.

"I'm fine," I called back, putting all my focus into walking. Moving. *You can do this, Ellie. You've come too far, now.* "Go —please! I'll…I'll find my own way back."

I didn't look to see if he obeyed my instructions. I simply urged my body forward through sheer force of will. Step by step. Sidewalk square by sidewalk square.

How ironic. I knew this part of the city—a rarity for me, despite having lived here my whole life. For instance, this road was one of the few I'd driven on myself. I knew the darkened park to my left. And I especially knew the cathedral looming above.

In the darkness, it watched my approach like a disapproving remnant from a past life. The life of a girl who consorted with vampires. Who'd sold her virginity to one. Who'd let herself be poisoned, tricked, and humiliated by one.

The stupid, foolish woman who might have even trusted one.

I shook off the thought as blurriness disrupted my vision and the gothic structure split into two. With every step, my body swayed, tossing my shadow over the path beside me. My breaths grated on the air, noisy and useless. I was weightless. My trembling hands grasped at my sides, desperate for stability.

By the time I reached the cathedral proper, the grounds were deserted. A lone streetlamp cast the only light to see by as I approached the mouth of the structure. The door remained closed, the sign still nailed to it. When I traced my fingers over its surface, they came away gritty with dust.

Well, you were wrong, a part of me hissed as I slumped forward, pressing my sweaty forehead against the wood. *You chased a shadow.*

But the funny thing about shadows was that they couldn't be stopped by something as mundane as a wooden door. A door that budged the slightest inch beneath my weight…

The wind picked up, tossing my hair around as if in warning, before I even palmed the wrought-iron handle. I pushed once, expecting to find resistance.

It opened easily, issuing a weary creak as if mourning its failure.

One peek over the threshold revealed an empty, cavernous interior with abandoned pews. Some entity took care to preserve the space, however. When I placed my foot on the wooden floor, my shoe didn't slide over a coating of dust.

Someone had been here.

Yet every ounce of sanity I still possessed warned me to turn back. To *not* push the door open wider or inch my way inside.

To run.

Because I had nothing to prove. And even more harrowing to admit—I had nothing to gain. Just more questions with no fitting answers. Like, if Dublin Helos was lurking within the city, then why wait so long to come collecting?

I owned part of his life, after all. Ten whole years. The devil himself shouldn't have been playing hide-and-seek while waiting for me to find him.

He should have been barging into Gray Manor like he owned the place, demanding I give him what I now owned.

His goddamn soul.

Shaking the thoughts away, I took another step. Thickened air irritated my nostrils and set off the reaction instinct could not—I recoiled. Harsh, rattling coughs forced me to cling to the door. Another set robbed me of balance altogether.

Light. Dark. The conflicting shades speckled my vision as everything spun and dissipated. Twisted. Faded.

And all I saw before the world went black was vibrant, terrible gold.

A BED OF ROSARY

François must have brought me home. Considering he had never been *inside* the house, it made sense that he wouldn't know where my room was. The gesture was enough to earn him a raise, though— even if I still slightly hated him.

He'd chosen a decent bed at least. The mattress conformed to my limbs, far too decadent to have been purchased by my mother. Perhaps it was one Georgie had snuck in as an act of rebellion? My nostrils flared, seeking out her scent in the silky fabric, but I wound up inhaling something spicier than her rosy perfume. Something…unnatural. Familiar. Like winter in physical form.

A part of me stirred in alarm, but logic quashed any suspicions before they could form.

You're dreaming, Ellie. Go back to bed. I rolled onto my side, fighting to return to the dreamless sleep I'd left behind. Just as my body began to relax, the bed frame jolted beneath me.

I lurched upright, my eyes flying open to a darkened room. Before I could write off the disturbance as a figment of my imagination, my straining ears picked up another alarming sign. Creaking wood. Footsteps? Heavy ones. They advanced in my direction, far too bold to be a burglar.

A list of potential visitors marched across my brain. Like my sister returning on her own for once? The grim reaper?

After licking my lips, I tested one theory by calling out, "F-François?"

Through the shadows, I sensed a doorknob rattle without a word of warning from the person on the other end. That ruled him out. Unease danced down my spine as I wrestled with the prospect of real danger. Perhaps terminating my entire security team hadn't been the best idea in retrospect? I couldn't regret it now.

Instead, I grasped at my surroundings for a weapon, finding only a pillow. I brandished it as the door opened and moonlight spilled in from a nearby window to illuminate the intruding figure.

A gasp caught in my throat. It wasn't a murderer or a robber —certainly not the lanky François.

He was a far worse entity.

Not real, I deduced. This apparition was just another phase in an all-too-vivid dream. But pinching my wrist didn't jolt me awake.

The Devil stubbornly remained, dressed in his usual soul-collecting attire—a flawless ebony suit crowned with a blood-colored tie. Pale skin contrasted harshly with the shadow surrounding him as did his hair—a gleaming shade of gold the sun couldn't outshine.

With this man's chiseled jaw jutting in the air, not even God himself would dare challenge him.

Let alone me.

Without invitation, he entered the room, and my heart stuttered as anticipation grew with every inch he gained. Admittedly, this was far from the meticulous, sly return someone like him was capable of performing. Almost as if I wasn't worth even a fraction of the effort. Still, I'd imagined this moment so many times, assuming what he'd say down to the last word. The general gist, at least. *Do be a good girl, Eleanor, and give me my contract book back, please and thank you.*

So a rebuttal was on the tip of my tongue before he even opened his perfect mouth. "You're slacking Dublin. That was far from a dramatic entrance befitting the big bad contractor—"

"You look like hell." He advanced another step, sweeping his gaze over me. "No wonder your doctor has been consulting experts the world over concerning your case."

"M-My what?" I blinked, confused. Weeks of fantasizing about this moment, and yet never did I imagine his first words would refer to my medical records.

"Here." One of his arms tensed, revealing something in his grasp. A knife? He threw whatever it was in my direction and I flinched, covering my head with my hands. Coolness brushed my calf, but no pain followed. Had he missed? I peeked through my splayed fingers, spotting a round object. A water bottle, of all things.

"Drink," he snapped. "I can hear your heart straining from here."

His tone was all wrong—deeper than I remembered, for one. Guttural. When I looked up, his mouth firmly resisted even the hint of that cruel, mocking smile I knew so well. The Devil was clearly vexed. Had I interrupted his self-imposed exile with my bloody excretions?

No matter. Matching his tone, I bit back with, "I thought your magic necklace was supposed to help in that regard?" I clutched at the item in question, straining the slender chain. "Or was that just a lie? A way for you to track me all along? I should have ripped it off the second you left—"

"You didn't." His gaze honed in on my throat. "Have you tried removing it?" He surged forward another step, only to halt paces from the bed. I had flinched without even realizing it. "Do you even know the lengths I went through getting the damn thing on you in the first place?" The slightest tremor disrupted his words. "Then again, maybe you *do* know? I'm sure she didn't specify those little terms all on her own—"

"She?"

"Don't play the fool." He inclined his head, exasperated with me already.

But the way he was glaring at me trapped any rebuttal in my throat. I'd almost forgotten this aspect of his persona—how dangerous he could seem when he wanted to, fitting the term I'd christened him with during one of our first meetings.

Monster.

"Removing the talisman disrupts its effects," he growled, a professor begrudgingly bestowing a lesson upon an ignorant fool. "I warned you—"

"I…" My mind raced to keep up as a million words formed and died on the tip of my tongue. In the end, I managed to voice only one pathetic question. "Why are you here?"

"A better question would be: Why were you *there*? To provoke me? Well, congratulations, you have. Is it my blood that you're after?" He nodded toward my extended wrist. "Or could it be that, once again, you're being manipulated by Raphael? Don't tell me that you didn't realize that was no ordinary restaurant?"

I swallowed hard, envisioning the elegant, rich décor of The Maria. Was he correct in insinuating an ominous reason for the splendor? That it was owned by the vampire Raphael…

Shaking my head, I tried to refocus. "I…I didn't. I didn't know you'd be there." Wait. Why was I on the defensive, explaining myself to *him*? I shook my head again. *Deep breaths, Eleanor.*

Obviously, this tactic was one of his many mind games. Mention my sister. Then pretend to care, and even throw in dear Dr. Goodfellow for good measure. How sweet.

I could admire his tact for not launching into demanding his contract back first thing. But what did one say to a creature who'd abandoned them without so much as a second thought, anyway?

Apparently, they said, "You know what? You don't have the right to ask me about a damn—" *Thing*, I meant to add before a violent cough racked my spine. I hunched over, grasping the sheets around me for balance. Sheets way too fine to ever be mine.

Wait… I blinked, finally noticing the rest of the room. One far too narrow to belong in Gray Manor. Even in the near darkness, I could tell that the walls weren't lilac, but made of stone. The bed beneath me was way too wide, the floors wooden. And Dublin…

Well, he looked way too at home in the center of the shadowed interior. Another step brought him closer still and I cringed against a wall of pillows.

"Where am I?"

"Your cough," he started as though I'd never spoken. "How long have you—"

"Where am I?" I forced myself to sit upright and ignored him in my quest to deduce my surroundings. Beyond the doorway, I noted a clue that answered my own question—a wall of breathtakingly beautiful stained glass could only belong in one type of venue. "So, you were lurking here, after all? How nice of you to finally answer the door." A full five days later. "It must have been hard to rearrange your very busy schedule."

His silence gave me my answer—*yes*.

"Well, in any case, it's a good thing you ignored me," I said, shrugging. "Otherwise, I might have struggled to fit you into my schedule. What with *time* being such a precious commodity these days."

The old Dublin I'd known would have scoffed at the bait and seen it for what it was—a deliberate reference to his contract book.

"Oh, I know," he countered, deploying an unexpected change in tactic. "You're a busy woman, it seems." His gaze settled along the neckline of my dress as he nodded. "Why, it is a miracle that I managed to catch you alone at all."

"So, you *were* watching me." I pointed an accusing finger at him. *Checkmate.* "You were spying on me—"

"And why would I do that?" He turned away, disarming me like one would a screaming child. "Pardon me, Eleanor, but I'm already behind schedule thanks to your little visit. What do you want?"

"I…" Bit my tongue. As always, his motives were as elusive as he was. Why would he stalk me? Despite all my suspicions, I still drew a blank. So I improvised. "You and I both know why I'm here."

"Oh?" His tone deepened further. "Do tell."

"You can threaten me all you want." I lifted my arms in a careless gesture. "Just drop the aloof act. Go on… Come out and ask me for it! I'd rather die than tell you, so prepare your poetic warnings—"

"What the hell are you talking about?" His eyes found me from over his shoulder, gleaming like hellfire. "Perhaps you hit your head when you fell?"

He sounded too damn serious.

"I…" My mind went blank. Could this be a trap? A trick?

Then a realization hit me with all the subtlety of a ton of bricks—he didn't know. Or he was a damn good liar. *Or…* Raphael was a far more cunning game master than I'd given him credit for.

As the seconds passed, his expression remained guarded, impossible to read. Left with no other option, I tore a page from my mother's playbook whenever someone had presented her with an uncomfortable truth.

I closed my eyes and willed it away.

"On second thought, it's nothing." I stood, shooing him with a wave of my hand. "I should really get back to Gabriel anyway." By some miracle, I managed to take a step toward the door without making a fool of myself by falling. I *limped* instead, bracing one hand against the nearest wall for balance.

Just as I reached the doorway, Dublin called out, "Your *letters*—"

I didn't miss how he'd stressed that word. So, my blood had made an impact after all.

"I haven't read them," he added, shattering my suspicion. "In fact, I only arrived back in the country hours ago. Though I'm sure you've been far too busy to notice my absence."

I bit my lip, tasting salt. So he claimed to have been gone all this time? It fit. The great and terrible Dublin Helos hadn't disappeared out of shame for what he'd done to me or to plot on how to retrieve his contract book. He merely went on vacation.

"Did they convey anything important?" he wondered.

"I… They're nothing. You can give them back."

I held my hand out and jerked it away once I spotted the red liquid smeared over the palm. But I was too late.

He seized my wrist in a grip so strong that it yanked me toward him. Flashing, his eyes fixated on mine. "How long have you—"

"Well, I'm leaving," I insisted, more than satisfied with this little reunion. Apparently, he hadn't poisoned me, a fact I couldn't dissect at the moment. So I snatched my hand back and continued to make my way to the door with my head held high and an air of indifference on full display. Things like "logic" and "reason" would only matter once he left me alone.

Which, of course, he took his sweet time doing. I could see him within my peripheral vision, standing rigid, his eyes on me.

"You need to see a doctor."

"I have a doctor."

"A *qualified* doctor—"

"Says who? I'll have you know, I've been *perfect* in fact, without your meddling, thank you."

"I'm sure you have," he countered. "Your friend Gabriel certainly seemed to be of the same mind. He looked liable to do more than take your *money*. Bravo, Eleanor. No one would guess that you were a virgin only a couple months ago. I'm sure that, in my absence, you've added a few more conquests to your ever-growing list."

I stumbled to a halt as my eyes went so wide that I figured he could see them dancing in my skull from his position.

"Don't tell me I've insulted you," he added.

"You…" I sucked in a breath, blinking rapidly. *No.* I refused to let him unnerve me. I needed to counter, regain my composure. Something cruel should have been on the tip of my tongue. Anything but, "You don't get to act like this. Not after everything you put me through—"

"Oh?" He came up behind me, casting a shadow that swallowed the pool of light I was standing in. "And what have I put you through?"

I gasped as his hand captured my chin, tilting my head toward him. With his height, only a sliver of his jaw was visible from this angle. And his eyes. They were silver, spitting fury like lightning.

"Do be a polite girl and enlighten me. You can start with the part where I saved your life."

"You left," I blurted, obeying his instruction like a good, pathetic contractee. "You left without even an evil speech by way of goodbye I might add—"

"You don't know, do you?"

A hitch caught in my throat. He sounded so furious at that fact. I came to him, crawling his way like a pathetic victim eager for more—and I didn't even have the sense to know *why* that fact irritated him so.

"Get off of me," I spat, slapping his hand away. "I'll tell you what I *do* know, though—I can press charges."

"On yourself for trespassing?" He moved his grip to my throat, barely applying pressure with flexing fingers. "Do try it, Eleanor. Or have you forgotten? You came to me."

I blinked. Something in his tone made my heart race, hammer a silent warning. "You came to me first," I pointed out, even more perplexed than ever at the image of him lurking in the dining room. "You *stalked* me.

Badly, I might add. You should try a disguise next time—"

"I can smell him on you, you do realize? Here." An icy gust fanned the exposed hollow at the base of my neck, his finger, drawing an accusatory line over the flesh. "You could have showered before coming here, at least. It would have made a more desperate impression. I'm sure you and your sister have some demand to make of me, especially after this little ruse. With her resources, don't pretend like you weren't alerted the second I returned, and I know for a fact that she has been keeping out of the spotlight. What is she planning? Let's not waste any more time. Say it."

"The man I met was helping me," I stammered, choosing to overlook his mention of Georgie—for now. If dealing with him had taught me one lesson, it was to stay focused. Ignore all bait. "I was—"

"Don't play naïve," he warned, applying more pressure to my throat. "You and I both know that he wanted more from you, Eleanor. *More* than your money. Perhaps a desire to corrupt the innocent heiress? It doesn't matter." His fingers flexed, with just enough tension to make me suck in a breath. "You forgot that you've already sold your body. Your soul. To me."

The way he'd said those two words... My brain melted. Disintegrated. Poor Dr. Goodfellow had every right to be concerned, because this was true terminal danger. I gasped like a drowning victim, flailing for a lifeline. In my hazy, scattered thoughts, I found one.

"Is this your trick?" I murmured despite the fragile cage of his hand. "Distract me? Pretend and then gloat—"

"Still the same old Eleanor Gray, as stoic as ever." He forced me to face him and my eyelids fluttered as I tried to withstand the intensity of his gaze. It was no use—I failed. "I did research into your dear Mr. Lanic. Why am I not surprised that you have a preference for dangerous, elusive men?"

A muscle in his jaw lurched, betraying the unbelievable. Hours back and he'd already inserted himself into my life, hunting down an acquaintance I barely knew.

But why?

"I…I thought you just returned to the country?"

"Your heart is racing, Eleanor," he snarled over me. "Perhaps you should see that doctor? I'm running out of contracts to extend where your life is concerned."

"Who says I need your help?" I pictured Goodfellow and her faked concern, but it was getting harder and harder to remember the weakness that had plagued me for weeks. The dizziness, or the coughing fits. Dublin Helos was the cruelest antidote to physical pain.

Around him, my thoughts were in more than enough turmoil.

"Where were you?" Dear God. The question slipped out, too puzzling to remain in my head, a weakness I'd mourn later. For some reason, an answer mattered more to me than shame. "Tell me. Or let me guess? Collecting more souls to add to your bounty?"

"My bounty? I was upholding *my* end of the bargain. I'm sure you know all about it." He waited smugly for a reaction I apparently failed to deliver. His frown transformed into a grimace. "Unless she really didn't tell you…"

I cocked my head. "Who didn't tell me—"

"Of course she didn't." He released me, raking his hand through his hair as if finally hearing the butt of a ridiculous joke; surprise, surprise, he wasn't amused. "When have you ever exercised self-preservation?"

Exasperated, I tried to retort, "You—"

"*You* broke the bargain." His grip returned to the nape of my neck. Using the contact like a leash, he yanked me closer. "Why? Did you fall into league with *him*, aiming to see just how far you can push me? You even smell different." His nose lingered near the crook of my shoulder. Drawing back, he shook his head and refocused his gaze on my mouth. In my quivering lips, he seemed to find an answer to the question he never voiced.

One too terrifying to ponder.

"You're too pale as well." He traced my pulse point with the tip of his thumb and my breath stuttered in response. "If you didn't remove the necklace…"

"I'm leaving." I tried to step past him, but he shifted, easily blocking my path. "Get out of my way," I demanded, trying to shove him back. I might as well have tried shoving the wall.

"No." He stepped into me, forcing me to take a hasty step back. Only for him to take another. Another. Before I could jerk farther out of his reach, his lips grazed my earlobe poised to deliver another insult. "You came to me first." Once more, he seemed to be speaking only to himself—but his hand crept into my hair, too firm to shake off. "Therefore, *you* voided the contract. I'm sure she's on her way, but it doesn't matter. I kept my end—"

"Stop!" It was my turn to utter, "What the hell are you talking about?"

"You let him touch you." He made it sound like the vilest of crimes. "I can forgive that. But not the innocent, childish games."

He tugged me closer. Too close. I tried to recoil, but his other hand latched onto the back of my scalp, trapping me in place.

"D-Dublin—"

"I will even pretend you didn't know about your sister's bargain," he hissed against my ear. "If that will embolden you to drop the act. Was he your plan for drawing me out sooner? Let me guess—Georgiana is waiting in the wings, ready to resurface?"

"G-Georgie?" I flinched at the third mention of her. Beautiful Georgiana consorting with Dublin about a bargain. A contract. "What did you—"

"I can forgive everything else. Even the flagrant disregard for your own welfare. Everything but this…" He eyed my throat as his upper lip pulled back from his teeth. The slightest hint of fangs teased the air, sending every nerve within my skin on red alert. "I gave you your life, Eleanor. I could concede that much. But your body? I don't remember relinquishing my hold over it."

"Stop!" I inhaled, once again fighting for clarity. "You're not making sense."

"Or you're too much of a prude to admit it." His mouth snapped shut, firm and brooding once more. "I'm starting to think I've misinterpreted your little evening. God forbid, I'd almost thought that you were foolish enough to challenge me. But lo and behold, you don't even have enough damn sense to realize—"

"Or you're too much of a pompous ass to quit playing games and just tell me what you want!"

The words had barely left my throat when he pulled me in, surging forward in the same swift motion. Our lips met and my body went haywire as his tongue eased my lips apart with a searching swipe that shattered my senses. Pushing him off was my sole aim for grabbing him in return, curling my fingers around his forearms.

But I'd forgotten…

What it felt like to be at his mercy. To have his mouth on mine. To feel his body—living stone impervious to my touch, resistant to my pathetic attempts to tame him.

He easily overpowered me, despite my grip on his arms. Two advancing steps of his herded me back. Back…until my knees struck the mattress and I fell onto the sheets.

He stepped between my splayed legs, robbing me of the chance to regain my bearings. Ruthless, his hand plunged beneath my dress, cupping me with no warning. No growled demands. Just vicious friction.

And it was as if my body ceased being *mine*.

Nerves unraveled, enslaved by his touch. The memory of him. Months alone and I'd never even tried to replicate the things he had done to me. I couldn't. Nothing compared to the stomach-churning sensation he sowed with every stroke of his thumb—ice over burning flesh. My teeth caught my lower lip as he rubbed, testing the thin lace of my panties, grinding the fabric into my skin. Helpless, my head reared back against my shoulders, a cry trapped behind my lips.

I couldn't resist the fire hissing to life within me, feeding on the motions of his fingers. Rough. Cruel. Relentless.

At the back of my mind, I knew I was hallucinating. This wasn't happening.

Dublin Helos wasn't groaning as he urged my legs farther apart, eyeing me the way Lanic had ogled my checkbook. Like I was millions for the taking, his alone to claim.

"I should have killed you," he whispered. One of his hands still raked through his hair, destroying his suave poise. Gone was the calm, collected contractor. In his place was a creature more beast than man. "I should want to kill you," he added, flicking his gaze up to mine. "The trouble you've caused me. The years. The chaos. The sacrifice. I swore to myself I'd never believe him, not for a goddamn second. But you…"

"I what?" I tensed. Was he finally referring to his contract?

"You *persist*. Weeks spent trying to prove that you were nothing." He chuckled at the absurdity of it, prowling forward, bracing his hands on my knees. "And I return to find you on my doorstep, ready for more." He shoved my dress over my hips and something rare splintered his anger, tugging on the corner of his mouth as he swept his gaze over me.

My legs twitched, ached to clamp together. Hide from him. As if sensing the thought, he traced a path down my inner thigh, observing every twitch of my spine.

"There is something wrong with you," he grated. "Something broken. It's like you truly are cursed. Corrupt. Like he planned you for me after all. He made you for me."

"Who?" My mind reeled. He was talking too fast. Hatred for him was becoming harder and harder to hold on to. And, God, I needed it. My fingers grasped the sheets as if I could find the emotion among them. "Raphael?"

"Why should I fight it?" he demanded, stroking his thumb up over my belly. My heaving breast. My throat. I trembled with every inch gained; drawn nails added a predatory fervor to each, pointed caress. "You are tailor-made to resist me every step of the way, aren't you?"

He lowered his head. A brush of ice against the flesh of my throat was my only warning before…pain. His teeth, I realized belatedly as his jaw nudged mine, urging me to arch, exposing more.

"You are mine, Eleanor Gray," he declared. "Body *and* soul."

Then…

He bit.

And everything went red.

Vibrant, beautiful scarlet rich enough to erase the gray my life had become.

I was too far gone to even care that I was drowning in blood.

DIAGNOSIS

A symphony of beeping machinery lured me into consciousness. Just from the way my nostrils twitched, I knew where I was before my eyes even opened.

A hospital.

Over the past year, I'd been in enough of them to envision the layout of this room entirely from assumption. A spacious one, judging from the echo. Private, most likely.

I wasn't alone, either—that had to be a first. Someone nearby was speaking in a hushed voice. My doctor?

Or perhaps *devil* would be a more fitting term.

"I didn't know who else to call," the man said, his voice easily placed. Dublin. My eyes were too heavy to open, but I could picture him paces away, scowling to match the gruffness of his baritone. "She trusts you, at least. Perhaps you can discover who the…cause of this may be."

"Cause? I should have never let you order me to stay away from her," a woman replied, her lilting accent distinct.

I knew her as well. My brain struggled to recall a name, but forming a solid thought at all felt like grasping at tendrils of smoke. All I could do was listen.

"Though it seems you haven't kept to that stupid 'bargain,' either," she said accusingly. "I thought you weren't planning on returning for at least a few years—"

"There was a complication," Dublin interjected. "A minor one. Once it is resolved, I don't plan on staying long."

"You mean a complication concerning Eleanor," the woman surmised. "I thought you might have been watching her—and you have, haven't you?"

"Only enough to know that she consulted a doctor who began contacting outside experts regarding her case. I decided to intervene before the chatter could catch Raphael's attention."

"Something you could order any one of your associates to do," the woman pointed out. "You could have asked me as well. Though, I should have visited her anyway, with or without your permission. Maybe I could have prevented her from… To be honest, I thought you were joking at first. I mean, Eleanor isn't exactly the type of woman one would expect to wind up in this condition."

"Are you implying that I'm incompetent? I ran the tests more than once," Dublin snapped. "I had them corroborated with several other professionals—"

"Leaving out one obvious reason why this doesn't make any sense, I am sure. Unless… You don't really think she's been with someone else since you've—"

"Are you insinuating another possibility?" Dublin wondered, and a part of me chafed at the grit in his voice. He sounded too calm—and in my experience, that was when he had the most potential for cruelty. "Don't be naïve, Yulia. There is only one logical conclusion."

"Dublin, I was only—"

"And don't insult my intelligence by pretending that you don't know the rumors spreading concerning her, either. Concerning my interest in her. That I lust after the weak little mortal like a wolf would a lamb. Is that what you think as well? I know Raphael in particular rather enjoys that theory—"

"Of course not!"

"My interest in Eleanor Gray extends purely to her bloodline," Dublin insisted. "Raphael attacked her for a reason. Her body reacted to him so violently *for a reason*. I intend to discover why before he can use whatever information he knows against me. Nothing more."

"Fine," Yulia conceded. "So, did you find what you were looking for?"

"The question isn't whether I did," Dublin snapped. "It's whether or not I believe the superstitious drivel in the first place. Don't tell me you do? Is that the real reason you fought so hard to make me notice Eleanor in the first place?

Not that it matters. It seems she hasn't lacked for male company."

"Dublin, I'm on your side," Yulia insisted. "I'm simply trying to understand. This isn't like you. Since when have you cared about what Raphael might think? And how would I know anything about the 'rumors' when you barely even talk about your past—"

"And I'm not willing to start now," Dublin growled. "Once I finish cleaning up this mess, I will leave. Tonight."

"On another wild goose chase?"

"No," he replied, but his tone had hardened. "I intend to take a more direct route, this time. Even if it means going to a monster we both despise..."

"Ah, so that's why you really asked me here?" Yulia's tone turned cutting. Hostile. "You don't give a damn about Eleanor now that she's moved on. You only want my permission to talk to *him*. The very monster *you* saved me from."

A deliberate pause left her statement hanging in the air. Finally, Dublin admitted, "Your permission? No. Your understanding? Yes. You and I both know that Dmitri possesses more knowledge in his twisted skull than anyone."

"Yes," the woman agreed. "Knowledge that he would barter for your soul—or, worse. Whatever answers he could give you wouldn't be worth the price you'd have to pay, trust me on that—"

"It's not merely answers I'm after."

Some internal part of me squirmed, alarmed by the emotion bared in his words. Concern? Or fear.

"You claim to be concerned for Eleanor? Well, the necklace should have preserved her life, but it hasn't. I could smell the sickness in her. If her health remains in such a perilous state, this could kill her. By merely attempting to feed from her, I almost did."

"I know," the woman whispered. "But you weren't yourself. We both know how hunger can affect you. I should have talked you out of ever giving up that stupid amulet in the first place—"

"So, she could die sooner?" Dublin countered.

"No, of course not! Although—"

"Although, *if you had, we wouldn't be in this dilemma.*" Dublin paused before continuing. "Don't look at me like that, Yulia, I know what you're thinking. We both know it to be true." An air of regret laced his words and it twisted my insides like a knife. "Alive or dead, Eleanor Gray seems destined to thwart all logic where safety is concerned."

"That's not what I mean! Look, I won't pretend like I have any other options, but anyone is better than that son of a bitch. Just wait a few more days and I'll try to find something myself. Even Saskia might—"

"Or Raphael?"

"No!" The woman choked out a tortured laugh. "I...I suppose going to him would be even worse than Dmitri. But just listen to me. If you can hold off for a few days, I will help you in any way I can, but I can't... If you do decide to seek out Dmitri, then please don't count on me to accompany you. Give me a week. I'm sure we can find the answers on our own. Please."

"...A week," Dublin conceded after a moment's silence.

"Good," Yulia agreed. "And as far as Eleanor is concerned, I'll do what I can to help her. Let me know when she wakes up, and I'll bring some things for her. God, I can't imagine how scared she must be—"

"I'm not sure if she even knows." Dublin sounded cold again. My tired brain tried desperately to piece together what he referred to. Something concerning me...

Something awful.

"W-What?" Yulia exclaimed. Seconds passed before she regained her composure enough to ask, "And, if she doesn't you will tell her *gently,* won't you? Without making her feel any worse? I mean, it—"

"I found her with someone last night. Perhaps I interrupted a congratulatory dinner?" A laugh undercut Dublin's chilling baritone. "I think we have both learned by now that Eleanor Gray deserves anything but pity."

"Don't be like that. You've hurt her once—you and I both know it. I doubt even someone of your fortitude has the willpower to do it twice. Especially about this. Just tread carefully."

A weighty silence didn't reveal his answer either way.

Finally, Yulia sighed. "I'm just asking you to think this through. Your decisions may have far greater consequences than even you could bear. Now, I need to get back to the club. That bitch Saskia will get suspicious if I stay away for too long. As far as your concerns go, give us a week to find our own answers before you go off again. A *week*. Promise me…"

~

I must have drifted in and out of consciousness, because when I finally blinked my eyes open, a figure loomed near the end of my bed, emanating a chill that resonated in my bones.

"Don't move," he warned.

One flex of my limbs and I understood why. Pain flooded my system, drawing a gasp from my lips. "Jesus Christ." I exhaled a shaky breath as the world gradually came into focus. "I feel like I've been hit by a truck."

"You're still healing," the speaker continued, his face a blobby blur. "You've lost a lot of blood. In your condition, you're lucky to not have suffered a worse fate."

Still healing? I turned, driven by an instinctive dread. And for good reason—more blinking brought an object lurking just beyond me into clearer focus. A long metal pole. Dangling from the very top was a bag of red fluid.

"A blood transfusion?" I deduced, horrified.

"Four pints lost," Dublin declared, stepping closer. The waning daylight was just enough for me to make out his expression—surly eyes and stiffened lips.

Dread unfurled in my belly. I knew that look. He was in a brooding mood.

"Count your blessings that you're even able to move."

"Get. It…" I had to suck in air to form each word. My fingers twitched on command but lacked the strength to rip out the IV. "Out. Get it out of me—"

"Do you understand what I just said? You hemorrhaged. You're weak." He wasn't using his clinical, doctorly voice anymore. "You've been out for nearly two days. There are corpses that portray more vitality than you."

And if I didn't know any better, I might suspect the devil was…exhausted?

His face revealed nothing discernible. As stoic as ever, he stood near a wide bay window overlooking an unfamiliar view of the city. From the bed, I caught snippets of the landscape beyond him: skyscrapers, bright lights. It was an area far from the reclusive hillside domain of Gray Manor—that was for sure.

And far from his cathedral where my last, hazy memories centered upon.

Mainly one image that chilled me to the bone.

"I bled," I whispered, hating how hoarse my voice sounded, "because you bit me."

"I did," he admitted, training his gaze on the view. "I shouldn't have fed from you, but the venom merely exacerbated your underlying condition. It didn't cause it—"

"Condition? Oh, don't tell me." I shifted to observe him fully. "You figured out my mysterious illness? What is it this time? Another blood disease?"

Despite my bravado, my voice broke. The world was spinning around me. Oddly enough, *he* was the stubborn anchor, as unmoving and rigid as the day we'd met. One of his hands fiddled with something hanging from his throat —shining, small, silver…

No, it couldn't be. I felt along my own neck, finding it bare —but too many thoughts battled for attention to care.

The man was an Indian Giver. So what?

So what if some of my last memories were of him scolding me as to the importance of that very necklace?

So what.

"Congratulations." I forced my hands together in a pathetic imitation of applause though it took nearly all of my strength. One pathetic clap was all I could accomplish. "What will I have to sell to you this time in exchange for the cure?"

"Cure?" he wondered in a dangerously soft tone. His shoulders were so rigid that I bit my lip. Odd. He should have been gloating. Not tense, his head bowed in contemplation. "If you want to take that route, then I need to ask you something," he warned.

"Why?" I tried to shrug off his caution. "Are you pretending to be my doctor again? I'm sorry to be the bearer of bad news, but I have a new doctor. A *real* one, who isn't inclined to drink blood in her spare time."

"You don't have any idea, do you?" He looked up, and nothing could prepare me for the ice in his expression. Dublin wasn't just brooding—it was so much worse.

He was *furious.*

"J-Just…" I stammered, wringing my fingers until a coherent reply finally formed on my tongue. "Just tell me, oh wise one. What's wrong with me now?"

His gaze cut away from me as he started to pace. "I don't know how else to ask this other than bluntly. Who have you been with, excluding me?"

Been with…

Fire heated my cheeks. His tone said it all. *How big of a harlot are you Eleanor, now that your virginity is a moot point?*

Needles of shame stabbed through my chest though I bit my lip to disguise my reaction. The only way to counter him was with a forced smile and more faked bravado.

"Other than you?" I coyly raised my hand and ticked each finger off one by one. "Why, Gabriel Lanic. My driver. My maids, before I fired them. My gardener. My security guards—"

"Enough!"

Shock rendered me senseless, and memories that shouldn't have been there popped into my head. Him, on top of me, his hands beneath my dress. More recently, him delivering a tortured observation in a callous whisper. *There is something wrong with you…*

I swallowed hard. This wasn't happening. I wasn't on my figurative deathbed while a vampire taunted me about intercourse.

"Leave me alone—"

"Answer the question," he snarled in a tone so hard I jumped.

"No one," I managed to rasp.

Rather than sneer at the admission, he…frowned. "Your modesty means nothing at this point, so I'd prefer if you didn't lie. Just give me a name."

"No. One," I insisted, clearly enough for him to absorb every single word. My cheeks were aflame, and I had to resist the urge to cackle hysterically. This was some mind game on his part, of course. Accuse me of being a moral-less harlot, right before coming in for the kill: I'd already given him my virginity, why not give him his precious contract as well?

"If there is a point to this," I added harshly, "then I suggest you get to it."

His brow furrowed and then his expression went blank. It was as if someone had flicked a switch, cutting off all emotion the bastard might deign to feel. Even rage. "I've arranged for you to see a doctor."

Something in his tone made me huddle beneath my blankets before I realized.

"What doctor?"

He had already turned on his heel and stormed from the room. Seconds later, a woman appeared in his wake. Slim and tall, her modest features and stern, wire glasses projected a knowledgeable aura even someone like Dublin Helos would defer to.

"Hello Eleanor," she said softly. "I'm Dr. Martin."

Minutes into a brief assessment, I had to admit that she seemed capable enough. She asked pertinent questions and thankfully wasn't as cheerful as Dr. Goodfellow. Hell, I almost felt as insignificant as a lab rat by the time she finished drawing vials of blood and left the room. But then, minutes later, she returned, lugging a sleek, square-shaped machine behind her.

"Ms. Gray," she began in a crisp, efficient tone, "I would like to get an abdominal ultrasound, if that is alright with you."

"An ultrasound?" It was a terrifying term, especially when paired with the high-tech machinery she expertly began to program. "W-why?" I asked, even as a part of me suspected what the answer may be.

Something far worse than a mere cough ailed me. A *tumor?* Rather than voice that suspicion herself, Dr. Martin took advantage of my silence to plug the machine into the wall.

"Ready?" The woman must have mistaken my panicked expression for permission, because she proceeded to turn the machine on.

And I squeezed my eyes shut.

I couldn't stop my hands from childishly flying up to cover my ears as well. But that didn't mean I couldn't feel. My hospital gown withdrew, allowing cold hands to feel my flesh underneath. An even colder substance greeted my belly a second later, biting through my numb skin. And then I sensed pressure, pressing up, down, around. Searching. Hunting. What for? A blockage, a tumor...or something worse?

I didn't know.

There was no cry of triumph, in the end, when Dr. Martin settled the probe near my pelvic bone. No mechanical beeping to alert those nearby of the machine's findings. Just a low, terrifying hum I heard even through my fingers. I was forced to press harder, shutting out everything but the steady, fast thrum of a heartbeat. My heartbeat?

My condition was more dire than expected if my heart was working so feverishly.

Seconds later, the pressure abated without fanfare. As if from miles away, I heard Dr. Martin murmur something to another presence who entered the room, their scent alone broadcasting their identity. Icy. Chilled. Winter. Whatever she said, it was succinct. Conclusive. As the material of my gown lowered, a soft touch ghosted my cheek and I let my hands fall.

"We're done, Eleanor."

"So…what now?" My eyes reluctantly opened to the white ceiling, blinded by the artificial light. I blinked to get my bearings, only to find Dr. Martin slipping through the doorway without so much as a word. But someone new stood in her place. My, what a difference a few minutes and tests had made. Silver eyes honed in on me with a chilling intensity that made me shiver.

"W-what?" Somehow, I managed to choke out a weak laugh. "What is it? How many months do I have to live this time?"

I was only half joking. From his expression, I discerned my condition wasn't too serious. Even he would show some ounce of sympathy. Right?

"What is it?" My voice ricocheted off the ceiling, high-pitched and breathless.

Finally, Dublin cocked his head. "There's fluid in your lungs," he said, sounding remarkably unconcerned by that fact. "You'll require treatment for it. You're malnourished. Your bloodwork is a case study in critical values. And—" He hesitated, turning the full power of his gaze on me once again. Just when I thought I might shrivel beneath the scrutiny, he added, "You're also pregnant, a little over eight weeks along. Congratulations."

I focused on how he said that word first. *Congratulations.* No one in the history of the world had ever sounded less sincere. Then, piece by piece, I dissected the rest…

Eight weeks.

"V-Very funny." I started to sit upright, coughing with the effort. I covered my mouth with my palm and flinched as warm liquid splattered it with every hacking breath. "I hope you got your laugh, at least—"

"Lie down." Only then did I realize he wasn't laughing. Or smiling. "I'm not lying," he continued. "Dr. Martin confirmed it. She is *never* wrong. Shall I phrase it differently? Your body is manifesting a growth of unconfirmed origin."

Despite the insanity leaving his mouth, he looked clinical. He looked detached. He looked every bit like the calloused doctor who'd intruded into my life all those months ago and left chaos behind.

"W-What…what does that even mean? Is that your way of saying I have cancer? Some kind of tumor?"

Anything but *pregnancy.* In this case, the term probably served as a stand-in for yet another made-up illness. Perhaps a blood disease lacked enough dramatic flair, so Dublin Helos had developed a new destructive narrative in his quest for more souls.

"What will it take to 'fix' me this time?" I wondered, switching tact to cut right to the chase. My gaze fell over his hands, waiting for the moment he'd withdraw some magical vial from his pocket. "I'll have you know that I much preferred the 'degenerative blood disease' narrative, by the way—"

"You do realize what I've said," Dublin interjected, still utterly emotionless. "Do I need to explain it to you?"

God, he sounded too serious. Too real. *Pregnancy, Eleanor. Reproduction. Spawn. Should I draw a diagram?*

"I..." A million words welled up behind my tongue. Oddly enough I could only croak out two at a time. "You're lying. You're wrong."

Which was worse? That someone could be so cruel? Or that someone could be so...stupid?

"You've made a mistake," I insisted, settling on the latter. Felt through the thin hospital gown, my stomach curved inward, mockingly concave. Empty... As my fingers drifted lower, they struck protruding hip bones.

"Mistake, no," Dublin said, running his fingers along the collar of his suit jacket as if flicking all implications of failure away. "I will say that the results didn't show up in the normal range. However, I had your blood sample tested. Of course, we'll do more conclusive tests, but the results strongly indicate… Well, I suggest you continue this discussion with the father. That might give you a bit more insight. I could bring him here, if you wish." His eyes cut to mine, devoid of anything remotely compassionate. "Just give me a name."

All at once, I fell back, striking my head off the edge of a pillow. The pain barely registered above a sudden need for clarity. "T-the what?"

"The father, Eleanor," he said, enunciating each and every word.

Father. As in, someone other than him.

And suddenly his previous line of questioning made horrible, perfect sense. *Who have you been with, excluding me?*

"You…you're serious?" As dizzy as I was, I felt the need to haul myself upright as I spoke. That question could only be delivered when I could look him dead in the eye. Piercing, fathomless eyes glared back. Blank eyes. The Devil's eyes. "Are you that inept of how biology works, in your advanced age, or are you just that damn cruel?" That was what I said in my head. The only sound to register against my ears, however, was a moan.

"Enlighten me, Eleanor," Dublin demanded, but his voice… An emotion I couldn't name stripped it down to grated words and harsh syllables—a dangerous baritone I knew all too well.

"Enlighten you?" I echoed, still struggling to understand the challenge. "Perhaps you should enlighten *me*?" I coughed again but the need for answers trumped all concern. My lungs were collapsing. My throat caved in on itself, capable only of spitting words out rather than letting any air in. "How. Could. This. Happen?"

"Sex with a man, obviously," he countered. But even though I only had weeks of knowledge to draw from, I knew him too well: that wasn't honesty. It was a rebuttal. An accusation.

Sex with a *human* man.

Because that is the only way you could possibly become pregnant.

I swayed as the world shifted. Suddenly, he was everywhere, blocking my path.

"You need to lie down."

His nearness alone stirred my body's instinctive flight or fight response. My heart screamed 'flight' but my pride, what little remained of it, wouldn't cow to his accusation. I needed answers. Any answer, and he needed to be the one to give it.

"Do the math," I panted against my palm. I knew he heard me, already piecing the timeframe together on his own.

In simple arithmetic, eight weeks ago resulted in a period roughly around the instance when I barged in on his suite, bleeding and half dead. When he cut me. When he kissed me. When he made me feel, for a second, that perhaps it all hadn't been a complete lie…

No! I pushed back my blankets and tried to stand. Trembling legs collapsed beneath me, and I would have fallen if a hand didn't cinch my arm at the last moment.

As if in a parallel universe, a woman walked by the doorway carrying a clipboard. She startled and looked up, only to turn away again. This moment was insignificant in her life. A chance meeting. A passing glance. Had she anything worthwhile to offer, how different a meeting might it have gone between her and the man behind me?

"Watch yourself!" Dublin's grip locked me in place, hard and punishing.

Through his flexing fingertips, I could sense everything he didn't dare say. Anger. Resentment. Fury?

"Get off—"

"Give me a name," he countered. "Or can you even remember? You had me fooled, I will admit. Oh, that innocent little virgin act was a stroke of genius, but in the end, it seems your hunger needed to be sated by someone."

"Stop!"

"No," he grated against my ear as I resisted his vice-like grip. It was as if the curtain had been pulled back and his poised, suave act splintered, revealing the true beast lurking underneath, demanding answers of his own.

"Tell me. Who was he?"

I laughed. I couldn't help it.

"Who?" His voice had devolved to a growl, lacking any semblance of polish though I couldn't understand why. Certainly not…jealousy?

No. Self-pity instead. Poor Dublin Helos. How had the devious Ellie Gray managed to trick him this time? First by tangling him within his own web?

And now this?

Another sound tore from my throat at the thought of it, though this time I wasn't sure if it was a cackle or a sigh.

"I may have sold you my virginity," I tossed back to him. "But pardon me, Dublin, if I still have morals." That was all I needed to say. Nothing else. Nothing bitter. Nothing real. Too late. More words spilled out. "You were the only one—"

My throat hitched and I grasped for the end of the mattress, leaning away from him. My chest heaved. It ached. God, I couldn't catch my breath. I couldn't catch anything. My senses. My sanity.

"What are you saying?" His voice reached me as if from miles away. I finally looked back.

He no longer glared, his jaw clenched.

A multitude of words sprung to my lips but just a handful escaped. "If I'm… If… You do realize that it would be because of *you*?"

The look on his face. I would never forget it. Like I just told the most beautiful lie. Like I had crushed his soul and self-worth in one fell swoop.

Like I had hurt him this time.

And God, I would have been lying if I claimed I took pride in it.

"Well? Say something!"

Instead, his eyes cut down to my chest, settling over my throat.

But anger and shame had control of my body and my mouth opened for one last petty blow. "Is this your way of payback?" I croaked. "For what Raphael did to you?"

Namely, what his adversary had given to me. A life for a life?

And still, he said nothing. So cold. So…frozen.

So, I did the only thing one could in my situation.

I lashed out, intending to slap him, only to grapple for his lapel as my stomach roiled.

And I vomited blood all over his white shirt.

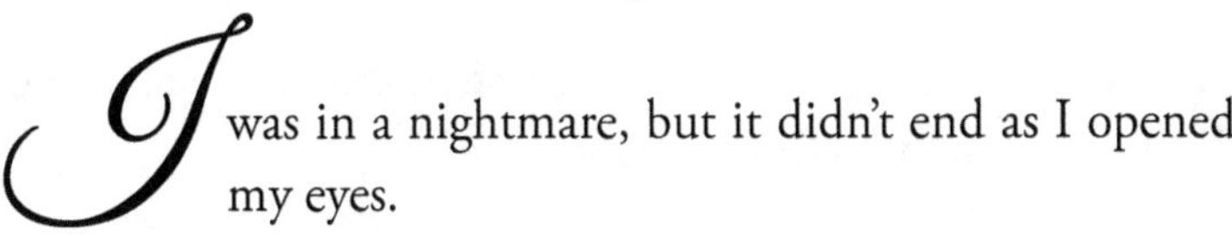

I was in a nightmare, but it didn't end as I opened my eyes.

I must have fainted. Dublin paced before my narrow bed, his back to me. We were still in that clinical, clean room with the door flung open to allow in the hustle and bustle of the rest of the hospital. The faint noises seemed miles away—another universe—mocking me as my reality crumbled to pieces.

"Raphael. He did this," Dublin growled, but the tirade wasn't directed at me for once. He glared instead, his gaze turned inward. "He knew. He...damn him. Damn." He tore his hands through his hair and I swallowed, too stunned to speak. He—the pompous, callous contractor—didn't act like this. Frantic. Unpolished.

Afraid?

Air wheezed from my chest, forming a strangled cough I couldn't suppress.

"Eleanor..." Dublin ceased his hurried pace and turned to me. "Let's assume you aren't lying," he said coldly. "And let's not waste time on petty indignation, either. This is important. What have you been eating?"

I stared at him, still convinced I was dreaming. None of this was real. It wasn't...

"What have you eaten?"

"Food," I croaked in response to the authority in his tone. "But even the thought of it makes me..."

My gag reflex triggered, though my body was too exhausted to follow through. I just choked on empty air. At least there was no blood.

Yet Dublin eyed me more intently than before. His gaze swept downward as if hunting for a certain reaction. "Think," he warned. "What have you tried drinking?"

"Water," I hissed, the obvious response. "And…"

A memory unfolded, too vivid to describe in words.

"What is it?"

His gaze was too severe to ignore. Almost as if he already knew just what images flashed within my mind. *My thumb sliced open. Blood. The taste of it…*

Gritting my teeth, I blurted out, "I pricked my finger the other day." The hand in question rested weakly by my side, my thumb still an angry, bitten red. "It bled and I…"

The knowledge that I was in a nightmare stripped everything of the dire urgency he seemed to feel—at least in my case. I sounded so bored, in a sense. I'd just professed a slight craving for blood. How blasé.

Evidently, Dublin wasn't of the same opinion. He turned on his heel and strolled for the door.

"W-Wait!" I struggled to lift my head from my pillow.

His footsteps continued down the hallway regardless.

There was nothing left to do but count my own surging heartbeat. One. Ten. Fifty. Too sluggish. Too fast. My lungs burned, shriveling beneath each breath I sucked in.

Focus, Ellie. Again, I tried to move a limb. A leg. An arm. Anything? Dripping sweat, I finally managed to raise the hand attached to the IV. First things first, I felt along my throat again, this time searching for bite marks. I found nothing apart from clammy skin. *Damn him.*

Dublin Helos wouldn't be able to swoop in and bestow another "cure" just in time to save the day. My attention reverted to the hanging IV, and I was about ready to rip the damn tubing out with my teeth by the time he reentered the room.

"Look at me," he commanded.

As I did, any argument I could have leveled died in my throat. A clinical, detached posture transformed him—now, he was a cold doctor with a theory to test. In one hand, he held a white Styrofoam cup with a lid and a straw sticking out of the top. In the other was a prepackaged plate of chocolate cake, like the kind one might find in a café.

"I told you I can't keep anything down." As I spoke, the heavenly scent of cocoa reached my nose as if to spite me.

"Sit up." He approached a bedside tray and pulled it closer. Then he offered the cup to me directly. "Drink."

I had a hunch that there wasn't water in that cup. My fingers twitched, unwilling to accept it. I wanted him to leave again. I needed to hate him again. That and silence were all I had left.

"Get out."

"Listen to me—"

"Why?" I scoffed, but he didn't budge.

His hand was unmoving, his gaze drifting from my throat to my wrists, sensing the frailty I couldn't even try to hide.

"You're dying," he warned. "Drink."

Before I could argue, a rare emotion flickered across his gray irises and I flinched. That look compelled me in a way even his surliest of growls could not.

I reached for the cup, wrapping my fingers around the smooth surface, intending to throw it. Before I made my move, he tipped his hand, guiding the straw to my dry, cracked lips. I tried to clench my teeth in defiance.

No!

This is insane.

"Eleanor, drink."

My mouth opened. Dublin didn't beg. Ever. It was a trick, obviously. Too drained to play his game, I relented. One sip. Purely for experimental reasons—the main one being so that I could spit whatever it was out in his face.

But the moment the warm, mystery liquid hit my tongue…

My throat contracted. More. Another sip. More. Long, desperate pulls. *More. More. More.* The desperate mantra drowned out everything else. Like shame, as I remembered how to make my limbs move and snatched the cup with both hands.

God, the satiation was indescribable. Terrifying. As if I had been dying of thirst only to stumble upon an oasis. A salty, bitter oasis flooded with sustenance that I knew instinctively hadn't come from him.

In the literal sense.

Stop! Agony tore through my skin as my conscience overrode hunger. I pulled back, gasping at enough air to spit out a single question he already had the answer to.

"No one was harmed."

Such a carefully worded statement, but it was enough. The straw slipped between my teeth again and I inhaled every last drop, heedless of the horror building at the back of my skull. It could wait. I could hate myself later. For now, my eyes slid shut, my stomach finally contented, and I blinded myself to all other thoughts and sensations—everything but this elusive sense of fullness. It was heaven, cushioning the blow when I finally resurfaced, as he snatched the cup from my hand.

"Eat."

He wheeled the bedside tray closer and unwrapped the slice of cake, which he shoved in my direction, along with a fork.

"I told you that I can't," I insisted. But something had changed. Once I inhaled the aroma in full, my stomach didn't rebel. I didn't need his assistance to sit up, either.

With the tip of the fork, I sliced off a sliver of dessert and settled the morsel onto my tongue. I'd barely convinced myself that projectile vomit onto the man across from me would be a satisfying reaction by the time I finally swallowed.

Rather than rebel, my stomach growled for more. One bite became another. Then a chunk. Then a piece ripped off with my bare fingers when the fork wouldn't suffice to gather up the crumbs fast enough.

Words couldn't describe what it felt like to taste an actual, solid meal after so long.

Words also couldn't describe the look on Dublin's face; it lingered for barely a second, but it was no less intense than his blank stare. Narrowed eyes containing the briefest hint of emotion. Revulsion?

Or fear.

Of *me*.

"What did you do to me?" Chocolate sprayed from my lips.

Quietly, he gathered the empty cup and the plate, tossing them both into the trash. His eyes met mine once again, the longest he'd held my gaze since I'd woken up. Like pools of ice, they reflected my hollow expression back to me. Wide eyes. Open mouth. Flushed, hollow cheeks.

In silence, he left.

And I closed my eyes, determined to wake up.

ADDENDA

lack hair.

Frail skin.

Haunting black eyes.

"I will make you a wager, Eleanor," he told me, his name every bit as beautiful as his youthful appearance. Raphael. "I will tell you what Dublin bartered for you—in fact, I will give it to you. As long as you help me discover something that he might value more…"

I should have run. I tried to. Red walls enveloped me, forming an elegant dining room, crowded by watchful figures with hooded eyes. I took a step and the scenery expanded around me, stretching forever. No matter where I turned, black eyes held me captive, boring deep to scrape my soul.

His hand captured mine, as quickly as a striking cobra. "I already have my suspicions."

He was so cold—shockingly, abnormally so. It felt as if death itself had taken hold of me.

"All you would be required to do is help me prove it to be true or false. Then I shall uphold my end of our bargain. Simple enough?"

A frigid thumb traced the back of my hand. As if drawn by an invisible force, my gaze drifted to his throat, where a serpent pendant hung. Its red eyes kept me in place as Raphael placed his hand over my stomach, imparting his chill into the flesh underneath.

"A simple suspicion," he repeated in a burst of breath so cold that I half expected frost to crystallize right there on my skin.

Then he lowered his head and bared his fangs…

I startled awake to a familiar scene—an empty room. Warm daylight streamed in through the massive window, unabated by the curtain someone had partially drawn over the view. My panic subsided as the fragments of my nightmare faded.

But I wasn't at Gray Manor. Noisy machines still monitored my body through various wires and devices—still in the hospital room, then. At least the IV was gone, as was the mysterious bag of blood.

I could recall those details, though my brain seemed determined to avoid remembering anything else. Thinking took a back seat to the desperate ache unfurling in my belly anyway. I sniffed and realized why. The bedside tray had been drawn up close to the bed and on it was a steaming plate of eggs, along with a Styrofoam cup. My selective memory gave me an inkling as to what might be inside it.

Something red that tasted like copper.

Not exactly the most charming of breakfast invitations. My "doctor" was exerting his presence into my life with little effort.

At least he wasn't here. I had no one to prove anything to. No one to judge. Just my own terrified thoughts playing a morbid commentary as I eyed the straw and pictured the liquid within.

This is insane, Eleanor.

You're hungry, Eleanor.

You're starving, Eleanor.

This is insane.

I clung to that last voice, the pathetic whisper of the person I had spent twenty-six years living as. Calm, reserved Eleanor Gray. The woman content to be a spinster. The heiress who needed no one. That girl wouldn't drink whatever was in that cup. She would cross her arms in stubborn pride and suffer.

Don't be so childish.

That newer voice was unwelcome, suspiciously masculine. To silence it, I sank back against the pillows and pulled the thin sheet over my head, smothering as much noise as the cheap cotton could. Almost as if to mock me...I felt.

Movement. Something. Deep down inside me, like the flexing of a muscle I didn't even know existed. It throbbed, demanding attention. Acknowledgment.

The longer I attempted to ignore it, the sharper the pain became. Insistent.

Drink.

I hauled myself into a sitting position. My hands trembled, outstretched before me, but it felt like ages before I gathered up the nerve to reach for the cup. I cringed with the first sip of lukewarm liquid. Before disgust could fully register, I was already swallowing the second. Third. An endless stream that didn't cease until the final few drops noisy crawled up the straw. My hands still shook as I set it aside and pulled the tray closer. The eggs were lukewarm, but I managed to redeem myself by devouring them slowly.

That hollow feeling in my stomach felt sated once I'd cleared the plate, but it still demanded…*more.*

"Eleanor?"

I looked over at the doorway and found a woman standing there. Her dark eyes softened as recognition seared through my chest.

A much more welcome sight than Dublin.

"Yulia?"

"Who else?" Her mouth cracked into the most beautiful smile. With her black hair slicked back against her head and her slender body clad in an ebony pantsuit, she looked as witchy as ever. "I've brought you something to wear other than those hideous gowns." She lifted her arms, each one displaying a dress on a hanger. "Which one do you prefer?"

Amid the chaos and turmoil I desperately fought to ignore, fashion was an abrupt, though preferable, change in subject.

One selection she held was a rich, modest black, made of silk. The other was a similar design but made of white lace.

"I'm partial to one in particular," Yulia admitted, fingering the white dress. "But I'm curious what you think." Her accent gave the words a lilting edge and I relished every note. I'd forgotten how lovely someone's voice could sound when they weren't growling threats or shouting insults.

Or peddling vicious lies.

"The white one," I blurted, pointing toward my selection.

"Of course. I see you still have your good taste." She gently set the chosen dress over the foot of the bed. Slung from her shoulder was a black duffel bag, which she set down at her feet. "Dublin asked me to design a few things for you," she explained while folding the black dress and tucking it inside the duffel. "Luckily I'd just finished some new designs that I managed to tailor in a pinch. Though I probably should get your measurements again…"

I'd been in the process of sitting up while she spoke, and her eyes settled over my concave stomach.

Memories gnawed at the edges of my skull. Snippets of a hushed conversation too terrifying to interpret—*poor Eleanor…*

"You should try it on," she said, gently dragging me back to the present. "Though I should warn you that Dublin made some…specifications."

"Like what?" I ran my hand over the surface of the white dress. It felt silky smooth—not laced with broken glass or any other devious tricks I could discern.

"Things he promised were utterly necessary." Her upper lip contorted in a grimace. "I'm sure you'll discover that soon enough. Here, let me help you."

She eased my gown over my head and guided me into a bathroom suite attached to the room. Facing my reflection in the mirror, I cringed. For a woman who'd needed a blood transfusion, I didn't have much to show for it. There were no bruises. No cuts. No broken bones to explain away my slow, sluggish movements.

But I was still rail thin. Too thin.

"I will definitely have to measure you again," Yulia deduced, observing me with a frown. "You're skin and bones—"

"It's nothing," I blurted, letting myself ignore my hazy memories of Dublin's diagnosis for a split-second. Something about a growth. Utterly trivial. "I'm sure anything you make will fit just fine."

"Oh." Yulia swallowed hard. Her eyes scanned my face, and her lips twitched, resisting a frown. "Did Dublin talk to you?—"

"More or less." I shrugged and turned my attention to the shower. As the water warmed, I tested the temperature with my fingers. Then I stepped beneath the spray, allowing the sound of rushing water to obscure the awkward silence.

Dublin deserved some credit. Pregnancy was an intriguing diagnosis, but no different from hemohemorrahgia—a complex lie designed to extort something at my expense.

That was *all* it was.

"It's good to see you again," Yulia called to me, her voice muffled by the shower spray. I snuck a glance at her while lathering my hair with the bottle of shampoo. "I should have visited you sooner. But..." She shook her head, her smile strained. "Do you need help? I'm dying to get my hands on those curls again."

I let her assist me—and I needed the help. For the first time in ages, water felt hot. My skin seared, painfully raw. There was no residual numbness radiating through my bones to shield from sensation.

But...

I froze, half dressed, transfixed on my reflection in a mirror hanging above the sink. A stranger stared back at me. I scanned her eyes, searching for the hint of a monster dwelling within her fragile frame.

A salty taste still lingered on my tongue, impossible to choke down.

"Eleanor?" A warm touch on my shoulder drew my attention to the woman beside me. "What do you think?" she asked while helping me into the white dress.

"It's perfect." The praise wasn't an understatement. Softer than gossamer, the material fit just as comfortably as any previous item of clothing she'd designed for me.

"I think so too. But damn." Frowning, she glanced at a watch on her wrist. "I wish I could stay longer, but Dublin will kill me if I don't finish at least a good bit of your clothing as soon as possible. In the meantime, I left a few things to tide you over." She winked and headed back into the hallway. "You should get some rest. I will check on you later."

By the time I had the sense to whisper, "Goodbye," she was already gone.

~

Semi-darkness greeted me as I opened my eyes. The ceiling was a swath of flickering shadow, and a lone fluorescent bulb illuminated the room, throwing the man standing at the foot of my bed in stark contrast.

Once again, he'd come armed with a cup of mysterious liquid and a bowl of food. Soup, it smelled like. Along with a thick slice of bread and another piece of cake.

"Eat," he prompted, placing the meal down before me.

Drowsiness rendered me compliant enough to accept the cup without complaint. It was already in my hand as I closed my eyes. Drank.

The moment I downed the last drop, he was there to ease it from my grasp. I opened my eyes and found him eyeing me from head to toe. I squirmed as he lingered over my face.

The rage was gone from his expression, but in its wake remained something far too close to concern.

"How are you feeling?"

"Fine," I croaked. "For someone who has cancer, anyway."

"Cancer?" So much for concerned. He went rigid, his eyes narrowed.

I nodded. "A tumor. That's what you implied, isn't it? I must have vampire cancer. Either that, or I am a harlot with no morals—"

"Eleanor…" His teeth clattered, but he snatched up the spoon rather than arguing. "Here."

Accepting it, I twisted the metal between my fingers. The polished surface displayed my reflection, but I barely recognized it. Wide, green eyes and a pursed, pensive expression. Turning away, I fished for any distraction. My scattered thoughts provided one. "Yulia brought me clothing." I gestured to the duffel on the floor. "But she said you requested an alteration. What?"

"How are you feeling?" he repeated without acknowledging my question. "I've asked Dr. Martin to reexamine you—"

"I have my *own* doctor." I fought to put some indignation into my tone and failed. My voice shook. I spent more time eyeing his suit than meeting his gaze directly. He hadn't changed, and the color scheme made him seem even paler than usual—a statue formed of ivory.

"Your so-called doctor, one Elodie Goodfellow," Dublin said.

Was I surprised? Perhaps. Frankly, I couldn't tell fury from shock.

"A medical doctor with more than a few mysterious donations in her bank account from undisclosed benefactors. I've taken the liberty of severing ties with her on your behalf and canceling your donation to St. Mary's. The fewer who have access to your medical records, the better."

My brain blanked at his audacity. One detail stuck out, however. "So, that wasn't you. The D.H. donor?"

He raised an eyebrow.

"D.H.," I explained. "One of the board members of St. Mary's hospital. A donor, I might add, who only appeared after Dr. Wallis vanished. Literally overnight."

I had two different brochures in my stash at home to prove it. One printed only a week after he'd supposedly left the country.

"That's why you went to see Gabriel Lanic?" He asked. "If I were to stalk you from afar, Eleanor, don't you believe I'd hide behind an identity more obscure than my initials?"

He had a point.

"I… Like hell I'll go to your doctor." With one hand, I shoved the blankets back and sat upright, facing the window. "You have no right to—"

"Do not fight me on this." His tone. I had never heard it quite so hard. As if maintaining this conversation alone had stretched his tolerance paper thin.

I twisted around to face him. "And why shouldn't I?"

He laughed, but his eyes were wide, his mouth partially open—a chilling display of ivory fangs. "You have a rare form of *cancer*," he growled. "And you think that just any doctor in the world can help you?"

"Like you care," I hissed. "According to you, I'm a harlot who should consult another man for assistance in this matter. Right?"

He didn't even look insulted. Or guilty. Or contrite.

He met my gaze unflinchingly and said, "You should pray that you accidentally wandered into another man's bed and developed your cancer. Otherwise…"

My stunned silence seemed to satisfy him enough that he left that statement hanging in the air. He tugged on the hem of his jacket, smoothing the edges, his poised, calculating self once more—but there were cracks. For one, he was still wearing that gray suit from the other day, but it wasn't so neat anymore. Dark splotches stained the suit jacket, rivaling the deep crimson of his tie. Strangest of all, my cross shone against his chest as if he'd never removed it.

Too much. Closing my eyes brought me seconds to regain control of my thoughts. *Focus, Ellie.*

He was something to focus on. My rage. My fear. This impending panic surging through my veins. Grasping for stability, I honed it all like a laser, pointed it directly at Dublin Helos.

"I'm sorry if you didn't realize this," I croaked. "But you don't own me. Not anymore. So take your insults and get the hell out!"

It was the last part of that statement that did it. *It,* as in made his jaw clench and his irises shrink around fathomless pupils.

"Your body is practically decomposing around you." His eyes lowered to my throat. "And you think this is the time to flaunt something as trivial ownership? If I didn't bring you here when I did, you would have died."

Died. He made that word sound too final. Not a joke.

"What are you talking about?" I asked.

His back stiffened as he turned away. "The talisman I'd given you…"

"What?" I demanded. "What did it do?"

When his gaze returned to mine, I barely recognized it. "Let's just say there was a complication I hadn't foreseen."

"So, that's why you took it back?" I watched it swing from his neck as my fingers brushed my bare throat.

"I brought you here," he said without confirming it. "I ran the tests. Trust me when I say that *cancer* is the last conclusion I would come to. So take this at face value. Or as a warning. Until this is resolved, I'm not letting you out of my sight."

Alarm bells went off in my head, but I remained silent.

"I don't intend to spend all of my time fighting with you, either." A deliberate pause punctuated the air before he asked, "Your sister—have you heard from her?"

Don't fall for it, Ellie, my inner voice warned. I didn't like how carefully he had phrased the question. Soft. Almost nonchalant, like a normal change of subject.

Funny, because it was my turn to laugh.

"I told her to leave," I found myself confessing without understanding why. "And she did. I told her I never wanted to see her again. And I haven't. So, no, I haven't heard from her."

"Not even a phone call?" His tone conveyed the suspicion he didn't voice—*I don't believe you.*

"No." I shrugged, eyeing my trembling hands. "Not even a phone call."

I had mulled over the various reasons for the silence. Maybe she hated me for not being the special, chosen one? Maybe I hated her. For leaving me when I needed her, and then coming back…

But only to clean up a mess she'd made.

Dublin would have never poisoned me without darling Georgiana. Despite everything, I thought I could ignore the deception—but betrayal was a strange animal. One day, all might seem well again. Those fresh wounds might even start to heal, scabbed over with assurances of love and heartfelt promises.

But a promise couldn't soothe the underlying infection for very long. Georgie, despite her apologies, had been unwilling to enlighten me on any aspect of her life. She didn't possess Dublin's penchant for brutal honesty, either, and every day that I saw her there, wandering the halls of Gray Manor as if nothing had changed…

The house *was* mine, technically, as was the fortune.

I just never expected her to forfeit it all so easily.

"You haven't tried to contact her?" Dublin pressed, his suspicion palpable.

"And what could I say?" I blinked and moisture spilled down my cheeks. In vain, I tried to banish the tears with a swipe of my hand. "Hello, Georgie. I'm… I have vampire cancer?"

It all had the makings of some sordid, morbid drama my mother would read when she thought no one was looking. I had *some* self-respect.

Enough to realize when another subject change was in order.

"How could this happen?" I directed the question his way, expecting a clear, succinct answer.

It's a tumor, Eleanor, honestly.

Anything but, "I don't know."

"Sorry?" I blinked, convinced I'd heard him wrong. I even patted my ears in case they'd become clogged.

"You heard me." His gaze shot to mine and nothing had ever terrified me more than his expression. Not the nightmares. Not the hunger. The hue of his irises flickered a burnished silver and in them I saw the truth before he uttered it out loud. "I don't know."

A sound trickled out of me that might have been another laugh. It definitely wasn't a sob. I hadn't fallen that far. Not yet. More tears weren't what spilled out of my eyes to paint my cheeks. Just sweat.

"What do you mean, you don't know—"

"Eat." He nudged the side table, jarring it closer to me. The bowl of soup wobbled, precariously close to the edge. "I can hear your stomach growling from here."

"No." I shoved the bowl away. "I don't want the damn soup. I want *answers*—"

"I don't know!" Thunderous, his rich baritone rang out, stinging my ears in its wake. He had shouted. *Was* shouting. "You want answers? Well, so do I. Do you think this is a common occurrence? Well it isn't. Neither is a woman who willingly sells her soul and can't seem to stay out of danger no matter the risk—"

"Sir?" Footsteps raced down the hallway and a woman in a white uniform peeked out from behind the door. A nurse. "Is everything okay?"

I almost envied her. She felt something. Fear, most likely. My physical senses might have returned, but my emotional nerves lacked reception. I still felt…hollow, even as a vampire raged a few paces away.

"It's getting late," I began while lurching to my feet. The nurse rushed forward to assist, but Dublin beat her to it.

His hand caught my arm reflexively, but I wrenched out of his reach, forced to grip the bed frame to steady myself.

"I'm fine," I insisted. "In fact, I should be leaving." I staggered for the door, pushing past him.

"Where are you going?"

"What does it matter?" I tossed back, limping over the threshold. "You can leave without a word, but I can't?"

It had to be late. The main lights were dimmed in the hall, leaving just a faint glow to see by. Up ahead, I spied an adjacent corridor that must have led to the central ward. Rather than head for it, I turned and advanced farther down the hallway. I needed silence. Darkness. Escape.

"I asked: Where are you going?"

Damn. A shiver racked my spine, instilled by the grit in the voice haunting me.

But I didn't give in. Left. Right. My feet moved dutifully, driving me forward even as my newfound strength began to wane again. Pride warred with basic human instinct. I needed to sit down. I needed—

"Stop." A pale hand slammed against the wall inches from my face and I had no choice but to stop. "I'm begging you. Begging that, for once in your life, you exercise *caution*." Though his tone was level, anger bubbled up beneath the surface of his polished persona. Like heat, I felt it sear my skin.

"So, now you care? Funny, considering that you left. Without a word. Without so much as a calling card. After you told me that the only reason you even bothered to tolerate me was to, and I quote, *'Get to the only Gray who mattered.'*"

"Should I tell you where I was?" He shifted to face me, and I took an involuntary step back. He towered above, his features in shadow. "I was trying to save your life, yet again. A task it appears that I take far more seriously than you do."

I swallowed. *Ah.* "What a convincing lie."

"A lie…" His eyes widened and then narrowed into slits. Against the wall, his fingers flexed, and a hairline crack appeared in the plaster. "You think you have the right to pout like a petulant child? When it was your sister who—"

"My sister who what?"

He seemed to hesitate before confessing, "Your sister who signed a contract of her own."

"Oh?" My heart throbbed, suddenly heavy, and I turned away. "Don't tell me you've been with her all this time? How lucky for you. You managed to score not just one Gray sister, but both—"

"No."

I cringed. His tone was far too soft.

"I didn't force *her* into a contract, Eleanor."

He let the silence linger, almost daring me to ask him to continue.

I didn't.

I couldn't.

So, his upper lip curled back from his teeth as he said, "She refused to let me near you—as you lay dying, I might add —unless I agreed to her terms."

Heat prickled up and down my spine as a burning sting stabbed at my eyes. "What terms?"

"I agreed to leave the city immediately," he said. "Cease all contact with you. If I refused, she would stand by and let us *both* watch you die."

"No." I blinked more rapidly, shaking my head. "You're lying."

He wasn't. We both knew it. Still, it helped somewhat to say as much. I could give Georgiana the benefit of the doubt she never extended toward me. I could pretend she actually loved me.

As long as I ignored the truth.

"Do you think I wanted to tell you like this?" he countered. "Trust me when I say this, but I don't enjoy playing the role of your monster."

"So, why come back at all?" I bit back. My heart raced as rage overrode logic. He wasn't the only one with secrets to tell. "No, don't tell me. We both know the answer—for your contract. Is that it? You want it back?"

Of course. His face would reveal as much. I smirked, ready to witness the truth in full view—his gaze widened, horrified. His jaw clenched, made of stone.

He wasn't gloating.

"You knew," I deduced, closing my eyes in defiance of everything his shocked expression conveyed. Yes, he had to know. "You want it that badly? Fine. Just admit it now. I'll shove the damn thing down your throat if you do."

But he said nothing. No quip. No insult.

"I-If we are done here, I'll just be leaving," I stammered weakly. One step was as far as I made it before I found myself shoved against the wall.

Gently. Cool fingers gripped my shoulders, trembling with the restraint needed to keep from bruising—his expression contained no such care, however. Even the suit couldn't save him—man became monster.

Rather than berate me, he reached into his jacket pocket. I hadn't noticed the bulge against his side before, which concealed something thin, made of silver. Two circular bits of metal capped off each end of it, and recognition hit me like a slap. Manacles.

"Are…are you insane?" I exhaled the question.

"I'm exasperated." He caught my wrists in his fist and casually tugged. Two involuntary steps brought me closer to him. In a low voice, he warned, "We can walk back to your room together. Or"—he hefted one end of the handcuff so that the metal caught the light—"I can drag you there."

I fought to keep my head held high, my chin jutting defiantly into the air. "You can't do this—"

In a blur of motion, he lunged. One sweep of his hand robbed me of balance, but before I could sway, I was in his arms. He surged forward, *carrying* me down the hall.

Heedless of any poor soul who might have been sleeping, I screamed. I kicked. I flailed.

"You can't do this!" I attempted to grab at the doorway as he turned into my room.

With little effort, he broke my grip and headed toward the bed. One shrug of his shoulders and I landed in an unceremonious heap over the crumpled blankets.

He snapped one of the cuffs onto my wrist while I was still stunned and secured it to the frame of the bed. I didn't even have a chance to resist. To fight. So I settled for lashing out like a child and kicked him.

If he felt the pain in his right knee, his face revealed nothing.

"You don't want to eat?" he echoed. "Fine." One swipe of his hand sent the tray of food crashing into the wall. Yellow broth slashed the white backdrop like paint and the cake went flying into a far corner. "You don't want to talk about this with some damn rationality, have it your way. Scream, Eleanor. Fight. You'll just give me a reason to gag you."

Shock deflated me. I cringed against the headboard as he stormed toward the doorway. A nurse was already there, gaping in shock.

"Get Ms. Gray something to calm her down," Dublin ordered as he pushed past her. He spared one last searing glance in my direction and snarled, "She's a danger to herself."

With what seemed to be an apologetic frown, the woman nodded and rushed off. Oddly enough, when she returned sporting a syringe, I didn't resist, allowing her to pierce my vein with little fanfare.

Like a good captive, I lay there, one hand chained to the bed, the other resting somewhere over my heart. It was racing. Pounding. Surging.

From unease or rage?

Who the hell knew?

Eventually, the wave of medication kicked in. My pulse slowed and my eyelids became heavy. When sleep came for me, I surrendered to it.

He might have won this round, but he'd already lost another.

When one was locked within a game of wits against a vampire, I'd learned that there was only one way to break a stalemate.

Someone had to bleed.

And I was already wounded.

~

The drug wore off in slow, ebbing waves. When my thoughts finally seemed coherent again, I peeled my eyes open, expecting to find myself strapped to the bed. Instead, both hands moved freely.

That wasn't all. The bedside tray had been righted, the mess cleared from the floor. Fresh food had replaced my ruined meal—another nondescript cup and a plate of bacon, eggs, and sausage. Draped over the foot of my bed was the black dress Yulia had brought along with a pair of my sensible flats and a black coat, also mine.

Unease goaded my heart into racing, but I choked the fear back.

Instead, I ignored the food in favor of getting dressed. My body felt stiff, each movement awkward and slow. By the time I fastened the last button on my coat, someone had entered the room to join me.

He was wearing black, I saw when I finally gathered up the nerve to look. A black suit. A blacker tie. His eyes glowed in harsh contrast, taking me in with one callous sweep. But he wasn't angry.

Even worse, he was unreadable.

"I suggest we change tack." He sat on a nearby chair and gestured toward the bed. "I'll open with a threat, since you seem inclined to play the role of prisoner. How much do you value your cat?"

"T-Tinkles?" Panic clenched my lungs, making each breath a struggle. "Where is he?"

"Safe," Dublin replied before I could assume the worst. "I will return him to you, of course. *After* we finish our discussion."

"Or?" Despite my feelings toward him, there were some lines even I had never envisioned him crossing. Then again, I'd never owned a piece of his soul before.

"Or I'll keep him," he warned. "We both know he won't mourn your company."

I bit my lip in anguish. In some ways, it was a far worse bluff than threatening his life. I would be the only one disenfranchised in this equation.

"What do you want?"

"I suggest we revert to our usual method of communication." He placed something onto the bedside table, beside the food: a rectangular, leather-bound book flipped open to a blank page. When my gaze returned to Dublin, he crossed his arms, transforming into his businessman persona. "We negotiate."

"Via a contract?" I backed away near the wall, keeping him in full view.

"Yes. I will apologize for last night if that's what you want."

"And what do *you* want?" I whispered.

He cocked his head and shrugged, smoothing his hands along the front of his suit. "I think it's best if you stay with me."

I didn't miss the marked shift in his tone. Cautious. As though I were a simpleton best communicated with via slow, careful wording.

"For your protection," he said. "You need proper medical care. I will make all the arrangements—"

"Don't pretend like you care," I warned. His words still hurt, smarting on my psyche like invisible scratches. "Just cut to the chase and tell me what you *really* want."

His eyes narrowed. "Should I come out and say it, then? I want my contract, of course."

Ah. It was a game of hide-and-seek I'd planned over two months ago. Back when bitterness had driven me to hide the leather book *where no one would ever find it,* or so the childish part of me had claimed.

Knowing Dublin, everything I had was probably in the gloved hands of one of his agents, being ruthlessly inspected as we spoke. Or he'd searched for it himself. Hell, maybe that was the reason his hair was slicked, damp in a way that eerily coincided with the rain lashing at the window beyond him.

But one obvious fact diminished my glee at the prospect.

"You didn't know I had it. Did you?" Suddenly drained, I crept forward and sat on the edge of the mattress, as far from him as possible.

"No." He glared through the window. "Raphael doesn't part with his trophies easily."

"So, what happens if I tell you? I wind up shackled to another bed? Or is this the part where you threaten me for real?" I squared my chin, fighting to sound brave. Even before I saw his jaw clench, I knew I'd failed.

"To kill you? How about we bargain instead, like I suggested? You want to stay at Gray Manor? Fine. You want to live in denial? Fine. As long as you remain under my protection, you can set whatever terms you wish."

"And as long as I return your contract," I added.

He nodded after a second's pause. "That as well."

I bit my lip. To relinquish the one morsel of power I held over him or not? *Knowledge is king*, my father used to say, during one of the rare moments when he wasn't heralding the importance of money. *Never surrender it willingly.*

"I'd like to know it's secure," Dublin insisted. "However, telling me its location won't invalidate your ownership."

I noted how reluctantly he added that last tidbit of information.

"Even if I tell you, it will change nothing," I felt compelled to say. "I still don't forgive you for insulting me—"

"And I don't expect you to. As for our agreement, shall we put it in writing?" he asked. "You agree to stay with me as well as reveal the location of my contract. In return, you set your own terms."

I attempted to meet his gaze and found no hostility in it. No real emotion, either. Just endless burnished silver. "Fine. I want… François gets to remain as my driver."

He raised an eyebrow as he reached for the pen. "François?"

"I hired him a few weeks ago. He's very…r-reliable," I stammered. Honestly, it was the principle of the matter.

François, though slightly hated, was still someone I'd hired on my own. Dublin could lock me away in a tower if he wanted, just as long as he let me keep what little of my life I'd managed to rebuild.

"Fine." He jotted down a line on a fresh page in the contract book. "What else?"

"And…" I swallowed hard, flexing my fingers against the mattress. "You apologize for what you said about me."

He raised an eyebrow. "If that is what you wish…"

"And," I added. "I want you to be honest with me. If I ask you something, anything, you tell me the truth. No secrets. No games. No lies."

"Agreed." With a stroke of his pen, he added another line. As he finished, his eyes cut to mine. "But I would like to second that request. You keep nothing from me. Nothing."

He held the pen out and shoved the book across the table.

I sighed, biting any more questions back. We were on a dangerous precipice, mere inches from falling off. Only God knew what waited down below, and I wasn't that inclined to find out for myself.

With a single stroke, I signed my name and watched him do the same.

And the sight alone shouldn't have imparted the most stability I'd felt since…

Well, since he'd left.

"So, what now?"

"Now?" He tucked the contract book into his pocket and stood. "You uphold your end—you come with me, no dramatics."

"And," I added with a sigh, "I show you where your contract is?"

He nodded. "Where is it?"

"Where else?" I countered. It was obvious in a sense—what imposing shelter would make for the perfect hiding place for a vampire's soul? "Home."

Gray Manor rose upon the hill like the disapproving relative most people complained about. The one bastion of my life that I could never seem to escape.

My only comfort was that Dublin didn't seem particularly fond of it, either. Stone-faced, he guided his car onto the property, following what little commands I gave. *Follow the main path. Then go beyond the house, beyond the gardens, farther…*

"Here," I croaked once we'd reached the very end of the property.

Looming before us stood what my mother had lovingly referred to as the Crowning Jewel of both heritage and home. Our family crypt. Even now, the structure held the same morbid fascination for me that it had during my childhood.

Made entirely of stone and almost simple in appearance, the structure contained Gray bodies spanning at least three centuries, back from the time of my great-grandfather many times over, James. Given what a diverse and interesting bunch we were, I almost pitied it.

"You hid it here?" Dublin wondered. He had leaned toward my side without me realizing and I flinched as his chill raised goosebumps over the back of my neck. A part of me wanted to hate him still—hate the fact that he could sit so close to me as though nothing had changed.

I snuck a glance at his face, alarmed by how neutral his expression seemed.

Apparently, we were both in denial of recent events.

"Georgie and I used to play here as children," I found myself muttering. Compelled by some need to explain the safety of my hiding place perhaps? Or maybe his skeptical frown amused me. "We used to sneak notes back and forth by stuffing them into this empty urn kept on a shelf for decoration." An ironic fixture, given my mother's general loathing of any frivolous displays. "Sometimes, I used to come here to think."

"You...*played* in a crypt?"

As his expression shifted, I wasn't sure what might appear. A wry twist of his mouth wasn't my first suspicion. God, it couldn't be a smile.

"Why am I not surprised?"

I turned away. I would take that as an insult rather than a harmless quip. Only he could make the cold boundaries I'd grown up obeying seem more trite than tradition.

In fact, he made everything about my past life seem trivial.

Like the days when I could sit beside someone and not recall what their touch felt like, rough with possession. I tried to suppress the thought, but my breath quickened anyway, signaling my unease like blood in shark-infested waters.

Thankfully, he parked the next second, choosing a spot near the shade of a weeping willow, and I used the task of unfurling myself from my seat belt to fill the awkward silence. When I finally pushed the door to my side open, Dublin was already there.

He warily extended his hand, as if expecting me to bite it rather than accept it. When I did the latter, he helped me to my feet. Together, we faced my childhood playground and I pretended like I wasn't affected by his scrutiny.

Neglect reduced the landscape to a wilderness of overrun grasses and weeds. Without its typical manicured appearance, the area resembled something right out of a horror film. The crypt itself was by far the most unsettling fixture. Square-shaped and framed by Romanesque pillars supporting a sharply pitched roof, it was an anomaly compared to the Gothic style of the main manor.

"You used to play here as a child," Dublin reiterated. "For enjoyment?"

I could sense the typical mixture of scorn and pity he usually showed whenever I mentioned personal anecdotes. This day, however, I decided to inhale the damp, humid air of the overcast day and give in to nostalgia.

He wasn't forgiven—but I could pause my ire for history's sake.

"Shall I give you the grand tour?"

The door wasn't locked. Ironic considering that most of the people buried here had spent their entire lives keeping their secrets under lock and key. Inside was a small entryway formed of gray marble floors and dark walls. A lone statue lorded over a spiral staircase built into the earth, leading deeper into the crypt.

"Is something wrong?" I looked back and found Dublin lingering beyond the doorway, his frown more pronounced than usual. "Don't tell me *you* have an aversion to death?"

"It's not that," he said gruffly. I waited, but he didn't elaborate further.

Sighing, I started forward without him. "I can bring it to you—"

"I would have thought you Grays had some elaborate protocol regarding your sacred structures."

I faltered and braced my hand against the wall for stability. Was that another joke?

"Do come in," I snapped rather than decide. "Welcome to the glorious Gray family tomb."

Without so much as a retort, he finally entered the entryway, and memories stirred as I led the way with him on my heels.

"My parents brought us here often," I admitted, brushing my fingers along the stone walls as my voice echoed. Dust coated my fingertips, depressingly thick. "It was the one thing I ever saw my father take pride in, apart from the fortune. He called it our 'enduring legacy.'"

At the foot of the stairs was a light that, once flipped, revealed the cavernous interior containing five chambers that branched from the central room. In the center stood another statue, one of a crying angel, her eyes downcast in sorrow.

"That's been here for generations," I remarked.

Slipping past her, I wandered the circular space and tried to see it as someone on the outside might. Like a vampire perhaps. In death, we Grays were every bit as interesting as we were in life. Our tastes in minimal design had changed little over the centuries. Such as a fondness for our namesake color.

I crept into the alcove designated for the most recent generation, aware of Dublin's gaze on the back of my neck.

"Is this the urn you and your sister used?" he wondered.

I peered over my shoulder and found him staring up at the old marble container on the shelf across from the somber angel. "Yes. It was one of the most reliable ways to reach Georgie back in the old days, if you can imagine that. I should look inside it." I started toward him, hope bubbling in my throat.

Maybe after weeks of silence, she would decide to reach out by recalling an obscure tradition from our childhood?

I changed course only when I noticed Dublin watching me. How pathetic would that seem?

Somewhere around very and depressing, I decided.

I turned instead and approached the wall where my parents were interred. Joined in eternal rest, they dominated the top two places. The layout resembled that of a vertical grid with each tomb marked by a stone placard engraved with the occupant's name. Per chamber, each wall could hold up to eight corpses in rows of two.

And, like any doting parents, mine had ensured that Georgie and I already had plots picked out beneath them. While we'd barely spent quality time together in life, we would spend the rest of our miserable eternity in close proximity.

How charming.

I trailed my fingers over my mother's engraved name, and I swore I could hear her scolding from beyond the grave. *My God, Eleanor, what have you done now? You were always such a dutiful child.*

"Sorry," I told her out loud, as contritely as one could while talking to herself.

Sinking into a crouch, I felt along the edge of the placeholder for my tomb. A sharp tug pried it loose enough to slip my hand into the space beyond. Tucked just within reach was a leather-bound book—and something else. I'd almost forgotten hiding it as well—a small plastic ring with a chipped blue bead in the center.

"Don't tell me you're too enthralled by nostalgia to remember why we're here?" Dublin remarked behind me.

Clutching the book to my chest, I stood. "I've got it." I turned and found him mere steps away. Extending the contract book with one hand, I quietly concealed the ring in my other. "My end of our bargain."

His face unreadable, Dublin took the contract from me and tucked it into the breast pocket of his suit.

Even though he'd mentioned as much earlier, I still felt tempted to ask, "So what does this mean?"

"The book is merely a symbolic token," he explained. "Your name is on it. Regardless, I find that it's best to keep these things close."

"Ah." I nodded along as if I knew the first thing about soul collecting. "Well, now you have it."

An uncomfortable silence stretched on for endless seconds. The longer we lingered, the colder the atmosphere felt. My teeth chattered as the monotonous scenery made me picture…well, decay.

"Yours?" Dublin nodded toward my earmarked tomb. "I suspect this isn't a new purchase."

"Oh, no." I followed his gaze and brushed my thumb over the etched letters of my name. "It was a Christmas gift. My parents presented them to Georgie and me when I was eight."

"A gift?"

"Of course." I chafed at his tone. As if such a thing weren't normal. "At least they had enough sense to realize that I didn't need any space beneath mine. I should have it engraved now: Eleanor Gray, forever alone."

Oh, the poetic justice of it all. One of the last Grays doomed to die a spinster.

"You believe that?" Dublin questioned in a tone that made me bite my lip. It was too stern. Too soft.

"Why shouldn't I?"

"You never envisioned yourself marrying someone? Anyone? You've never wanted children—"

"I'm tired." Sighing, I turned to him, swiping my dust-covered fingers on my skirt. "Now that you have your precious…"

He was looking at me so strangely that I lost my train of thought. It was different from his usual scowl—eyes narrowed, mouth in a firm, odd line. Something flickered across his gaze, too elusive to name. Before I could, he marched toward the central chamber, beckoning with a wave of his hand. "Let's go."

Perhaps talk of tombs was too morbid, even for the undead? I tucked my ring into my purse and then followed him, uneasy. As he mounted the stairs, I couldn't resist slipping my hand into the urn on my way past. Unsurprisingly, I found nothing but dust.

Georgie was probably galivanting on a beach somewhere with a new lover, her pathetic sister forgotten.

"I'd rather not spend the rest of the day among your deceased family members, if you don't mind," Dublin called from above.

When I finally rejoined him, he was waiting for me outside the building and I steeled myself for a plot-twist-style reveal. *Ha!* He had been lying all along. This was the part when he'd entrap my soul for eternity. I could only hope he didn't drug me first before spiriting me away.

"Get in," was all he said, wrenching the car door open for me.

Confined again, I had no escape from the thoughts that months alone had kept at bay. Things like memories of him I wished to smother. His touch. His taste.

The night he returned…

My lips burned and I brushed my fingers along them, tracing the remnants of him. Had that kiss been another twisted game?

A way for him to lower my guard.

Again…

Stop, Ellie.

Rolling my window down and inhaling fresh air helped somewhat. Or at least the biting chill put everything back into perspective. Once again, I'd signed a portion of my life away, though I wasn't quite sure what I'd bargained for in return. In all honesty, I didn't need his protection. A squadron of security guards on my family's payroll would have sufficed—though, admittedly, not as effective as a vampire.

But sufficient.

I didn't need him.

"Where are we?" I asked as the car finally slowed before a building in the heart of the city. A secluded high-rise accessible only through a security gate and a garage activated by a keypad.

"Somewhere safe," Dublin replied before exiting the vehicle. He circled to my end and offered his hand to help me stand.

Wary, I followed him into the building, observing everything as objectively as I could. "You certainly haven't changed," I blurted. "My house would have been just fine, you do realize?"

It was a lie.

"Your house looks like it should be condemned," Dublin replied, tugging me along.

I tried to regain my anger, but I was too busy gaping at our surroundings to remember to be insulted. Dublin had always had a flair for elegance, but this…

Black walls and marble flooring created a hushed world of darkness. Elevators lined in gold led to the upper floors. There was no lobby. No grinning receptionist. Just a silent trip up to the tenth floor, where we exited into a darkened hallway. At the end awaited a black door that opened the moment Dublin approached.

A woman stood behind it, her smile warm. "Good evening, sir," she greeted while stepping aside, allowing Dublin and me to enter what appeared to be a private suite.

I glanced at her from the corner of my eye, hating how my stomach tightened with every detail observed. Blond hair formed a neat bun at the nape of her neck, displaying beautiful features subtly enhanced with makeup. Her modest black dress did little to disguise her curves. A strange sense of déjà vu warned that I knew her.

From where?

It was only when she gestured for my coat that I remembered. *Katherine.* That was her name. The woman whose contract he managed. He'd saved her from Saskia and her henchman if I remembered correctly.

And now she was apparently at his personal beck and call.

"Thank you. That will be all, Kate," Dublin told her, sending her scurrying off across the spacious entryway.

Kate. The nickname echoed inside my skull. The same man refused to call me Ellie, professing a hatred of "unprofessional" monikers. And yet, this woman was *Kate*.

"Nice to see you've had company." The statement slipped out, but I didn't know how I intended it to land. As an insult? A jab? Something innocent, I decided when Dublin trained his gaze on me. Merely a harmless question. "Last I remembered, you lived alone."

Whether out of an unwillingness to fight or simple disinterest, he gritted his teeth against a reply and stalked forward to throw open two double doors directly across from us.

Beyond them was a sight so unexpected that my mouth dropped open, all else forgotten.

A room formed the center of the suite, one almost entirely encased in glass, each massive window displaying a harrowing scene of the city. Multicolored swaths of skyscrapers bathed in nightfall created a fantastical landscape of neon and navy.

"Does this meet your expectations?" Dublin wondered, his tone as smug as ever.

Perhaps for good reason, considering I had to physically nudge my mouth closed with the tip of my finger.

"It's fine." As I spoke, I crossed the room, wandering as close to the glass as I dared. Awe turned out to be no match for pride, however. "It's *beautiful…*"

"There is no family crypt," he added. "But hopefully it will suffice."

Was that yet another joke?

"Luckily, my pre-chosen tombstone isn't going anywhere," I said. "Who knows, by the end of the month, I may be enjoying it the way my parents always intended." A smile shaped my mouth. "I should pick out my coffin tomorrow, I suppose. A nice, sensible, boring one fit for a spinster."

I was breaking my resolve to stay angry again. Perhaps hating him took too much effort? Still grinning, I looked over—but Dublin wasn't laughing. Instead, his eyes cut to mine, imparting a chill that made me shiver.

"We need to talk."

"Oh?" I returned my attention to the view and braced my fingers over the glass. "About what?"

His scoff warned that he wasn't playing along this time— but anger I could stomach. His low tone alarmed me far more. "I think you know what."

Did I? *No*, I decided, shaking my head. "I'm tired." I turned toward a random direction. "Is the bedroom this way?"

"Eleanor."

Before I could take a step, his hand fell over my shoulder pinning me in place.

"I've played along until now," he admitted. "But I lack the energy to pretend anymore."

"Pretend?" I asked innocently.

"Yes, pretend—as though you don't know what really ails you. It isn't cancer."

A part of me felt relieved that I couldn't see his face from this angle—and that he couldn't see mine.

"My contract was one aspect requiring clarity, but now we need to discuss—"

"I don't want to talk about this now," I said. "Frankly, I'm not in the mood for more personal attacks on my character, either—"

"Can you blame me?" His strained tone turned cutting. "Put your pride aside for a second. This isn't a little game, or a fantasy, or a contract that you can confront by stripping naked and turning the tables. This is your life. For whatever reason, I'd rather not see you squander it in denial."

"As if you care." Because he didn't obviously. At least, not beyond some ulterior motives he had yet to reveal. Sighing, I tossed out potential answers, saving him the trouble. "Allow me to guess why. Raphael has put a bounty on my head? Or maybe your aim is more selfish than that? You get your precious years back as long as you—"

"I'm trying to talk to you reasonably. You decide to provoke." His grip tightened, straining the fabric of my dress. I could feel the ridge of every finger and memories triggered. Sensations I didn't want to recall. Emotions I didn't need. All of them descended at once, constricting my chest in a vice. "Look at me." He spun me to face him. "You demanded an apology. Fine. You have one."

God, I trembled at what I saw in his gaze, lurking beneath the gray irises, so faint that it could have been a figment of my imagination. Hate?

Or something far worse. *Guilt.*

"But I won't humor you anymore. I refuse to let you mock me as well." His tone deepened and I understood the true source of his irritation. I had the nerve to taunt the great and terrible contractor with two concepts that seemed to affect him more than any other. Life and death. "According to Dr. Martin, your condition is not fatal. And yet you still choose to refer to your mortality as casually as the weather? Fine. But first, face the fact that you *may* have a tumor. Or—"

"Stop." I had to clench my hands into fists to keep from slapping them over my ears as he snarled his next words.

"*Or* something far different. If I can acknowledge as much, why can't you? Say it."

"Fine. Something *unnatural.*" I blinked, surprised as moisture slid down my cheeks. "So unnatural that you accused me of having loose morals rather than believe it. Is that what you want me to say? I would rather have a tumor—"

"I had every reason in the world to deny it," he pointed out. "Or at least deny that I had any part in it. Can you admit that?"

Maybe I could… If life and death weren't the very tools of his trade.

"So, why believe it now?"

He laughed, spitting out each chuckle through clenched teeth. "Perhaps because I've ceased being surprised by anything where you are concerned? And I don't want to fight with you, but I won't watch you lie to yourself, either."

More tears spilled from my eyes though I wasn't sure why. "Why not? Tormenting me is what you do best, after all."

"Stop trying to bait me into a fight." He reached out, tucking a stray curl behind my ear.

I went rigid—there was no gentleness in the act. He lingered as if daring me to recoil, so I dug my heels in just to ensure I didn't.

But then he remained, taunting me with seconds of contact. So, I gave in and tried to swat his fingers away. "I'm not the one who attacked your character—"

"You are now," he said.

"Oh really?" I laughed. "How?"

"By pretending like you don't see it." He stepped in closer, and I had to crane my neck to hold his gaze. "Forget the rest. You ask why I care? Don't you dare act as though you don't know—"

"What?" I demanded.

"Why I returned despite intending to spend at least a full damn decade abroad." He lowered his mouth to my ear. "What Yulia knows. Saskia. Raphael. They all see it. Mocked me for it. I even told you once, my intentions toward you, didn't I?"

That he had.

"I want you, Eleanor Gray..."

Lies. I swallowed hard, resisting the memory. "Told me what? That you have a fetish for innocence? That I'm the one who toys with you? Who kisses *you* out of nowhere and leaves on a whim—"

"No." He withdrew, his eyes flashing. "That I have an irritating impulse to *not* watch you die. Even if you aggravate me every damn step of the way. Even if it's a goddamn struggle just to keep my sanity around you. It's like you want me to—" He broke off and let me go. "Fine. Run. Play the only role you seem willing to play."

"Wonderful." I turned on my heel, gritting my teeth. "But don't pretend like this is my fault. I didn't leave you. I didn't accuse you of—"

"Damn you." His grip clamped down like a vise on my forearm, dragging me back. The second I winced, he released me only to shift his weight to physically block my path. "You enjoy this, don't you? Pushing me to the goddamn brink. The harder I try to keep my composure, the more you chip away at it. Is this what you want?" He fingered the neckline of my dress, seizing the fabric. "Fine. Perhaps I had every right to question your integrity? I'll offer you another ultimatum—drop the naïve act or we will both discover just how innocent you really are. You named a whole list of others you've supposedly been with—but how many were lies?"

My hand lashed out, colliding with his cheek. *Thwack!* He didn't even flinch—but I did as his thumb toyed with a delicate strip of lace.

"Let go," I whispered. My hand stung as if to warn me away from slapping him again. "Get off!"

"No." He wound the material more tightly around his finger, forcing me on tiptoe to keep it from ripping. "Admit it out loud, your true condition—"

"Or?" I rasped, hating how my voice broke.

He twisted the lace again. "Or I'll lose my patience."

"Stop!"

"Fair enough." His expression blank, he tugged.

Fabric unraveled like wisps of smoke as my dress slipped from my shoulders. Before my eyes, Yulia's creation fluttered in pieces to my feet. Even in shock, I knew he was the cause of the malfunction.

"What are you doing?" I rushed to cover my breasts with my hands, but Dublin didn't even give the appearance of shame.

His gaze raked over me, lingering on the flesh my fingers struggled to shield. Disgust, I could stomach, even if it stung.

While a part of me may have cringed from it, my pride would remain intact.

But his lips parted instead, and my breathing hitched. Alarm bells sounded within my skull, warning me away as he angled his body toward me. Pinprick pupils made his eyes seem even brighter. Burning. Impossible to meet head-on.

It was a dangerous expression. One that triggered a million terrifying sensations I shied from acknowledging. Heat. Heaviness in my limbs that made it harder to stand.

And an ache in my chest that grew more painful by the second.

"*Finally,* you have the sense to be afraid. Or not." His nostrils flared, and he scoffed. "I should have known. As always, this excites you more than anything else. You *enjoy* what you do to me."

Enjoyment? Was that the name for how my heart lurched in time with his callous laugh?

He took another step. I jolted back until my spine went rigid against the unyielding wall of glass behind me.

"Get away from me," I croaked.

He laughed again. Then he lunged, slamming his hands against the glass on either side of my head. In the same motion, his knee nudged my thighs, forcing them apart. Slowly. The fabric of his pants teased snatches of my skin, making me jump with every deliberate nudge.

"You put on a good enough act." He brushed his thumb along the trembling corner of my mouth, tracing my frown. "But your heart betrays you always. It rarely hammers in fear. Instead, your pulse dances with excitement."

My head spun as I desperately tried to regain clarity. Sanity. Anything. "Stop—"

"Then face what you really fear. Do you enjoy mocking me? Parading me through a crypt and spewing poetic notions of death? This truly is a game to you."

He swiped his hand over my belly and I cringed, resisting his touch. But then his fingers drifted lower. Lower, plunging between my legs.

And I forgot how to move. How to breathe. Paralyzed, I was a slave to his reaction.

A hiss caught between his teeth. "Damn you." Eyes glowing, he looked down at his fingers. "Of course you're wet already. Of course you crave this."

A deeper groan resonated in his chest as he flexed his wrist, caressing the part of me only he had ever claimed. I closed my eyes, my lips bitten and raw. Noises escaped my throat regardless.

He was ruthless, utilizing sinful, featherlight passes of his thumb. My head reared back against the frigid glass, a groan ripped from my lips.

"Look at me." His forehead nudged mine until I met his gaze. Both eyes were wide. Unfocused. Less devil now, merely an angel fallen from his perch, hell-bent on dragging me down with him. "I'll destroy you before you destroy me. I will. So stop daring me to. Death is a fucking game to you, but life? *That* makes you run scared. So say it." His mouth found my earlobe, grazing the tip in a silent plea. "Put a name to your *tumor* or forfeit your body if you're so determined to die anyway. Say it or you're mine."

"Why are you doing this?" My eyes were overflowing. All I could see were shadows—dark and light, swirling around us. "Stop."

"Then say it."

My lips parted. I croaked, "C-Cancer."

"Fair enough."

A zipper hummed, sounding miles away, and real panic descended.

"Let me go," I said breathlessly.

He didn't, placing his hands on my hips with a gentleness that contradicted the hate radiating off him in waves.

I should have been screaming. Clenching my legs together.

But when he flicked his thumb along my inner thigh, they spread for him with no resistance. It was as if my body rebelled against my brain, welcoming the pressure inching inside me with no restraint. His hips slammed against mine and my spine arched, driving him deeper.

He stiffened as if waiting for me to shove him off. Scream. Fight. My mouth found the crook of his shoulder instead, stealing his scent in ragged gulps. He raged inside me, so rigid, forcing my numbed flesh to conform. Burn.

And it was an agony some sick part of me relished. Raw friction. Communication he couldn't fake or deceive through.

His body stripped him bare and only like this were we ever matched.

Two desperate, pathetic souls.

Groaning, he rocked his hips and my breathing faltered. He was too deep. Too consuming. My nails dug into his shoulders, my face hidden against his skin—but he wrenched on my skull, forcing me to face him.

"Two months," he declared against my parted lips, his eyes heavy-lidded. "Weeks of torment. Being haunted by this." He growled in time with another slow, searing thrust. "Your skin. The feel of you. The sound of you…"

Lies. I fought the wave of pleasure, my eyelids fluttering—but then he jerked, slamming into me. Mind-numbing fire ripped down my spine, feeding on my blood like gasoline, and I went limp.

"I should have killed you the first time," he said. "It's what you wanted, wasn't it?"

The words he said didn't matter. Each gritted note in his voice set off a chain reaction. Nerves crackled. Short-circuited. I whimpered, grasping him tighter. My hips shifted, urging him deeper. Harder. More.

He hissed, rearing back. Then he lurched into me. "Restraint. You take it from me. Always. And you think you can hide from me? From this." Harder. Sharper thrusts made every fear and doubt dissolve into nothing. "But I own you, always. Body and soul."

His thumb invaded between my legs, and I saw white with each stroke he delivered. Every muscle contracted, contorting me like a puppet on violent strings.

All the while, his thrusts quickened. Faster. Too fast.

My head fell back against my shoulders, my eyes on the ceiling as pleasure built.

"I've had centuries to prepare for you," he growled as I convulsed, mindless. "Years beyond your understanding. Do you think this means anything? No." He stiffened, grunting against the base of my throat. "You mean nothing."

His arms caught me as my thoughts drifted. As if from far away, I could hear him talking still. To me? Or himself?

"I won't let *you* be the end of me. I won't…even if it means I have to ruin you first."

came to in frozen arms. Dublin's. For what felt like ages, he carried me, but I lacked the strength to even open my eyes. When his body finally withdrew from mine, a cloud of silken sheets provided a clue as to our destination. Forcing my eyes open confirmed it—a bedroom, darker than the main space. A sliver of moonlight served as the sole illumination, giving his limbs ethereal definition as he stood back.

My heart lurched in my chest. God, he resembled an angel more than ever as his eyes swept over me, his jaw tight. But his grated, hollow voice was pure hell.

"You should be fine," he said, almost to himself. "I cleared it with the doctor. Your labs had improved, and she didn't recommend against it."

Sex, I realized in the depths of my addled brain. He had gone through the trouble of discussing sex with his mysterious doctor. An image of my dress came to mind, how easily he'd removed it…

I didn't want to jump to the obvious conclusion. It was too insane. I wanted to sleep. Forget.

But some cruel sense of curiosity wouldn't let me. Struggling for breath, I croaked, "Yulia—"

"I lied to her," he admitted, easily catching onto my train of thought—the lace had been one of her mysterious alterations.

But the fact that *he* had requested such a detail presented a scenario I couldn't fathom at the moment. I closed my eyes instead, desperate to reconnect with my limbs. They were jelly, disobeying any command I issued. I could only lie at his mercy, blind to his expression. Eventually, he left anyway, his steps resonating through the silence.

Only to return minutes later.

I jumped as warm liquid dripped against my inner thigh. My eyes flew open to watch him kneel over the mattress, a rag in hand. He ran it between my legs as reverently as a worshipper cleaning off a cherished altar, and the insanity of it…

I trembled, but he didn't look up, intent on his task. But something in my silence made his jaw tighten and his fingers stall.

Finally, he grated out a single request. "Say something."

"I'm dreaming," I whispered, clinging to that thin possibility. Otherwise, my brain throbbed with too many thoughts to process. His touch. His words. His rage…

"I won't let you destroy me."

But then he stood, tossing the rag aside, and turned toward the door. Guilt didn't belong in this specter—it made him feel far too real.

"Wait," I croaked.

He froze near the threshold of the hall. Within a heartbeat, tension transformed him into a creature of muscle and bone. An unrivaled statue of perfection.

But his gaze revealed a crack. Something elusive that made my thoughts twist into knots when I tried to decipher it.

So I didn't.

I closed my eyes and willed everything away. Everything but the childish ache worming through my chest where my heart might have been.

In the end, all I could muster up the strength to voice was, "Why? Why leave?" I added, choking every word out. "Then come back. Then kiss me. Then…" My body hummed, riding the wave of lust even as my mind raged in turmoil. "Why?"

I waited.

But footsteps broke the silence rather than words.

He left.

And, alone, I squeezed my eyes shut tighter and fell into the darkness eager to consume me.

~

I awoke in a decadently furnished room accented in shades of ebony and emerald. Solid oak furniture clashed with the modern-style windows and light fixtures—much like I did, in a sense. An old-fashioned creature in a world far ahead of its time.

A heavy emerald canopy loomed overhead, fanning around a bed adorned with silken sheets and lush pillows. A window to my right overlooked a view of the city no less stunning than the one visible in the main room. Overcast daylight streamed in, illuminating a wooden wardrobe in the corner and a door partially opened, which I assumed led to the hall.

That shadowy doorway presented a reality too terrifying to face. Not now. I contemplated staying here forever, unmoving, ignoring reality for as long as I could—though it wasn't as if my body shielded my ignorance for very long. Only a strip of silk covered my naked limbs, and an ache throbbed between my legs. The images of last night loomed, inescapable.

Sitting upright was the only way to banish them. Groaning with the effort, I stood as well and found a robe draped over the end of the bed. I drew it around myself and crept from the room. It was a short distance to the center of the suite, but I didn't find Dublin lurking there.

Instead, a glass table near the edge of the room had been set for one, containing a plate of sandwiches and a lidded cup. I devoured the food without stopping to savor it. Then I paced to keep any wayward thoughts at bay.

Eventually, I wound up wandering throughout the rest of the spacious suite in search of a distraction. He hadn't spared any expense, though that said little given his wealth. There were plenty of rooms lurking behind closed doors. A kitchen. A wide parlor with a billiard table and a piano.

None of it felt like him though—unlike a makeshift apartment hidden within a church.

This place resembled…

Well, a neat, clinical *cage*.

A sudden thud pierced the silence, and I spun around to find an ivory shadow lurking beyond the doorway, dressed from head to toe in steel gray. His closed-off expression was far too dangerous. Cautious. The man might as well have been on tiptoe.

But sleepless hours spent tossing and turning on an unfamiliar bed could put a lot of things into perspective. Like the stark, cruel state of my current reality. And how much better it felt to ignore it.

All of it.

"I'm going to pretend that last night never happened," I blurted. For some reason, my voice sounded raspier than it should have, but it got the point across. "Whatever you said. Whatever we did—it doesn't matter. It never happened."

There. Like magic, I'd willed all the tension away. Sighing, I tilted my head to observe a painting hanging on the wall. A naked angel standing as the sole survivor on a ruined battlefield. How lovely.

"Eleanor…" Dublin fixed me with a strange look. Suspicion? Well, he had no reason to be.

"My cat," I croaked, switching to more important matters. "Where is he?"

I could have kicked myself for forgetting about him yet again in the tumult of events.

Dublin stood there for so long that I started to wonder if he'd turned into stone. Finally, he sighed. "He's in the room beside yours."

"Really?" I raced down the hallway in a direction I'd missed during my first exploration.

Sure enough, a peek into the room beside mine revealed another suite, and curled up on the floor was Tinkles. My beautiful darling looked healthy, whole, and as surly as ever. He blinked at me, flexing his claws. Approaching him directly was a reckless act, but after days away, I couldn't resist.

"Darling!" I sank to my knees and threw my arms around him—but my skin wasn't immediately skewered by his claws.

In fact, something wet and warm stroked my cheek, so unexpected that I flinched back. His tongue, still protruded from his mouth, the culprit of the odd sensation. I had no clue how long I sat there before a familiar shadow appeared in the doorway.

"What did you do to him?" I demanded.

"Come and eat," Dublin said, ignoring the question. Without another word, he left.

After I made sure Tinkles had adequate lodgings—irritatingly, his room was even larger than the one he had in Gray Manor—I returned to the main room and found the table set with another cup and a plate of steaming vegetables and fish.

Dublin retreated to a far corner, his arms crossed while I sat and downed both offerings without complaint. He wanted to say something, I sensed, so I avoided his questioning stare. Presenting me with food at all was no doubt his attempt at getting a rise from me, allowing him to ruin our fragile truce. So I scraped my fork against my plate for emphasis. *See?* I wanted to gloat. Everything was nice and cordial. No need for any horrible reminders of events that didn't matter.

Because they had never happened.

"There is something we need to discuss," he began as I choked down the last morsel of food.

Damn. Fighting to keep my face neutral, I set my fork aside. "Like what?"

"You claimed you wanted answers… Well, do you?"

Answers. That wouldn't break my rule, per se. It would be harmless information I could choose whether or not to believe.

"Y-Yes."

"Good." He rummaged through a nearby sideboard. After withdrawing something from a drawer, he faced me again, revealing the object settled on his palm—a leather-bound book, dark with age. "You can start with this."

He dropped the book onto the table, and I eyed it as one might a bomb.

"What is it about?" I scanned the cover, more puzzled than ever. "There's no title."

"Consider it part of a private collection," Dublin explained, flipping it open to a yellowed page. "A ledger of sorts."

He was right. At a glance, I could tell that it wasn't a normal tome. It was handwritten for one—a series of lines penned in shockingly familiar script. Names and dates. Reading them, I felt my brow furrow.

"James, Agatha…Mary…Edward." I met Dublin's gaze, an eyebrow raised. "These are my ancestors' names."

"Yes." The firm line of his mouth revealed not even a hint of his intentions. Good or bad. "Every last Gray for over three centuries. Dead, alive, or otherwise."

"Ah…" I nearly choked. No wonder he knew so much about my heritage—he'd studied it. Though a better question was: Why? "So what am I, the tenth Gray to fall under your spell? What, do you keep a list of your conquests to reminisce over?"

As much as the thought irritated me to indulge, I couldn't help but wonder if Georgie was written in his little book as well.

He raised an eyebrow. "You still don't realize the gravity of what you've done, do you? Allow me to enlighten you, Eleanor, but most people—spinster or otherwise—do not sell their soul on a whim."

"You sold yours to Raphael," I pointed out, though I didn't intend it as an insult. Going off his stiffening jaw, I suspected he took it as one anyway. "I just want to understand. Why?"

He made me sound so horrible for forging a contract—but what might tempt the infamous Dublin Helos to embrace virtual servitude?

"It wasn't a decision I made out of boredom, I can tell you that," he said coldly. I looked at his face and braced myself for one of his glares, but he wasn't staring in my direction anymore. "And it certainly wasn't one I took lightly, even now."

"It's not like I had a choice," I said, eyeing my hands. They were shaking. "Not the first time, at least…"

Signing his contract had been a life or death decision then —mainly because, unbeknownst to me, he had poisoned me to the brink of death.

"I believe your lineage may provide answers as to this… situation," he said, changing the subject. "See if you can recall any forebearer with an unusual legacy."

"How would I know?" I asked.

He looked back at me. "I'm sure your parents, who gifted you a gravesite as a child, regaled you with plenty of tales of your ancestors. Do you deny it?"

My silence gave him my answer. He was right. In lieu of normal childhood games, Georgie and I had recited the names of our forebearers as reverently as schoolyard rhymes.

"Read," Dublin commanded. "Scour your memories for any relatives that stand out."

"You think this…" I swallowed hard, choking down the word *cancer*. "This condition has something to do with my bloodline?" I could have laughed. It sounded *that* sordid. Until I remembered my sister's secret life, that is. I grimaced as the true depth of my ignorance resonated like a slap. *You're so pathetic, Ellie.* "How?"

"I'm not sure." He eyed me for so long that I felt numb when he finally turned away.

"You're lying." I wasn't sure exactly why, which was the confusing part. But Dublin rarely backed down from a fight —unless he had more to lose by playing his hand. "I remember when you taunted me about knowing James, my ancestor, personally. But now I find out that you have a literal book on my family, and you're acting like it's just a normal way vampires pass the time."

By tracking centuries of genealogy. For the fun of it.

"What aren't you telling me?"

"I have my own avenues to hunt," he confessed without turning around.

"Like?" I sat forward as he crossed the room.

Staring broodingly from the windows, he looked more the stereotypical vampire archetype than ever. Eternally tormented. A snippet of a past conversation crossed my mind, uttered in a woman's voice. *"If you do decide to seek him out, don't count on me to help you."*

Just who was he trying to avoid?

"Don't I have a right to know?" I pressed.

"Rumors," he replied. "Even I have enough pity not to bore you with them."

But there was more, I suspected. So much more. Not only was he lying, but he was hiding something.

"What kind of rumors—"

"Sir?"

We both spun in the direction of the foyer, where the soft, feminine voice had come from. The blond from last night stood there, framed in shadow, dressed ironically in a light-pink dress. My eye twitched. Dublin would have a conniption if I were to wear such a color.

But in this instance? He inclined his head, his expression neutral. "What is it, Kate?"

There was no scorn lacing the single syllable. No derision. No hate.

Kate.

"Your appointment is here," she said while folding her hands primly before her. "Should I show them in?"

"No." Dublin's eyes flickered in my direction as he spoke. "No... I'll meet them personally. Thank you, Kate."

She nodded and left the suite.

"I guess you won't be joining in on the Gray family history book club," I deduced, trying and failing to sound civil.

"I didn't think you'd be so amicable." The bastard had the nerve to sound surly that I had the gall to thwart his expectations at all. "I will be gone for a few hours." He seemed to hesitate before moving toward the front door. "Read the book."

His true command was easy to interpret: *Stay here. Stay out of trouble.*

Be a good little captive.

"If I have to immerse myself in centuries of dreary family history, it's only fitting that I commence such torture in Gray Manor," I pointed out.

Somewhere familiar, far from his beautiful, luxurious high-rise where a stunning blond could enter and exit as she pleased.

Somewhere I could remember my life's destiny as a grouchy spinster.

"You will stay here," Dublin said without turning around.

I swallowed, tapping my fingers over the surface of the table. "A short trip wouldn't be a bother to you. I could call François?"

He gripped the handle of the front door. "That we will discuss when I return."

I swallowed again, tapping my nails more frantically. So much for remaining cordial; my attempts were straining at the seams.

Desperate, I tried a new line of attack. "We did agree that he would remain as my driver."

"We will discuss it later."

Before I could argue, he stormed from the suite, slamming the door in his wake.

So much for cordiality.

Rather than pout, I flipped the book to a fresh page and started to read. It was a surprisingly enthralling task. Who knew that one could find morbid comfort in scanning the many variations of Margaret, Eleanor, and Mary passed down throughout the years?

I wondered if Dublin had stalked any of them. Drained their blood or taken their virginity? The thought became less amusing once my eyes settled over one of the last names in the book.

Georgiana Gray.

Tears pricked my eyes before I understood why. Did I miss her? My thoughts were so scattered that I couldn't tell. Hell, I wouldn't even know what to say to her.

Perhaps I could only write it down.

Upon rising to my feet, I approached the sideboard Dublin had fished the book from and found a silver pen nestled in a drawer. I ripped a blank page from the journal and filled it with line after line of text. Moisture spilled down my cheeks, obscuring the words, and I didn't even try to make sense of them. In a twisted way, I felt the same impulse that had driven me to write Dublin.

Desperation?

Folding the page, I returned to the room I'd awoken in and scoured it until I found my shoes and my purse on a chair in the corner. Yulia's clothing conveniently stocked the wooden wardrobe, and I chose a garment at random. As I dressed, I did my best to squash any guilt. *He* was the one who'd suggested we bargain, after all. I had upheld my end so far.

Proving I wasn't a prisoner was the least he could do to uphold his.

Regardless, I didn't call François as I slipped from the suite and crept into an elevator. Even I knew where to draw the line.

Apparently, so did Dublin—no one rushed from the shadows to stop me. The first floor was as deserted as when we entered, but the door wasn't locked when I tested the handle. Escaping the garage and locked gate was surprisingly easy as well; none of them required a code to exit from. On the main street, I managed to flag down a cab on my own—only to realize as the man dropped me before Gray Manor that I didn't have any cash.

After shoving a check into his hands, I escaped the vehicle without gauging his reaction. His muttered curse gave me a clue. Still, I tried to banish all guilt as I skirted the manor proper. Waning daylight bathed the grounds in a bluish, eerie twilight, and a screen of mist obscured the mausoleum, thinning the closer I came. A storm must have been brewing.

Once inside, I approached the urn and dropped my missive inside it.

Then…

I lingered, wringing my fingers at the prospect of returning to Dublin's alone. Was he still with his "appointment?"

Or Kate?

Shrugging the concerns away, I craned my neck to appreciate the subtle detail of the mausoleum's interior. Delicate reliefs of angels and demons decorated the crown molding, shaping the stone. Within minutes, I found myself inching from room to room, mentally pairing the names I passed with the ones scribbled in Dublin's ledger. *Agatha. Mary. James II and III and IV…*

Dublin had tracked them all with an alarming level of detail, birth years and death dates included. On closer reflection, the fact that he had studied my bloodline at all definitely deserved more scrutiny.

Perhaps the journal was his subtle attempt at irony. A reminder solely directed at me—I wasn't the only Gray to catch his interest. Therefore, I wasn't important. In the grand scheme of Dublin Helos and his devious intentions, Eleanor Gray was nothing more than a single scribbled anecdote among pages of them.

But this name *wasn't*.

I frowned as my fingers traced the unfamiliar series of letters engraved in stone. Not a name at all, it appeared as I strained my eyes to read it, but a phrase.

Memento Mori.

Latin? I couldn't recall its meaning off the top of my head. Carved within plain sight, it dominated the space placed between my Great-Great-Aunt Maria and Uncle George in a section of the chamber where the light struggled to reach.

A slight roughness in texture differentiated it from the smooth graves nearby. The stone here felt older, more tattered than George's tomb and he'd been dead for at least two centuries.

Driven by an impulse I couldn't explain, I felt along the edges of the epitaph, tracing every divot in the worn stone. At the slightest bit of pressure, something shifted in a way it shouldn't have.

Unease prickled at the back of my mind, warning me away. Secrets, once uncovered, rarely revealed useful information as far as I was concerned. Just more deception. More lies. I tried to move—forsaking the intrigue—but my feet remained stubbornly rooted in place. It was the damn chamber, its mystery feeding a question I couldn't shake.

What would a Gray deem important enough to hide within the family tomb?

Eventually, the curiosity became too much to resist.

I rolled my sleeves up and tugged again, bracing my feet against the floor. The placard budged another inch. Another. Sweat dripped down my neck as I applied even more pressure, straining the muscles in my shoulders. More. More…

Until, with a thud, the lid of the tomb came away altogether. I jumped back, fearful of the prospect of a coffin lurking beyond. A cloud of dust obscured any contents, triggering a furious coughing fit. Hunched over, with my hand pressed over my nose, I peered through the darkness.

The dust cleared gradually, revealing a cavernous space in lieu of some ancient deceased Gray. I pulled back, prepared to write it off as empty, but a glint of silver caught my eye before I could.

Intrigued, I sank into a crouch, squinting to make out the object. Whatever it was had been tucked too far back to observe from my position.

I had no choice but to reach inside.

My heart raced as I cautiously inched my fingers deeper within the tomb, feeling along the marble bottom. My arm was in nearly up to my shoulder by the time I finally brushed something cold. Slender. Familiar?

I withdrew it, holding it up to the light, and a gasp tore from my lips as I identified just what it was—a cross. Dangling from a thin chain, it looked identical to Dublin's. It could have been the exact same one.

But the shape differed upon closer inspection. The tips were pointed instead of squared, and a series of letters had been etched into the metal. A name? I couldn't read it, but as the talisman's weight settled over my palm, it was impossible to shake the sense that it was so much more than a casual piece of jewelry. Dublin guarded his more fervently than his own contract. Perhaps, in his obsessive need for control, he'd hidden a spare here?

Among the decaying bodies of a hundred Grays.

I mulled over the potential answers, none of them comforting. So lost in thought, I almost missed the slight noise at first. It shattered the quiet, reverberating from the upper level. A hiss. A thud.

Footsteps.

I bit my lip, assuming the intruder's identity. Dublin Helos himself, arriving just in time to smack my hands for disobeying? I tucked the cross into my fist and turned toward the central chamber, fully prepared to face my scolding.

Do I need to get the manacles, Eleanor?

"You saw her come in here?" a man whispered—but his voice was too soft. Not Dublin's.

Panic froze me in place as his steps continued their hurried descent.

"The lights are on," another man pointed out. "And keep your voice down. We don't want to scare her."

"Ms. Gray?" the first man called out, his raised voice echoing to the farthest reaches of the crypt. "We're…friends of your sister's."

Georgie. But something in his tone made me creep back toward the empty tomb and I traced the rim with trembling fingers.

"I don't think she's here," the second man deduced. Both sets of footsteps sounded like they'd settled near the base of the stairs. Mere paces away from my corridor.

"Let's fan out just to be sure."

My pulse surged, hammering against my eardrums. As footsteps approached my section of the chamber, I crouched, inching into the open space in the wall. Dust and grime clung to my skin. It took everything I had to shuffle back, peering through the opening of the tomb.

"Anyone down here?" A shadow darkened the doorway, his silhouette large, betraying a muscular frame. Seconds later, a slender figure appeared beside him. "I don't think she's here," he said. "Let's check the house again. The kid said someone came onto the property. If she managed to escape, it's only a matter of time before they track her down."

"You think she escaped?" the larger man replied.

"Of course. He isn't stupid enough to let her wander around alone. At least if she is in here, he won't be able to track her anyway. We can keep watch."

He. *Dublin?*

"I'm surprised he hasn't killed her already. Or sold her." Their shapes retreated from the doorway and I heard their footsteps as they crossed the central chamber. "But it's only a matter of time. He's already summoned the *other* one. I hear the bastard is on his way now. Helos must know she's gone."

"Doesn't this feel strange to you though? Looking…well, hunting down a Gray? Especially since no one's seen Georgiana since—"

"We don't question," the smaller man hissed. "And whatever reason there is for it, I don't really want to know. After what she's been through, she might be better off… Come on."

Their steps faded to silence. In their wake, my thoughts spun. Too much information clamored to be reconciled all at once. Georgie. Her "friends." Their intent—hunting me down.

For what?

And Dublin…

A dull pain seared through my palm, so I loosened my grip on the cross, wincing as warm liquid dribbled down my fingers. I'd gripped the necklace so hard that it had broken the skin. The coppery scent of blood tainted the air, as vibrant as an SOS beacon. I imagined Dublin tracking the smell, using it like a map to find me.

Or not. Deep down, I knew that the fact I'd left his property at all was a miracle within itself. Perhaps he didn't *care* enough to come looking.

Enough! I shook my head to clear it and inched forward on my hands and knees. My entire body trembled as I climbed from the tomb and approached the central chamber, clinging to the wall for balance.

A glance revealed that the space was empty. Taking a chance, I lurched to the stairs, straining my ears for any hint of noise. The upper level was deserted as well, but the heavy door had been left open, allowing a draft to blow loose branches and leaves across the floor. Each sound echoed like whispered admonishments. *Run, Eleanor!*

But to where? Darkness loomed beyond the doorway, impenetrable this deep within the property. I couldn't even see the silhouette of the house.

Or anything for that matter.

I hesitated, racked with uncertainty. A part of me considered taking my chances and crossing the property anyway. Logic warned against it. I should hide instead. Wait for Dublin.

No. The second intrusion of him into my thoughts made me grit my teeth. No longer would I sit around playing the perfect victim, always awaiting his rescue.

I started forward, my muscles tensing to run. I didn't even see the hand rushing from the shadows to grab me until it was too late.

"There you are!" Harsh fingers clenched my forearm, wrenching me forward, but my assailant loomed beyond my sight, too strong to resist.

I lurched, ripped off-balance, and landed on my knees. Instinct took over. I lowered my mouth to the unfamiliar grip, bared my teeth, and bit. The figure hissed in response, shoving me aside, and I spun, failing to regain my balance. *Wham!* Stars exploded across my vision as ringing bells banged a symphony in my ears. Pain came in slow, nauseating waves, each one stronger than the last.

"Damn! Are you all right?" A face appeared before me—tanned and handsome, balanced among a cloud of dark, curly hair. "Ms. Gray? Can you hear me?" Concern constricted his features as he flickered in and out of focus. So real one second. A ghost the next.

Until the world vanished altogether.

And I was alone.

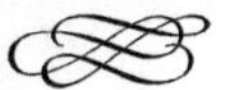

"Ms. Gray? Can you hear me?"

I groaned, blinking my eyes open to a shadowy space lit only by a circle of orange light cast by a bulb hanging from a grayish ceiling. Damp, dank air alluded to an enclosed space with little ventilation. Somewhere underground? The crypt?

"Please, say something."

I stiffened as my gaze settled upon the figure crouched beside me, his face half bathed in shadow.

"Thank God! You're awake," he breathed as our gazes connected. "How do you feel—"

"Where am I?" Panic shook my voice, but I was beyond feigning bravery.

As I struggled to regain my bearings, my gaze darted around the room. It was small, formed of water-stained walls that resembled concrete. A floor composed of the same material sported a rusted drain a few feet away from me. Otherwise, there was nothing else in sight but a wooden door in a far corner.

"Safe," François said. "Try not to move. You hit your head pretty hard."

My head. I attempted to lift it to no avail. My entire body felt heavy, weighted down as if by stones. It took three tries before I could move my arm more than a fraction. When I finally brought a trembling finger to my forehead, warm liquid coated the tip.

"You're bleeding," François admitted, grimacing. "A little pressure and it will stop in no time though." His wide-eyed expression contradicted the confident tone. He was a good liar as well as an expert driver, it seemed.

But hemorrhaging to death was the least of my problems.

Dublin was going to kill me anyway—if he weren't already resigned to my death. Stone walls and distance weren't enough to slow him down. This long without his sudden intrusion could only mean one thing.

What if he wasn't coming at all?

"Please don't move!" François reached for my arm as I tried again to sit upright.

I cringed from him, able to control my limbs with more accuracy. "Stay away!"

But he was the least dangerous of threats to my life.

The world pitched wildly beneath me, and I almost laid back down. My stomach roiled in time with my throbbing skull—a constant melody of pain. Making any solid observation was a struggle.

But I noticed François' hands just fine—namely the weapon glinting in one.

"Are you going to kill me?" I wondered, surprised by how calm I sounded. My heart lurched and I almost couldn't resist the urge to panic. Scream. Fight. Something in his gaze kept me still, however.

"No! Of course not." He eyed the knife in his grip and gulped. Then he shoved it hastily into his pocket without taking care with the blade. The way he flinched led me to suspect he'd cut himself. "I came to help you."

But those men had revealed one bitter truth during their banter. *"The kid said…"*

"Do you work for my sister?" Posing the question at all hurt.

But his contrite frown stung more. "I work *with* her," he admitted. "But she isn't why I'm here now." He glanced over his shoulder, his brow furrowing. "In fact, I need to move you—"

"Don't touch me!" I scrambled back, desperate for a weapon. I might have had one already. The firmness within my grasp alerted me to the fact that I was still holding the cross. Odd. After everything in the crypt, I should have dropped it. Upon closer inspection, I noted its odd shape.

The long, thin arms of the cross seemed designed to conform to my fingers regardless if they formed a fist around it or not. Readjusting my grip, I brandished one of the pointed ends. "Take me home now," I rasped. "And I will forget this ever happened."

"Home?" François cocked his head, his eyes wide. "You don't have any idea what's going on, do you?" He chuckled helplessly, raking his fingers through his hair. He was still wearing his nondescript driver's uniform—a plain black suit and white undershirt—yet he was sporting one glaring violation of the manor's dress code.

Blood speckled the collar, painting it red.

"Ms. Gray." When he met my gaze again, his eyes reflected something far worse than betrayal: pity. "I don't want to scare you, but by getting to you first, I may have just saved your life."

No. I ignored the confession. It was too horrifying to think about just yet.

"Tell me," I blurted, changing the subject. "Have you always been a member of Georgie's…club? Where is she by the way?"

"The Grayne?" He shot me an odd look. "To be honest, I thought you knew. Your sister tasked me to look after you while she went away. A damn good job I've done of that." He eyed me from head to toe, frowning at the blood drying on my hands. "I need to get you to a doctor—"

"Why?" I demanded. "If Georgie had you watch over me, then why are those people looking for me? Friends of yours?"

He looked away, his frown even more pronounced. "It's complicated, Ms. Gray."

"Complicated." I laughed, thinking over all of the drastic, terrifying, horrifying events I'd been through in the past few days—Dublin's return notwithstanding. "Complicated doesn't cut it. Explain. Now!"

"Okay! Okay!" He held his hands out before him in a placating gesture and sighed. "All I know is that I was ordered to protect you. Your sister asked me personally. Then you went missing that day, by the church…" He waited as if expecting an explanation.

One I never gave.

Sighing again, he soldiered on. "After that, I was contacted by a member, but it wasn't your sister." His eyes narrowed as though he were still processing the information himself. "She hasn't contacted me in a while, mind you. But that day, my directive changed. If you returned to the house, I was to inform another member immediately. *Not* your sister. In addition, they said I would be removed from your direct detail. No one could tell me why. It didn't feel right, so I kept an ear to the ground. At the same time, I learned that a certain powerful figure had returned to the city. Someone with a rather gruesome reputation and a connection to you. Let's just say I put two and two together."

That mysterious, dangerous figure needed no introduction —Dublin Helos.

"Who were those men?" I asked. "What do they want with me?"

"Let's just say the kind of people who don't get assigned to babysitting detail," François admitted. "I'm just glad I could get to you first."

"Why?"

He grinned sheepishly and shrugged. "You were different than what the rumors made it seem. Not some naïve, insane lady who fell prey to vampires—" He broke off, coughing into his fist. "I mean...I know your sister wouldn't want this. Until I hear from her, I'll do as she asked. That's all that matters."

"Where is she?" Her avoidance of me was one thing. But if even François hadn't heard from her...

"I don't know," he admitted. "But trust me, she can handle herself. If you don't mind me saying this, miss, you should focus on yourself."

I blinked, my eyes burning. From guilt? Or maybe pain. When liquid began to dribble down my cheeks, I knew from the consistency that it wasn't tears.

"I...I need more than a doctor," I whispered. The nearest wall was my only stability as the world seesawed beneath me and I clung to it, my knuckles whitening. "It won't stop."

François hissed and shrugged his jacket off, wadding up a sleeve. "Here. Try this."

He pressed the fabric near my left temple, but the bleeding didn't slow. If anything, the pressure seemed to encourage more to drain. With every passing second, I felt dizzier. Thinking took deliberate effort and any coherent thought lacked the urgency I needed to possess. They floated within my skull, increasingly silly. For instance, *If I were a surly vampire, where would I be?*

The cathedral? The manor? In Hell?

Somewhere far from here because he doesn't give a damn about me.

"We can try a hospital," François suggested. "I know one beyond the network."

"I need more than a hospital." I shut my eyes in defeat.

There was no use in denying it. I finally let myself face one fact that had been gnawing at the edges of my psyche all this time. Dublin Helos, for whatever reason, hadn't come breaking down the door. Had he finally washed his hands of me for good?

Or were my circumstances even more dire than I could comprehend?

"No one can find you here," François said as if reading my mind. "Not even *him*. This place is protected. So was the crypt. Vampires can't enter without permission."

"How?" Perhaps Dublin's loathing of my childhood playground had been based on more than annoyance? I shifted, attempting to sit unassisted. "It doesn't matter. I need to find—"

"Honestly, Ms. Gray I shouldn't take you anywhere. Or at least somewhere that isn't safe." His gaze darted toward the door again, and his hand brushed over the stashed knife.

"I'll die," I said, sounding eerily calm at the prospect. "Without Dublin, I'll keep bleeding." More liquid ran rivulets down my cheeks as if in emphasis. "Please."

"Damn it!" His jaw clenched, François stood and lifted me into his arms without warning.

Despite his lanky frame, I felt secure. Enough that I went limp, conserving what little energy I had left.

"Close your eyes," he demanded. "I've already broken one too damn many rules anyway. Just hold on to me."

I complied, gritting my teeth as he raced forward, jostling my body in the haste. I could hear doors opening and closing, and eventually, the still atmosphere gave way to fresh night air.

"I hope you don't mind if I've been using your car," he muttered before he released me onto a surface that felt like the leather back seat of the Rolls.

I opened my eyes, noting the familiar interior, as François rushed into the driver's seat. The car jolted into motion just as I realized one key fact. "I don't know where—"

"I know," François said without elaborating. "*Everyone* knows where he is."

Stunned, I could only watch the scenery change beyond the window, becoming brighter as the lights of the city replaced the manor's overgrown grounds. Too bright.

You're hallucinating, my inner voice warned as stars danced across my vision. *Stay awake, Ellie…*

When the car finally came to an abrupt stop, I knew I was dangerously close to fainting. Keeping my eyes open at all was a struggle, and I lacked the strength to open the door on my end.

I reached for the handle in vain. But then the entire structure vanished like magic. Or through violence—a monstrous sound resonated with the power of a bomb exploding. Crunching metal. Shattering glass. François' startled shout.

But each terrifying noise faded the second I looked up into a pair of silver eyes glaring from the face of a monster. The sight of bared teeth and protruding fangs set every nerve in my body on end—but in a way more terrifying than fear. *Relief.*

"Dublin…" I didn't even see the moment he reached for me.

I only knew that I was in his arms within the space of a heartbeat, trapped in a stony embrace.

We were near a deserted road. From beyond the cage of his arms, I saw a car door resting on its side, its window shattered. The rest of the car, however, remained whole. Alarmingly pale, François gaped from the wreckage, still buckled into the driver's seat. Beyond him, I expected to find the looming façade of the high-rise—but this building was made of brick. Square. A warehouse of some kind?

Dublin offered no explanation. He moved so fast that I barely processed the layout of the building at all before I found myself thrown onto a soft surface.

"Look at me." He gripped my chin, his eyes narrowing over my forehead. "Damn."

Hissing, he withdrew something from his pants—a switchblade that expanded into a gleaming knife. With no hesitation, he drew the blade across his wrist and pressed the wound to my lips.

"I don't even know if… Just drink."

I flinched at his harsh tone—frozen with fury. Regardless, my lips parted on command.

And all thought faded as the taste of him hijacked my dulled senses.

I floated, suspended on a wave of ecstasy only his blood could bring. Magical, bubbling ecstasy. Comforting. Suffocating, like the world had been boiled down to a single essence, mine alone.

But eventually, I had to resurface.

And reality held no such joy.

Dublin was already jerking his arm away as if my skin were poison. In the same motion, he rebuttoned his cuff link and slipped his suit jacket on. Armor, I suspected. Strong enough to cage in the emotion spilling from his eyes like fire—rage.

His mouth opened and closed with a sharp snap. Then he turned away, tearing his fingers through his coifed hair. Beyond him, an unfamiliar room unfolded, composed of dark walls and wooden floors polished to gleam.

At least it seemed unfamiliar at first glance.

The light fixtures caught my attention within seconds— silver, shaped like snarling serpents coiled around bulbs that cast pale light. A certain venue came to mind, one I had tried to visit mere weeks ago while searching for Dublin, only to find that it'd vanished.

The Den.

"Look at me."

My savior stood at the foot of the surface I was resting on— a large bed shrouded in black. The sole piece of furniture, it dominated a relatively bare, but no less elegant, room. Ebony walls displayed little decoration, devoid of any windows. Almost as if to make up for it, an eye-catching chandelier dangled from above. Matching the style of the other lamps, it consisted of an array of coiled, silver snakes.

Memories stirred on the periphery of my psyche, each one more dangerous than the last. The only way to vanish them was to focus my attention on the man eyeing me as though he wished more than anything to take every drop of his blood back.

"Are you that determined to die?" His hair hung loosely, framing his thunderous expression. Dressed in a mixture of black and scarlet, he resembled the Devil more than ever. Hungry for my soul. "If so, admit it now and I'll do it myself."

"N-No." I swallowed as my gaze lowered to the knife still brandished in his grip. "I…I'm sorry—"

"Sorry?" He snatched my hand and only then did we both realize I still had something clasped within it.

The necklace. It slipped from my fingers and landed on the bed, caked in fresh blood. Even so, I could finally make out the four letters scratched into its surface—MERO.

I started to reach for it, but Dublin snatched it first. His hand shook, his eyes wide and unfocused. It wasn't a spare, I suspected. He eyed it the way one might a ghost. A remnant from his past he hoped to never see again.

"Dublin!"

I jumped as a door in the far wall flew open, revealing a panting woman who raced inside. Yulia, barely recognizable in a red dress that hugged her slender shoulders. Her dark hair rested atop her head, coiled in an elegant coif—a night-and-day contrast to her usual style.

Stopping short, she noticed me and sighed in relief. "Oh, thank God! You found her. Is she all right?"

"She's fine." Dublin didn't even look at her. He glowered, holding my gaze in a way that nothing—not even fearing for my life—had ever made me feel. Miniscule. With a subtle flick of his wrist, he tucked the necklace into his suit pocket.

"I'm so relieved." Yulia braced a hand against her chest. Then she stiffened and her gaze darted to the doorway. "But you need to get her out of here. *Now*, before he—"

"Oh, I don't think you'll be leaving any time soon, Dublin." Another woman entered the room, letting out a chilling, girlish laugh that set every nerve in my body on end. Loose curls spilled down her shoulders like fire, enhancing the less vibrant scarlet of her dress.

Her name easily came to mind. *Saskia*, Dublin's main adversary in the inner workings of the club he had once traded my soul to. Anemia.

"Oh, you've thoroughly done it now." She cocked her head in my direction as a smile played over her ruby-colored lips. "In fact, I do believe you'll both be joining us for this evening's activities. You *and* Eleanor."

"No." Dublin lunged toward me and grabbed my arm, yanking me upright.

Still dizzy, I staggered after him, fighting to keep my balance. Luckily, his blood was already replenishing my weakened muscles. I remained standing at least as he started for the door, dragging me in his wake.

"We're leaving—"

"He's already on his way," Saskia crooned. "After all, you *did* call him." She tapped her chin with the tip of a manicured finger. "Or should I say you barged into my establishment, threatened my Mikhail with bodily harm, and demanded I summon him for you or—and I'm paraphrasing—you'd *kill me with your bare hands?*" She smiled, but her eyes blazed with barely concealed fury.

Sure enough, a man was lurking in the doorway, just beyond the reach of the lights. Handsome and pale, his name came to me instantly. *Mikhail.* His mouth lacked the smug sneer I remembered, however. Scarlet smears painted his face and his neck in a startling contrast to his dark suit and his ivory shirt. Blood, I suspected. From a wound that had already healed.

"So yes, you will stay," Saskia said sweetly. "And *he* should be arriving within minutes. Actually, he's even called ahead to request your presence *personally.*"

Dublin stopped short, and I had to dig my heels in to prevent myself from colliding with him.

"I said get out of my way." He swiveled his gaze in Saskia's direction and her smug grin wavered a fraction.

Only to reform a heartbeat later, more beautiful than ever.

"What on Earth shall we dress little Eleanor in?" she wondered, turning her attention to me. Wincing in disgust, she scanned my rumpled dress, splattered with blood. "She looks well enough, considering the fuss you made. Still so plain, though I'm sure I can do something with her." She rubbed her hands, and I recalled an unsettling piece of advice Dublin had given me once.

"Saskia is a succubus. She cannot actually read minds—merely the subconscious fears and desires of those around her."

"Come here, my dear—"

"No. *I'll* dress her." Yulia stepped forward and took my hand. She tried to pull me out of Saskia's reach—but an iron grip on my opposite arm kept me rooted in place. "Dublin," she said softly. "I'll watch out for her." She brushed her fingers along my arm in brief reassurance. "I promise."

He let me go. Before I could look back, Yulia was dragging me through the doorway, past a scowling Mikhail.

"Darling Yulia to the rescue," Saskia remarked, sighing like a child denied a treat. "But will her magic work this time? After all, you brought her *here,* Dublin." The way she stressed the word implied a nefarious connotation. Something that made her haughty tone shake with more than just anger. Fear? "*You* called Raphael from his rest, all the way here. And for what? Though it is no matter. You may be the all-powerful Cael, but within these walls, even you are just like the rest of us. Under his rule."

"Come." Yulia steered me forward.

I looked over my shoulder, catching a mere glimpse of the room. Dublin was framed by the doorway, as rigid as a statue. His eyes flickered to mine and my entire body went cold at what I found in them.

Nothing. Not even anger.

Not hate.

Not even concern.

He was beyond feeling anything at all.

AMUSEMENT

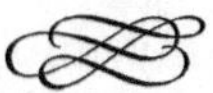

"Damn, damn, damn!" Yulia raced around a wide room, snatching items from various racks of clothing.

The space we were in resembled a dressing room, so similar to the one in the original club where we'd met. Red walls and floors a dark shade of wood served to enhance the allure befitting the club's mysterious name. At least the moniker I remembered it as—*Anemia*.

In the prime position to display my reaction, a large, golden mirror hung across from us, above a marble vanity.

"I hope you're all right?" Yulia inquired mid-lunge. Her chosen prey was a garment from an overflowing closet. Frowning, she held it up for inspection and then tossed it aside. Then she rummaged for something different, her eyebrow furrowed in concentration.

"I'm fine," I lied. The mirror provided enough evidence to contradict me—my bloodshot eyes stared blankly, my hair matted and damp. Scarlet streaks painted my cheeks and my neck, staining the bodice of my dress.

"Thank God," she muttered. "Finally!" On what had to be her fourth trip around the room, she found a garment that made her nod in approval. Pivoting on her feet, she returned to me and lifted my chin. "Oh, Ellie."

Her irises contracted with pity as she unfurled her selection and held it before me—a long dress made of black silk. While conservative in some aspects, it had a dangerously low neckline that reinforced its purpose in a club like this— a place where souls were bartered and sold on a whim.

Even Dublin's.

"It will have to do." Without waiting for my opinion, Yulia started to tug off my soiled clothing—a task made easier once she found a strip of lace along the neckline and pulled.

There was no other way to describe how the fabric came apart other than like magic. Or expert tailoring.

"Here." She helped tug the new dress over my head, and before the silky material had even settled at my waist, she already had a wet rag in her hand and was dabbing at my shoulders. "Dublin will be angry," she warned in a level tone. "I'm glad you're okay, but you need to realize what is at stake now. The fact that he even came here is—" She bit off the rest of her words, her mouth wrinkled. "Where were you? We thought…" For the first time, she seemed to realize just what substance she was dutifully cleaning off me. Her mouth dropped open in horror and the rag slipped from her fingers. "Are you all right?" She felt along my forehead, inspecting the flesh. "Were you hurt? Dublin didn't seem alarmed, so I thought—"

"I fell," I croaked. "He…he gave me his blood. I'm better now."

"Oh." She drew her hand away and stooped for the rag.

Cautiously, she continued her ruthless cleansing, but her expression wavered, more strained than before. Her lips twitched as if fighting to contain any more questions. Then she left the room in silence and returned with a basin of warm water and a fresh set of rags.

The water, she used to wash the blood from my hair, before forming the semblance of a bun that my short locks would allow. After securing it to the nape of my neck with pins, she stood back and sighed. "I guess you're ready."

But I stiffened, unwilling to move.

"What's happening?" I asked. Something terrible, judging from her grimace. Something involving a man I would have given the Gray fortune never to see again—and the figure Saskia implied would be arriving soon.

Raphael.

"You were gone for hours." Yulia's anguished expression only strengthened the guilt lancing through my chest. "I've never seen Dublin like that. Ever. He thought those radical fools had taken you, perhaps."

Radical fools? The Grayne?

"I don't think he was being rational," she continued in a rush. "Maybe he assumed coming to *him* was his only choice?" She turned away, cradling her chin in her hand. "At least he found you first, before it was too late. I tried to stop him. He *promised* me he wouldn't ever sell more of his time—"

"Let's go."

I turned and found Dublin in the doorway, his face expressionless. His gaze flicked over me once, conveying no disgust. He didn't even bother to utter a mocking quip. He merely beckoned with a nod before advancing down the hall.

"Go," Yulia whispered while tucking a curl behind my ear. She squeezed my arm reassuringly and urged me forward. "It will be okay."

My stomach churned as I staggered a few reluctant steps, leaving her behind. Up ahead, Dublin continued without waiting for me, already halfway down the narrow hall.

His taste lingered on my tongue as my body thrummed with his blood. Every drop prickled beneath my skin, so potent that it burned. In a sense, drinking from him had always been painful. Overwhelming. In fact...

I usually fainted.

I swayed on my feet as I tried to reconcile why I hadn't. A swallow racked my throat as I looked down, surprised to find my hand against my abdomen, the fingers trembling. I wrenched it away, forming a fist, and when I looked up,

Dublin was watching me. The moment our gazes connected, he turned and continued forward.

I crept after him, and far too soon, we entered a spacious room decorated in shades of black. Like a lecture hall, leather seats framed a makeshift stage—a circle of light illuminating the very center of the marble floor. It was a chillingly familiar setup. Much like a showroom, perfect for various wares to be displayed for purchase.

Human wares.

"Stay close."

I jumped as Dublin grabbed my hand, dragging me to his side.

"Say nothing," he told me.

Across from our position, a contingent of people was already flooding in from a different entrance.

Leading the mass of beautiful, elegantly dressed specters was a man almost too perfect to be real. Stunningly pale, his face was that of an angel's, frozen in time. An angel who had been barred from Heaven for too damn long.

Instead of wings, an ebony cloak shrouded most of his slight body, blending in with the long, black hair falling down his shoulders. With a flick of his lips, he greeted me with a nod.

"Eleanor Gray."

I shuddered beneath his scrutiny. Centuries of life had stripped his dark eyes of any expression. Only a chilling aura set him apart from those in his retinue, Saskia and Mikhail among them.

The closer he came, the tighter Dublin clenched my hand until I had to grit my teeth to keep from crying out.

"Raphael," he said coldly.

"Dublin," the other man replied. His voice was so soft, yet it resonated clearly over the hushed murmurs of those around him. "How lovely of you to join us. And with dear Eleanor." He extended his hand to me. "I wasn't sure when we would meet again."

I eyed his slim fingers as the memory of our first meeting flashed across my skull. He'd felt so cold. Like death.

A pointed nudge to my side jarred me back to the present. Glancing at Dublin, I saw him jerk his chin in a silent command. *Do it.* Left with no choice, I placed my hand over the ancient vampire's and winced. He grasped my fingers without warning, bringing them to his lips.

"I'm curious as to the nature of this visit," he murmured, lifting his head. But he didn't release my hand. Instead, he drifted toward another corner of the room, forcing me to follow.

I sensed Dublin right on my heels, silent, my other hand still in his.

"Not to be blunt, but I was under the impression that Dublin had ceded all interest in you," Raphael added. "He claimed to have cut off all communication. Leveraged his contacts so that poor Saskia had no choice but to move from our previous location. The last I'd heard, our dear friend had left this marvelous country entirely. I must confess I understood his aversion. Your bloodline has always been mired in needless superstition." He sighed. "So, imagine my surprise that the first time he deigned to contact me in weeks happened to concern *you*."

I glanced at the man in question, but he wasn't even looking in my direction. His eyes were fixated on the center of the room, his jaw slack with disinterest—even as he kept time with my every step.

"In fact..." Raphael paused before a leather chaise and lowered himself onto it, gesturing for me to follow. When I did, he took my hand again, stroking the palm of it with his thumb. "For Dublin to call me here, this hour of the night, I would have thought you were in danger." His empty eyes cut to my face, scanning it with reptilian curiosity. Without revealing whether he discovered anything of interest, he shifted his attention to Dublin. "Did I assume wrong?"

"No," Dublin replied. He remained standing paces away, angled slightly toward the center of the room. "It was...a misunderstanding. Nothing more."

"Ah." Raphael nodded and patted the back of my hand. The seemingly playful gesture contrasted with his chilling, frozen smile. "*Nothing.* How wonderful. Then, Eleanor, my dear, you must have entered here of your own free will, under no claim to speak of."

Claim. Dublin stiffened at the word. By the time I'd blinked, he had returned to my side. Startled, I took the hand he was offering, allowing him to pull me to my feet. Raphael released me, but each pad of his fingers glided over my flesh like a serpent in retreat.

"She was just leaving," Dublin said, maneuvering me to stand behind him.

"Leaving?" Raphael uttered a sound too cutting to be a laugh. "Oh, no. The entertainment has just arrived. Do stay. Both of you."

Dublin stiffened. "I—"

"I insist," Raphael added, flicking his hand in a dismissive gesture. "Why, look! The show is just beginning."

As if his acknowledgment were the cue, a woman entered, pale and slender. Dressed in a sheer, white slip that barely reached her knees, she was a stark contrast from how I remembered the women on auction dressing. Not overtly sexual, to put it bluntly. Though her purpose was painfully reinforced by the sheer fabric of her dress—pale skin and flushes of pink peeked, fully visible beneath. Her large, green eyes stared out blankly, framed by curly, dark hair. The style chafed my nerves, uncomfortably familiar. *Too* familiar.

"A lovely creature," Raphael remarked, his lips quirked in another mirthless smile. "Don't you agree, Dublin?"

Without warning, Dublin released my hand. Suddenly, the space between us widened as he stepped aside, and my heart surged. A few feet yawned like an ocean to separate us. I tried to meet his gaze—anything but reach out directly.

He ignored me.

"Ah, yes," Raphael continued as though he'd received a response. "The last auction you participated in was such a success that I've had Saskia replicate your ethereal aesthetic. I hope you don't mind." Only when his eyes flickered in my direction did I realize he was speaking to me.

My stomach churned as I faced the girl again. One word could summarize her "aesthetic." *Me.* Everything from her chin-length curls to her slender frame resembled mine. Specifically, how Yulia had dressed me the night Dublin had bartered for my contract.

"I am curious what you think, Dublin," Raphael wondered. "I must say, this style has been a boon for the club. So many seem so curious as to the appeal. What with your discerning tastes, anything you desire must be remarkable."

Murmurs of agreement rose up from those seated nearby.

"You see?" Raphael gestured with a wave of his hand. "I believe the consensus is unanimous. Shall we begin? Saskia, my dear."

"Yes, my lord." Grinning, Saskia stepped forward, advancing on the girl. Once close enough, she brushed her hand along the girl's cheek, tilting it to reveal the side of her throat.

I was reminded of an auctioneer displaying a piece of jewelry for a buyer's discretion.

Circling around to stand behind the woman, Saskia ran her fingers along the flimsy neckline of her shift next. As if waiting until just the right moment, she tugged, allowing the sleeves to fall down the girl's shoulders.

My cheeks heated as I looked away. But Dublin didn't. He stared along with the rest of the room, his eyes conveying nothing. A dangerous thought crept into my brain, impossible to silence—was he inspecting her as well?

"Exquisite," Raphael murmured in a way that made my throat tighten. "But I sense that Dublin doesn't approve? Too short?" he wondered. "Or too thin? No matter. I do believe Saskia has cultivated an entire selection to match these *specific* tastes." He clapped his hands together and four more women drifted into the room, each one more waiflike than the last.

Only slight variations in their height and their size set them apart. Overall, they all were thin with large eyes, short dark curls, and delicate white dresses. It was like looking at a distorted mirror, reflecting variations of me from a million different angles.

All of them slightly prettier.

Slightly thinner.

Slightly more appealing.

"Pick one," Raphael suggested, still speaking to Dublin. "Any one you'd like. Her contract is yours. My gift to you. My only request is that, in return, whatever time you spend with your new acquaintance is time that I would get to spend with dear Eleanor. Alone."

Crackling tension electrified the air. Even Saskia stiffened, her throat contracting around a swallow. Though, no matter what, her sly grin remained firmly in place.

"Well? What say you, Dublin?"

"To your offer?" Dublin faced him, his eyes a burnished, cool silver. Given his lack of emotion at all, one might have thought Raphael had presented him with a blank piece of paper. Not a woman. "No. I'm afraid we have a previous engagement to attend to." He reached for my hand, yanking me forward to close the distance between us. "We'll take our leave."

"An engagement," Raphael echoed. "Perhaps one having something to do with why you demanded my presence here, only to bring Mero's rats to my doorstep?"

It was as though a switch had been flicked. In an instant, the atmosphere thickened further and the entire room seemed to shrink back, scurrying within the shadows.

Only the two men withstood the unbearable tension. Dublin stared unfazed, while Raphael casually sat back against the leather chaise, folding his hands on his lap.

"We've been together long enough for you to know that there are few things I cannot tolerate, Dublin. Having my time wasted is one, though I know that the respect between us is far too great for such an insult." His endless eyes flickered in my direction, flashing with rare interest. "But the second is secrets. Especially when they concern a mutual old friend of ours. Don't tell me you've forgotten him already. Mero."

Silence fell. In a room of strange, undead creatures, something warned that I wasn't the only one holding my breath.

"Even as he waged his little war against both of us, utilizing his human pawns, I have remained a loyal and neutral party," Raphael insisted. "I have even toed your boundaries, haven't I? After all this time? The Grays were but mere mosquitoes buzzing on the periphery, until one of them decided to bite my flesh. I had every right to retaliate, then. Didn't I?"

A second passed without a reply.

And his eyes narrowed. "Answer me."

"Yes," Dublin hissed.

"Good. So, is it too much trouble that I wish to enjoy a few mere moments with an old friend? Even if he apparently has no further use for my services?"

This time, when his gaze slithered in my direction, he lingered, tracing a path up and down my body. There was no lust in the dark pupils. Just calculating, detached observation.

"I even came when you requested, prepared to assist you in any way that I could. All for the sake of dear Eleanor." He tilted his head thoughtfully. "I let you have her when you asked despite the risk. You knew the second you bid for her that you would be breaking *his* precious rules. The Gray family was to remain untouched, always. Do you remember?"

He waited until Dublin made a growled sound of acknowledgment in the base of his throat.

"Yes. As long as you did, he would remain in the shadows. I know you wrote off his threat as mere superstition, but I never did. I even warned you, didn't I? I even offered you others. You refused. So please"—he smiled again, all traces of hostility erased—"allow me to learn your tastes so that I may replicate them more accurately. Choose."

"I…" Dublin's grip loosened over my hand only to bear down more tightly than ever. "I'm afraid that none of your offerings interest me," he said so dismissively that I flinched. "Perhaps I'm just not in the mood for distraction, or perhaps your curator hasn't done her job well enough."

"Is that so?" Saskia hissed through her teeth. "Then why not enlighten us all?" She waved her arm toward the guests. "What exactly excites you, Dublin? Do tell. Is it the pale, bony exterior? The childlike demeanor?" She sneered in my direction and laughed. "Please don't tell me it's her stunning beauty."

"It's simple," Dublin replied with a shrug of his shoulder. "It's the one thing you can't cobble together or clumsily recreate: a pure, pedigree bloodline."

Saskia glared at him, her upper lip curled back from her teeth.

"He is right." Raphael sighed in defeat. "Alas, we always did share a fondness for such…" He traced his mouth with the tips of his fingers as if reliving events too horrifying to picture. But then his small smile faded. "There is another," he added.

Dublin went rigid once more, crushing my fingers.

"The other Gray girl. The one *I* wanted procured. The one you claimed I could not have." If a man like him could pout, I'd name the downturned tilt to his mouth as such. Rather than petulant, he looked more serpentine than ever. A predator denied a satisfying meal. "You did not flaunt your boundary for her—"

"Because she was not foolish enough to sell herself to me," Dublin snapped. He eyed me pointedly and sighed. "I must beg your pardon. She's weak." His apparent explanation for my trembling legs. "I've fed from her too much. She lacks stamina. We should go."

"You'll leave soon enough," Raphael insisted. "*After* the entertainment. Saskia."

"As you wish." She returned to the naked woman and positioned her to better face the crowd. "Offers for this one? I will accept payment only in years—"

"Years?" Dublin interjected, his tone hard.

"Yes." Raphael stroked his chin and nodded. "A peculiar arrangement, but again, you have inspired us to try new methods of business. Our new policy is, rather than bartering for a few wasted nights, we trade our beautiful specimens for years of service. One year of the buyer's for a year of hers. It is only fair."

I nearly choked in recognition. Trade in years—a cruel variation of the bargain Dublin made for me. But something told me it was more than that. So much more.

One of the shadowy guests raised his hand.

"Two years," he declared as casually as if bargaining with play money. Not time.

"A fair start. Any other takers?" Saskia wondered.

Another man raised his hand. "Ten," he said. "For this one and that one." He pointed to another girl. "Each."

"Ah!" Beaming, Saskia clasped her hands together, her demeanor shifting into that of an expert saleswoman. "And what about this charming girl. I must admit I'm not too fond of this 'aesthetic,' but she is lovely, isn't she? Do I hear an offer?"

With every second I watched the twisted event unfold, the more numb I felt. My eyes were fixated on the women, refusing to leave them for an instant. Did they even care that years of their lives were being bought and sold around them?

Apparently not. Each one faced the room with little expression. None flinched. Squirmed. Whimpered. Not even as one of the "guests" stepped forward to claim his prize. He was tall, unnervingly handsome, with eyes so amber that they bordered on ruby.

"Congratulations." Saskia crooned. "She's all yours, though, as per custom, you are allowed a taste before finalizing. Here." She snatched the girl's wrist, extending it.

In response, the man bared his fangs before lowering his head. As the ivory tips sank into her flesh, the girl gasped. But not in pleasure.

She wrenched her arm away, coming to life with another hollow cry. "N-No!" Her eyes blinked rapidly as if she were waking up from a dream. Whatever she saw made her face pale and her eyes widen with horror. "No! No! Let me go! Let me go!"

The man withdrew, his gaze questioning.

Saskia merely sighed and snapped her fingers. As if from nowhere, two men swooped from the shadows and grabbed the girl on either side. Within seconds, she had vanished, though her cries were still audible, echoing off the walls.

"Let me go! Where am I? Let me go!"

"Our new policy requires that we recruit a different breed," Saskia admitted. She flicked the hair of another woman, who remained unmoving despite the commotion.

And their blank expressions took on a more sinister meaning.

"These girls are a bit more skittish and might require a… softer touch. But they are yours alone to break. Do I hear another offer?"

I turned, moving blindly, my stomach heaving. Logic and self-preservation vanished. I could only cover my mouth, solely focused on finding somewhere—anywhere else.

"Don't," Raphael snapped, his voice ringing with authority. "Saskia will attend to her. You and I have a private matter to discuss. Did you truly think I wouldn't realize who you were looking for? The witch. Even though you've pretended not to all this time, you've believed in his curse. Haven't you? I assume that is the reason you ran, the moment I tested that so-called superstition…"

I should have gone back—but a gag ripped from my chest and I raced down the hall until I found an empty room. The next second I was on my hands and knees, vomiting onto polished wood. The gleaming surface displayed my reflection in mocking relief—wide-eyed, frantic. Pathetic. Guilty.

Even now, faint cries echoed off the walls, and I hunched over in shame. That poor girl.

All of them.

They were here because of me.

"Oh, do get a hold of yourself, darling."

Stiletto heels stabbed the floor in tandem as someone advanced on my position. Cloying perfume flooded my nostrils even before a pair of pale legs appeared within my line of sight.

"We all know that Dublin is besotted by the innocent-little-girl act," Saskia harrumphed. "But my God is it tiring! Though I must thank you. Even with that goddamn necklace, he's easier to read now than ever. Shall I share?" She giggled maniacally. "He was always surly before, but now? His thoughts are so devious that deciphering them is child's play. Hungry. Lustful. All those things he acted so *above* feeling before. All because of you."

She crouched down and tapped my chin with the tip of a pointed fingernail.

"He thinks about fucking you," she explained, her lips quirked. "And not in any romantic, poetic sense. You're but a trophy to him. He relives corrupting you over and over. How you felt. Your delicate little body shuddering beneath his. How you squirmed and flinched with every thrust. He felt so powerful then. It's rather hilarious."

My cheeks burned at the picture she'd painted. Nothing in the world felt more violating than having those words flung in my face.

"Or pathetic, actually. He hates you. Despises you. Craves you. Obsesses. It's madness, really. One might think the man had never been laid before." She sighed and pulled her hand away. "But you know what really gets his cold heart pumping?"

She waited as if expecting an answer. Then she chuckled.

"Your *sister*. The pretty one. He thinks of her often, though he guards those thoughts a bit more securely than the ones of you. Perhaps he's fucked her as well? Don't tell me you didn't know… You didn't! Oh, to see the look on your poor face." She licked her lips in glee. "But now it's time to go crawling back. The show must go on, my dear." She snatched at my arm and stood, yanking me upright. "Don't resist. I mean, honestly—"

She broke off, wrenching her hand from me as if burned. A series of unsteady steps propelled her back so suddenly that she struck the wall. Just as quickly, she recovered, and before I could even react, she grabbed me again, sliding her grip down to my wrist. Her thumb pressed against my pulse point as her eyebrows furrowed. When she met my gaze, I didn't know how to read her expression. Something made her bite her lower lip as she finally let go.

"Clean yourself up." She turned on her heel and retreated to a far corner. We were in that dressing room, but Yulia was nowhere in sight. "Here."

I flinched as Saskia shoved something beneath my nose: a white handkerchief.

I took it and warily dabbed at my mouth. Then I gagged as the image of that girl replayed. Over and over and over…

Desperate, I scanned the room, my stomach heaving.

"Do it in this, at least!" Saskia shoved a round basin into my hands.

A wastebasket that held crumpled napkins and a fresh wave of vomit. I recognized chunks of my meals from earlier and cringed, disgusted but partly relieved.

At least it wasn't blood.

"Come." Saskia beckoned with a crooked finger and started toward the main chamber. "He won't tolerate our absence for long," she warned as I lingered.

So, I followed, my heart pounding with every step. I didn't dare look up from the floor in front of me. I couldn't see those women. Their faces.

But I could hear. Frantic breathing. A smothered whimper.

And then Saskia's pleased giggle as she donned her ringmaster role once more. "A beautiful girl to be sure," she called to a man eyeing one of the women. "And I can tell you enjoy her taste. How does five years sound?"

"Keep your head down." The warning entered my ear as a familiar hand cinched my wrist, tethering me to a body chiseled from stone.

"Until next time," a voice called out, dripping with false politeness. Raphael.

"Next time," a woman seconded, Saskia. "Oh, and, Dublin? To new beginnings. For both you *and* Eleanor."

Veering away from them, Dublin steered me through the club until we finally reached the exit.

I barely had the chance to inhale the fresh air before he shoved me into a waiting car and appeared in the driver's seat. As the door slammed behind him, I had enough sense to keep my mouth shut. To keep my expression blank and choke down my horror. I blinked back any tears, but I knew my heartbeat betrayed me, thrumming with shock and terror.

Dublin drove recklessly, cutting into the paths of other vehicles without a damn given for etiquette. He glowered at the road, his body rigid, his knuckles stark white over the steering wheel. The areas where he was gripping it bulged inward, and I feared the damn thing might snap in half as the car finally came to a stop.

Before I could reach for my seat belt, he opened my door— the right way this time—and I was in his arms. Rigid with tension, he carried me into a building I vaguely recognized: his high-rise. The ascent to the suite lasted seconds as he took the stairs in lieu of the elevator. When he finally hauled me into the foyer, Kate was nowhere to be found.

I was alone with him, a fact that he cemented by locking the door as he set me down, leaving me to sway with fragile balance.

"Where did you go?"

I bit my lip, hating the display of weakness. I should have been haughty and defiant, jutting my chin into the air. As it was, I could barely breathe without gasping. Panting. Whenever I closed my eyes, I saw them. Whatever horror they were currently facing was my fault.

All my fault.

"Look at me!" He gripped my chin, wrenching me around to face him, but what he saw in my eyes made him frown and release me. "Were you aware of him all along? 'Protecting' you?" he wondered, sneering the word. Turning his back to me, he started to pace. "Perhaps he's the one you've really been fucking. Is it his?"

Hurt mingled with shame, searing my cheeks. "Who?" I croaked before an answer came as if whispered in my ear. "François."

"Yes, *François*," Dublin snarled, his voice booming.

I had never seen him like this. Smiling. Glaring. Vicious. Cold and blazing in one terrifying display.

"His kind don't risk themselves lightly. And certainly not for a vampire-fucking whore as they would call you."

I winced as the insult landed as intended. But I couldn't even muster up the energy to feel insulted. "Where is he?" I despaired at my driver's most likely fate. Still, I clung to a fragile hope even as I gritted my teeth to steel myself against the answer.

It came, uttered in a tone as cutting as a blade. "Dead. Or at least he *will* be once I'm through with him."

"Please don't." I stepped forward without thinking, reaching for his hand. "It's my fault. He didn't mean—"

"He didn't mean what?" Dublin growled, snatching his hand away. "To lie in wait to ambush you? To carry out his orders like a willing little pawn? You're lucky he didn't run a stake through your chest—his kind are foolish enough to believe in that myth."

"He helped me," I insisted, fighting to keep my voice level. "And I'm sorry—"

"Sorry?" He threw his head back and laughed more deeply than before. "*You*, the innocent, naïve, selfish Eleanor Gray, are sorry. Tell that to those women who will be sucked and fucked because Raphael likes toying with me! Isn't this the part where you cringe in haughty indignation and call me a monster for allowing them to be sold in the first place?" He paused as if waiting for that very argument.

It stung to realize that, in another world, I might have lived up to that expectation. I would have blamed *him*.

"No? Well, I couldn't do a damn thing without presenting you to him on a silver goddamn platter anyway. So, congratulations. Once again, you've made me look weak before that creature. Once again, I've gone against my better judgment to save your life. And all you can say is you're sorry?"

My lips parted, but instead of another apology, a cry escaped. And I broke. Tears spilled from my eyes as sobs ripped from my chest. I swayed, bracing my hands against the wall in a fight to stay upright, but my knees buckled, depositing me onto the floor.

"I'm sorry," I whispered, though he could have been gone for all I knew. Still, it had to be said, if only to cement my own horrid sense of guilt. "It's my fault. I'm sorry. I'm sorry. I'm so, so sorry—"

"Don't cry for them." Dublin grabbed my arm, hauling me to my feet. Without allowing me to find my own balance, he pressed me against the wall, trapping me there with one hand on either shoulder. His eyes a burnished silver, he resembled the "old friend" Raphael referred to more than ever. Someone utterly devoid of humanity.

But then he frowned, brushing his thumb along my cheek. Yulia must have missed a spot, somewhere hidden behind my ear, because his finger came away red with blood that should have been dried by now. He eyed it like it was the most alluring and repulsive thing in existence.

"You should be crying for yourself," he hissed while swiping his hand along the side of his suit jacket. "Those women will suffer their pain. They'll reconcile their choices with whatever price they bargained their souls for. In the end, they'll convince themselves it was worth it. But you?" He caressed my throat with a single finger, tracing my surging pulse. "You sold yourself for nothing. You sold yourself to *me*—and I am not like those other fools who take their orders from Raphael. Do you think you're any different from them? Those women?" He cradled my windpipe, forcing my head back until I met his gaze. "Do you think I wouldn't take any single one of them over you? I would." He stepped into me, lowering his head until our foreheads touched. "I would."

The fabric of my dress bunched at the waist, captured in his fist. I shivered as he tugged. With a violent rip, the material gave way altogether.

And with every bared inch of me, Dublin stiffened further, tracking the gown's descent until it reached the floor.

"Your body affects me no differently than theirs," he growled, his voice thicker. "You don't appeal to me more. This pale, thin, shapeless body doesn't fucking haunt me." He found my nipple, grazing it with the tip of a fingernail until I jerked as if yanked on a string. "You mean *nothing* to me."

His mouth brushed mine and my lips parted. Ruthlessly, his tongue swept inside, harsh and punishing. I could feel the prickling tease of his fangs even as they protruded, catching the edge of my tongue. All the while, his body caged me in, rough through the fabric of his suit. Repelling me even while providing strength. When my knees buckled, holding on to him was the only way I managed to stay upright.

The harder he kissed me, the more my thoughts spun, senseless. There was no seductive method to this madness. Just him gripping my waist, pulling me into him, grinding his body against whatever part of me he could reach.

Until he stopped, leaving me balanced on a precipice.

"This is the part where you agree, Eleanor," he hissed, drawing me into his arms.

The interior of the suite blurred and distorted until I found myself shoved onto the bed in that emerald room, bathed in the multicolored glow of the city lights.

"This is the part where you reinforce that I couldn't possibly have any interest in fucking you." As he spoke, he tugged my legs apart, easily slipping between them.

Fabric swished and fluttered through the air, so quickly I barely registered it. His jacket. His shirt. His pants. All shed within seconds.

My eyes were still on the crumpled pieces of fabric when he slid his hand between my legs, easing the tip of a finger inside me.

"And this is the part where I pretend like you're wet for me alone," he continued as I gasped at the intrusion. "That deep down you relish what I do to your body. That you crave it. That the naïve, prudish innocence is just an act." He ventured deeper, and my nails caught at the silk beneath me, scrambling for purchase. "I convince myself every goddamn time." He groaned as my body quaked, gripping him in trembling waves. "I make myself believe it, even though I know it's a lie."

Another finger. Too much—but the pressure was nothing compared to his expression. Eyes narrowed with hatred even while I writhed, full to the brim with him.

"Women like you are more evil than I even would ever claim to be. It's why you hide through life pretending that you have no appeal. It's why creatures like Raphael try to replicate you. It's why five hundred years of fucking life hasn't tormented me like you do." He drew his hand away, slamming his full length into me instead.

I moaned, my back arching, eyes closing as every nerve came alive with awareness of him.

"The way you feel is sin," he hissed, rearing back for another sharp, punishing thrust. "It's hell. And he made you, didn't he?" He captured the back of my throat as if to coax the answer from it, but I was too far gone to speak. "He made you. To tempt me. To make me crave you. To the point of madness, I crave you…"

God, I didn't even know if he was referring to Raphael or some other creature. I was beyond coherent thought. Fire built within my blood with every burning bit of friction— and his words were gasoline. My spine lit the match, curling and driving me into each pass of his hips.

And then ignition.

Any sound I made was swallowed by his lips parting over mine, taking every strangled cry. It went on for an eternity…

Pleasure bordering on ecstasy. Sensation rivaling pain. Too much. All at once.

And then everything shattered. I fell apart, reassembling over twisted, sweat-soaked silk. When I regained my senses, his mouth was in my hair, his arm over my waist.

And he spoke to me, murmuring words too softly to hear.

But then I made the mistake of relaxing into his embrace, brushing my fingers along his arm. Abruptly, he sat up, pulling away. In a daze, I watched him lunge through the dark, dressing so quickly that he was already in the hall by the time I registered him lifting his shirt.

Gone in an instant.

TURBULENCE

I lay there in a daze for so long that I couldn't tell if it was still night or day when I finally heard a voice drift from down the hall. Dublin's low rasp, resonating with authority.

"…the plane ready. I want to be airborne within the hour. No delays…"

Then minutes passed, and I sensed he'd started a far different conversation.

"I'm sorry," he growled, sounding fainter than before. His tone had softened, containing a mixture of emotions—some easily recognizable, others more obscure. Guilt? *And* defiance. "I don't have a week! I know Saskia suspects. It's only a matter of time before she starts whispering into Raphael's ear. With this, he'll have enough leverage to tack another six hundred years onto my debt—if only to keep him from turning her into his pet. Is that what you want?"

He paused, allowing someone to answer. Through a phone, I suspected, because I didn't hear another voice nearby.

Finally, Dublin sighed. "It's either Dmitri or Raphael—" The other speaker must have interrupted, because he swore so darkly that I trembled. "I will never sit back and watch him parade her like some sick conquest. Hate me if you'd like. But Dmitri was there at the beginning. If anyone would know what this means, it's him—"

Another interruption drew a hiss of disgust from his throat.

"You think I don't care? Don't you *ever* question that again, Yulia. You and I both know what this has cost me. So, fine. Cast your lot in with Raphael if you'd prefer him as your protector. Just know that I have never forsaken you, and I never will."

He went silent again, for long enough that I suspected the conversation had ended. Heavy, slow footsteps alluded to him pacing. A picture came to mind—him glowering while raking his hands through his hair, furious because of me. I'd made him do something that had even Yulia against him.

But what?

No answer came by the time his footsteps advanced toward my room. Just beyond the doorway, they stopped.

"Get dressed."

His tone stiffened my spine—so cold that it rivaled the chill in the room itself. Cautiously, I sat upright as he retreated, and I had to reconcile the million things I wished to ignore.

The inside of my legs felt wet. My knees were jelly, wobbling as I attempted to stand. I had to cling to the bed frame just to keep from falling.

I made my way to the wardrobe and fished out one of Yulia's dresses. Then I felt along the wall until I nearly tripped over my shoes discarded on the floor. After pulling them on, I entered the hallway, where Dublin loomed in the center room, his back to me. Wordless, he gestured to an open doorway—a bathroom, I realized as I crept closer.

Inside, I quickly washed and ran my wet fingers through my knotted hair. I'd barely stepped over the threshold when I found him in the foyer, wrenching the door to the suite open.

A curt jerk of his chin was my sole cue to follow. Together, we traipsed down the steps and exited the building to darkness. It was either late at night or early in the morning. Bathed in moonlight, his car idled up ahead, but this time, a driver sat before the steering wheel. Dublin ushered me into the back only to slam the door behind me and claim the passenger's seat for himself.

As the car took off, I wrung my fingers over my lap, desperate to find a distraction from the tension thickening the air. I looked down, eyeing myself critically. My dress was a gray one, relatively shapeless, though no less elegant than any of Yulia's other creations. In a way, it fit the somber atmosphere so well that it could have been curated for this moment. My trademark costume as Dublin's dowdy archnemesis, destined to torment him to no end.

Minutes of driving became hours. Eventually, our journey extended beyond the city, but Dublin never revealed our destination and I lacked the courage to ask. Instead, I consoled myself by staring from the window as dawn painted the horizon in brightening shades of lavender and pink. Gradually, the trees of the countryside gave way to neatly trimmed fields designed for a sole purpose.

One that became clear as the driver entered a maze of wide, rectangular buildings and finally pulled up before, of all things, one item even my family didn't possess: a plane, slim, white, and most definitely private.

"Ready for takeoff, sir," the driver remarked as Dublin climbed out and approached my door.

He wrenched on the handle and offered his hand—but his mood hadn't softened during the ride. If anything, the rage had solidified in his very bones, rendering them rigid against me.

"And the arrangements?" he asked the driver while approaching the plane, tugging me along.

The door to the cabin hung open, a set of stairs leading to it. From this angle. I noticed a smiling woman in a crisp black uniform waiting at the top, her hands folded before her.

"Everything has been taken care of," the driver assured. "Have a safe trip, sir."

Dublin maneuvered me to stand before him, ensuring that I had to climb the stairs and enter the plane first. An elegant interior greeted me, well beyond the luxury of the few first-class cabins I'd been in throughout the years. The space resembled a lounge rather than a vehicle designed for transport. A plush, dark carpet accented gunmetal-gray walls, and instead of rows of uniform seats, a black leather couch hugged one wall across from a flat-screen television. Parallel to it, on either end of the room were matching recliners. A doorway straight ahead alluded to additional compartments.

The aircraft even possessed its own attendant, it seemed.

"Welcome, miss," the smiling woman greeted warmly. "Welcome, Mr. Helos. Can I offer you wine or—"

"That will be all," Dublin said, and she promptly scurried off to some unseen hiding place.

Pushing past me, Dublin claimed the couch for himself, leaving one of the recliners for me. Conveniently, both faced away from him, as distant from his position as the space would allow.

My face heated as I marched toward my imposed exile. Memories of last night flooded my thoughts, each hazy image more confusing than the last. Paired with his stony reception today, I suspected that it all was some new, twisted mind game.

Congratulations, he was already winning. I had no idea how to combat him this time. My usual defense—stripping naked and daring him to consign me to Hell—didn't appear to be an option this time.

"Sit," he snapped, fastening a seat belt over his waist. Purely for show, I suspected. "We're about to take off."

I scrambled onto the recliner and buckled myself in. Minutes later, we were hurtling down the tarmac and then airborne.

And it seemed as though the farther we left the Earth behind, the more frantic my thoughts became. Saskia's taunts echoed viciously inside my skull, outlasting the hum of the plane's engine.

"He relives it. Over and over… But you know what really gets his cold heart pumping? Your sister."

"Can I get you anything to drink, miss?" The female attendant asked, suddenly appearing by my side. Balanced on her hand was a silver tray containing a variety of beverages.

I started to shake my head. "No, thank you—" But I broke off as movement caught my eye.

Dublin. He cut his gaze toward the tray, fixated on a beverage in particular. Without thinking, I grabbed the item consuming his interest—a bottle of water. With a few swift pulls, I drained it, aware of him watching.

By the time I returned the empty bottle to the tray, however, he was already back to ignoring me.

When the attendant retreated out of view, I finally gathered the nerve to face him. He eyed the world visible beyond the windows, his arms crossed. At a glance, one might name his posture petulant—but it was so much more than that. Callous. Disinterested.

Cold.

One would never guess that last night he'd sworn that I'd tempted him to madness.

Lost in thought, I rummaged through my purse. Within seconds, my fingers cradled a small object between them: a cheap ring of plastic gold sporting a cracked turquoise bead. I slipped it onto my finger as I refocused my gaze on the creature sitting across from me.

"Saskia told me something," I croaked, breaking the silence. "Several somethings. Confusing things."

"And you believed her?" He didn't even bother to utter his customary scoff; I wasn't worth the effort. "Do I need to remind you that she thrives on deception?"

"No," I admitted. "B-But…"

For the first time, I closed my eyes and allowed myself to relive the images I'd been suppressing. His kiss. His touch. The way he'd held me like I was something he wanted to break and cherish in one twisted breath. Like he craved me as he claimed.

Such a startling contrast to the way he was acting toward me now—like I was something repulsive. A burden he felt compelled to suffer.

Which one was the truth?

For some reason, he assumed I knew.

"Don't bother yourself worrying about Saskia and her lies." Leather hissed as he shifted, presumably starting to stand. "Now, if you're finished, I need to speak to the pilot—"

"She told me you think of me," I blurted out. My eyes were still closed, but in some ways, the blindness enhanced my ability to perceive his reaction.

His harsh intake of a breath he didn't need. The tension crackling in his muscles, his joints stiffening. The man could convey a symphony of emotion when he wanted to. Namely rage.

"That you think of sleeping with me," I added before he could deliver the cruel retort that I knew was poised on the tip of his tongue. "Is that true? Is it?"

His silence became unbearable. So I opened my eyes, hating how they burned. "I could stomach the sex if that were all you wanted," I confessed—and it was the truth. Bartering myself to him had been a mere transaction, nothing more.

Or so I'd tried to claim. Over and over, I had fed on that lie.

"If wanting me was as simple as desiring a pawn in a game, then fine. If my virginity were a token prize to you, I could understand. I could even understand if you had a fetish for innocent little virgins like Saskia sniped. But..." I racked my brain for the right words. Something far more dignified than what wound up spilling out instead. "But stop teasing me. Please."

He stared expressionlessly, so intent. So silent.

Ah. So this *was* another game. A part of me sighed— partially frantic, partially relieved. If only he would admit as much, then all of the confusion could cease. The memories. The ache in my throat as I remembered his touch. The throbbing pulse between my legs when he crept into my thoughts at night. All of it would stop as soon as he said the magic words.

You think I'd lust after you? Think again. Your money is all that is appealing about you. It's your sister I truly want. It's always been her.

When his jaw twitched, I held my breath in anticipation. Finally…

"Why does it terrify you?" he wondered as if truly curious. "The thought that I might want you."

"Why?" I gestured between us with a wave of my hand. "Because I'm *me*. And you're you."

"A monster?" Heavy-lidded, his gaze became more unreadable than before.

"No!" I stammered, too confused to convey what I meant. My only salvation turned out to be the bluntest of terms. "You could have anyone you ever wanted. Beautiful, perfect women." And God, it stung to admit that. More than it should have. "Anyone. Like…Georgiana. Don't tell me you haven't considered her."

Saskia herself had hinted at as much.

"Just tell me and I could understand."

Rather than go slack with relief, his jaw tightened further, his eyes narrowing. Not in anger. More thoughtfully, as if the answer to a puzzling conundrum had just presented itself. One so obvious that he was openly skeptical of it.

"You truly believe this?" His tone conveyed more than he said out loud. *That's why you've been ignoring reality? Living in denial?*

"Of course!" I had to laugh, choking out the pathetic sound. "I have eyes, Dublin." *So just admit it,* was the part I held back. *Please admit it.* "If sex is all you want, fine. But don't pretend like you want something more beyond that."

"Like?"

I wrung my fingers in exasperation. "Like something requiring the serious discussions of *tumors* and what they might mean. I can't… I refuse to play that kind of game with you. You accused me of being in denial, but maybe I'm being realistic? I am not ready to handle something like this." It stung to say it, but at least I could. "And neither are you. The sooner we agree upon that point, the easier this will be."

There. I broke off, panting and satisfied with the extent of my confession.

Now, it was his turn.

"Come here," he commanded, beckoning with a crooked finger.

I lurched, fumbling with my seat belt. Once freed, I crossed over to him, maintaining my balance with the gentle motions of the plane. He shifted, leaving enough space beside him for me to sit, and I did, sighing.

Finally, he would say it. But rather than speak, he took my hand and unfurled every finger. Then he placed it on his lap, right between his thighs.

My palm seared, instantly registering what lay beneath it. Firmness. Hardness. Evidence of something that made my stomach clench and my teeth snap together. In shock, I tried to pull away—he gripped me even tighter.

"Perhaps I've humored your naivety for too long," he mused, sounding eerily calm despite the part of his anatomy proclaiming anything but control. "Do you truly believe that I intended to announce my return at all? Let alone to you?"

I squirmed, uneasy. It sounded so obvious when stated out loud. His abrupt resurfacing hadn't been a trick, or a mind game like I'd assumed, but…

Impulsive?

"How did you even know?" I asked, playing along. "Where I was?"

"Believe it or not, finding *you* was not my priority." A low sound trickled from his throat, too terrifying to be mistaken for a laugh. "My sole intention for returning at all was to convince Goodfellow in person to relinquish your case. My efforts to block her attempts from afar had proven ineffective and she is no fool. When she began consulting experts in the *occult*, I decided to intervene."

I swallowed hard at the dangerous shift in his tone. "She was just trying to help me."

Judging from the stern tilt of his mouth, he did not agree.

"She risked drawing attention to you. Good intentioned or not, she put your life in danger. As long as you wore the talisman, I could sense your location, so I knew you were in no immediate harm at least." He fingered the necklace in question. "But when you suddenly wound up in an area of the city where I know Raphael exerts his influence, I followed. Only to discover your meeting with Gabriel Lanic and..." His grip on me tightened, applying even more pressure against my hand. "I refuse to let you pretend like you don't see what the whole damn world has. What it's mocked me for," he warned. "That you haven't felt every inch of it slammed inside you. If anyone is playing a game here, it isn't me. Goddamn, a part of me wonders if you somehow planned it, if only to make me out to be a fool..." He flicked his wrist, forcing me to feel more of him. All of him, swelling against my hand. "So, no, Eleanor, I'm afraid your supposed innocence isn't a fair enough excuse." He released me, shrugging my presence aside as he started to stand again. "Now that we've gotten that established—"

"Then why leave in the first place?" I demanded, eyeing my hand. It burned and the fingers were trembling, impossible to control. "If you want me so damn much then why leave at all? And don't use Georgiana as your excuse. You don't take orders from anyone."

The fact that he would return merely to exert his control over my life in something as trivial as medical records proved that fact.

"Why?" He paused and his eyes flashed as if the question required serious contemplation. "Perhaps I don't enjoy being at the mercy of a woman who would sooner spend eternity with her cat as a companion than admit her attraction to me?"

"Attraction?" I whispered hoarsely.

He chuckled and began to rise to his feet. "We once established that you've learned more than a few tidbits on sexuality from romance novels. Use that knowledge to draw upon what might cause a woman to become wet—"

"S-Stop." Plush carpet cradled my knees as I sank to the floor, all modesty forgotten. If he wanted to play tricks, then I'd sink to his level. Prove it once and for all—he was lying.

"You use sex like it's a game," I blurted. "Like the whole damn world knows the rules when only you do. You kiss me when you want to. Leave me when you want to. But I'm the one at fault? Even now… You're trying to confuse me for a reason," I decided, shaking my head. "You always throw sex in my face just to manipulate me. You did it at the auction, and in the cathedral, and when you came back."

Each time he had taunted me with a taste of desire.

Only to yank it back the second it suited him.

Even now.

"You're saying these things because you know you can turn the tables," I said.

He didn't move, his gaze impossible to read. "So what will you do now, Eleanor? Run away. Make me hunt you down. Pretend I was always the monster?"

"No." My hands fell over his thighs and hesitation paralyzed me for a heartbeat. Until he tensed beneath me, still seated. God, I could almost hear him hissing a dare. *Do something, Eleanor. But don't fool yourself. You lack the nerve.*

"I want to prove it to myself once and for all. You're lying and I'm not afraid to face the truth this time." Biting my lip, I tugged at the fastenings of his pants to no avail. My hands shook too badly to undo them, but he didn't laugh and shrug me off. He tugged the zipper down himself, his eyes slits, conveying confusion and a warning.

You're playing with fire.

But I was too tired to heed it. I lowered my mouth instead, flinching as his fingers latched onto my scalp. He started to tug, but his grip went slack the second my tongue connected with the silken flesh beneath the cotton of his pants.

Such a vulgar act. I had only ever performed it once before in my entire life.

Only ever with him.

Yet nothing could compare to the feel of it. Having him at my mercy. Exploring his body far beyond physical touch. I could taste him, spice and winter. I could feel him, hard and unmoving. Thickening. Thicker.

And I knew in an instant that I had made a horrible miscalculation.

He didn't shrug me off the way some prudish part of me insisted he would. The smug, confident Dublin Helos would *never* surrender an argument due to such a base impulse.

And yet, I could hear him growling with every tentative flick of my tongue. Soon, he began to buck into every taste, betraying a lack of restraint that made my breathing hitch in anticipation. When his fingers cinched a fistful of my hair, I nearly sighed in relief. I'd won. His rejection would prove it. I all but hissed in triumph as his opposite hand latched onto the nape of my neck—but the touch wasn't resisting. His fingers clamped down, *restraining,* as if to prevent me from pulling away.

And for whatever reason, I didn't…

My eyelids fluttered as my tongue lapped along the crown of him. His blood was addicting, but this was an even more potent drug. *Power,* however briefly it lasted. There was something terrible in his taste. A flavor that made a groan catch in my throat and my stomach clench. Something too elusive to name—I could only chase it, gradually taking more and more of him into my mouth.

All I could.

Dazed, I made the mistake of looking up, seeing him stare down on me, his eyes slits, his jaw so tight that it could have been chiseled from stone.

It was like that very first night. Something shot between us, hot like fire. Electric. Suddenly, he flexed his grip, wrenching me upright. Up, onto his lap. Cupping my knee in his opposite hand, he spread my legs apart, forcing me to straddle him completely. There was no mistaking what pressed against my inner thighs now, pulsing against the fabric of my dress.

No pretending that I wasn't the cause of every inch.

And that knowledge confounded everything I knew about myself—everything I knew I wanted. His nearness made me yearn in ways I barely understood. For his taste. His rage. His need.

Everything.

I shivered as he batted the skirt aside, sliding a thumb beneath my panties. The gusset was no match as he yanked, ripping the thin material right down the middle. Slowly, his thumb burrowed between my folds in its place.

As he applied the slightest hint of pressure, the world ceased to spin.

"*This* is what you do to me." He lingered and my entire body trembled, balanced on the pad of his finger. I sucked in a breath, my eyelids fluttering. If revenge was his aim, well he had won. I was unbearably cruel for making him feel even a fraction of this.

A single, lazy flick of his wrist fed tendrils of fire ripping through me like drops of gasoline. There was only one word for it, and groaning, he murmured it, "Insanity…"

Still vengeful, he stroked me again. Slower. Harder.

"Madness." A grunt edged his words and a part of me knew why. With every caress of his thumb, my breathing quickened. My hips twitched, chasing the pressure and he felt…

Harder. Thicker. Firmer.

Because of me. My body was reacting to him in a way those romance novels he once taunted me for reading referenced. I looked down, observing the confident way he manipulated my body. He pulled his hand back slightly, taunting me with the evidence that I wanted him just as badly.

Needed him.

Craved.

As if aware of the thoughts, he encircled my throat in his entire fist, forcing me to meet his gaze. I swallowed hard, riveted by the sensation of his fingers. Still stroking. Thrusting.

Like I was an instrument at his mercy, one only he could ever tune.

My back arched at the intrusion, but he held me against him as if daring me to watch. How his pupils constricted when I moaned. How his tongue flicked along his lower lip as if to capture the sound. The way he groaned—truly groaned. As if in pain every time I rocked my hips, chasing the firmness just beyond reach.

Our eyes met again. Then foreheads. Mouths. Frantic, I inhaled him, letting his tongue battle mine even as insecurity threatened to shatter the numbing haze of lust.

This isn't real.

It isn't you he wants, Eleanor.

He doesn't want you.

"I won't let you play the innocent this time." Baring his teeth, he positioned me above him, stopping short of lowering me onto him directly. He grasped my hand and lowered it to the tip of his cock. "Take what you want from me. Admit it."

My fingers curled and I marveled at the feel of him. I flexed my fingers and he hissed. Curled them and he nearly came off the couch. I guided him against me and he bucked upward at the same time. He entered me in one slow, tenuous motion and it was sin. Him inside me was pure, hellish sin. The world slowed. The noise of the plane quieted and the rest of the universe ceased to matter.

Just this.

My hands fell over his shoulders, straining for leverage as he cradled my spine, guiding my movements. Slow. Harder. Deeper. So deep…

I stopped caring if the lust barreling into me was real. I only needed to feel it. My moans were broken. Loud. Shameless. In the back of my mind, I knew his pretty attendant could hear me. The whole damn plane could.

But they could also hear *him*.

He grunted with every thrust, his hands scrambling for purchase over my waist, gripping me tighter. Tighter…

I gasped as he stood, lifting me in his arms. Pivoting on his heel, he spun me around and then pinned me down so that I was facing him. My back arched against the leather of the chaise as he rocked his hips, thrusting in from a newer angle. One too intimate. Too close.

He nipped my lips as if to steal away any doubt before it could form. In its absence, fire seared through my veins, building until…

Explosion. My body bore down, gripping him so tight that I saw stars. Nails drawn, I clung to him, my fingers laced through his hair as wave after wave of pleasure ripped me apart.

In the aftermath, he went limp, his arms around me. Skimming along my jaw, his mouth found the crook of my shoulder next, his fangs delivering the barest tease of pressure.

Then he stiffened.

"Sir?" a soft voice sweetly called. "We will be experiencing some turbulence. The pilot requests that you buckle up for safety."

He shrugged me off him, maneuvering me onto my side. A strap of leather fell across my waist, easily secured by his quick fingers. Before I could even register the loss of his touch, he resettled beside me, so close that my face rested against his chest.

As reality reasserted its presence, it became almost impossible to swallow down an irrational panic. Prudish shame nibbled at the flesh of my cheeks, reddening them. Moisture slicked my inner thighs. I could still feel traces of him lingering inside me, and my poor, addled brain struggled to process it all without reverting to the instinct that only now I could admit was a defense mechanism —*denial.*

Dublin's hand tensed over my lower back as if waiting for just that reaction. God, it was as though he could truly read my mind, anticipate every action.

So I bit my lip and then blurted out the only question I could. "Should I be worried that your attendant doesn't seem to mind when you have sex in your private airplane?"

He went still. Then he shrugged. "She's seen worse. Trust me when I say that this may be a welcome change of pace for her."

Something told me he wasn't referring to sex.

And my desperation for any random—*safe*—topic grew. "Where... Where were you born?"

He stiffened further, but his hand remained, bracing me to his side as the cabin shuddered, buffeted by a sudden tempest.

"Eireann," he finally said once the motion settled. "Or Ireland—some called it that, even back then."

A rather obvious realization dawned on me. "Is that why you go by Dublin?"

He shrugged, his fingers fanning out along my spine. "A bit cliché, but it gets the point across."

I had to admit that it did. But there was more to it. The truth lurking within his name that I'd discovered on a whim what felt like a lifetime ago. How, when unscrambled, the letters composing Dublin Helos formed a morbid phrase —*is hell bound.*

"Why don't you live there?"

"Let's just say..." He trailed off, deep in thought, and a part of me tensed. I'd accidentally triggered something delicate. I held my breath as he withdrew his hand, but a heartbeat later, his fingers brushed my shoulder, teasing the edges of my hair. "I haven't earned the right to return."

In my right mind, I might have never pressed him for more. But as the plane jolted again, his arm went around my shoulders, keeping me secured despite the fact that he hadn't bothered to fasten himself in.

"How long has it been?" I asked if only to distract from his nearness.

"In years?" He tilted his head as if he had never thought back to count the time before. "Centuries?"

"Oh." I swallowed. Spending even a full year away from Gray Manor seemed too long to fathom. Not out of fondness perhaps—but duty. It was my legacy, the one thing in existence resolutely mine.

I tried to picture how it might look after centuries of absence. Of one day returning to find my family home a husk of its former self. Would I mourn it? Probably.

And the thought made me realize that anything Dublin might have cherished in his homeland was now most certainly dust. He grabbed my hand and I realized I'd been toying with the object on my middle finger—a cheap, plastic ring.

He eyed it wordlessly, raking his thumb across the bead's dull surface. As he released me, he shifted, pulling me more firmly to his side. The belt fastened around me offered enough slack that I could draw my knees up and rest my head against his shoulder.

"Why did you leave?" he asked, his gaze still on my ring. "When you went to the manor? Let me voice my crude assumption now. François is your lover and you were planning to escape to France and live out your eternity in marital bliss."

I nearly choked. "That's a very...specific suspicion."

"That isn't a denial," he pointed out. A muscle in his jaw flexed, stiff with tension.

"Well, you were meeting with *Kate*," I pointed out. "I remember her, you do realize? The woman whose contract you managed for Raphael. You must have thoroughly enjoyed her 'services' in order to invite her to live with you."

I loathed the raw emotion that leeched into my tone.

My cheeks flamed as his eyes cut down to mine. "You're jealous of her." He phrased it like some momentous revelation.

"And you're jealous of François," I countered—though I didn't truly believe it, even as the words left my mouth.

Not until I saw his face. His mouth flattened as if he had hoarded all emotion behind a mask. It was an expression he only deployed in the rarest of circumstances.

When I'd caught him off guard.

I swallowed hard as he became stone against me. "Do I have reason to be?" he wondered in a dangerous tone.

"No, but do I? If I happened to care that you had a beautiful woman indentured to you for all eternity in your luxurious penthouse—"

"Raphael used her like a pawn, the same way he utilized the others."

I cringed and my indignation diminished somewhat. *Others.* Those poor women made to look like me and paraded before him. Why? As part of some sick, twisted game?

Or perhaps something far more sinister…

"By keeping her close, I could negate his attempts to control her," Dublin explained. "Nothing more."

"And François is my driver," I said thickly. "Nothing more."

He shifted slightly and I wound up leaning against him even more. "So how did you wind up bleeding in his care?"

I sighed too drained to argue. There was no point in lying now. "I was trying to send a message to my sister."

Did he believe me? I couldn't tell. His face revealed nothing.

Cautiously, I continued. "I took a cab and slipped a letter in that stupid urn in the simplest chance she might remember she has a sister and come looking for me. I didn't want her to worry."

How pathetic, all things considered.

"I was in the crypt when two men came in. Something about them felt off so I hid. When they left, I tried to leave and François found me."

"Did he hurt you?" I flinched. His voice was too soft. Too low.

"No," I fervently insisted. "I fell. He helped me. And when I asked, he brought me to you."

"How long have you known him?" Again, he used that alarmingly soft tone and I wondered just how naïve I'd been all this time not to realize my "driver's" identity on my own.

"Just a few weeks. I didn't know he was working for my sister. I swear I didn't."

But he had known. He nodded once as if confirming his own dark suspicions. Which of course he didn't bother to convey out loud.

"Is he dead?" My voice broke in anticipation of the answer.

"No."

"Good." I squeezed my eyes shut, too relieved to watch his reaction as I added, "Please don't hurt him."

He said nothing for so long that I feared I'd done it—broken this fragile moment. My heart ached at the thought. This time had felt so different from our other brief truces. I could still remember the way he'd looked at me, his eyes burning, his lips hollowed around a groan.

"And the necklace?" he said before true panic could set in. "Where did you get it?"

My belly tightened. His tone was more cautious than ever, laced with something so rare that I marveled at the sound. The same cold, detached note he utilized only around Raphael.

"It was in a tomb," I confessed. "An empty one. It didn't have a name on it, just a phrase. Latin, I think."

"Latin?" Dublin echoed hoarsely. He sat forward, dislodging me from his side. "What did it say?"

"Yes. Um… *Memento mori.* That was it. Do you know what it means?"

I watched him, startled by his reaction. He was staring off as if seeing something far beyond this space. Far beyond this reality. A wistful tilt to his mouth betrayed his true nature more than ever: a creature unmoored by the constraints of time.

"Remember death," he declared, uttering the phrase with a chilling sense of finality. Slowly, he sat back and his hand hooked around my waist, drawing me against him once more. "It means remember death."

"That sounds like something a Gray would want on a tombstone," I admitted, trying to picture the mysterious culprit. "Perhaps they got their necklace at the same sale you got yours?"

A lie of course. The way he fingered the thin chain—always without seeming to realize it—revealed its personal nature. He hadn't bought it at some thrift shop. No. It held far too much sentiment. A gift?

Though that presented more mystery as to why its twin just so happened to have been hiding within my childhood haunt and family mausoleum. For *years*, judging from the dust surrounding it, if not decades. Centuries?

"Unless of course," I added, shrugging away the morbid connotations, "you gave it to some poor ancient Gray woman you seduced." Though most likely not within an airplane traveling to only God knew where. I could claim that scorecard, at least. "She stole it, because we Grays are nothing if not spiteful, and left it somewhere only one of her poor, bumbling descendants would be able to find it. Was it Agatha?" I wondered, naming one of the members of his thorough list. "You did write her name rather peculiarly—"

"You are a singular creature." He gripped my chin, tilting it so that I faced him. Lips pursed, a ruthless sweep of his gaze was all he required to decipher me. "To be honest, if there were more than one of you with your abject lack of self-preservation, I'm sure your bloodline wouldn't have lasted this long. Poor Agatha would have already wandered off a cliff on a whim."

"Or an evil vampire would have goaded her off," I croaked. Because he had the gall to profess that he had an interest in her that extended beyond her plain looks and massive fortune. "Poor Agatha—"

"*Agatha* would have written me a check during our first meeting," he countered, suddenly serious. "*You* insisted upon your own terms, no matter how reckless and inane they might be. The first time I offered you an out, you stripped naked and demanded you have your way." He pulled me closer and his thumb swiped my lower lip as if in punishment. "I told you to make yourself unappealing at the club. So you decided to dance in a way that made me offer up more time to that bastard Raphael just to keep you out of his reach. I turned you away for your own good, yet you came marching back with your chin in the air, daring me to have you again."

He sighed, such a hollow, tortured sound. "Then I leave the country to try to regain my sanity, only to return and find you on my doorstep. And again, when I try to *finally* let you go, you get on your knees and suck my cock." Awe painted his voice, as did anger, and hopelessness, and eternal frustration. "At every turn, you confound me. At every attempt to ignore your albeit lacking charms, you find a way to hook your claws into me. You called me the monster, but frankly, I must admit that I am at a loss when it comes to you. A part of me suspects that if I *did* kill you, you'd merely come back to life, giggling with glee that you'd finally managed to break my resolve." His other hand came to cradle the side of my face, brushing the stray curls back. "I'm confounded by you," he reiterated. "So I have decided that the only way to survive you with my sanity intact is to utilize you. As I see fit."

My breath caught at the raw lust his tone revealed. As if chasing the reaction, he worked the tip of his thumb between my lips, seeking out my tongue.

"And how is that?" I managed to ask.

He seemed to mull it over. "I will no longer resist your impulsive inclinations. I'll merely combat them. The next time you question my supposed lack of attraction to you, I will take it as an invitation over an insult."

I drew my thighs together, aggravating the slight ache between them. "Oh?"

"I'll strip you naked," he mused. "For a start, at least. There is no use in humoring you like one would a sane woman. You thrive on this—corruption. I think it's what you've wanted all along."

I thought back to our very first meeting, when he'd barged into my bedroom and presented a choice: life or death?

"Stripping naked or dropping to my knees does seem to be an effective way to render you speechless," I admitted. Then my teeth skewered my lip. "As is presenting a, let's say *unlikely*, challenge to your understanding of vampire biology."

He remained silent for so long. I flinched when he finally moved and settled his hand along my hip. Outstretched, his fingers grazed the flat of my belly. The sight triggered a flurry of emotions too complex to name. They thickened my throat and obstructed my breathing—overwhelming in every aspect.

"Regardless of what happens between us… I don't want to face this alone," I admitted, my voice hoarse.

"You won't. It is true that this 'challenge' is unexpected," he finally confessed. "Though, I would ask that you not make a habit of deconstructing my concept of reality."

"What did Raphael mean?" I asked. "When he said that my bloodline is cursed. That you knew someone who—"

"It doesn't matter." He brushed his mouth along my jaw, taking his time in the advance toward his true destination. I inhaled raggedly, my lips parting even before his finally settled over mine. This kiss was slower than the others. Deeper. Savoring instead of frantic. His flavor lingered on my tongue, and I took my time deciphering every subtle nuance of it. He was a creature born to be deciphered.

He could taste as unyielding and relentless as ice in some aspects one moment. Then hot like winter spice the next. Sweet like wine, all the while laced with a bitter, dangerous hint that made my stomach constrict and heat spread through my belly.

When he started to pull back, I followed, craving more. His blood was an addictive substance, but even it was unmatched compared to him.

"I really do need to speak to the pilot." The raw regret in his tone soothed any sting of rejection I might have felt. He looked tormented as he pulled away and stood. Surprising me, he reached for my seat belt and unfastened it before helping me to my feet as well.

Instead of toward the cockpit, he led me down the length of the cabin and into a space dominated by a bed. Something I suspected a vampire's private jet might otherwise not contain.

"You need sleep," he said, urging me onto the mattress. "The bathroom is there." He nodded to a small door just beyond the bedroom. "I shouldn't be long."

I watched him go. Even disheveled in his polished suit, the man remained unmatched in poise. Doubt, that terrible fucking thing, was harder to quash without his mouth to silence it, however. That vicious voice returned, slightly louder than before.

You think he truly wants you? It's all lies, Eleanor.

The only way to banish the thoughts was to enter the bathroom—unusually spacious with a wide sink and enough space to wash myself in comfortably—strip my soiled dress, and attack my body with a warm, wet cloth. I washed slowly, swaying in time with the plane's various jolts and tremors.

I was doubtfully eyeing my dress, considering whether to wear it at all or just leave the bathroom naked, when someone knocked softly on the door.

"Miss? Mr. Helos requested that I bring you some of your belongings so that you can make yourself as comfortable as possible. We have about eight hours until landing." The attendant opened the door and offered an array of items balanced on a tray. A length of black material that resembled a robe. A fresh dress. Slippers and various toiletries.

I accepted them all gratefully and dressed in the modest black shift and the silken robe. When I reentered the bedroom, Dublin still hadn't returned. I climbed onto the mattress, gasping at the quality—divine. Before I knew it, I was groggily stirring to awareness and finding a presence looming over the bed.

"The plane won't crash, I hope," I murmured as another bout of turbulence rattled the cabin—though honestly the mattress was so luxurious that I barely even felt the disturbance at all. "Is everything okay with the pilot?"

Dublin said nothing, his face expressionless. Closed-off.

Unease made me swallow as I scrambled upright. "What's wrong?"

"What exactly did you tell your sister? Perhaps you've had a line of communication to her all along? I had my men check for your little note. It's gone." His voice was so cutting that I ran my fingers along my throat just to make sure he hadn't drawn blood. "Tell me now. Did you mention the contract? Gloat over the fact that you own me like a dog on a leash?"

I shook my head. "What are you talking about? What's wrong?"

"We're being followed." He eyed me pointedly, as if waiting for a confession.

When all I could do was sputter wordlessly, he turned on his heel and stormed into the main cabin.

"Wait!" I started to follow but he stopped short, his voice like a whip.

"Don't. Stay in here. Get your *rest* while I try to ensure we both don't end up killed."

I stared after him, my mouth agape. He crossed the central cabin, disappearing through a doorway at the other end.

I crept toward the threshold, his rage an invisible line that kept me from stepping over it. Doubt became full-blown paranoia. And then dread.

My heart felt a bit like that goddamn Gray family crypt. Dusty and chambered, filled with a million dark, shadowy spaces. And every time I let him in, he slammed the door on his way out.

COLD

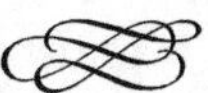

*I*t seemed that we landed hours later. An eternity perhaps, suspended in time and space—the perfect environment for Dublin's anger to fester into full-blown apathy when he finally appeared outside my unofficial prison cell.

"Come," he said. Dressed in a fresh suit entirely composed of black, he didn't even resemble the man I'd clung to just a few short hours earlier. He was a stranger who dabbled in the trade of souls—but mine was already far beyond his reach. "We need to move quickly." Suspicion lanced from him, honed like a blade.

So I parried in the only way I knew how: with equal vitriol.

"I'll move," I snarled, my hands on my hips, "just as soon as you tell me where the hell we are."

He lunged, snatching my wrist, and yanked me across the main cabin.

"Get off of me!" By the time I'd managed to wrench out of his grip, we were already descending the steps onto a secluded tarmac, seemingly in the middle of nowhere.

A car waited nearby, another stern-faced driver standing at the ready. But Dublin's silence couldn't obscure everything. Evening painted the sky a stunning ochre shade, for one. Like fire, smoldering down to ebony embers speckled with starlight. Given that we'd left the city only early in the morning, it shouldn't have been this dark yet.

"Where are we?" I demanded as I continued down the steps.

Dublin said nothing, but the moment I reached solid ground, he grabbed my arm, all but hauling me to the car. I sputtered as he shoved me into the back seat—but this time, he followed, slamming the door after us.

I scrambled as far away from him as I could, squeezing myself against the opposite door. He didn't even spare a glance in my direction.

His attention on the driver, he commanded, "Go."

"Where are we?" I demanded. Somewhere far, far from my home I suspected.

Foreign air lingered in my nostrils, far crisper than the stench of the city. Twisted trees lined the road and loomed above, easily displacing any view of the sky. In some ways, it felt like a parallel universe, one frozen in time.

"I'll keep our location to myself for now," Dublin said in a tone that made me grit my teeth. "Just in case you decide to write more letters to your sister. And here I was, assuming she might be in danger. I actually considered offering my services to assist you in finding—"

"Something happened," I deduced. "Just tell me. If I did something wrong—"

"*You*? Make a mistake?" His eyebrows furrowed in mock shock. "The woman who's gotten more people killed in her wake in a month than most will in a lifetime?"

Pain ripped through my chest, so potent that I pressed my hand against it as if that might lessen the blow. It didn't. Once again, my defensive mechanism threatened to deploy. I wanted to say something equally harsh, enough to combat the way my eyes burned. But as I observed my hand in the waning daylight, something displaced even my anger.

"My ring." Panicked, I felt around my seat, finding nothing. "It's gone. Go back! I must have left it in the—"

"Did you not hear me when I said we were being followed? Yet you suggest we go back for a worthless trinket. And you still claim you don't have an ulterior motive?"

I bit down on my tongue so hard that I tasted copper. Aching, I brushed my naked finger with my thumb as I tried to reconcile why a *worthless trinket's* loss was troubling me so much. Especially when the man who'd given it to me didn't seem to give a damn either way.

"You're right," I admitted, turning away from him. "It's worthless trash. I truly hate you, and I spilled all of your secrets to a sister who abandoned me without a word. *And* I hope her spies blow us both up because, obviously, I have a death wish. Hopefully my *cancer* will speed along that outcome, at least. So tell your driver to hurry up to wherever we're going. I'm bored."

He said nothing, but I cut myself off from any senses that might decipher him. Instead, I did what I should have done all along—trusted my suspicious, doubtful instincts. Oh, how right they were.

But admitting as much hurt more than it should have. I hunched beneath the pain of it, wrapping my arms around my chest in a vain effort to mitigate the ceaseless throbbing.

But it didn't.

All I could do was whisper out loud the confused, pathetic questions circling my brain in an effort to weakly combat the self-loathing.

"You want me to trust you, but how can I when every time I try you push me away, or insult me, or disappear?" Oh God. My voice was trembling, breaking openly. Tears stung my eyes, impossible to blink back. Oh well. He'd accuse me of lying regardless. I had nothing left to lose. "I confessed to you that night in the cathedral how you made me feel. You left days later, and I'm the cruel one? But now you return and I'm not only supposed to believe that you might give a damn, but that I might be—" No. I bit off any more. That was too pathetic. "I think it's best if from now on we just…"

Exist in a silence so heavy that I didn't have to finish defining it. We fell into our roles far too well, retreating to opposite ends of the car, glaring from our respective windows.

He never offered a word in his defense or otherwise.

And I was too tired to demand one.

~

Our eventual destination awaited at the end of a paved driveway lined in trees and illuminated with orange lanterns. When my gaze fell over the structure, I gasped aloud as the driver finally came to a stop.

Poor Gray Manor would blush in shame.

Composed of stone, a sprawling mansion gleamed in the moonlight as if crafted from a fairytale. Light spilled from every window, painting neatly manicured lawns, complete with bubbling twin fountains placed on either side of the cobblestone driveway.

I still gaped as Dublin exited the car without a word. His hand appeared seconds later. Warily, I took it. Had he decided to apologize? I eyed his expression, hunting for any softness as he guided me up the path to the front door. There, a man wearing a stark black uniform ushered us inside.

"Show Ms. Gray to her room," Dublin commanded him, releasing me. He turned on his heel and stormed out the way we'd come.

I watched, flinching as the door slammed behind him.

"This way, miss."

I turned to the butler and tried to shift my attention to my surroundings, letting their beauty negate any pain.

Breathtaking was the operative word. I'd thought his beautiful penthouse suite was impressive, but this was luxury on an entirely different scale. My mother would approve of the plain-but-quality oak-paneled walls and polished floors. The golden light fixtures illuminating wide, open hallways with high ceilings and furniture in shades of emerald and ebony, however?

She'd scoff in disgust at those.

My room, unsurprisingly, was no less elegant. For all his moods where I was concerned, I couldn't accuse Dublin of compromising my comfort out of spite. The bed looked heavenly—solid wood, carved with extravagant reliefs of roses and vines, draped in a ruby canopy. A wide window displayed a view of yet another garden, its details obscured in the darkness.

"Goodnight, miss," the butler called before leaving the room and closing the door.

I swallowed hard, blinking as my eyes started to prickle. It was funny how silence could bring everything into painfully clear focus. Like the fact that I was alone again.

That my lips were still swollen—again.

That the inside of my thighs ached and I couldn't tell if it was from pain or just the shame of rejection.

I wanted to be angry. Or bitter, or hateful. I wanted to storm about the room and declare just how unaffected I was by Dublin Helos and his switchblade rage. I wanted to do anything but crawl onto the mattress and huddle beneath silken sheets as moisture spilled down my cheeks once more.

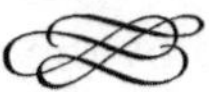

*M*orning came with the intensity of a punch —literally. Ruthlessly aimed, it slammed against my abdomen and the pain jolted me from a fitful sleep. Gasping, I rolled onto my side, clutching my stomach. Every breath hurt. It was as though my lungs were in a vise grip. An invisible fist squeezed only to release. Again. Each vicious cramping wave left me writhing over the sheets.

"What's wrong?" The door flew open and Dublin rushed in. Pale dawn light painted him in shades of gold, making him seem more angel than Devil. He wore a fresh gray suit, his hair slicked back, his overall appearance perfection.

Gritting my teeth, I sat upright and placed my feet on the floor, my back to him. "Nothing," I said even as another wave of pain stole my breath away. My eyelids fluttered as I inhaled through my nose, gripping the sheets so tightly that my nails pierced the fabric. Eventually, the tension subsided, and I attempted to disguise my rigid posture with a shrug. "I'm fine."

He didn't move—and his concern irritated me far more than it should have. *Now* he wanted to care after accusing me of being a suicidal traitor. Yesterday's Eleanor might have forgiven him, swayed by the display.

Not me.

"I'm fine," I hissed, biting the words out. "And I'd rather be alone now, if you please. How else will I contact my sister via telepathic Morse code and give our location away?"

He moved—a series of slow, heavy footsteps that paused near the threshold. "I'll be gone for the day," he told me, his tone devoid of warmth once more. "When I return tonight, be ready. There is clothing in the wardrobe—"

"Fine," I snapped, deliberately avoiding asking him where he planned on taking me.

"And…"

I could almost taste his hesitation, cracking his callous façade.

"If you need me, ask for me."

"I won't." I eyed my fingers lazily, inspecting the nails. They were trembling and I balled them into fists to hide it—though the act was in vain.

He was already gone, marching down the hall and then the staircase.

Alone, I crawled onto the center of the mattress, tense in anticipation of another bout of pain. I'd never felt anything like it before. Was this a new phase of the cancer I'd deliberately avoided thinking about until now?

Fear goaded my pulse into a frantic thrum. I tossed and turned, wavering on calling for Dublin after all. My lips parted. Closed. Parted again…

If I did call for him, it wouldn't be out of weakness. Just in case I truly was dying, he deserved to be told what an ass he was to his face. That was all.

When footsteps approached my room, I sat upright, wondering if my thoughts alone had conjured him. But no. A smiling woman wearing a plain gray dress approached the foot of my bed, holding a tray. On it was a simple breakfast and a nondescript black cup containing a suspicious-looking liquid.

Once she left, I ate quickly, tasting nothing. The food helped. After a few minutes passed devoid of any cramping, I paced before venturing from my room to examine the manor proper.

Something told me that Dublin hadn't bought this property on a whim. There was too much of his personal style embedded within everything from the subtle silver accents to the almost cathedral-like architecture. I suspected he had owned the place for a while, a fact that intrigued me more than I wanted to admit. It was easy to forget just how old he was. And how wealthy. How powerful.

The man possessed a string of unknown credentials—being a doctor included. I'd witnessed firsthand his procurement of an orphanage, and he seemed to own countless buildings and enterprises. A collector, in a sense. If I wanted to be morbid, his interest in me made perfect sense—a man so wealthy and bored that he collected properties and money like candy. What else was Gray Manor but a token to add to his list?

And what was I other than a fun diversion?

Stop, Ellie. I rubbed my arms, shivering. A chill lingered over the lower level as if no one had thought to heat it. Considering that a vampire owned the place, who would?

Seeking warmth, I returned to my room, and there I lingered, no better than a bird in a cage.

~

In my quest to prove as a fitting antagonist to Dublin, I did my best to appear only *somewhat* presentable before he came for me. The resulting look required one of Yulia's dresses—mysteriously found within the room's only wardrobe. Floor-length and composed of black lace, it sported a modest though no less elegant neckline. After a halfhearted bit of styling with my wet fingers, my curls no longer stuck out in all directions, so that was a plus—and about where my efforts extended.

If he expected more, that was his problem.

As night fell, I finally descended to the foyer. Only to find Dublin already there waiting. One look at him reinforced just how futile my pathetic attempts had been.

The air left my lungs, driven out by the formidable silhouette he cut. His suit was black, crowned by a silver tie that made his eyes nearly unbearable to meet head-on. So I stared at his chest instead, noticing a ruby-red corner pocket.

"How are you feeling?" he asked as I descended the final step.

A quick, disinterested glance in his direction was the only response he received. In silence, he extended his arm for me anyway. As we exited through the manor's main door, flecks of rain fell from an indigo sky and I shuddered.

It was colder here than in the city. My teeth were chattering within seconds, lending an eerie backdrop to the howling wind playing through swaying trees. Where exactly were we?

Dublin provided no explanation. Using my grip on his arm, he guided me down a paved stone path toward a circular driveway where a car waited. A new driver stood at the ready, and I felt more disoriented than ever.

"Where are we?" I finally asked.

While I couldn't see Dublin's face from this angle, I recognized the subtle clenching to his jaw just fine. I wasn't the only one capable of giving the silent treatment. Fine.

Biting my lip, I withheld any further questions as he guided me into the back seat of the car and climbed in beside me.

He leaned forward to mutter something to the driver and the man nodded, flicking a dial on the console. Then he sat back, staring in any direction but mine. It wasn't long into the drive that I realized we weren't far from civilization after all.

Though one very different from the world I'd grown up in. Judging from the few street signs we passed—all written in the same obscure language—I seriously doubted that we were still in the country. Beautiful renaissance-style architecture cemented that suspicion. Buildings framed in Romanesque columns, and ruby tiled roofs cast a surreal atmosphere, almost as though we'd stepped back in time.

"Can I ask where we are now?" Awe colored my voice, but I struggled to swallow my irritation as Dublin remained silent. The hostility between us felt as palpable as the heat flooding the car's interior from the vents.

Later, I'd let myself mull over the fact that he must have requested as much for my benefit—it wasn't like he was the one shivering. At the moment, I didn't even bother to thank him but stoically faced ahead.

Until the driver finally pulled up before a grand building made of tan stone, built in a stunning mixture of classic and renaissance architecture. My mouth fell open. As Dublin circled around to my side of the car and helped me out, I still gaped.

"I plan on meeting someone here." He finally spoke, lowering his mouth to my ear as we joined a throng of beautifully dressed patrons queuing up to enter the building. "Stay close to me."

The venue was a theater—a fact that became obvious the moment we passed through the grand entrance and entered a lobby draped in hues of red and gold. It was a luxurious sight far beyond that of even the vaulted theaters my family frequented.

Without bothering to stop near the box office, Dublin led me up a set of stairs, draped in scarlet runners, that deposited us within a secluded hallway. Gilded doorways lined it, shrouded by hanging ruby curtains. Near the very end of the corridor, Dublin pulled me through one, revealing a small, enclosed space with a breathtaking view of a circular stage below.

It was a private box. Four red velvet chairs lined in gold were positioned near the balcony. Placed on each cushion was a cream-colored program revealing the details of tonight's show—written in the unknown language.

"Have a seat," Dublin commanded, pulling out the nearest chair for me. "He should be here soon."

He didn't look very excited for this meeting. I wasn't the sole reason for his thunderous expression, apparently. Though before I dared to ask, his clenched jaw warned that he wouldn't divulge any details of our mysterious guest. Rather than press him for any, I busied myself with perusing a program I couldn't even read.

Eventually, Dublin settled onto the chair beside mine, and beyond us, the theater began to fill. One by one, nearly every seat became occupied with a beautifully dressed patron—all but the two empty ones beside us. By the time the curtained entrance to our box finally shifted, the main lights had already begun to dim.

The man who entered—with a chilling smile and blood-red hair—was a vampire. I knew even before his grin widened to reveal sharpened fangs. A poisonous chill proceeded him, setting every nerve in my body on edge. In his wake stood a tall, blond woman wearing a floor-length navy gown. A thick strip of black velvet obscured her throat, forming a fashionable choker, and a matching headband held the curls back from her face. But the style only enhanced her lifeless, glassy eyes as they drifted aimlessly around the room.

"Dmitri," Dublin said gruffly. He stood and shook the hand the man had extended in his direction—but his shoulder flexed as if he were applying far more strength to the gesture than protocol called for.

"Dearest Dublin! I was surprised to receive your invite." Surprisingly lilting, the other man's voice betrayed a distinct accent. Russian? "And I must say that I'm even more intrigued to find you have your own guest. I was intending to share." He gestured absently toward the blond.

She staggered, giggling at nothing.

"There's no need to share tonight," Dublin said, but even I didn't miss the subtle warning in his tone. He extended his hand to me and I took it—but even I had enough sense to realize that it wasn't a loving gesture, but a possessive one.

"Relax, Dublin," Dmitri urged with another hearty chuckle. "Do sit. We have so much to discuss. You as well." He gestured to an empty chair and snapped his fingers before his companion's nose.

The dazed blond stumbled forward and obediently claimed the seat beside him. At the same time, a hum from the orchestra warned that the show was starting.

The four of us watched in unnatural silence as the curtains lifted and the actors took their places. It was an opera. One performed by singers who bared their souls upon the stage —but it wasn't the typical tragedy.

A young girl lamented her fate—doomed to love a man she could not have. Her anguish easily translated the language barrier, and I could follow the plot as easily as if someone were whispering it to me in my ear.

Her lover belonged to a faction far beyond her station. Their love was all but impossible, yet he had been willing to forsake it all.

For her.

Together, they escaped and were even blessed with a child along the way.

But ultimately, their romance was doomed.

A man her lover cherished like a brother tracked them down. Unwilling to accept their union, he slaughtered the woman and her unborn child, leaving her lover to mourn them alone.

And plot his revenge…

By the time the final scene before intermission drew to a close, I felt chilled to the bone, my throat dry. Even Dublin sat unusually stiffly, his gaze fixed on the stage. Something told me that this particular production had been chosen specifically.

For him.

"Marvelous! Marvelous!" Dmitri exclaimed, clapping his surprisingly slender hands. "They were going to perform a ballet," he added as the lights returned to full brilliance and the curtains drifted shut. "Something about a swan. I casually slipped the director some inspiration, however." He laughed, his teeth glinting like ivory in the orange glow of a hanging chandelier. "Dublin has always nursed a fondness for the arts," he told me with a wink. "Theater. Music. What was that phrase you used to spout? *Music is the only damn thing humanity possesses worth saving.*' He was a different man back then though, called by another name."

I shuddered in remembrance of it. *Cael.* A creature even Saskia had feared.

"I hope I've impressed you both," Dmitri added, fingering the collar of his scarlet suit.

"It's entertaining. That's for damn sure," Dublin replied. His tone was anything but impressed. He sounded uneasy.

Feeding off the grim emotion, I shifted, uncrossing my legs. Re-crossing them. I couldn't keep still. Dread formed a physical pressure, crushing my stomach. More cramping? I brushed one of my hands against my belly, just for a second —but even as I drew it away, Dublin had already snatched my wrist.

Casually, he settled my hand against his lap instead.

"So, what has brought you here?" Dmitri wondered, eyeing us, a smile playing on his red lips. "All the way to *Italia*. I know you prefer the States—"

"Remember that favor you owe me?" Dublin interjected.

"Ah…" He nodded. "And how is the dearest Yuliana?"

"Consider this a collection call," Dublin hissed, ignoring the question. "You want to remain in hiding? Well, my friend here has a morbid fascination with vampires. In fact, she's too curious for her own good. You know more about our kind than anyone. So, *humor* her."

"Lies," Dmitri scolded with another hearty laugh. His eyes glinted, a mysterious mixture of brown and green. "I'm surprised it's taken you so long to try and weasel out my many secrets, old friend. But you've never expressed an interest before. Especially not after my 'exile.'"

"*I* have no interest," Dublin insisted. "However, my companion has a rather naïve outlook on our condition. Her innocence amuses me, but I've grown tired of having to humor her questions. Enlighten her."

It was a dare. One Dmitri seemed more than willing to accept.

He shifted in his seat to offer me his hand directly. As pale as snow, his palm glowed in the soft lighting. I eyed it, motionless, until I sensed Dublin's gaze on my throat, issuing a silent command. *It's okay.* But when I finally placed my fingers within Dmitri's, his clamped over them in a vise grip.

"Such a sweet girl," he murmured, his smile widening. "Where on Earth did you find her?"

"Don't talk to me," Dublin snapped. "You answer her."

"V-Vampires seem…n-nice," I managed to croak in the silence following their banter. Mentally, I berated myself for sounding so damn naïve—but then I felt Dublin nudge my shoulder. *Keep going.* "D-Do you get married?"

"Marriage? Oh, she is darling!" Dmitri chuckled in amusement. With deft grace, his fingers skimmed my palm and I shivered.

He felt even colder than Dublin.

"Marriage is a very human concept, my dear," he explained in an almost fatherly tone. "When you've lived as long as we have, something as trivial as a ring ceases to hold any true value. There is much more stock placed in loyalty. Obedience. Isn't that right, my darling?" He glanced at the blond, but I doubted she'd even heard him. Had she been drugged? If so, something told me that the poison in her veins wasn't what most women used to chase a high.

Her dreamy smile concealed the taste of something a bit more…organic.

"What about children?" Dublin wondered offhandedly. His expert skills of manipulation were on display, steering the conversation while he still feigned disinterest. "She's mused on that before."

"Has she?" Dmitri's eyes snapped in my direction so quickly that I recoiled. "What a strange question, my dear." As he spoke, his frigid fingertips continued to stroke my hand, and it took everything I had in me not to yank it back.

"I… It's just something I saw in a movie once," I stammered. Not a total lie. In the early days of my self-imposed loneliness, I might have decided to torture myself by renting every vampire-based movie known to man. All of them. "Can vampires—and humans—have children—"

"Of course not." He released his grip, allowing my hand to fall. "At least nothing that I could dare call a 'child.'"

A cold, icy feeling resonated through my stomach. "How…how so?"

"It would be an abomination, my darling." He flicked his fingers to dismiss the mere idea. "A nonviable creature. There have been stories, terrible things." His eyes sought mine, gleaming with callous amusement. "Thankfully, such creatures are rumored to have mercifully died within the womb. And there is almost always a curse within play, those nasty things. Why, any of my kind foolish enough to even *attempt* to sire a living child would most surely forsake his eternity."

"Forsake?" I asked in a whisper.

Beside me, Dublin was stone. Had he known any of these rumors? I couldn't tell from his expression—hard and unreadable, stone once more.

In a sense, I probably resembled him. I couldn't breathe.

"He'd become forever damned." Dmitri shrugged. "A creature doomed to never die, no matter how the world may decay around him. A terrible bargain, I'm sure. Especially in exchange for such a twisted parody of nature. Oh, I wouldn't trouble your pretty little mind with such horrors." He mimed shooing away an invisible fly. "Best to not even think of such things."

"Oh." It was all I could say—just a gasp disguised as something intelligible. Twisted images filled my head before I could block them out, giving vivid life to his brutal imagery.

Death. Dying. Deformed.

"Though Dublin would know better than I," he added, chuckling. He inclined his head at the man beside me. "Right, old friend? After all, I believe that Mero was the first to—"

"Don't," Dublin warned, sitting forward. "Do not mention him."

"Ah." Dmitri rubbed his hands together with barely concealed glee. "We still aren't allowed to say his name, I see. Not even his given one? Oh, well. His little friends certainly seem emboldened these days. I hear even the bothersome Gray girl has taken a side for once. Either that or vanished. The *other* one, of course." He eyed me pointedly, his lips quirked. "Georgiana, I believe her name is?"

"Side?" I croaked. Something in how he'd emphasized that word…

It terrified me to my core.

"Well, I'd consider it more like a lack of objection, one might say. Though it could be as the rumors claim and the poor girl has simply disappeared, gone without a trace—"

"Enough," Dublin bellowed. "This isn't the time for your mind games."

"Mind games? I'm sure *you* learned the truth well before I did, what with your network of little spies. *Mine* told me that you were on your way the second your plane landed. And while you didn't bother to introduce your guest, I know *her* name well enough." His head swiveled in my direction. "Eleanor Louise Gray, the second-to-last living heir in the entire Gray line, barring her uncle of course. My my, Dublin, you didn't think to tell her that her own sister has signed her death warrant? That is rather cruel, even for you."

"What?" The room bled into formless color around me. Only Dublin's face held any real definition—his mouth strained, his eyes turned away.

"I said *enough*," he growled.

"Pity. I could tell her so much more." Dmitri lifted his hand to my cheek. "Such a pretty little thing—"

"You touch her and I'll kill you." Dublin didn't even look like himself anymore. Hunched forward, he radiated an ageless power, every bit as commanding as Raphael.

Dmitri's smirk never wavered, but he shrank back, contritely bowing his head. "I meant nothing by it, Dublin," he simpered. "The rumors have buzzed with how much of a liking you've taken to her. I wouldn't *dream* of harming her—though I do wonder how long it will be before…"

"Before what?" Dublin hissed.

"Before the owner of her bloodline comes searching for his little toy. They've followed you here, though I'm sure you know that. I don't think they even know why they need her dead. Mere soldiers following orders. *His* orders. How ironic that her sister may have volunteered to carry them out—"

The room spun as their conversation divulged into distorted noises and hushed voices. Nothing mattered but a single thought I couldn't suppress. Georgiana wanted me dead?

Or…she was missing.

"…must ask why you care about this one anyway?" Dmitri added, his voice regaining clarity. "Everyone knows that you kept an unusual interest in the other one. Such a beauty. If I had to place money on which woman you might desire, it would be—"

"Eleanor!" Dublin reached for me as I knocked the chair over in my rush to stand, hitting the floor on my hands and knees.

Air clawed its way into my lungs as I hauled myself upright using the wall for balance and threw myself between the gap in the curtains shielding our box.

The hallway beyond was deserted. Spinning and distorted. No matter where I looked, all I could see was endless red. It dripped from the walls and coated the floor. Drowning me…

Fabric snatched at my hands as I ran, feeling along the wall, desperate for a door, an exit. Anything. In the end, I staggered into an empty box and spotted a vase of roses. I ripped out the flowers by their stems, lowered my mouth over the neck of the vase, and—

Watery liquid erupted from my throat. The force of each wretch brought me to my knees, and it was all I could do to clutch the vase to my chest and heave.

I cringed into the shadows as heavy footsteps approached my corner and someone drew the curtain back.

A lingering chill lowered the atmosphere, identifying the intruder as clearly as if he'd shouted his name. But he said nothing, advancing toward my corner with broad strides. He crouched instead, sweeping my hair back as another wave of vomit spilled into the vase. When my stomach finally had nothing left, he took the vase away.

"Don't," I pleaded when his hand brushed my shoulder. I scurried out of reach as if burned. My face found the safety of my palms and I hunched into myself, too tired to keep the tears at bay. "Don't touch me—"

"Eleanor, look at me." He sounded too soft. Too gentle. "Look at me—"

"I can't take this." My voice bordered on shrill, alarmingly high-pitched. Broken. I couldn't get enough air. My lungs were deflated, impossible to fill. God, I needed him to leave—only then could I break. "Get out! Just leave. Get away!"

"You're hyperventilating. Breathe!"

"Stop!" My hands muffled the plea, but I couldn't look at him. "Just leave me alone. Please. Leave me alone. I can't… I can't take it anymore—"

"You can't? I knew that very first day," he gruffly admitted. "That first day when you met my gaze, completely unafraid. I knew." Heedless of my plea, he remained, still restraining my curls. "I knew you'd torment me to no end. I knew that you would thwart even my most well laid plans. I knew then and there that one encounter with you would never be enough."

His voice was deeper than ever. Gone were the harsh bravado or bitter anger. This was Dublin Helos in a way I'd rarely experienced him.

Open and honest.

Yet I wanted to scream loud enough to drown him out.

"Please, go—"

"I'd met your sister before you," he continued. Even level, I could never overpower the gritted cadence of his voice. "A beautiful creature. If there were any Gray doomed to tempt me, it would be her…" He trailed off, and nausea constricted my throat as I imagined everything he'd held back.

Him with Georgie, laughing at my naivety. Stinging tears fell without restraint, but in a sick, twisted way, there was peace in the agony. Finally—*finally*—he was telling me what I'd wanted to hear all along.

The full truth.

"I've avoided your kind throughout the centuries for a reason, the Grays, but…something made me confront her directly when she grew bold enough to challenge Raphael," he continued, unconcerned as I shook my head in a silent plea. "I expected… She was beautiful, yes, but she aroused me no more than any other beautiful, talented soul I'd traded for centuries. In a way, I pitied her—the most interesting creature to spring from your bloodline since James and I was immune to even her charms. Still, I decided that selling her to Raphael would be a waste, so I intervened. Her dowdy, plain sister would make a useful pawn, but it would be for her benefit in the end. In one fell swoop, they'd both be spared, and I would have the last laugh over a creature I'd grown bored of serving. My plan was infallible—until I saw *you.*"

His voice lowered to a hiss. Me, Eleanor Gray, the bane of his existence. So infuriating that he couldn't even refer to me without rage constricting his voice. He grabbed my wrists, wrenching me upright, tearing my shield away.

I closed my eyes instead. Facing rejection was easier this way. If only he would just get it over with. Stop twisting the knife.

"I get it," I insisted. "I've always gotten it—"

"Do you?" His voice dripped directly into my ear, preceding the sensation of ice brushing my earlobe. His mouth? "I saw you and I experienced an irritation unlike anything I'd ever felt. This pathetic mortal woman had the nerve to spite my plans through sheer stubborn denial. Rather than come to me begging for life, you shrugged me off. Turned away. *You* looked me in the eye and merely scoffed at what I was— even your sister hadn't done that." He sounded more incredulous than impressed. "No…you were determined to spite me, even then, and I knew… No one could imagine such a doom."

The coldness of his finger swiped at my cheek, brushing away a fresh wave of tears.

"And even now you'll still deny it. I all but tell you out loud and it's as though you slam your hands over your ears, childishly refusing to hear it. Then I push you away and you react as though you're the one who has been wounded. Regardless, I am a fool."

The stark admission startled me into opening my eyes. He looked so hollow, Dublin. A frown replaced his polished persona, his eyes narrowed. Gingerly, he brought his hand to the side of my face, tilting my jaw for his inspection.

"I am…sorry," he confessed, but the words lacked true sympathy. It was almost as if he wasn't used to saying them. In real time, he was relearning how to feel something as simple as empathy. "For doubting you. For hurting you—"

"You didn't!" I scoffed. "You're trying to get inside my head —you're always inside my head!"

And I wanted to rip my hair out in frustration. My fingers curled, nails drawn, and I started to raise them, but he renewed his grip, stepping forward in the same smooth motion.

"Let me go," I hissed.

His eyes flashed, and I waited for a cruel retort. He lowered his head instead, brushing his mouth against my forehead. Shock paralyzed me—his end goal.

"You're in no state to be alone," he murmured against my flesh, but his tone made me recoil. Soft again. Deceptive again. He sounded too much like he cared. "That's why you are this way."

"I'm always alone," I pointed out, my voice hollow. "Always. Even my sister…" I couldn't even say it. "And I'm dying, and I'm scared, and I'm alone. I'll always be alone—"

His mouth found my lips, sealing them with a single motion. I faltered, flicking my tongue against his. It wasn't fair. His taste teased my senses, a tempting drug, potent enough to take the pain away.

It hurt. My heart. My head. I couldn't focus on everything Dmitri had said all at once or I'd go insane. I *was* going insane.

"Look at me." He gripped my chin, tilting my head back, and met my gaze. His tongue traced his lower lip, reminding me of a predator wondering where to strike first on vulnerable prey. "You asked me once, why someone like me might be attracted to someone like *you*." He brushed his thumb against my mouth but nothing more.

I inhaled raggedly, wanting…needing. Something. Anything.

As if aware of that, he angled himself even farther away from me. "I suppose that's part of your appeal. Your innocence. You don't even know what you do to me, do you?"

I bit my lip as our gazes connected. His burned, impossibly bright.

"Your smell. Your taste. You pretend that I bought you from Raphael to rescue your delicate soul from any other, but deep down, you know the truth: I wanted you for myself."

"Lies," I croaked. It was all I could say.

And he laughed. "What did I promise I'd do the next time you countered me?" He pretended to mull it over, stroking his chin, even as he advanced.

I held my breath.

With deliberate slowness, he fingered the delicate silk over my shoulder. Then he tugged, easing the fabric down until my breasts threatened to slip free. "I said I would strip you naked."

I watched in slow motion as my dress continued its guided descent. I didn't recognize my body anymore. Flushed pink with arousal as if coming to life for him alone. Even as my mind was in turmoil.

Even as the world shattered beneath my feet, I belonged to him.

"And you questioned…" He shook his head, eyeing me the way one would a feast. Someone starving—but there was a flaw with his meal. Frowning, he grazed my cheek with his thumb, smearing the tears still streaming down it. I could see his thoughts shift—lust becoming pity. The contrast made my head hurt.

So I lunged forward, risking my balance to reach for the fastenings of his pants. "I don't want to think," I confessed as he stiffened. "Please. I don't need coddling or sympathy. I just want…"

Sensation. His mouth on mine, his hands between my legs, delivering a dose of pleasure so potent that I'd shudder, arching wantonly into his touch.

Grays did not perform or require physical acts of comfort. We endured. "A strong inheritance is the only embrace you ever need," my mother used to say.

So he didn't hug me. He merely held me close instead. Close enough for me to cling to the front of his suit as though I were drowning. Close enough to bury my face against his chest and smother whatever sounds I made. I was shaking—that's why his arms tightened around me, keeping me there, keeping me from completely breaking apart.

His hand caught my throat, but there was no violence in the gesture. Guiding me to face him, he met my lips with his. Chilling. Frozen. Distracting. My arms went around his neck, drawing me further into the kiss. Sloppy, bruising, skin against teeth.

I needed more. Only this could make the harsh interior of the theater and the agony in my chest disappear. Only he could make it stop. With more pain—his teeth grazing my tongue. His hand plunging between my legs.

More. More. More.

I rocked my hips into every touch, not giving a damn for anyone around to hear the groan that tore from my lips. It clashed with the opening lines of the orchestra. The opera was continuing, somewhere in another realm that felt eons away.

In my world, there was only him. Ice and fire. Skin and silk, twisting, rubbing, claiming.

Dublin.

"Please," I croaked as he withdrew. My fingers shamelessly reached for him, clinging to whatever they could. "Please, I need you—"

He stood and snagged my wrist to haul me upright after him. One shift of his weight shoved me against a wooden sideboard pressed against the wall. It held only a vase of roses, which he easily batted aside. Then his hands gripped my hips, hauling me onto the smooth surface while he forced his bulk between my legs.

I spread them easily, allowing him to peel back the sleeves of my dress. My body spilled out from the silk, eager for his touch, and he devoured me with ravenous, groping hands.

My nipples stiffened for him, roughened by the merciless sensation of his chest against mine. Our mouths reconnected. Devoured. Fabric tore. Cool air assaulted my skin, preparing me for ice as he undid the fastenings of his pants. The flat of his hand caught my lower back, dragging me closer as he lunged, entering me in one thrust. Hard. Brutal. No mercy.

No care.

Just need that outlasted the soreness from the last time he'd taken me like this.

A scream caught in my throat, smothered by his palm. My head fell back. All I knew was pleasure and pain as I let my eyes close and rode every deep, punishing thrust.

With every one, I clawed at him, demanding more, more, more. Everything.

Only he had the power to erase my mind.

All I had to do was feel.

All I had to do was fall.

But even the Devil couldn't extend the violent descent from Heaven.

Eventually, we both crashed, breathless and senseless. His mouth was on my neck. My hands were clutching fistfuls of his suit jacket, but even buried inside me, crushing me with his weight, he wasn't close enough. His presence couldn't snuff out the fear. The guilt. The doubt.

"Look at me." He caught my chin in his palm, forcing me to meet his gaze.

I saw nothing there but silver. It blinded me just long enough for him to shrug his suit jacket from his shoulders and draw it around me. There was no one in the hallway beyond the private box as he helped me from the sideboard and pulled me out after him.

Any usher we passed said nothing but a cheerful greeting, and the rest of our surroundings blurred as he led me through winding corridors, then out into fresh air. Eventually, we entered his car.

The driver pulled off without a word, returning us to that secluded manor in the hills. I wondered if he owned it. I wanted to ask. Something trivial. Something mindless that might devolve into pointless small talk. My lips sprang apart, but by then, he was already hauling me out onto the curb and up the front walkway.

The door opened automatically, held by an unseen figure. I could only make out a blur of formless features before I found myself being dragged up the stairs. Into my bedroom.

There, in the darkness, he shoved the jacket from my shoulders, leaving my body bare. One bruising kiss robbed me of my senses. Then the mattress struck the back of my legs before he shoved me onto it fully.

Another kiss stopped time, kept eternity at bay.

I moaned, arching into every touch, every stroke, extending the barrier between reality.

Silk and ice became my world.

The only thing that mattered was feeling.

As long as he stayed.

IN THE GRAY

Sleep was the one realm Dublin couldn't follow me into, and alone, I traversed a hellscape of memories with nothing to shield myself from the pain.

Shadowed specters watched me, peeking from beyond a darkened veil. Only snippets of their faces were ever visible, but I knew their identities well enough.

Georgie. My parents. Death.

They all taunted from the abyss, cackling at my attempts to chase them away. But sprinkled in between their insults was a cruel truth that never ceased to echo.

Deformed.

Abomination.

Unnatural.

I startled awake, but reality was just as unwelcoming: a labyrinth of twisted sheets threatening to suffocate me. My fingers fanned out desperately, finding only empty, frozen space. Alone, I writhed, screaming my throat raw—but no real sound came out. Just gasping, broken whimpers. Sobs. Cries.

Despair weighed on my chest, crushing every ounce of air from my lungs.

I couldn't breathe.

"I'm here." Cold fingers caressed my spine, banishing the terror. Their owner rested beside me, and his mere presence was enough to keep the darkness at bay.

Tension drained from my limbs as gulps of air entered my chest. Drifting from my back, his hands cradled my hips, pulling me against the firmness of his body.

But the contact wasn't enough. I squirmed until his grip tightened and comfort became possession. Grasping fingertips. Scratching nails. I was a slave to whatever he could make me feel.

Pain. Misery. Mercy.

Anything.

I craved it all.

And much like the doctor he pretended to be, he delivered each necessary dose. In his arms, hours unfolded like seconds. I endured them in a daze, aware of him leaving only long enough to let me catch snatches of sleep or to shove food into my mouth.

Eventually, I started to refuse even that much.

But my Devil persisted, unwilling to see me in Hell just yet.

"Eat."

I cringed as he pressed something to my lips despite how hard I pursed them shut. Then I rolled onto my side to escape him, but he merely circled the bed, remaining in my line of sight. Balanced on his hand was a steaming plate, but I felt nothing even as the smell tickled my nose.

"Eleanor, eat."

I shook my head, eyeing the ceiling in lieu of his darkening expression. "I'm not hungry."

"You're starving." He matched my apathy with aggression, his tone bordering on a growl.

But I couldn't muster up the fear to heed him.

Numb, I buried my face against a pillow. Exhaustion preyed on my psyche, warning that sleep would come for me again. I didn't even have the strength to fight it.

"Look at me." He fisted his fingers through my hair, forcing me to face him.

For the first time, I noted how these hours had changed him. His eyes glowed, his fangs hanging freely.

Yet he still played pretend, trying once again to tempt me with a morsel stabbed on the end of a fork. "Eat."

"Why?"

His throat jerked, but his lips trapped the answer. *Because you'll die.*

"I'm fine."

"Look at me." He reached for my arm, but I didn't mean to swat his hand away. The plate fell from his grip anyway, smashing into pieces at his feet.

"I'm sorry," I whispered, closing my eyes against the mess I'd made. Guilt slipped through my numb armor regardless, heralding dangerous, whispered thoughts. Desperate, I tried to banish them, gritting my teeth in concentration. *Don't think. Don't.*

Nonetheless, Dmitri's words echoed in my skull anyway. *Deformed. Dying. Horror.*

I hunched away from them, clinging to the sheets, craving oblivion again. But already, Dublin wanted nothing to do with me.

He stood, crossing the room to snatch up the broken pieces of a porcelain plate. The sight of his back was a familiar one, all things considered. But God…not now.

My voice broke. "Don't leave me—"

"I'm not," he hissed even as he approached the door and wrenched it open. His gaze met mine as he crossed the threshold, honed like a knife's edge. "But you *will* eat."

The door slammed in his wake, but my boneless limbs kept me from chasing after him. I crawled to the edge of the mattress anyway. I was that pathetic. I'd fallen *that* far. His nearness alone could keep the thoughts at bay. The fear.

I would have done anything to extend it. Anything.

The sound of his returning footsteps made me tremble with relief. When I looked up, I found that he held more food. This time, a platter of apple slices, cheese, and fresh fruit.

"Eat," he commanded, stopping short just beyond my reach.

I squeezed my eyes shut. In vain, beads of moisture escaped, clawing down my cheek. "I can't…"

"Look at me."

The gritted cadence of his tone held sway. I obeyed just in time to find him brandishing a knife in his other hand. Naked, his skin gleamed like marble, and it seemed laughable that anything could hurt him. Even the blade he dragged across his collar bone.

Crimson bubbled up in a single line, painting him in gore like a true predator. After stalking closer to the bed, he set the tray at one end of the mattress and then lifted an apple slice.

He brought the red end of the fruit to his wound, letting his blood taint the apple's ivory flesh. Then he lowered the offering to my lips, ignoring how they twitched in defiance. "Open."

It wasn't fair. My body craved pleasure—distraction—but my mind only wanted an escape. Oblivion. A drop of his blood could serve both purposes.

Aware of that power, he taunted me, pressing the fruit more firmly against my mouth. "Eat."

A drop of moisture grazed my lip. Burning. Tempting. Sweet.

My tongue darted for it, rebelling against my pride. When he threatened to draw the apple away, I finally pried my jaws apart.

"Good," he murmured as one reluctant bite became two.

I licked my lips, ready for more. Even the hint of his blood was…

Explosive.

Warmth blossomed in my veins, battling the chill persisting in my heavy bones. With a burst of renewed energy, I drew my knees up to my chest and sat upright as my thoughts clouded, deliciously dizzy. But nowhere near high enough.

Thankfully, he already had another apple slice in hand. Fresh blood painted its milky interior, and I didn't require coaxing this time.

"Good."

The guttural praise resonated in my skin as his free hand cradled my cheek. He used the contact to tilt my head back and fed me another slice. Then another. With every tentative swallow, his thumb stroked my jaw in a rewarding caress.

I wasn't sure how much I ate before I finally refused the next morsel, legitimately full. In silence, Dublin removed the platter from the bed and set it down in some distant corner of the room.

I watched him, uneasy again. I should have been high on cloud nine, giddy and detached from the world. But I wasn't. Reality remained way too close. Even his blood couldn't push it away for very long.

"Lie back," he commanded as if reading my mind. "Trust me."

Confused, I fell against a pillow, eyeing the ceiling. The slow thud of his footsteps matched my pulse, quickened by the second. Only it ceased amid a growl as his hand caught my thigh so he could drag me to the edge of the bed with no warning.

Panicked, I grabbed at the sheets, nails drawn. "W-What are you doing?" I tried to sit up, only to be rewarded with a sharp pain that flared along my knee. His fingers, pinching ruthlessly in warning.

"Lie back."

In my weakened state, I had no hope of denying him again. My spine went limp, forcing me to crane my neck down just to see him. Like a true predator, he crouched at the end of the mattress, his head lowered as his hands pinned me in place, pressing down on either thigh. Aware of me watching, he hovered there as if tracking my pulse through feel alone.

A jealous creature, he hoarded my every reaction to him— every breath to scrape from my throat. The twitch of anticipation racking my spine, impossible to suppress.

The soft moan that escaped as his fingers bit down, melding his touch with the slightest hint of pain.

His eyes flicked up to mine once, conveying a silent warning: *Surrender.* Then he lunged so quickly that I could only *feel* him driving between my legs. My eyelids fluttered at the alarming mixture of sensations—not his hands. Not the part of him I'd barely grown accustomed to feeling inside me, either.

This newer, deadly heat came like a lightning strike. So sharp. So potent. My brain struggled to match sight with feel… Only as I saw his head rock in time with the relentless pressure could I finally give his weapon of choice a name.

His *tongue.*

Thoughts scattered. Fears vanished. As if injected with a lifespan's worth of his blood, I transformed, a greedy, broken creature. Senseless, I could only watch. Gape. From a handful of romance novels, I knew what he was doing. Something every bit as vulgar as the act I'd performed on his plane.

But he didn't lick, too coy to avoid naming the act in his head. His tongue battered me open, sowing friction with every taste. Fire. Lying still was impossible—I writhed as if my spine were a string.

And he ruthlessly tugged with every stroke. Nothing was sacred to him, no place beyond his reach. My Devil dove into my soul, taking whatever he could claim and sowing discord in his wake.

He was sin.

And I was a corrupt, lost soul desperate for damnation.

My fingers curled, clutching the sheets to their breaking point, until the sensation changed. Deepening. Thickening. His finger? His *thumb*. Pressing, pushing, swirling.

A slave to every motion, my back bowed urging him closer. Closer. Closer. Too senseless to beg, I tried to demand more, lurching forward to grasp at his hair. Impervious to pain, he shrugged my attempts off and continued his exploration at his own leisurely pace.

My pleasure was at *his* discretion—not mine. As if to prove as much, he captured an aching bit of flesh between his teeth, threatening to bite. I jerked, my back bowed so violently that the top of my head was all that remained on the mattress.

Lost in his hell, he refused to allow me to come down, pushing me higher and higher with every sharp, pinching nip—but I wasn't the only one lost in the onslaught. His savoring groan reverberated through my flesh, and I shattered.

Stars prickled behind my eyes, punctuating explosions of pleasure as they ripped through every muscle and nerve.

Drugged with the million different reactions, I faintly heard him mutter, "Refuse to eat again and I'll never…"

He didn't say what. Nonetheless, the threat resonated, paired with the violent, dangerous note in his voice. So I ignored it all and focused on feeling. On breaking. On flying.

He coaxed me so, so, so high.

Then let me fall and watched my descent with glowing eyes.

Even panting and breathless, I knew when he pulled back from me. My body ached, desperate for more. I *needed* more.

The mattress dipped beneath his weight before I could mourn his absence in full. One of his hands cupped my waist, drawing me into him, as the other caught my skull. While he pinned me in place, he made me suffer a different form of contact. Another first.

Intimacy.

But sex I could stomach. I could pretend, once I woke up, that none of it had meant a damn thing.

Not this. Nestling my face into his chest, still panting, felt ten times more addicting. More dangerous.

Not even the headiest drug could compare to the haven of his embrace. He could desolate me with *this*.

But I was too weak to resist the destruction.

And he was cruel enough to know as much.

~

Cold. That was how I awoke. Cold and sore. Hungry and lonely. It was like being transported to only a few days ago and nothing in the world terrified me more than having to relive that reality. Solitude. There was only one cure and my fingers scoured the sheets in search of it.

Dublin.

I found nothing, not even when I peeled my eyes open to an empty room bathed in the gray glow of dawn.

Fear unlike anything else shredded me to my core. A sick part of me welcomed it. Misery was what I really craved. What I needed to feel. I could chase a reprieve all I wanted, but this…*this* was my fate.

Abandoned once again.

Perhaps this time he'd left a note behind? I scanned the room, finding only a gray robe slung over the end of the bed. When I climbed off the mattress and pulled it on, I realized the door to my room was ajar as well. Once in the hallway, I made out the faintest notes of music and hope guided my motions, a pathetic lifeline.

I followed the sound, creeping down the stairs and through a maze of rooms until I reached one at the very back of the house. Contained within was a lone piano placed before a row of bay windows. Devoid of curtains, they displayed an unobstructed view of a small garden overrun with sprouting roses.

Hunched on the bench was a figure wearing only a pair of wrinkled black pants. I'd never seen him so disheveled. So…tired. His bare torso caught the light, displaying the numerous silvery lines speckling his skin. Scars was too ugly a word to call them. Merely…decoration, deliberately chiseled there by whatever artist crafted this stunning creature.

The moment I stepped foot within his domain, the music ceased on a single plaintive note.

"You were sleeping," he said without turning around. The emphasis he placed on that word betrayed another meaning —*sleeping* free from nightmares, for once.

A part of me recognized the words as his reason for leaving. Which felt…odd. Even odder was that some of the irrational fear eating through my chest abated.

There was a word for women like the one I was becoming. Clingy. *Needy.* My mother used to gossip about a socialite she'd known once, who'd actually had the gall to take offense when her husband's work hours grew from days into weeks. *She has his estate. Why should she care?*

Perhaps because poor Mrs. Perriweather suffered from the same irrational darkness that plagued me? The fears lurking within the shadows of her psyche, threatening to swallow her whole if someone—anyone—wasn't there to keep them at bay. All they had to do was stay, just long enough for her to find herself again.

However long that might take.

This feeling was temporary, I was sure of it. So why couldn't I cross the threshold until he beckoned me closer?

My hesitant footsteps were quickly swallowed by the notes of music that rose to a crescendo as he continued to play. I'd misjudged his skills as simply *good* before. Talented. Only now could I appreciate the full wealth of emotion he layered into every single note. He didn't look down at the keys once as he sat with his posture erect and his eyes on the window. He didn't merely play. He *bled*.

He never stopped, even as I perched myself on the end of the bench. I wasn't sure who closed the distance first. Which body shifted to bridge the gap. All that mattered was that my head was on his shoulder and I huddled into the contact while his fingers still flexed to stroke the keys.

"What song?" I asked as softly as I dared.

"Something Puccini," he explained. "*Vissi d'arte,* I believe. A bit dramatic for my tastes, but it gets the point across."

"The point?"

"Here." He grabbed my hand, manipulating my fingers where he wanted. With quiet motions, he guided me to strike the keys in tandem, and the melody continued.

I suspected that a million answers to my question lurked within the tune spilling out around us. Including what Dmitri himself had hinted: *Music is the only damn thing humanity possesses worth saving.*

Closing my eyes, I tried to listen—but nothing rivaled his voice and I was too greedy to deny myself it. "What does the title mean?"

He hesitated, the music faltering slightly. "'I lived for art.'"

"What is it about?" The mixture of sharp and low notes conveyed longing. Pain.

"In short?" He inclined his head and ceased playing altogether. "*Nell'ora del dolore.*" His mouth grazed my throat, allowing his voice to enter my ear, lowered for me alone. "*Signore, perché me ne rimuneri così?*"

He sat back, continuing the melody unassisted. Something warned me against pressing him for clarity. Not yet. I listened instead, somehow sensing the meaning in every strained tone before he translated, his gruff baritone melding with the music.

"In this hour of grief… Lord, why do you reward me thus?"

His tone barely wavered, yet he conveyed the passionate plea effortlessly. The pain. The desperation. Did he truly feel that way? Or was he merely interpreting the agony written into the music?

I watched his fingers fly across the keys. My teeth tore at my bottom lip, but I barely felt the pain. Sighing, I leaned against him, sensing him shift to support me.

"I'm afraid." My voice fell to a whisper, nearly swallowed as the music swelled. "I'm so afraid. I don't want to die."

He had been wrong about my supposed death wish.

I wasn't ready.

The music slowed, becoming an array of scattered notes, seconds apart.

"You will."

I flinched at his tone, but his fingers drifted through my hair before I could interpret it as an insult.

"Sadly, I'll be there to witness it, I suppose. When the time eventually comes. In fact, I imagine it to be a rather boring affair, given your track record." He cocked his head as if picturing the moment and sighed in disappointment. "Oh yes. You shriveled in old age, laid out in your precious little manor, irritating me until your last breath. Predictable until the very end."

My lips twitched into a painful expression. A smile? "Who said I'd even let you in through the front door?" I croaked. "I *do* have standards, you know. I'd prefer my mourners sniffling and tearful if you please. Not smug and irritating."

"Tearful?" He nudged my jaw with the pad of his thumb, eyeing me with an eyebrow raised. "Hopefully not from boredom. Did you not hear my first request?"

A sound ripped from my chest that I recognized only as he started to play again. A laugh, hollow and broken. But real nonetheless.

And it chilled me to the bone that he had the power to conjure such a reaction from me at all.

 $\mathcal{I}$ startled awake at the exact moment the melody died in a jarring array of clashing notes. Beside me, Dublin lurched to his feet as footsteps raced in our direction.

"What is it?" he demanded.

I turned, following his gaze. An unfamiliar man stood in the doorway. Dressed in nondescript black, he conveyed the readiness of a soldier.

"There's someone at the…" A thick accent made it impossible for me to discern the rest of what he said, but Dublin hissed through his teeth.

Before my eyes, he transformed—a monster again. "Are you sure?"

The man nodded.

"Eleanor." Dublin didn't even look in my direction. "Get upstairs. Now."

Standing, I drew my robe around me with one hand. Dublin headed through the doorway and I followed in his wake, moving straight for the staircase.

I nearly missed the figure strolling boldly across the foyer to meet us. Blood-red hair would have rendered him striking —even without the vibrant emerald-green suit complementing the color of his eyes.

The vampire from the opera house. Dmitri.

"I suggest you let her stay, Dublin," he said, his upper lip quirked. "Considering that what I have to say concerns *her* more than it does you."

"Move." Dublin lunged, all but dragging me up the remaining few steps. "Get to your room—"

"I know it was rude to intrude," Dmitri continued, unaffected by our retreat. "Especially considering how much effort you put into your protection. It might amuse you to know that you weren't *quite* as discreet as you thought. As always, the rumors precede you."

Icy hands met my shoulders, pushing me down the hall. He didn't even waste energy on words this time. The command was clear. *Go!*

"But never in a million years—and I think you'll appreciate the joke—would I have expected this. Did you really think I wouldn't notice?" Dmitri wondered, sounding legitimately amused. "That thing growing in her stomach?"

The world shifted underneath me, and I staggered to a stop, clinging to the wall for balance. Behind me, Dublin went rigid, his grip a vise on my forearm.

"I'm surprised you risked bringing her to me directly," the man below added, raising his voice for our benefit. "Then again, I do remember your rather possessive nature. Regardless, I knew the moment I saw her just *why* you'd sought me out after all this time. It certainly wasn't to humor her with trivial stories."

"Get out."

I risked looking over my shoulder again as Dublin released me and advanced toward the mouth of the staircase. I only caught a glimpse of his expression from my position, but I recoiled at the sight. His eyes practically glowed, a chilling shade of silver.

Soulless.

"I could hear its *heartbeat*, Dublin," Dmitri crooned, his voice trembling. "A marvelous sound if you know what to look for. Steady. Strong. This is all so very interesting that I couldn't resist flaunting your rather elaborate security."

My thoughts swam aimlessly, desperate to process two words. *Steady. Strong?*

"What do you want?" Dublin demanded, snapping me from the confusing turmoil.

"I want…merely to satisfy my own curiosity," Dmitri said. Excitement bubbled from him. He sounded on the verge of laughter. "It's not every day that such a rare case study lands upon one's lap. And it isn't every day that a man who once proclaimed a lack of a soul goes through so much trouble to protect a mortal woman—"

"I would assume that you more than *satisfied* your curiosity already," Dublin interjected. "You chose your words carefully, didn't you? Knowing just which wounds to prod. Did you want to shatter her mind the way you break the rest of your toys?"

Dmitri's reply took seconds to reach me, deceptively demure. "All right, I admit it. Perhaps I was *exaggerating*."

"Exaggerating?" My voice broke as something snapped inside me. Something raw and violent that made even someone like Dublin Helos an insignificant obstacle in my path. "Why do you care?" I was halfway down the staircase before I knew it, stopped only by a single icy grip on my arm. "Why? You said that…that…"

"That you were carrying a deformed, doomed, worthless creature?" He blinked his multicolored eyes just once. "Well, it's simple, my dear. I lied."

Red. That's all I saw. All I could taste. Anger. Rage. Blood.

Now I knew how Dublin could switch from man to devil so easily.

Madness.

It was the only word capable of describing it. Poised, quiet Gray girls didn't give into fits of hysteria. We seldom launched ourselves down a staircase toward a creature who could easily break our necks with the strength in his pinky. We never shouted—and certainly not the tumult of words spilling from my throat. I couldn't even decipher them all, just one plaintive howl that echoed incessantly off the walls.

"What do you *mean* you were lying?"

"Eleanor, stop!" A grip of steel cinched my waist, lifting me from the ground. I resisted senselessly, my legs kicking at nothing. "Stop!"

When I finally felt the floor again, I swayed, unable to keep my balance. All I could do was cling to the nearest source of stability within reach—firm, frozen flesh. He held me, even as the tears spilling down my cheeks painted the flesh of his chest.

"What does he mean he was lying?" I couldn't stop demanding it. Screaming it.

"I won't let him hurt you," Dublin insisted, his entire posture possessive.

But it was far too late for that. *Hurt* was the only way to describe it—being yanked from one extreme to the other within the span of only a few days. From despair, to numbness, to…hope?

Hope was the most bitter of the three to swallow. The most painful. I choked on it as Dmitri's chilling laugh resonated off the walls.

"Look at me." Dublin captured my chin, commanding my attention. "Five minutes. Give me five minutes."

He cut his gaze to my bedroom door and I knew instinctively what he meant. Five minutes to reestablish control. Five minutes of secrecy with the man who seemed to relish in mind games designed to drive me insane.

Five minutes of *trust*.

When I finally stopped shaking enough to stand on my own, he let me go. Watchful, his gaze tracked my every tortured movement as I entered my bedroom and closed the door behind me.

Five minutes.

I could have lingered, straining for every snippet of their conversation like an eavesdropping child. God knew I wasn't above the action. But…

I turned away, observing the room clearly for the first time since returning from the Opera.

Crumpled bedsheets covered the mattress I'd barely left in three days—but telltale signs revealed how someone had done their best to take care of me. There was an empty glass on the nightstand, once containing the water they'd urged me to drink in my stupor. Another pillow rested beside mine, utilized by someone who didn't even need to sleep. He had shared the cold bed with me anyway.

My throat tightened with too many emotions to decipher at once. After everything, the least I owed him was five damn minutes. But then what?

"I lied."

"I lied."

I couldn't focus on what that confession might mean. I decided to shower instead. Hours of despair clung to my skin, more unbearable than any stench.

I found an adjacent bathroom and drew a bath as hot as I could stand it. A groan tore from my lips as I sank beneath the rushing liquid. It felt good. It *felt*. Ignoring my five-minute deadline, I took my time, washing my body with some lavender-scented soap and a washcloth I'd found in a cupboard.

Without observing my reflection, I ran my fingers through my wet hair once finished and then redonned the robe.

By the time I returned to the foyer, it was well past five minutes. Regardless, Dublin waited for me at the bottom step. He was still wearing only the black pants. Nonetheless, he appeared as imposing as ever. His gaze roamed my body in silent scrutiny, tracing the contours of the robe. If he didn't approve of the outfit choice, he didn't say so. When I held my hand out, he took it, drawing me to his side.

As we advanced down the hall, his clenched jaw betrayed a warning. *Be on your guard.*

Dmitri was waiting in a small sitting room, holding court from a leather chair positioned near a curtained window. "Allow me to apologize, my dear," he said to me. The amusement flicking in his eyes contradicted the contriteness of his tone. "I had no intention to startle you."

"You didn't?" I'd never known how disdainful I could sound. Not even Dublin had drawn that snarl out of me. "Then what was your intention?"

His smile widened. "To test a small theory." Uninvited, his gaze cut down to my stomach and I found myself obstructing his view with the flat of my free hand.

"What theory?" How to drive a woman insane with as little effort as possible? Because as much as it confused me to admit it…

I'd gone insane. Only now could I climb out from the chaos of my own thoughts and see the smoldering ruins for myself. Days spent in bed clinging to a vampire for emotional support. I didn't know whether to laugh or cry. Cry perhaps?

Because those three days had been the first time in my life that I'd ever had *anyone* to drain for emotional support. Like a leech, all irony aside.

And more baffling, Dublin had let me take every last drop I'd needed.

Shame flooded my cheeks, setting them on fire as I glanced at him beside me while he glowered as stoically as ever.

"What theory did you want to test?" I finally demanded of Dmitri.

He raised a reddish eyebrow while stroking his hairless chin. "A hunch," he said vaguely. "The truth is that your condition is rarer than you realize. There are only rumors, many of them…disturbing." He smiled. "Though I am now positive that dear Dublin knows better than any of us—"

"Don't," the man beside me warned. "Peddle your lies again and I'll rip your tongue from your mouth."

"As you wish." Dmitri nodded, lifting his arms in a gesture of surrender. "Frankly, I understand your skepticism. Such is the nature of hearsay, you see. More often than not, you'll find it circulates merely to serve a certain advantage. Much like a rumor being murmured about *you,* dear Eleanor."

The line of my mouth tightened in foreboding anticipation. I had enough sense to recognize a dangling carrot when I saw one. No doubt, another "exaggeration" would serve as the punishing stick should I take the bait.

So I said nothing, yet his grin took on a more satisfied tilt.

"Some speculate that you might be in possession of something… Let's just say something *intangible* worth more than you can possibly imagine."

An answer came to my mind instantly. A prize tempting enough to spark the greed even Dmitri's cool grin couldn't disguise. *Ten years.*

"Dmitri…" Dublin's tone deepened well beyond a warning.

"Well, yes. Anyway, while the information is scarce, I've always had a fondness for tracking down the sources of any rumor to catch my ears." He clasped his hands together, balancing them on his knee. "It just so happens that I stumbled across a few tidbits of information that might interest you about your current condition."

"How do I know you're not lying?" A better question might be why my voice broke over the thought of it. Answers, good or bad. Ignoring my "cancer" until now had been a foolish, childish whim. I could see that.

But could I stomach the truth?

Dmitri sighed and reached into the breast pocket of his suit jacket. "Easy," he warned as Dublin stepped between us, shoving me behind him. "I bring gifts, as promised. A bit of light reading."

When Dublin didn't rush to disarm him, I assumed whatever he was holding must have posed some semblance of legitimacy. Skirting the formidable body before me, I observed his offerings.

Two slender leather-bound books. They looked old, more worn than Dublin's mysterious Gray family tome. Yet as the light reflected off their stained covers, I couldn't suppress a shiver.

"You sense it, don't you," Dmitri murmured smugly. "Knowledge that our beloved Raphael wouldn't dare allow to circulate that Den of yours. I am more than willing to share of course." He withdrew the books slightly beyond my reach. "For a price."

"And now you can leave." Dublin placed his hand over my spine. In that simple touch, I sensed a silent promise—*This isn't the end. I'll find another way.*

"So soon?" Dmitri chuckled. "Dare I say I'm not surprised. One could only expect you to be skeptical. Perhaps I can divulge a glimmer of what I've learned? Something tells me that you've already gleaned that small detail involving fresh blood?"

I flinched, betraying the truth, and he nodded. "Ah… There's more, of course," he said, his tone suddenly serious. Narrowed in thought, he flickered his gaze to Dublin. "But first, I have to ask. Very few events could trigger such an occurrence from what I've read. Dear Dublin, tell me that you didn't try breaking your little rule for her, did you? Forget your little hang-up about feeding from a live host, but to go a step further—"

"I warned you once about your lies, did I not?" Dublin said so softly that I shuddered, fingering the edges of my robe.

"Lies, yes," Dmitri admitted. "But this is just a mere question." He took a step forward, honing his gaze on my throat. Whatever he saw made him frown and that simple expression transformed him entirely. Gone was the sly intruder. He resembled a scholar mulling over a puzzling mystery.

And somehow that made him more intimidating than ever.

"You haven't fed from her in a while," he mused aloud. "For all your loathing of the act, you must have feared for her life, I suspect. I'd heard Raphael tried feeding from her. That could… But that wouldn't explain why she didn't die. No. Though if you *did* try to turn her—"

"Enough!" The bellowed command resonated through the manor's foundation, and I found myself bracing my hand against Dublin's shoulder.

"Don't!"

He swiveled his head in my direction, eyeing my fingers coldly, but the tension in his body eased just enough for me to breathe again. For whatever reason, I sensed that the contact had kept him from lunging.

"And I will take my cue to leave." Still smiling, Dmitri bowed. "Such a shame that we couldn't come up with some kind of agreement," he lamented as he headed for the entrance of the room. "What a shame. I had so hoped your child might survive unharmed."

I staggered an involuntary step toward him. "Wait!"

Obediently, Dmitri lingered.

Dublin simmered. "A word?" He took my arm, dragging me into an adjacent room.

The door slammed behind us, rattling in its frame, as I found myself spun around, forced to face him directly.

"Listen to me." Something within his gaze made goosebumps creep over my skin. Unease. Wariness. Those rare few emotions he only displayed in the presence of Raphael. "You do not want to play his game," he warned. "Yulia was right. I should have never even—"

"I need answers." It sounded like such a pathetic contrast to his caution. As if answers could ever change what a part of me already knew deep down.

Some things you couldn't change. Studying the sordid reasoning behind them didn't make the truth any easier to stomach. Yet, at the same time, ignorance could be unbearable torture.

"I need answers." I couldn't disguise the bleating, pleading note in my voice. But the longer I observed Dublin's face, the more I realized that I might not have been the only one desperate for a lifeline. "I will admit that I don't know your history," I added. "But please. This isn't cancer. I…I don't want to pretend anymore. So, you can gut him like a fish with your bare hands when this is over, but I *need* answers."

"Should I be on my way?" Dmitri called from across the room. A glance over my shoulder revealed him standing in the doorway, observing his right hand with dejected interest. "I suppose I must—"

"Wait!" It terrified me, how desperate I felt. Desperate enough to beg. I reached for Dublin's hand, squeezing it so tight that I was sure, despite his superior strength, he still felt the pressure. "*Please.*"

Like always, his blank expression gave me nothing to cling to. I floated in uncertainty for what felt like an eternity. Then…

"What the hell do you want?" He advanced on the other man, using my grip to tether me behind him. "No riddles. No games. Just lay out your terms. Now."

Once more, Dmitri seemed to drop the carefree act. His eyes found me again, sparkling with undisguised interest.

"I merely want to observe," he said. "And conduct my own research. Why should these ancient bastards"—he hefted the journals—"have all the fun, eh? To put it a bit more bluntly, I simply want to come along for the ride."

If anything, that response made Dublin stiffen further. Remnants of winter emanated from his gaze, freezing me down to my core.

Wisely, Dmitri seemed well aware of the delicate line he was toeing. "And I'll even play nice," he insisted. "No mentions of the past—for now. *And* I wasn't even lying when I mentioned that little bounty on her head. I'll even go further and share another tidbit of information—they fully intend to collect on it. Soon."

He let the word hang there, gauging my reaction, which—surprisingly—was more subdued than Dublin's. I simply stared at him as my brain struggled to process the reality. While the man beside me nearly broke my hand.

"Damn." He released me, forming a fist. I swore I heard bone crunch and meld within the span of a second—he had clenched his fingers *that* tightly.

"The funny thing is he is more than aware that his human soldiers can't harm her as long as she's under your protection. Oh, Mero—I mean, *he of whom we will not speak*." Dmitri made finger quotes as Dublin snarled in warning. "You remember how he loved his deception? His games? Though he preferred poison over intrigue. Oh, the things that man could do with poison." He sighed as though reliving a cherished memory. Then he cleared his throat. "So, if he truly wanted her dead, she would be. Therefore, her death isn't his main goal, for now at least. Which means his ultimate plan is a bit more abstract. In fact…the sister is missing, correct? I'm sure he knows the value of that life to her." He nodded toward me. "Oh, come now, don't you see it? He's deliberately trying to provoke you—"

"Enough." Dublin didn't shout that time, but the low, raspy baritone seemed to reach even deeper, clawing open the part of me that recognized the beast he truly was beneath his flawless skin.

"And I'd wondered why," Dmitri mused, completely unperturbed. "I admit that I had to rack my brain for quite a while to come up with the solution. After all, why come out of hiding after so damn long? Raphael is of no interest to him, and we know how much he craved his peace. But then, if I may be so cliché, the answer appeared right in front of me."

He stepped closer, grazing my cheek with an icy finger. "Was that his one condition to end that bitter war between him and your master? Stay away from those under his ownership. But you couldn't resist, could you? No, after years of atonement, you *dared* to defile one of his precious, sacred Grays. Though I'm sure that was his plan all along."

A hand brushed my hip, knocking me off-balance, and I found myself staggering out of Dmitri's reach. Dublin stepped forward, filling the space I'd left behind.

"Touch her again and I'll keep the arm," he promised as casually as most men might comment on the weather. "And the next time I choose to hunt you down to whatever corner of the world you've run to, you'll owe me more than just a favor."

"Fair enough." Dmitri met the cold expression directed his way with a surprisingly chilling one of his own. "But now, down to business." He clapped his hands, all smiles once again. "When do we leave? Dare I request we take my jet? It's climate controlled—"

"Is there a point you're trying to make?" Dublin countered.

Dmitri blinked. "Why yes, I suppose I did forget to mention that particular detail. Those friends of yours... Well, they've decided to launch an attack here, on this very estate you think no one else knows about. Right...*now*."

As if to accent his words, a sudden barrage of noise resonated in the distance. Shouting?

"Go get dressed." Dublin shoved me toward the stairs and I didn't hesitate.

Once in my room, I snatched a dress at random from the closet and pulled it on while staggering down the stairs. I had to have been gone less than a minute, yet Dublin was already dressed, appearing by my side as if from thin air.

"Stay close." He took my arm, tethering me to his side as two armed men came from the shadows to flank our position. His calm demeanor warned me that they worked for him.

Had they been here all this time, lurking out of sight?

"I see you decided to play him at his own game," Dmitri remarked. He grinned, apparently entertained by the air of urgency. "Using your own human pawns. Certainly creative if not necessarily prudent. May I suggest again that we take my jet—"

Dublin pulled me forward, and within seconds, we were exiting from the front door. I didn't know what to expect as I took in the scenery waiting beyond. Weak daylight filtered down through storm clouds, adding a silvery sheen to the breathtaking landscape—but despite Dmitri's warning, there was no one else in sight.

Apart from Dublin's driver standing at the ready.

Not particularly hurried, Dublin guided me into the waiting car and the driver sped off. Every now and again, however, he spared a wary glance at the figure seated beside him.

Somehow, Dmitri had insinuated himself into the passenger's seat. Occasionally, he decided to provide casual commentary. "Again, I must insist we take my jet."

Dublin seemed murderously determined to ignore him, glaring from the window instead. Eventually, we reached a remote area where the hills gave way to grassy lowlands and desolate fields. In the distance, I made out the shape of a building on the horizon. An airport hangar?

No sooner did the thought cross my mind before—

Light. Noise. *Bang!*

A tremor rattled the earth. I screamed as the driver swerved severely to stay on the road. Dublin flung his arm over my hip, pinning me in place until the motion subsided. Just as the driver righted himself, black clouds began to billow over the horizon. Smoke. Soon after, tendrils of orange flame licked at the sky as if alive.

"Well." Dmitri delicately cleared his throat. "I suppose it's a welcome coincidence that I had *my* private jet moved to a lesser known runway not too far from here. Isn't it?"

BLOODY HELL

*D*mitri's climate-controlled private jet proved to be surprisingly…cheerful. In a contrast to Dublin's monochromatic color scheme, tanned leather created a cozy backdrop, punctuated by hints of elegance. Like the grinning, glassy-eyed flight attendant already on board, waiting to serve crystal flutes of champagne.

Ignoring her, Dublin marshaled me into a recliner-style seat by a window and claimed the one beside me, effectively serving as a barrier between me and his "old friend."

Dmitri didn't seem to mind. He unfurled himself into a seat near the back of the cabin, grinning like a well-fed cat. Something told me that turning our back to him at all was a risky endeavor.

But Dublin consumed my sole focus, and I couldn't spare an ounce of concern for anything else. Tension radiated from him in waves. I suspected little was due to Dmitri's presence. No…

My heart raced as I brushed my hand along my front, watching the fingers settle against my stomach. Panic danced on the edges of my conscience, urging me to deny. Ignore. Pretend. Facing the truth of my "tumor" terrified me more than anything in the world.

More than Dublin.

More than Raphael.

The mere possibility shattered my safe, cautious mind state. I'd been groomed to spend most of my life alone, sans even human children.

But now?

The thought of another reality terrified me. Almost as much as the threats building against it.

"Who is Mero?" I whispered, still eyeing my splayed fingers.

Dublin flinched, but he'd had long enough of a reprieve from the question.

So had I.

Though perhaps we both were no match for the topic in the end. After all this time, I'd thought I'd witnessed the full spectrum when it came to the emotional range of Dublin Helos.

Anger. Guilt. Rage. Pity.

But the expression contorting his features now was unlike any I'd ever experienced. Pained.

"One might call him the *founder* of the Grayne," he rasped in a tone devoid of emotion.

Not for the first time, I truly understood the vast gap between us forged by more than mere age. Sheer *centuries* of distance. He looked eons older in the space of a heartbeat. Ancient.

"I thought you said my ancestor James was the leader of the Grayne?" I remembered as much from his impromptu history lesson delivered the night before my fateful meeting with Raphael.

Though, to be fair, that was all I knew about this mysterious order that had consumed part of my family. Any attempt to pry a single bit more from Georgie had been met with deflection and stonewalling.

Until we both couldn't take anymore.

"He was," Dublin said. "Mero was…let us just say the catalyst to your predecessor's sudden fervor when it came to hunting my kind. In the grand scheme, Mero knew that his human pawns would be all but useless against a foe like Raphael. You were merely a vehicle."

"You knew him?"

"I did." And that was that. He closed up. Turned to stone. Something told me that even bringing up our contract now wouldn't get him to soften to me again on the subject.

So I changed tack. "How did you know? About the blood," I clarified. It was something that had always bothered me beneath the surface. Perhaps I hadn't admitted it to myself until now. "That I would have to…"

"You were dying," he said simply. "You claimed that food held no appeal. In the name of saving your life, I took a risk and decided to… Let's call it thinking outside of the box."

"And what about *your* blood?" I observed the bluish veins twisting beneath his skin. "You told me it wouldn't work anymore. That it couldn't heal me."

Yet here we were. His blood had already saved my life ten times over since his return.

"And," I added as something else rose to the forefront of my thoughts, "it used to overwhelm me. I would be out for days, but now…"

"There is something I need to tell you." He turned away, staring beyond the luxurious cabin into a world I could never follow.

Biting my lip was the only way to brace myself against whatever he might reveal. But I was no match for his touch; he captured my hand, swiping his thumb across the palm. And just like that, I was disarmed.

"That day Raphael fed from you. His venom hurt you, didn't it?" he asked without meeting my gaze. "More than as just a mild discomfort."

"Yes…" I cringed at the memory. One bite and it had felt as though my insides were melting around me even as my heart struggled to beat. "But yours didn't."

"That's because he killed you."

I looked up in confusion, but he still faced away from me. Purposefully, I realized. Whatever tinged his gaze now, he didn't want me to see.

"I… What do you—"

"Your heart stopped beating," he explained, as detached as though reciting a well-known tale from heart. At the same time, his fingers tightened, holding mine firmly captive. "I heard it. I saw it. You were gone before I could even reach you. And in that moment, I had to make a *choice*." His voice grated over the word, conveying more than the usual definition. *Choice.* Something life changing. Life altering. "You wouldn't understand. There was no time to think. No time for hesitation. For once, I was—" He broke off and released me, but he didn't pull away. His fingers formed an open cage, almost as if he expected me to recoil first.

For whatever reason, I forced myself to stay.

"What choice? What did you do?"

When he didn't respond, I eyed my naked fingers, too numb to process my emotions. Was I horrified by the potential answers? Shocked?

"Let's just say I pushed your body beyond its limits and I nearly killed you in the process. All for nothing, because I failed anyway."

I swallowed hard, too uneasy to even press for answers. Did he overdose me with his blood? Give me too much venom?

"But I'm still alive," I pointed out before swallowing the lump that had risen to my throat.

"Yes." He sighed, deflated of all tension. "You came back. Still breathing. I assumed I'd made a mistake. Perhaps it was the venom? The why didn't matter. I decided to leave in search of answers. In my absence, I ensured the necklace would protect you."

"But what you told me was a lie, wasn't it?"

Its purpose hadn't been solely to keep me alive.

"As long as you wore it, I could find you," he admitted, finally lifting his gaze to mine. "No matter your location."

Deep down, maybe I'd known that. In some ways, it had been easier to let myself pretend my survival could be so simply insured—a magic necklace slipped around my neck just in the nick of time.

But in his world, *nothing* came without a price.

"I didn't realize my miscalculation until I tried feeding from you," he admitted, referring to the night I'd found him at the church. "You reacted violently. Not to mention that you were weak. Malnourished and… When your *cancer* was discovered, in a way, I wasn't surprised. Merely by attempting to change you, I had unknowingly encouraged a new breed of 'life' to take root. Mero always did have a rather ghoulish sense of humor."

I exhaled sharply in a poor excuse for a laugh. It was a morbid joke, even for a vampire.

"I know it was wrong to deceive you." He reached for my hand again, and a part of me scoffed, eager to write him off. But he had never sounded so raw before. *So* open.

And for whatever reason, I couldn't pull away.

"Why didn't you tell me?"

"How could I?" He laughed darkly, shaking his head. "When I didn't even understand myself?" He eyed me warily and reached out with his thumb. When I didn't cringe, he brushed my cheek, lingering against my skin. "I still don't. Years of servitude to that bastard, yet he's never toyed with me. Toyed with *lives* just to test me. Not like this."

And perhaps that fact alone was Raphael's driving motive.

But trying to understand the man at all made my head throb. I cradled my palm against it, rubbing my aching temple.

"I need time to process this," I said softly. "I just... I need time—"

"I understand. But there is one thing you mentioned that I would like to explore in further detail." He cocked his head, his eyes narrowed. "What did Raphael say when he gave you my contract?"

I sucked in a breath. "He said that if I helped him prove something, he'd give me what you bargained for."

"Damn him." Lurching to his feet, Dublin transformed once more into stone. Ruthlessly focused, he scanned the length of the cabin until he eventually found Dmitri.

The other vampire was seated in the same spot, balancing the giggling flight attendant on his lap.

"Do you have an ability to communicate with the ground?" Dublin demanded. "Where?"

"A satellite phone, of course." Dmitri inclined his head toward an alcove at the very back of the cabin.

Without a word, Dublin crossed over to it, leaving a trail of rage like a storm cloud.

"I hope you ring lovely Yuliana," Dmitri called after him, smiling sweetly. "I do so hope to see her." As he turned to me, his grin widened. "There is no use in torturing yourself, dear. Come sit with me." He patted the space beside him.

"No, thank you." I crossed my arms, fighting to keep any of the turmoil ripping through my heart from showing on my face. "I'm fine."

Accepting defeat, Dmitri sighed. "Suit yourself. It's much harder these days to make this old voice carry far, but I suppose I must try. If you want answers, I am willing to trade."

Trade. The way he'd said the word almost reminded me of Dublin—full of mysterious innuendo. And I knew better than to take any bait he might offer.

"I know more than you realize," Dmitri added. "Like the fact that you are hungry. That you've been starving yourself and your child for far too long. That if you continue to be so reckless with your health, the results may be disastrous."

"Helpful advice, considering you claimed it was an abomination," I snapped. But as Dmitri raised an eyebrow, I realized I was shielding my belly with both hands.

"Ah, but that is where you misunderstood the meaning of the word, my darling." He chuckled once and leaned back against the leather cushions of his seat. "*I* am an abomination. As are Dublin and Raphael. Powerful, unfathomable creatures are always glitches in the grand design, or so I choose to believe. I will admit that even I do not understand the nuances of your predicament. Why would you require blood, for instance, when from what I can tell, you are persistently mortal? Perhaps the requirement is meant solely to mock him with what you may never become? Ah, but who could envision such a cruel torment?"

With that, he turned his attention to his giggling flight attendant and nuzzled her throat. Then he wrenched her head to one side and—

I turned to the window and didn't dare take my eyes off the view until Dublin returned. He occupied the seat beside me without a word, resolute in whatever mood had been building in him since the moment Dmitri had arrived.

It all had to do with that name. The figure who had driven us out of the country and was no doubt awaiting our return.

The man who seemed to want me dead, though I didn't even know why.

Mero.

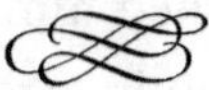

"Eleanor."

A gentle pressure settled over my shoulder, jarring me awake. Blinking, I gradually pieced together my surroundings. Somewhere small. Darkened. Confined. A car—*his* to be exact. Dublin himself was driving, and a glance at the back seat revealed that Dmitri was nowhere in sight. I was sitting up front, slumped within a leather seat, my head propped against a firm, muscular forearm.

"We're in the States," Dublin explained while manipulating the steering wheel. "Not far from the city. It's been about an hour since we landed. I didn't want to wake you."

Oh? I scrambled upright and peered through the windshield. Dawn painted the horizon in a mixture of pink and orange hues.

Already, I could sense my body protesting the change in time zone. Exhaustion weighed my eyelids down, and my stomach rumbled, voicing its displeasure at having been denied a solid meal in nearly a week. An unwelcome reminder, Dmitri's warning invaded my thoughts.

"If you continue to be so reckless with your health, the results may be disastrous…"

Gritting my teeth, I banished him with a shake of my head. "Where to?" I asked Dublin, steeling myself for another whirlwind journey.

Another high-rise? Another distant country?

"Somewhere safe," was his reply.

He was still wearing the same black suit, his hair only slightly mussed from the journey. I eyed his expression, hunting for a clue to feed on. A frown. A raised eyebrow. Anything.

The man didn't even blink, remarkably closed-off.

"What about the books?" I didn't spy them in the car anywhere. "And answers. And what if—"

"I'm handling it," Dublin gently insisted. "You've been through a lot. At least allow yourself a few days to readjust —in fact, consider it nonnegotiable. I promise arrangements have been made in the meantime."

Yet not even five minutes later, he parked and exited the vehicle without waiting for me. Or a word of explanation. Frozen with shock, I gaped after him, struggling to process our destination.

"Safe?" I hurried from the car, craning my neck to eye the structure before us in disbelief. "Here?"

As though Gray Manor wasn't what loomed up ahead, Dublin leisurely strode to the front door.

"Trust me when I say that I can protect you here as well as I could anywhere else."

But there was a caveat to his statement, I suspected. One betrayed by the subtle clenching of his jaw. This newfound protection had come at a price.

One he refused to reveal as he opened the door and ushered me inside with a wave of his hand.

"You have nothing to fear," he insisted as I hesitated beyond the threshold.

I wasn't sure if the words were meant to be comforting. They weren't, considering that everyone from my sister to her mysterious club apparently wanted me dead. *Plenty* to fear in all respects.

Returning here at all—especially after what had happened in the crypt—felt like slathering myself in butter, ready for the slaughter. I eyed Dublin's neutral expression as doubt strained my worn, battered nerves. My trust felt all but indebted to him after the way he'd cared for me. Yet...

"Trust me." He reached back for me as his eyes met mine again. The stoic grip on his emotions wavered, allowing a hint of softness to ease the stiffened corner of his mouth.

"I've ensured your protection. Not even a spider could enter without my permission."

His confidence soothed my fear just enough for me to mount the front steps after him. Once we crossed the threshold, the house didn't transform into a horrific trap at least. No monsters sprang from the shadows to attack. In fact, the dour interior greeted us with little fanfare, and any fear quickly turned to suspicion.

"You've had people here," I accused.

In my absence, someone had cleaned the drafty foyer and figured out how to restore heat to the house. In honor of the dreary, overcast day, a fire roared in the drawing room, basting my skin with heat as he led me past it.

"I'll have them stay out of sight," Dublin proposed with the air of a kindly benefactor humoring his bothersome charge. "I wouldn't dream of standing in the way of your apparent independence."

I swallowed hard, biting my lip. Just how much of my month in self-imposed isolation had he deduced so far?

"Given how long you've survived without your staff, I'm sure you don't even require a maid anymore," he added.

Ah, *that* was a definite jab.

"You're wrong," I snapped. God help my instinctive impulse to needle him at every turn—though he had asked for it. "I am an *heiress*, after all. Whoever shall bathe me, and clothe me, and put me to bed?" I did my best to channel my mother, who would have pointed out those very dilemmas in horrified indignation. "Why, look." I wiggled all ten of my fingers, pouting. "I have delicate hands."

"Is that so?" He seized my wrists. A ruthless tug brought me closer to him, rendering me at the mercy of his gaze. "One of your defining attributes," he murmured, turning his attention to the prized hands in question. "Worthy of protection. So, from now on, I suppose I will be the one to bathe you, and clothe you, and put you to bed." His serious tone cast doubt on if he truly intended the proposal as a joke.

Laughing, I shrugged as though unaffected. "Via one of your contracted proxies? Kate, perhaps?"

He blinked. "Naturally, only I would ever be permitted to touch you. Such an important heiress couldn't be trusted to the care of just anyone."

My heart seized and I took the tiniest step back. Running away was my first, cowardly instinct. He could have this round. I had no trouble admitting how poorly unmatched I was in this arena. Nothing in my pathetic verbal arsenal could counter the sensual gleam flicking across his gaze.

But then I remembered just how sinful his touch could feel. One dose of those sordid memories banished all logic.

"Well, I do own your contract," I blurted, my face heating. "It's about damn time I put you to work, isn't it?"

"That you do." The grit in his baritone resonated down my spine. I'd barely processed the lust contained within it as he stepped in even closer, forcing me to crane my neck just to maintain eye contact. "Though, frankly, Eleanor, you've been rather lax in exerting such ownership. No commands to do your bidding. No humiliating assaults on my autonomy. I have to wonder…do you even have it in you?"

I shuddered, recognizing both the dare *and* the threat he'd posed in one go. Did I have the gall to command him? Would he really listen if I tried?

And if I didn't take the bait, could I stomach the million terrifying questions still looming overhead? My decision took mere seconds to settle upon.

"I…I'm hungry," I croaked, jutting my chin into the air. "Make me something to eat. *Slave.*"

"As you wish, *mistress.*" He released me and inclined his head. "What would you like?"

"Baklava," I blurted, recalling how the old chef used to despair whenever my mother had requested that particular dish. "From scratch."

He crossed his arms, unimpressed. "What else? Surely you want more than just a dessert."

"Spaghetti, then," I countered. "With meatballs *and* homemade noodles."

"Interesting choice." He nodded in earnest. "What else?"

"Baked Alaska." I was just being ruthless now. "And some fish. I prefer to have it gutted, descaled, and filleted in front of me."

"As you wish. Shall we?"

He grabbed my arm and steered me into the old servant's alcove. While I watched, he made several calls in rapid-fire succession. Each one progressed way too quickly for me to make out much. When he finally hung up, I found myself dragged into the kitchen, where he shoved me onto a stool and then proceeded to hunt for supplies.

Had I been inclined to help him, I honestly wouldn't have known where to begin. He didn't seem to require much assistance as he fished various pots from the cupboards and pulled utensils from drawers. If anything, the bastard seemed a tad too confident in his actions, as though he knew my kitchen far better than he should have.

Not long after, a courier appeared, laden with groceries, and Dublin spread out his bounty over the countertops. After shedding his suit jacket, he set to work. Begrudgingly, I soon realized that my impromptu menu had been ignored. In lieu of pasta and tomato sauce were fresh apples and vegetables, some of which I'd never seen, and a loaf of delicious-smelling bread.

"Should I have you whipped for your insolence?" I wondered as I sat forward, propping my chin on my hands, enthralled by the sight of him.

Who knew the big, bad contractor could make for a capable domestic?

Oblivious to my thoughts, he remained intent on his task. His fingers flew from ingredient to ingredient, sorting them as he went.

"I decided to exert a bit of creative control," he confessed without a hint of guilt. "Your nutrition means more to me than fear of your legendary wrath, oh *mistress*."

I let the taunt slip by unchallenged, unwilling to explore the unfamiliar sensation lancing through my chest. Instead, I peered at the assembled ingredients with a frown. "Well, what *are* you making?"

He reached into a brown paper bag that had yet to be unpacked. From it, he withdrew something wrapped in butcher's paper—a large, completely whole fish. After selecting a knife, he proceeded to slice off the creature's head. As his gaze met mine, something that might have been amusement lifted the corner of his mouth. "You'll see."

I crossed my arms. "Fine."

Damn him. Watching him cook shouldn't have been nearly so fascinating. The man possessed an alarming skill with a knife. With unnatural ease, he chopped veggies, washed herbs, and shifted things from pots and pans. It wasn't long before a delicious aroma filled the entire room and I eagerly sniffed, lightheaded in anticipation.

Though, to disguise my interest, I made sure to sigh loudly at random intervals. "Does your sudden concern for my 'nutrition' mean no evening brandy, then?"

I was just being petty now, but Dublin was prepared for me.

From another paper bag, he fished out a bottle that resembled champagne at first glance. "Sparkling cider," he explained, setting the bottle down. "I wouldn't imagine denying such an esteemed heiress of her customary nightcap."

Touché, Mr. Helos. Resigned, I waited patiently while he finished. As he removed the final boiling pot from the stove, he looked back as if noticing me there for the first time.

"Shouldn't you be getting dressed for dinner, mistress?" he inquired, raising an eyebrow in mock surprise. "I wouldn't dare to presume that you eat in casual clothing like some common riffraff."

Apparently, he too was capable of channeling my mother from beyond the grave.

Throwing my head back, I performed a haughty appraisal of him with a sweep of my gaze. "How could I? My lazy servant hasn't offered to dress me yet."

"Ah, I beg your pardon." He stepped around the counter while wiping his hands on a dishcloth. "How unacceptable."

I stiffened as he advanced on my position step by dangerous step.

"Can you walk up the stairs on your own?" he wondered. "Or are your feet as delicate as your hands?"

A flame jolted to life in the pit of my stomach. As if fed by gasoline, it spread, feeding an inferno only he could ever spark. Nothing else affected me the way he could with a single searching look. Nothing except his touch.

"I...I can walk," I conceded, rising to my feet. I swayed. Finding my balance at all was a feat of sheer willpower on jellied limbs.

"Good." Dublin inclined his head toward the door with a gentlemanly nod. "After you."

I led the way to my bedroom, where I was alarmed to find that not only had someone cleaned it, but the door to my wardrobe was hanging open, mysteriously brimming with new clothing.

"Yulia works fast," I blurted, recognizing her handiwork in the delicate satins and artfully applied lace. A red dress in particular drew my eye. The moment my gaze settled over it fully, Dublin had already yanked it out by its hanger.

"Turn around and raise your arms," he said, manipulating the fabric in his hands.

"Shouldn't I be the one issuing commands?" I couldn't even muster up enough air to sound truly indignant.

"I am simply eager to serve."

A shiver ran down my spine at that chosen word. The hoarseness I thought I'd heard in it was simply my ears playing tricks.

"Arms." Impatient, he took it upon himself to spin me around. Then he tugged the zipper of my dress down.

Gradually, the fabric slid down my hips to pool at my feet. "Step."

Shivering from head to toe, I took two steps forward, freeing my ankles from the discarded fabric.

"Now…" His fingers fanned across my torso, radiating possession. "Hold your breath."

I looked back in confusion. "W-Why?"

He shook his head, but his fingertips flexed against me in silent encouragement. "Do it."

So I inhaled, trapping the air inside my lungs. While I slowly exhaled, he drew his hands up to my shoulders, smoothing the hair from my neck. A tendril of ice grazed the exposed flesh. His mouth? Nuzzling…

Just when the lack of oxygen became uncomfortable, he slid the new dress on over my head. The moment he drew up the zipper, I let my lungs expand.

"Why?" I wondered. The gown fit fine, even as my chest heaved frantically against the fabric. I was breathless—that was why I was panting. Of course that was why.

Rather than some pre-prepared quip, Dublin tugged on the dress, adjusting it. It was only when I turned to face him that he finally relented.

"I wanted to hear your heartbeat." His gaze was on the violet wall behind my head, his jaw clenched.

"And?" I rasped.

"It is…adequate." He met my gaze, holding it for so long that I felt senseless when he finally turned away. "Come and eat."

He made me sit at the dining room table while he returned to the kitchen. Moments later, he reentered with a full-blown meal on one of my mother's prized porcelain plates.

"Does this offering please you, mistress?" he wondered while placing a set of silverware before me.

He'd prepared fish in addition to an array of steamed vegetables and various side dishes too exotic to name.

Scowling, I took a bite, fully intending to lie. Unexpectedly, rich flavor broke my resolve, and I shoved in another forkful before I could stop myself. Another. In the midst of my chewing, Dublin pressed a cup into my hand. Aware of its contents, I did my best to choke down the warm, wet liquid before returning to his meal with vigor.

"Is everything to your liking?" he asked innocently, well aware of his victory.

A helpless moan tore from my throat as my unofficial verdict. It just wasn't fair. The man could cook like the devil.

Once I'd cleared my plate of every last crumb, he made a show of pouring the sparkling cider into one of the crystal flutes that I was fairly certain my mother had sold her soul for.

I took a sip. Made a face for the sake of putting up a front of displeasure. Then I drained the rest.

Barely concealing his triumph, he cleared the table while I stood. From this angle, he resonated a presence my childhood home struggled to contain. In the glow of the chandelier, his chiseled features stood out in harsh relief. Beautiful.

Unattainable.

Who are you kidding, Ellie? a part of me snickered. *As if he could ever want you.*

And maybe that vicious little whisper was right? I was halfway to the doorway when his voice reached me, low with warning.

"Where are you going?"

I lingered over the threshold without looking back. "To bed." My tone fell flat, deliberately stripped of innuendo.

All insecurities aside, sex within these walls was definitely *not* an option anyway.

My mother and father had lorded over this house once. Their prudishness was etched into the wood. Hell, even now, I could feel their judgmental eyes on me, casting shame for the way my heart picked up speed at the low, dangerous tone that reached me next.

"And have me risk another whipping?" He was behind me in an instant. His chill basted the back of my throat and my body reacted. Tightened. Tensed. Craved. "You are to be bathed and put to bed," he reminded, throwing my own words back at me. "Or do you not remember?"

I wanted to back down right then and admit defeat. He would always win when it came to games like this. Dangerous games. He was a man who'd staked his entire livelihood around sex. There was no way in hell I could best him in that arena.

It would be foolish to try.

Sighing, I tried to convey as much. "No matter how many times we…" I trailed off, exasperated. "It's like my brain won't let me believe it."

But he wasn't looking at me—not directly. His eyes traced a path up my hip and settled over the cleavage bared by the low neckline of my dress. My heart lurched against my rib cage as if trying to save itself from the onslaught of sensation that assaulted me. Too late. Heat blossomed in my veins. My throat went dry. Moisture gathered in sensual places.

But one word from him made my belly clench, all thoughts of doubt and propriety forgotten.

"Upstairs."

I turned automatically and staggered toward the staircase. He followed, keeping his distance during the entire long, winding trek to my bedroom.

Once inside it, he continued to advance, backing me toward my bed. His eyes burned too damn brightly. Maintaining contact for long was impossible. I tore my gaze down to his chest, seeking a reprieve. I found one. The contours of his body strained beneath his shirt, hypnotizing me with every shift in fabric as he came closer…

Closer…

An icy finger lifted my chin, forcing me to look up. His expression was guarded again, devoid of even the smugness I'd come to associate with him. When his lips finally parted, all he said was, "Is there anything else I can do for you, *mistress?*"

My answer rode a gasp. "P-Put…put me to bed."

In return, he seized the front of my dress and yanked, ripping the material without the aid of Yulia's tricks. The next second, he had me against the wall, his lips on mine, and there was nothing left to think about or worry over.

He controlled every motion, guiding my lips apart with his own to coax my tongue into submission. Coaxing—that was the only way to describe it. He teased the shame away, reawakening all those strange, unfamiliar sensations. I panted, breathless in the aftermath. Mindless.

Starving in an entirely different way than I'd been earlier.

When he finally did "put me to bed," it was in the literal sense. My back struck the mattress. He followed, settling over me, nudging my legs apart. Like a true subservient, he stripped down entirely for my benefit, watching as my lips parted and my eyes widened at every inch of chiseled muscle revealed.

Then he lunged into my touch, offering up his body to explore as I wished.

The mattress moaned beneath our combined weight, obscuring any sounds smothered into the sheets.

And my poor parents could only watch on in despair from beyond the grave.

MASTER AND PROTECTOR

The next morning, I woke up alone. Ruffled sheets betrayed that someone had shared the bed with me during most of the night, leaving recently enough that the space beside me still resonated with their chill. I sighed, smelling him in the sheets, his scent mingling with mine.

For now, a voice hissed at the back of my skull.

I rolled onto my side to escape it, but doubt nibbled away at the pleasurable ache dissipating from my limbs.

For now… But how long until you drive him away again?

"Stop," I scolded myself out loud, rising to my feet.

After dressing in a plain gray shift, I descended the steps and found Dublin lurking in the foyer. He was wearing black now and my tongue darted along my bottom lip in appreciation. Damn that color. It emphasized his eyes like nothing else.

And as they flickered in my direction, that terrible, doubting voice went silent.

"You there, servant." I pointed at him, my chin in the air. "I'm famished. Make me something to eat."

He inclined his head graciously in mock servitude. "What would you like, *mistress*?"

"I want…" As I descended the remainder of the steps, my hand shot out, demanding assistance.

He stepped forward, cradling my palm against his—but then my act slipped as my stomach growled. I truly was hungry, and even the prospect of spending hours watching him slave over a meal was no match.

"Grilled cheese," I blurted, naming one of the few meals that even I knew didn't require much fuss.

He raised an eyebrow. "In lieu of filet mignon and braised leg of lamb?"

I'd surprised him. Triumph left me beaming as he led me toward the kitchen.

"Yes, and not only that," I added, stroking my chin. Cooking the meal himself would be far too easy. This time, I had another challenge in mind. "I want you to teach *me* how to make it."

"As you wish," he agreed. "I'm sure even someone of your delicate nature can learn how to slice a loaf of bread."

I grinned wickedly; the poor man had no idea how daunting a challenge he'd just undertaken.

~

"Even slices," Dublin instructed.

I chafed at how damn patient he managed to sound—despite the fact that I'd already butchered at least two loaves of bread. Relentlessly gentle, his fingers slid over my spine as he adjusted my grip on the blade with his opposite hand. I tried not to agonize over what served to be my fifth attempt.

"Try again."

"Okay…" I inhaled with determination and lowered the blade. What began as a semi-clean slice quickly resulted in a deformed chunk of mush as the knife slipped and smashed the loaf entirely. "Damn it!" I tossed the blade aside and tore at my hair. "I give up!"

My own challenge be damned.

Ironically, this task had proved to frustrate *me* more than Dublin. And the more aggravated I became, the more insufferably patient he seemed determined to be.

"Try again." He returned the knife to my hand, sealing his grip over mine. Parting, his lips brushed my throat as he warned, "You apply far too much pressure. Now"—he positioned what little bit of bread remained before me—"all you need to do is guide it…"

He flexed our combined grip and the result was a perfectly uniform slice.

"Now, you."

I did my best to copy his easy, effortless motion. Lost in concentration, I closed my eyes midway and reopened them only when the blade hit the cutting board.

"Finally!" I exclaimed in relief. My prize wasn't as neat as his, but at least it was useable.

"Good. And now for the next step." Dublin moved to a different section of the counter and coated the slices in butter. Then he slipped a slice of cheese in between them and fried the creation in a hot pan.

I grinned with unabashed pride as he finally placed the meal on a plate. "Next time, I want you to teach me how to fillet a fish," I joked as I followed him into the dining room.

He had enough sense not to respond.

While I'd been distracted during the bread debacle, he must have conjured up the steaming bowl of tomato soup, which he placed beside me as well. One sniff and I registered the unusually salty undertones to the tomato aroma. It betrayed an ingredient not found in most variations of the dish.

"Where's Dmitri?" I wondered as I lifted a spoon. Given his request to "tag along for the ride," his absence puzzled me more than I wanted to admit. While he was no comparison to Dublin physically, I couldn't deny that the man possessed more than enough skill in manipulation to be a threat nonetheless.

And while my sanity wasn't the healthiest to begin with, I'd never heard voices.

Certainly none so persistent. So insidious. Even as I ate, a cruel taunt echoed on the outskirts of my thoughts. *He doesn't want you…*

Clearing my throat, I pushed the unease aside and refocused on Dublin. "Don't tell me his promise for 'answers' turned out to be yet another lie?"

"He's around," Dublin said coldly. "He'll return soon enough. I won't have him toy with your hopes again. Therefore, I suggested that he ensure his information be *accurate* before sharing it."

"Or?" I risked asking as I fiddled with my sandwich.

His eyes narrowed, glowering beyond me. "Or I'd slice him into pieces thin enough to fit within the pages of his goddamn books."

Ah. A threat far too specific to be a mere boast.

Rather than linger on the topic, I busied myself with sipping from my soup and devouring the surprisingly good sandwich. Perhaps the full belly lulled me into a state silly enough to question, "Have you ever been in love?"

I flicked my gaze across the table, gauging his reaction.

He gave me little to go on. Merely a furrowed brow. "Love?"

"Something beyond mere lust." I waved my fingers through the air. "In your old age, I'm sure you've plied plenty of women with heartfelt poetry and roses." I laughed, but the joke turned out to be at my expense.

Of course, he'd had others. He'd all but alluded to it.

"Roses are a bit cliché," he countered, sounding bored at the prospect. "I'd like to think I have more creativity than that."

I shrugged, turning my attention to my plate. "You sent me one that first day, remember?" Along with a written choice. *Life or death?*

"They make for an effective tool to craft a grand entrance, I will admit." He laughed. "Though I would like to believe I'd profess my love in something a bit more impressive than a rose."

Something he'd never give to you, that doubtful voice hissed. I shook it off like a bothersome fly.

"Like?" I asked Dublin.

He said nothing.

"You know, Georgie's many lovers—the ones she risked sneaking in the manor—would leave roses for her as gifts, smuggled into different rooms," I said. "Sometimes, they'd assume my room was hers—which goes to show that brains weren't high on her list of attractive attributes. Every time I saw a rose on my floor, I knew… It was never for me."

What a melancholic admission. After a sigh, I sipped more soup and then shoved the rest of my bread into my mouth.

"Do you miss her?" Dublin wondered.

His voice was too soft. I could stomach his concern when it came packaged within an elaborate joke—but it was another thing entirely when he didn't bother to disguise it at all.

"Georgie?" I stared down at my hands, blinking rapidly. "I…"

He only cares because he wants her more. And you know it.

"Stop!" I rubbed at my forehead.

Dublin's hand brushed my wrist. "Are you all right?"

"I'm fine." I set my empty plate aside as proof. "I'm just… tired, I think."

"Should I assist you?" He grinned, utilizing his dangerous mixture of charm and smug amusement. With unmatched grace, he stood and approached my chair. "Or are you willing to bruise your delicate feet by walking yourself?"

I choked out something that passed for a laugh. "I wouldn't want to tire out my weak servant so soon. I'm fine. I think it's the time zone change."

He let me mount the stairs alone, but I could sense him watching. Even as I entered my room and closed the door, I knew he was listening down below, waiting for any hint that something was wrong.

So, willing to put him at ease for once, I calmly shed my dress and pulled on a robe. Then I carefully lowered myself onto the bed with a contented sigh for his benefit.

But I didn't dare to close my eyes. I couldn't. Shadows painted my room, swallowing up the violet beneath a sea of impenetrable darkness. My breath tainted the air in puffs of white. And the voices persisted, louder without his presence to smother them.

Silly Eleanor.

Stupid Eleanor.

Fucking you is all he desires. Fucking. Fucking.

You don't matter. You or that thing growing inside you.

Abomination. Abomination.

I tossed and turned, burying my face against my pillow. Air caught between my lungs and my throat, unwilling to move. I was suffocating. Gulping for breath, I inhaled and struggled to regain my bearings. *Breathe, Ellie. You're being ridiculous.*

"Eleanor?"

"I…I'm fine," I blurted even before I found Dublin in the doorway, poised forward as if to lunge. "I promise."

He didn't seem convinced. His grip remained on the doorknob as his gaze scanned the room in a cautious sweep.

"I'm just tired…" I let my eyes drift shut and my head fall back against the pillows.

If my act convinced him, he didn't let on.

As stubborn as a guard dog, he stood there even as I felt myself finally drift off.

But the voices chased me, hissing into the void.

He doesn't care.

He doesn't want you.

He could never love you.

~

Breakfast came in the form of a cup of red liquid shoved beneath my nose the moment I peeled my eyes open. Quite the departure in service from last night —though I wasn't particularly compelled to complain.

Groaning, I sat upright and obediently drank. Watchful eyes chased every single swallow until the last drop danced over my tongue. Then my servant withdrew the cup without warning and left the room.

"Sleep," he commanded from the hall before unease could even take root in his absence. "I have some business to attend to, but I'll be back."

I must have dozed off again. The next thing I knew, my eyelids were fluttering open and the sun painted my room in shades of gold.

But Dublin was still gone.

His promise echoed in my thoughts, becoming a mantra. *He will be back. He will be…*

Or not.

For all I knew, he could have left again. Abandoned me again. His kiss, his touch—it all could have been a trick designed to lower my guard. Because the walls of this manor reinforced the truth more than anything—I was no different from any other Gray, and I held no real appeal beyond this storied fortune.

And Dublin Helos wouldn't want you, a vicious voice seconded from inside my skull. *Stop kidding yourself, Eleanor. It's pathetic. You're pathetic.*

"No!" I stood and paced, tearing my fingers through my hair. I was being irrational. Pathetic. I…

Don't matter.

Something caught my eye, lying on the floor beside my bed, discarded. I stooped to retrieve it, confused as I found myself holding a beautiful white rose glaringly out of place. I brought it to my nose, inhaling the delicate perfume.

And the longer I observed it, the more dread solidified in my bones. It wasn't for me. No. Just like in the old days, it had been left for someone else. Someone beautiful he'd smuggled into my room while I'd been away. *That* was why he stayed. There was always someone else.

"What are you doing?"

Dazed, I looked up, still holding the rose to my chest.

Dublin stood in the doorway, his eyes wide, fixated on the item contained within my hands. *Proof,* a part of me despaired.

"Eleanor." Racked with guilt, his voice shook, unnervingly soft. "Put it down."

"Why?"

When I pressed the rose to my chest, he lurched a step closer. "Don't! Put it down. *Now.*"

"Tell me *why*?" I tightened my grip even more. His reaction only reinforced my suspicions. He was lying to me. Deceiving me.

"Eleanor." His voice deepened imploringly. "Put the knife down!"

Knife? Confused, I eyed my hand and gasped in horror. The leather hilt of a slim dagger trembled within my fist—not a flower. Honed to a lethal point, the tip grazed my throat with every frantic breath I took.

"Oh God!" Panicked, I threw it aside and hunched over, staring down at my hands. "I'm sorry! I think… I think I'm still dreaming. I—"

"It's okay." He knelt before me, easing me into his arms. From over his shoulder, I saw the knife disappear, tucked beyond my reach. "What were you thinking?"

"I…"

He pulled back, forcing me to meet his gaze before I could form a coherent explanation. Yellow sunlight spilled in from the window, almost blinding as it reflected off his features. How could I tell him the truth?

I'm hearing voices, Dublin. Voices in my head, and they won't stop.

They won't stop…

"I'm fine," I croaked. "I…I was cleaning up."

"Cleaning up?" He sounded more cautious than ever.

It wasn't until I followed his gaze down to my chest that I realized why. I was trembling.

"Yes." I staggered to my feet and shook my head to clear it. The paranoia had been the mere remnants of a nightmare. Yes… "I need a bath. That's all," I decided, staggering toward the bathroom. "I expect you'll have lunch waiting for me, slave."

I didn't look back to see his reaction. I raced into the safety of my tub instead, running the water as hot as I could stand. Lavender-scented soap helped erase the unease somewhat.

When I finally reentered my bedroom, I wasn't shaking anymore. Heat kissed my clammy skin, displacing some of the unnatural bitter cold.

And I felt fine.

I was fine…

Liar, that voice cackled from within. *You're going insane, Eleanor.*

You're going insane.

QUIET

The following days passed in stiff, tense stillness. Desperate to put the knife incident behind us, I fell into my role more fervently than ever—the obedient ward under a monster's control. I didn't dare so much as breathe the word "answers" or mention Dmitri.

Yet, with each passing moment, our delicate routine strained at the edges.

For one, Dublin stopped serving me anything requiring silverware, insisting more often than not that I drink my meals. If I asked him why, he evaded giving me a solid answer—and, as if to disguise the concern, he tried distracting me with taunts.

Insults, even.

"If you become any thinner, I won't have anything to hold on to the next time you decide to straddle me while airborne."

But I knew he was worried—and that terrified me more than hallucinating a weapon into a rose. When he looked at me, his expression became hollower than ever. Trying to maintain eye contact was a game of averted, downcast glances. Eventually, the man began to resemble a living statue in my presence more than a protector.

Always on guard. Always watching.

Even worse, I could sense what little glimmer of trust we'd built up slip further away. The quest for answers itself had cemented our unnatural union, yet each day without them felt like another unwelcome shove off a cliff toward an unknown drop.

Maybe the delusions were my body's way of trying to warn me?

You aren't ready for this.

You can't handle this.

You shouldn't prolong this.

"...consider your time up," Dublin snarled. He sounded faint, as if his voice were coming from down below. But, bellowed like thunder, each word reached my ears clearly even as I lay in bed, too drained to eavesdrop. "You have an hour to return with whatever 'answers' you have. I won't even waste my breath on a threat. And if I learn that you've somehow harmed her..."

Murder resonated in his tone and some numb piece of my soul stirred in response. Me. He was afraid for me.

Faked of course, the callous voice in my skull taunted. *Lies.*

"Something is wrong. I talk to her and it's like she doesn't even hear me. I've never seen her like… Do you think I haven't? I've taken the precautions. I've restricted her meals. Any blood I give her has been vetted to Hell and back. But if you are behind this, then know that I won't stop at merely killing you—"

Lies. Lies. Lieslieslieslieslies…

"Eleanor. Look at me."

I flinched; he sounded closer now. From the doorway, I realized as I turned toward it. Without an invitation, he entered my room, consuming the small space with his presence.

"How are you feeling?"

"Fine," I insisted. "Just tired." To prove as much, I shifted, placing a pillow over my head, my eyes squeezed shut. Nonetheless, I sensed him step closer—remaining far away enough to judge me unmolested should I ache to touch him. Far enough away that *he* didn't have to touch *me*. "I'm fine," I repeated hoarsely. "I just need rest."

"You're not sleeping."

I winced at his accusatory tone. Was he angry?

Of course he is.

Alarmed, I lifted the pillow enough to observe him. Stern frown. Blazing eyes. Hell yes, he was angry.

Because he hates you.

"You need to eat."

"Like you care." My words echoed the voice hissing in my head, but I was too tired to ignore them anymore. They were the only truth to be found within these walls lately. The only answers I had to cling to.

His lies. Lies.

"I wouldn't be here if I didn't," he stated bluntly.

But that voice overpowered him. *He's lying. He's…*

"You're lying," I whispered. "Like you really care whether or not I live or die—"

"Oh?" His expression darkened, his eyes flashing with warning. Any other day, I'd rush to heed it. "You don't want to play this game with me. As you recall, our contract specified honesty. I'm demanding my fair share now. Tell me what's wrong."

"Nothing," I insisted. Because saying it out loud would have been far too insane. Too real. If I had to gauge his reaction in real time… I wasn't sure if I could handle the truth I might find.

Because he hates you.

Hates.

Despises.

Obsesses.

And you know it.

"I'll come back later." His voice cut through the chaos for a heartbeat's reprieve—but then he turned for the door and the whispering intensified. I barely heard him growl, "You need to get some rest—"

"No, you know what I really need? I need *answers!*" I sounded so damn tired. So worn. A hundred-year-old woman howling from her deathbed. "I need the truth. And you're hiding it from me, aren't you? You're keeping me here. You're waiting, aren't you? Waiting for me to die—"

"Eleanor." His face was stone, but that of a statue carved in the guise of concern. Eyes too wide, mouth too tense. "Listen to yourself."

"I know why." I wrenched my blankets back and stood, pacing as everything became clear. His motives. His true intentions. "You're just waiting for me to die. You want me to. You don't give a damn about me—"

"Eleanor…" Confusion crept into those hollow eyes, a more terrifying sight than the visions. "I think you need to lie down—"

"No!" I cringed against the wall as he took a step in my direction. "Stay away from me!"

He doesn't care about you, the voice warned, growing louder. Deafening. *He doesn't. It's obvious.*

"You don't care! Get out!"

But he didn't look smug, like a villain called out in his vicious grand plan. He looked at me like I'd grown three heads. Like *I* was the monster.

"Get out!"

"Eleanor—"

"Get out!" I lunged for my bed, grabbed a pillow, and threw it at him.

When he easily sidestepped it, I snatched the vase on my bedside nightstand instead. It smashed against his chest, the broken pieces speckling the floor, as sharp as knives. But he remained, so I hurtled a picture frame at him next. A lamp.

Each weapon betrayed a shifting intention—less to repel him and increasingly to *hurt*.

"Get the hell away from me!"

When I aimed for the doorway again, another pillow in hand, he was already gone. I swayed, my weapon slipping from my fingers. Maybe he'd never been there at all? Maybe…he was already away from the manor, leaving me again.

Abandoning me again.

He didn't give a damn about me. All he wanted was…

No. I tugged at my hair, desperate to clear my thoughts. My memories portrayed someone far different than what the voices painted. Someone who'd held me at my darkest moment. Who'd claimed to crave me. Protect me.

Voice breaking, I called out for him. "Dublin? Dublin!"

No response. My room remained empty—or was it?

No. Something was at the foot of my bed. Moving.

"D-Dublin?"

He didn't come, and the noise strengthened, intensifying. Soft. Sweet.

I crept along my bed frame, drawn forward as if hypnotized. When I finally spotted the creature lying on the floor…

Shock brought me to my knees. I couldn't breathe. I couldn't even scream.

It was a baby. Someone had left her there naked, her tiny limbs perfectly formed—and an emotion unlike anything I'd ever felt drowned me.

She wasn't a grotesque monster. No abomination.

She was beautiful.

Lively. *Alive.*

And as I gaped, her hands grasped at the air for me, her impish grin infectious. But the longer I stared, the more demanding her cries became. Insistent.

She needed me. I needed to hold her.

Cautiously, I drew closer, bringing a trembling hand against her tiny head and the cap of golden curls that shielded it. The strands felt like silk, a hue I'd only seen one other person possess. But her eyes… They were a blazing, burning green.

Like mine.

"Shhhh…" I tried to slip my hand beneath her tiny body. To hold her. To soothe her. Everything would be all right. She was safe. No one would ever hurt her. No one.

But my fingers disobeyed and encircled her throat instead.

"No!" One by one, they clenched no matter how hard I tried to stop. "No! No!"

Tighter I clenched, until her beautiful babble ceased mid-song. That delicate face turned blue, those tiny limbs frantically flailing.

"No!" I tried to pull away, clawing at my frozen wrist, but it wouldn't budge. I tugged harder, scraping with my nails. "No! No! Stop!"

My grip wouldn't loosen, and her tiny body grew limper by the second. Lifeless. With every heartbeat, the color faded from her rosy cheeks.

And I'd lose her forever.

"No! No! No!" I scanned my room, desperate for help. But salvation appeared like magic in my hand—a jagged piece of broken glass, honed like a knife.

And there was no time to hesitate. I slashed, unconcerned as the sharpened edge bit into my wrist. Deep. Deeper. Blood spilled, splattering the floor, but I didn't matter. Only she did. I needed to save her.

But even the violence didn't loosen my grip. The next cut went so deep that the blade scraped bone—but not deep enough. So I slashed again. Again. Still, my fingers wouldn't loosen.

And she wasn't moving anymore. She wasn't moving…

"No!" I wailed, trying harder. Cutting deeper, slicing into any part of my arm I could reach. "No! No—"

"Eleanor!"

A cruel hand stole my weapon, struggling to contain my flailing, kicking limbs.

Teeth bared, I fought like hell, but I was no match. "Let me go! Let go! I can't leave her!"

But when I looked down, she had vanished.

And in her wake: red, red, red. The floor became a sea of it, frothing beneath my feet.

Endless amounts of blood.

"No! I didn't mean to." I choked out the confession, my heart breaking as much as my voice was. "I did it. I didn't mean to. I didn't want to hurt her. I couldn't save her—"

"What's wrong with her? Eleanor! Eleanor, look at me!"

I barely recognized the sound of Dublin's voice—ragged, distorted by a horror I couldn't begin to fathom—but I couldn't see his face. Though his words lashed at my eardrums, I barely heard him. Just darkness and noise. That goddamn noise.

You're pathetic. Pathetic. Pathetic. Pathetic.

Desperate, I tried to claw at my ears, but with my body restrained, I could only scream, "Stop! Make it stop, please!" I didn't know who I was pleading with. Dublin? God? Anyone? "I can't take it. Make it stop. Make it stop! Make it stop—"

"Dmitri!"

"I have it. Shhh, my dear," another voice crooned sweetly into my ear. "A little pinch… There. This will take the pain away, I promise."

I was only vaguely aware of a burning sting along my arm.

And then…peace.

"You are restrained," a man warned as I floated on the cusp of consciousness. His voice served as a steadying anchor, drawing me back when I only wanted to drift.

Dublin? No. Someone sly, their accent thicker.

"Try not to panic," he insisted. "You're wounded, and frankly, I'd rather not have to bandage you *again*. So deep breaths and all of that. Prepare yourself, my dear. It isn't pretty."

I stirred, fighting to remember how to control my limbs. All senses felt cut off from my brain as if locked behind a wall with no key. In vain, I tried to flex my hands. Blink. Anything.

"You were poisoned," the speaker continued as my thoughts spun, still hunting for a name. "With something known as Ergot—best to get that out of the way. It's a rare compound known to inspire all sorts of nasty things in those who ingest too much of it. Paranoia. Hallucinations. Psychosis. It builds up in the blood, you see. Slowly, over time. Months. Years. Though, judging from your recent state, you've managed to receive a full dose in mere weeks. An impressive feat, I must say. Admittedly, I should have guessed from your rather thrilling reaction to my little lie that your mental state may have been exceedingly delicate." He sighed in admiration.

An image formed in my brain of a handsome, angular face. Hair the color of blood. Shifting eyes.

"No bother! I'm not the only one who overlooked your symptoms. Helos may be an arrogant bastard, but I know he tested the blood he gave to you. You're just lucky he caught on before you finished severing your hand. *That* might have made things a tad unpleasant."

I finally managed to open my eyes. Blurred and unfocused, it took them several seconds to clearly interpret the figure before me. But that mocking grin required no introduction. *Dmitri.*

"Where…" My throat ached as I tried to speak. "Where is Dublin?"

"Off getting more bandages in case you reopen your wounds, I suspect," Dmitri replied. He almost resembled a different person without his playful sneer. "You scared the hell out of him. Dare I say, that's quite the feat, given the man's rather fearsome reputation." He didn't even chuckle. Hell, as his eyes took on a wistful gleam, he almost appeared…impressed? "And yes, this is a lot of information at once—I apologize—but this is the fifth iteration of this damn speech I've delivered and I pray, for both our sakes, that you aren't faking your sanity this time."

Faking? I eyed the room beyond him, increasingly uneasy. It wasn't mine. And the rich, golden décor didn't resemble something Dublin would own, either. It boasted of more exotic tastes, far beyond typical elegance. Above me, a vaulted ceiling sported a gruesome fresco—a horde of angels slaughtering an opposing army.

I swallowed hard, tearing my eyes from the chaotic scene. "Where am I?"

"Hell," Dmitri replied. Sitting on a gilded chair near the bed, he snatched a book from a nearby table. With a casual flick of his wrist, he flipped through the pages. "I never thought I'd ever see a day when Dublin would willingly return to the enclave, to be honest." He eyed me with a thoughtful frown before turning yet another page. "Then again, I never thought I would *join* him in said enclave. You, my dear, have provided quite the adventure."

Enclave? I tried to sit up, but my arms resisted any movement. Literally—not for lack of trying. The harder I strained my wrists, the more I felt the weight of resistance. Something encircled each one, rendering them immobile.

"Manacles," Dmitri admitted. "Or at least silken ones. Your Dublin refused to let me use the metal pair after you tried slipping out of them."

I couldn't remember anything he'd mentioned. Panic bubbled out of me on a single word. "W-Why?"

"To keep you from killing yourself, of course." Sighing, he set his book aside and propped his chin on his fist, sitting forward. "Ergot is a powerful poison. It lingers in the blood and renders the mind susceptible to all manner of disturbing hallucinations. For instance, when you had no luck cutting your hand off, you tried clawing out your throat. As you can imagine, it made for quite the mess. You're lucky that I happened to arrive in time," he added smugly. "There is only one antidote for Ergot, and I happen to be among the few in the world skilled enough to make it. Which reminds me…" He tutted with his tongue and stood, smoothing his hands along his suit, a brilliant indigo. On the same small table as the book rested a teacup, which he lifted by the handle and lowered to my lips. "It's time for your next dose, my darling. Do drink up."

I clenched my jaw shut.

He sighed heavily. "Come now, Eleanor. I really don't want to force-feed you your medicine." His eyes flashed a menacing green. "*Again.*"

His words were too much to process all at once as a million realizations washed over me. *Tried to kill yourself. Ergot. Blade. Poison. Dublin. Gone. Gone.*

When he lowered the cup to my mouth again, I squirmed helplessly, resisting my binds. "Get away from me—"

"It's all right."

That voice… I turned toward it, my heart aching—but when I finally spotted Dublin advancing toward me, he looked…

Haggard.

Hollow circles swallowed his eyes, though he didn't require sleep. The unusual color enhanced the planes of his face in gaunt relief. For a horrifying second, he looked every bit his age. Centuries of pain and exhaustion clinging to a human form. Then his eyes met mine and his entire expression softened.

He became my Devil again, wary and distant.

"Drink it," he said, nodding to Dmitri. "It's all right."

A part of me wanted to rail against the commands. It wanted to shriek and scream and demand answers.

Why was my skull on fire? Why was I shivering even beneath mounds of blankets? Why did my throat taste like dirt?

And why, oh why, was my arm throbbing like hell?

My throat provided another dose of agonizing pain. The skin burned with every breath as if rubbed raw. Or, if Dmitri was to be believed, *clawed* at by a madwoman with brittle nails.

"Eleanor," Dublin rasped. "Drink."

For the moment, I chose the safety of his baritone over questioning. As Dmitri returned the rim of the cup to my lips, I obediently pried them apart. The liquid within smelled pungent, as if tinged with a million different spices. With the first sip, I realized where the gritty taste in my mouth had come from.

"It was a very clever method," Dmitri mused as I gulped at the tea. "Slow. Sustained over multiple hosts. He must have started not long after you began supplying her fresh blood." He eyed Dublin, smirking. "I used to muse which one of you two might best the other when you eventually did resume your trite little war games. Believe it or not, Dublin, but I always had my money on you. Mero could be cunning, but he had his boundaries. Even if he *is* using the other Gray girl as a pawn, like I suspect, I doubt he's killed her. Yet. *You*, on the other hand, were ruthless—"

"Enough." The growl lacked any of the intensity I was used to. In its absence, Dublin resembled a mere shadow of his former self. A specter on par with Raphael—a hollow soul, somewhere in between the man and monster. But as he turned his attention to me, some semblance of the Devil I knew returned again. Namely in his eyes as they flickered with an unreadable mixture of emotion. "How do you feel?"

"Tired," I rasped, my voice breaking.

"You should be right as rain in a few more days," Dmitri insisted. "Ergot is resistant but not infallible—"

"I need to speak to her alone." Dublin didn't even look at him, expecting his will be obeyed.

"Fine." Dmitri shrugged and headed for the doorway. "Though perhaps now isn't the best time to mention that you shouldn't trust all you see or hear, Eleanor," he told me with a playful wink. "The Ergot is still in your bloodstream, after all."

His laugh echoed in his wake, but Dublin's voice easily overpowered it.

"Tell me what happened." He sat on the edge of the bed, his back to me, but his hand settled over my hip, palpable even through the heavy blankets. "From the beginning. Everything."

"I was hearing voices," I admitted. My throat felt sore from disuse. Just how long had I been beneath the spell of the drug?

"What did they say?" he prompted.

I hesitated, swiping my tongue along my dry, cracked lips. "That... That you hated me. That you didn't want me." I realized now just how insane it sounded out loud. "I think I knew I was being irrational, but I couldn't help it. It felt so real. I could hear it—"

"Telling you that I couldn't love you?" He didn't meet my gaze. Instead, he eyed the far wall, his jaw clenched. "You screamed that line the most."

I closed my eyes, hating the vicious memories as they teased the edges of my psyche. "How could this happen? Dmitri said—"

"You were poisoned," he said over me. "Right under my nose and I didn't even see it until it was almost too late."

As my eyes reopened, I found him watching me, lingering over my face. "Why?"

"To punish me." He sounded more resigned than vengeful. "I suspect that was his design all along, as far as you were concerned. Punish me."

"Why?"

"Why?" He laughed, shaking his head as if unsure how to even phrase the answer. "He… I loved him like a brother once," he admitted softly. "I trusted him above all others. Always. And you are his vehicle to punish me." The hand he rested over me withdrew, becoming a fist he slammed onto the mattress. "But he's overplayed his hand, and if he tries to hurt you again, I will kill him."

"Dublin…" I'd forgotten how formidable he could sound. How dangerous when confronted. Blazing silver eyes cut me to the bone as he held my gaze. "What about Georgie? Dmitri said she might be—"

"You need to focus on yourself for now," he warned. "Trust me on this."

It was as close to begging as a man like him might ever come—and despite his nearness, I sensed he could drift from me farther than ever if I pushed him away now.

And I wasn't the only one who needed him.

"I saw things too." The words almost hurt to say, conjuring a memory sharp with a pain I'd never ever felt. Longing. Fear. Guilt. "I saw… She was so beautiful…and I killed her." Panicked, I flexed my fingers, grasping at nothing. "I killed her—"

"It was a nightmare," he said, but it wasn't the truth. A nightmare was comparable to what I'd witnessed, but I'd rather burn alive than feel that pain again. "The drug should help you sleep without any more dreams. Get some rest."

I steeled myself for him to leave, but he found my hand, still bound to the bed, and grasped it tightly. He remained like that for only God knew how long.

Long after I surrendered to unconsciousness again.

CONTAMINATED

The vicious specter of doubt chased me through a nightmarish maze. I couldn't escape it, assaulted by its cruel taunts. *You're pathetic, Eleanor. Pathetic...*

I awoke, gasping as panic formed a noose around my throat more restraining than the binds still pinning me in place. Straining my shoulders, I struggled to sit up, blinking my eyes open to the morbidly decorated ceiling above. A twisted sense of relief slowed my frantic heartbeat by a fraction. I was still in that room.

And someone remained beside me, brushing the sweat-soaked curls from my face.

"You're safe."

I turned toward the sound of his voice.

He hadn't moved from his position on the side of my bed, even though I sensed I'd slept for hours at least. "Eleanor?" He sounded worried.

Should he have been? I wasn't sure. I needed to move. I needed to think.

"I…I think I just need to use the restroom…"

The corner of his jaw twitched, betraying his thoughts in a way I'd never been able to interpret before: suspicion. He didn't trust me.

"This isn't the first time you've woken up seemingly lucid," he murmured, more to himself than to me. His eyes narrowed over my hands as they grasped at the sheets, yet he made no attempt to free me. "How do you feel?"

I took my time answering. He was cautious for a reason, and I sensed a need to make my reply as coherent as possible.

"Sore," I admitted finally. "And my arm hurts. And my throat."

Some of the tension constricting his brow eased. "Your wounds need to be healed, but you've been refusing to drink my blood. Dmitri's had to rebandage you at least four times. It's a miracle you haven't bled out. We couldn't even inject you because you fought like hell every time, even while sedated." His mouth softened further.

Was my Devil impressed?

But his words only emphasized what Dmitri himself had hinted at. *This is the fifth iteration of this damn speech I've delivered…*

"I still feel strange," I added hoarsely. "Like my thoughts are scattered and… But I don't want to hurt myself."

His gaze flickered to my right arm, tracing the length of bandage wrapped from wrist to shoulder, but the pathetic note in my voice must have been enough to overcome his concern. For now.

He approached the limb closer to him. With some sleight of hand I couldn't make out, he undid the manacle—a strip of thick, black silk—and placed it on the nearby end table. I flexed my fingers carefully, hissing as blood returned to them. But I kept the rest of my body still, avoiding any sudden movements. Watching me like a hawk, Dublin circled around to my opposite side and did the same.

Freedom hurt. I groaned as I stretched my limbs and attempted to sit upright. Dublin assisted me, utilizing his touch where I lacked the strength. Despite how my muscles were throbbing, it felt good to move. Even while being observed with an intensity most men might reserve for a lab rat.

Unnerved by his concern, I decided that my best option was to utilize it. "Help me up."

I extended my uninjured arm, allowing him to pull me to my feet. From this angle, the rest of the unfamiliar bedroom unfolded before me. With every detail, the unease within my skin grew into an itching dread. It was large, as cavernous as Dublin's cathedral. Dark walls lacked a window, instead sporting exquisite macabre paintings depicting images of war and violence.

Marble floors were adorned with Persian rugs woven with intricate designs composed of gold and ebony threads. A fireplace—black stone carved into the open maw of a serpent—yawned against the far wall and the fire roaring within basted my skin with what little heat I felt.

"Come here." Dublin approached, his hands raised as if to ensure he didn't startle me.

Once satisfied by my reaction, he lifted me into his arms, and within seconds, we were in an adjacent bathroom, the interior of which was no less extravagant than the bedroom. And just as imposing.

A large sunken tub had been cut within the center of the marble floor. Dublin set me down near the edge of it. His touch lingered along my arm as if to gauge whether or not I'd suddenly try attacking myself. Then he withdrew to the corners of the room, fetching various supplies.

Overall, the layout resembled how I figured an ancient Roman bath might. Golden columns accented the space at various intervals, and a large mirror consumed an entire wall alone. Once I saw my reflection on its surface, I failed to muster up the energy to even gasp. My skin lacked definition, my cheeks sunken and hollow.

I looked more dead than alive.

No wonder Dublin seemed unwilling to leave me unattended for very long. He returned to my side and guided me into the basin of the tub. There, he stripped my thin nightgown and ran the water.

The nuances of his expression eluded me once more, so I observed my skin instead. A thick length of bandages covered my right arm from wrist to shoulder. Crimson splotches betrayed signs of fresh bleeding, but I wasn't brave enough to check the wounds underneath. My throat was another matter. I ran my finger over it, sensing uneven, inflamed skin that matched the violent array of scratches my reflection revealed.

"You need blood," Dublin warned as the water lapped up my sides. "You need to eat."

He sounded hesitant and I couldn't help but wonder why. Though maybe I already knew. I'd been so hysterical that he'd had no choice but to bind me just to keep me from hurting myself.

"How was I poisoned?" I asked as he settled behind me.

"Methodically. You were never given blood from the same person twice," he said. "From the outset, I knew to source anything I gave you carefully. Every drop came from donors I considered to be the highest quality and least susceptible to corruption. For you to receive the dose you did, each one of them must have consumed trace levels of the poison long before I drew a drop from their veins."

His gruff tone conveyed just how elaborate a scheme the level of planning revealed. Someone cunning enough to outsmart even his best efforts.

All part of a systematic scheme meant to infect me.

"Anyway, I'm not offering you *human* blood this time." As he spoke, he withdrew something from his pocket. A small, thin blade—small enough, I realized, that should I grab it, I wouldn't be able to do much damage to myself. "Do be a good girl," he said as he slashed the blade across his wrist, drawing a line of blood. "You've bitten *me* with every attempt before now. Admittedly, it wasn't very pleasant."

"I did?" My skull throbbed. "I can't remember."

He stroked my cheek. "Drink."

A million questions bubbled beneath the surface as I eyed the smooth skin of his wrist. Like how did he know if his blood alone would even sustain me? What happened if he was carrying the poison as well? And most importantly, was there some proper etiquette to follow while feeding from a vampire?

In the end, his free hand caught the back of my neck, guiding me forward.

My lips parted, allowing a sliver of liquid between them. The moment his taste registered, I no longer required coaxing. I lunged, gripping his arm to keep it in place as deep, ravenous pulls racked my body. Perhaps the fact that I was starving was the catalyst, but he tasted better than good. Better than sin. I drowned in his flavor, craving more...and more...more...

It was like surfacing from an eternity spent submerged beneath water when I finally came up for air, unbearably full. Regardless, my tongue was already chasing what few drops I hadn't managed to swallow.

Fully prepared, Dublin brought a wet cloth to my chin and dabbed it along my bottom lip. "Already, you look better," he murmured, a rare hint of praise.

I glanced at the mirror, which seconded his claim. Color gradually returned to my skin. The pain lessened. I didn't feel quite as dizzy, and my thoughts felt easier to grasp and decipher.

Like the threat still looming above our heads, for instance.

"What about you?" I eyed him over my shoulder. "What if the poison is in your system—"

"It doesn't affect me, which is why I didn't sense its corruption until it was too late. No matter… From now on, I will take the necessary precautions."

What they might be? He didn't explain, leaving it at that.

By then, the water had reached a comfortable height, and he set about washing me thoroughly from head to toe. My body sang beneath the ministrations, and once again, I wondered just how long I'd been strapped to the bed.

Which brought up an even bigger question.

"Where are we?" I supposed deep down I knew at least part of the answer—nowhere good. Much like the bedroom, a decidedly 'serpentine' theme continued even in here. The water fixture on the bathtub was in the shape of a snake, spitting water in the place of venom through golden fangs.

Dublin ran a cloth across my shoulders, seemingly too intent on his task to respond.

I tried again. "Dmitri said something about an enclave—"

"You're safe," he said, parting my hair with his fingers.

A moan caught in my throat. I arched into his touch before I could help it, relishing the surprisingly pleasurable sensation of his chill on my scalp.

"You no longer seem determined to harm yourself, at least."

I shivered, glancing at my bandaged arm. There was no use in avoiding it any longer. Gritting my teeth, I fingered the end of the strip and began to unwind it as Dublin's hands stilled.

Once the entire length had come undone, pale, untouched flesh was revealed underneath. The properties of Dublin's blood never ceased to leave me speechless. A few sips of it and I was already healing. Yet I had no trouble imagining the carnage that had marred the limb just minutes before. Damage *I* had done. The crumpled bandage conveyed as much, splattered with alarming amounts of scarlet liquid.

"It felt so real," I whispered in horror. "All of it."

"Even the doubts?" He sounded unusually calm as he continued to detangle my matted curls. "That I didn't care about you? That I couldn't love you?"

"Yes." I hunched over myself, drawing my knees to my chest. I eyed the mirror across from us, marveling at the scene it showed. Dublin Helos, crouched in the water behind me, studiously arranging my damp curls. "It doesn't matter. I know that—"

"Should I say it now?" His mouth lingered over my shoulder as he moved his attention to washing my back. "To counter him should he ever steal inside your mind again? At least then you'd have heard it once."

I couldn't breathe—equally alarmed *and* fearful. Even now, doubt festered somewhere inside me, fighting to resurface. Once acknowledged, it gleefully feasted on my unease. *His love would be a lie. A lie...*

"No," I insisted, shaking my head. "I can ignore it."

"I suppose you might require some token to assist in that quest." Lowering the cloth, he lifted my hand from the water, extending the fingers for his inspection.

In confusion, I looked down, frowning as something caught the light. Something small, encircling my finger.

Recognition prickled through my chest.

"My ring..." Only it wasn't. A fact made apparent as I drew it closer for inspection and realized the gold band shone far too brilliantly. Real? A delicately thin band, it encased a stunning blue stone far too beautiful to be formed of cheap plastic.

A replica, but one recreated of materials that I sensed were a million times the worth of the original design.

"Love is an archaic concept, I must admit." Dublin sighed, brushing his lips against my throat as he spoke. "But I suppose we could name it that. What I feel for you. *Love*, in a sense."

As his fingers traced the pulse quickening in my arm, I quaked, too stunned to speak.

"So remember that the next time you dare to slice into this flesh. Every inch belongs to *me*."

My lips parted, a startled laugh escaping them. Only he could turn a romantic confession into a threat. But the reaction made him brace me more firmly, his body molding to mine.

His thumb brushed my jaw, urging me to face him. "Look at me."

His eyes burned, nearly impossible to meet head-on—but in this arena, he offered no reprieve. Our lips met, the kiss slower than any other. Deeper. In it, I sensed more than he could ever convey out loud. Anything. *Everything.*

Enough to silence the remnants of the voices the way sunlight scattered roaches.

"I dearly hate to interrupt..."

I jumped at the intrusion. Before I could cover myself with my hands, Dmitri appeared near the mouth of the bathroom. Not even a heartbeat later, Dublin stood toe-to-toe with him, obscuring any view he might have glimpsed.

"Pardon the interruption," Dmitri simpered as he was promptly herded from the room. "But I figured that you would prefer hearing this from me. *He* requests an audience with you and her." He waved in my direction over Dublin's shoulder. "I take it one of his little spies told him she was up and moving. You knew he wouldn't wait for long. Not when you've come crawling back so conveniently into his control."

"Who?" I croaked, snatching for a nearby towel. Dread thickened my throat as I stood, drawing the material around me. Again, I suspected that a part of me already knew the answer.

"You didn't tell her?" Dmitri remarked, practically *singing* with glee. "Oh my. Well, this will be quite a shock. I'll save you the trouble. Raphael requested your audience, my darling Eleanor. Though I take it you've met our dear, dear mutual friend already?"

That I had.

"He suggested you dress for dinner," Dmitri added as his giddy footsteps retreated. "Oh…and, and Eleanor?" He poised his next statement as if knowing the exact moment I'd flinch in response. "Welcome to the enclave."

LOST

ublin toweled me off in silence. As if conjured by magic, he pulled a black dress on over my head and guided me into a pair of matching heels. He said nothing, his expression stony—though, to be fair, I wasn't inclined to ask too many questions.

Whatever this "enclave" might be, I suspected that its real purpose lacked any mystery in one context: This place was Raphael's lair. Somewhere beyond the club where the ancient creature held full sway.

And where Dublin did not.

I eyed my ring as he swept my wet hair back from my face to observe his handiwork. Satisfied, he took my hand and steered me from the bathroom. As we crossed the threshold of the bedroom and entered the unknown, he pulled me closer. Enough so that his bulk obscured my view of our surroundings. I could only make out a floor a milky shade of marble and blood-red walls accented in gold.

As blinded as I was, the trip through unseen corridors felt as disorienting as being led through a maze. While blindfolded. In the dark.

Eventually, the corridor must have expanded into a larger, more open space judging from how our every footstep echoed like a gunshot. My ears caught whispered conversations from unseen figures. When Dublin finally drew to a stop, he tugged me to stand beside him.

And when I finally scanned our surroundings unobstructed, my shock transformed my expression, impossible to contain.

We were standing in a throne room. One decorated in swaths of scarlet and gold. More disturbing frescos adorned the walls and high ceilings. Images of angels slaying demons and fiery portrayals of Heaven and Hell.

Like an angel himself, a lone figure was sitting upon a raised dais positioned with the commanding presence of a throne. Raphael. His shoulders draped with a scarlet cloak, he looked every bit as chilling as when I had seen him last. His skin was a thin sheet clinging to bluish veins, enhancing the hollow bones of his eternally beautiful face.

"Eleanor Gray." His faint tenor slithered against my eardrums, conjuring imagery of death and decay. "I am pleased to find you safe and sound…as promised." His dark, lifeless eyes flickered toward Dublin. "You were wise to come to me, as well as to reveal such a miracle. Such… gifts must be guarded at all costs—"

"She is still under *my* protection," Dublin interjected. His hand gripped mine tight, boldly conveying possession. "Barring whatever agreement may be between us."

"And what a marvelous job you've done." It was impossible to discern from Raphael's blank smile whether he meant the phrase as a genuine compliment or an admonishment.

The figures on the outskirts of the room collectively flinched, providing the answer. A *threat*.

"But I do not humor Mero and his toys like you have. Now do you realize the danger he represents? I warned you once when he chose to forsake this life. My Cael, I *warned* you." His voice resonated more strongly. "You should have destroyed him along with his abominations. And yet you let him scurry in the shadows, protecting him even as he taunts you." Something that may have been genuine emotion made his eyes narrow a fraction. "It saddens me to see what you have become, old friend."

"You've always seen time as a commodity," Dublin replied, matching his detached tone. "You command thousands of years' worth of it. A *lifetime* at your disposal, yet that is all you choose to do with it: hoard."

"You mean without *living*?" Raphael issued a chilling, whispery laugh, his disdain for the concept palpable. "As Mero did. Back when you rightly chastised him for forgetting his true nature. Oh, how I wish I had been there. To help you command your senses without this pointless guilt." He shook his head, gazing expressionlessly at events far beyond this room. This century. "While I sit here now, you and I both know whose soul carries a deeper stain upon it. But ever since that day, you've tried to appease him, haven't you? Obeying his inane rules. Until now. Suddenly, you seem determined to consume everything dear Mero cherished. His little pawns. His Grays. Even his old pet… I know you've been trying to find her."

His eyes flickered with renewed interest as Dublin went rigid. "Has it truly come to this, my friend? Hunting a witch in the hopes that what? She could undo the curse she placed at his behest? *Ignorance*," he chided, clasping his pale hands over his lap. "Then again, so was the mere belief that saving dear Eleanor from Mero's curse would be as simple as turning her. Did you think I didn't realize?" A cold sound trickled out of him, a soulless imitation of a laugh. "I knew from the moment you resisted Saskia's attempts to sell her just what she meant to you. Your *prize* in Mero's game. I can only imagine her appeal."

His attention cut to me with the swiftness of a slicing blade, further scattering my thoughts. *Turned?* That word teased the fragile order of my psyche. I trembled, deciding to ignore it. Not now. I couldn't examine it now.

"I admit I was skeptical at first," Raphael continued. "When I heard of his curse. I should have anticipated its power, however. *His* little witch was a rare creature. Such arcane talents she possesses." He sighed, lifting his slender shoulders in defeat. "How I regret not claiming her for myself. You think *you* are the only one hunting for her? Perhaps the next time you come prostrate before me, I'll name her as my price."

"You want to berate me?" Dublin inquired, stepping forward. "Fine. But *none* of your anger concerns Eleanor." He released my arm, his posture stone once more. Only his eyes reflected life, and I suspected that what little humanity remained in them was wasted on the glance he spared in my direction. "She needs rest. Let her go."

"So desperate to shield your true nature from her *still*, Cael?" Raphael's lips twitched in amusement—but in the end, he nodded and raised his hand in a silent command. "*You.* Show Ms. Gray back to her quarters."

A slender figure stepped forward, his head bowed, his red hair gleaming.

"There." Turning to Dublin, Raphael murmured, "I assume this is agreeable with you?"

Dublin said nothing. But he didn't react when Dmitri appeared by my side and reached for my hand, either.

"As you wish," the vampire simpered with mock piety. Even before Raphael, he lost none of his coy amusement.

Dublin on the other hand…

When I looked back, my Devil no longer existed. A stranger was standing in his place—a tormented creature who answered to only one name.

"Well, Cael," Raphael murmured. "What do you have to say for yourself now?"

Dmitri murmured into my ear, "Let us make our escape before the shouting begins, eh?"

Moving quickly, he guided me back to the room I'd woken up in.

"Do have a seat, my dear." He gestured to the bed but remained standing while I perched myself on the end of it.

I was too uneasy to care as he watched me, his eyes gleaming.

"You're shaking." He sounded positively pleased by that fact. "But try not to pout too much, my darling. While the men chat, we can hold a conversation of our own."

"What kind of conversation?" I eyed him sharply, an eyebrow raised.

"Ah, now, that is the question." His eyes glowed an ominous golden hue in the firelight. "You want answers, I presume. More than dear old Dublin has given you, yes? Not that I can blame him, of course," he admitted with a sigh. "This is such a very sore subject for him—"

"What do you want?" Even as I bristled in annoyance, I couldn't deny that he was right.

I wanted answers. But I also wasn't naïve enough to assume he'd give me anything for free. Something warned me that even his assistance during the aftermath of my poisoning had carried a price tag.

"You misunderstand me, my dear one." His smile did nothing to ease my suspicion. "I merely want to wheedle myself into your good graces."

Common sense told me to ignore anything he had to say. To wait for Dublin. To play my hand if I had to. But that same part of me warned that I could maintain my innocence for only so long…

"Who is Mero?" My lips felt dry. I had to drag my tongue along the bottom one.

"Mero?" Dmitri laughed. "That's the wrong question, my dear. The rather boring history between him and Dublin doesn't matter. Not a bit. What you really should be asking is where do *you*, and your child, fit into the grand scheme?"

"M-Me?" But I was well aware of my role—I was a liability to Dublin. A burden he had gone out of his way to bear. His pawn requiring protection.

"Oh, but that's where you are wrong," Dmitri claimed as if reading my mind. "You need to go deeper than that. Right to the beginning. Ask yourself, do you know why only Dublin could feed from you, though I am well aware that is no longer the case? Why is it blood that sustains your current condition, as if to mock his very nature?"

My eyebrow rose. "How did you—"

"Rumors," he said with a dismissive wave of his hand. "Answer the question."

I shrugged; the answer didn't seem to have the makings of a trap. "He said his venom made it so that only he could—"

"*That* is what he told you?" Barking out a harsh bit of laughter, Dmitri slapped his hand against his knee. "You can't fault the man for creativity, though I suppose it is true in some sense. But really, Eleanor, use that critical mind of yours. Go deeper than that. What happened when another vampire fed on you? Someone other than Dublin?"

Someone like Raphael.

My throat went dry. "I…" Even as my voice failed, I knew that my horrified expression revealed the truth. *I died.*

"Dublin has never offered to turn another mortal," Dmitri murmured, his tone suddenly serious. "Never. Not once. Not even in his most…shall we say, his *heyday* as a man who made Raphael quake in his cape." He smirked at the memory. "I think, all along, you've already suspected as much," he added knowingly. "The real catalyst for your pregnancy. The blood you require, though you remain mortal still. Mero, I suspect, had counted on him breaking his one rule all along. For *you.* But it's corrupted you far beyond what poor Dublin intended. While not a vampire, you are…changed."

He eyed my belly. "You just haven't bothered to admit it to yourself. You know there's more to it, and I will tell you what—it is your bloodline. You Grays have been cursed for centuries. Everyone knows it. Especially Dublin. Before you, he has spent years ensuring that none dared feed from any of your kind. Did you know that? It's why the Grayne still exist—he lets them thrive, purely out of courtesy to Mero, the dear friend he betrayed."

"How?" I whispered. "How did he betray him?"

He waved his hand dismissively. "Oh darling, I'm sure you saw my beautiful opera. You are no fool."

I tried to picture the morbid performance and its grisly themes. A man had escaped those in his faction, only to have everything he'd fought for ripped away by someone he trusted.

"Mero was the first to crave another life," Dmitri said as though settling in for a long tale. "A different life from the hell he'd consigned his soul to. I suppose ruling hand in hand with the ruthless Cael took its toll. Rather than trade in lives, he wanted to *live*. And he craved it so badly he found a cunning little witch talented enough to give him and his mortal lover the life he so desired. There were a few caveats, of course."

He lifted his hands in a makeshift scale, raising one while lowering the other. "A terrible price would be paid by both parties involved. I assume they considered it a worthy sacrifice however, in exchange for an abomination in every sense of the word. But then what happened, my dear?" He chuckled darkly when I flinched. "Come on. Continue the tale."

As he had taunted, his opera revealed the answer. The villain of the story had slaughtered a woman and her unborn child in the name of duty.

"Dublin killed her," I choked out in a whisper. "The woman. Didn't he?"

God, I wanted him to laugh, proving I'd been wrong.

"Yes," he said instead, displaying his fangs in full. "And in his grief, Mero founded the Grayne, utilizing your dear ancestor in the process. At his behest, his witch cursed your entire bloodline, though some might say 'protected.'" He scoffed. "Serving within the Grayne was a mere small part of the deal your ancestor made. Mero would protect every Gray to follow, just as long as a few descendants contributed to his lunatic cause. For years, he has maintained that bargain, always watching from the shadows. And in guilt, Dublin has kept even Raphael from destroying them. Though now I have to wonder if perhaps his motive all along was *fear*?"

He searched my face for any reaction. In the end, he sighed. "What better way to punish the man who stole everything you desired than to ensure that he too one day will dare to crave the same simple, honestly boring, wish? *Love.* A family. A reason to endure these wretched, lonely years. And then, were you such a man, you would get to rip it all away."

Pausing his story, Dmitri waited, as if expecting me to realize something. To *feel* something. I just felt numb.

"I see I may have to spell it out for you, dear." He inhaled sharply. "Dublin's always known that one of your kind might set Mero's devious revenge into motion, I suppose. And now..." He gestured toward my stomach. "Have you wondered why he has accepted your condition so easily? It isn't usual—I can tell you that. Or why he hasn't killed you, despite the obvious danger you pose? Why he can't even bear to face the truth by telling you the very things that I am now? Or why the *one* soul you care for more than him perhaps has vanished and he hasn't even offered to help you find her?" He leaned forward, and almost in a whisper, he declared, "You are his doom, Eleanor Gray. Always have been. Always will be."

He stood and stretched his arms over his head in a mock yawn. "I will leave you to your rest," he said before exiting the room. Near the threshold, he paused long enough to add, "Pleasant dreams."

TOKENS

With my thoughts raging in turmoil, I couldn't sleep. I sat hunched over the side of the bed instead, so lost within myself that I barely heard Dublin when he finally returned. Whatever he saw in my expression made him stiffen with one foot poised over the threshold.

"What's wrong?"

God. The sight of his cautious, careful frown banished some of the agonizing tension in my chest. Gone was the stranger from the throne room. He resembled *himself* again, radiating his usual mixture of fury and frustration—but still *Dublin*, the bastard soul collector extraordinaire who'd stolen into my life uninvited.

The man who had corrupted me in more ways than one.

The man who had lied to me.

Tears spilled from my sore, bloodshot eyes, streaming down my cheeks before I could keep them at bay. Despite the roaring fire, my teeth chattered. Tremors racked my hollow frame, yet all I could manage to rasp was, "I'm fine."

"You're not." He spun on his heel, aiming for the door, "I'll get Dmitri—"

"No." I shook my head until he stopped, his back partially to me. "It's not the poison."

Just horror.

Just anger.

The worst part? I didn't know whether to direct it all at him or myself.

"Dmitri," Dublin hissed, this time without concern. Suspicion laced every uttered syllable. "What did he say?"

Anxiety clawed through my blood, sowing bitter regret. How funny that my demand for answers had come back to bite me—after weeks of questions and unintended answers, I doubted I could withstand any more revelations.

"Did… When Raphael bit me…" I closed my eyes as the memory threatened to unfold in painful clarity. "Did you try…t-to turn me?"

"That sly fucking bastard." His voice was a low rasp. "What did he tell you?"

And for some insane reason, I found myself laughing. "That I am destined by blood to destroy you."

"Is that all?"

I bit my lip. His tone was all wrong, suddenly neutral. Confused, I opened my eyes, gaping as he shrugged.

"Frankly, Eleanor, I'd like to think that my doom lies in something a little more formidable than you." He crossed over to my position and stroked his chin, eyeing me with a sweep of his gaze.

"Don't lie to me," I countered. "Is it true?"

He raised an eyebrow. "Is what true?"

"The curse." I ran my fingers through my hair, parting the curls. His reaction didn't fit the morbid, somber tale Dmitri had told. If anything…God, his lack of concern made it all sound so silly when put into perspective.

So silly. So morbid. So very much like Dublin.

"That my family's bloodline was *cursed* by a witch so that one of us would ultimately result in your destruction. Is that ringing a bell?"

"Not particularly?" Dublin frowned as though seriously mulling it over, hunting for that obscure detail among the centuries clouding his ancient brain. "Eleanor, I get damned to Hell on a weekly basis. You can't really expect me to remember *one* witch from—"

"There's more." I stared at my bare toes rather than face him. "That the reason why you could feed from me had nothing to do with venom. No other vampire can. That's why Raphael's bite killed."

"Raphael killed you because he grows more sadistic with every year he's aged." His upper lip curled from his teeth in disgust. "Toying with mortal lives is a game to him. Think of it as a child ripping the wings off a butterfly merely to watch it squirm."

"Then…why are you drawn to me?" I wondered helplessly. Magic would certainly explain it.

"Why?" He raised a golden eyebrow as though I were a simpleton asking why the sky was blue. "Honestly, for the same reason a lion might be drawn to a psychotic, bold, fearless little lamb who acted so peculiarly from the rest of the sheep. I think I'd have to be blind *not* to notice you merrily skipping into danger."

"But…" Doubt returned, planting itself firmly in my chest.

"In fact"—he swiped his finger along the length of one of my curls and then snatched my wrist, inspecting the ring glinting on my finger—"I'd say you are the very opposite of what a curse might conjure to tempt me. I've always despised the color green." He peered into my eyes with a frown. "I also prefer skin that has some definition to it. As well as sun-kissed hair—"

"You mean like Georgie?" I was too stunned to feel offended.

"Yes," he mused, the corner of his mouth lifting. "If some witch designed one of you Grays to 'doom' me, as you put it, it would be *Georgiana* who'd fit the bill. Beautiful, sane, agreeable. A cliched, whirlwind love affair would commence, I suspect."

"Do you know where she is?" My eyes stung. Blinking didn't banish the sensation. His ring threatened to crush my finger. It suddenly felt so heavy. "Have you both just been toying with me this entire—"

"No." He grabbed my chin when I tried to turn away, forcing me to face him.

"I don't know where she is now exactly, but the day I met her, she didn't infuriate me," Dublin went on callously. When I tried to wrench my head away, his grip tightened, holding me captive, forcing me to see. That alarming shift in his gaze—I sensed he *wanted* me to see it. "She doesn't make me question things I have never questioned. She didn't make me sell my soul to Raphael after one ridiculous dance. She didn't arouse me to the point of madness. So if Dmitri meant 'doom' as in 'liable to drive me insane,' then you, Eleanor Gray, fit *that* bill perfectly."

Furious, he swiped at a bead of moisture rolling down my chin, crushing it.

"Come. Raphael doesn't keep his dwelling as well ventilated as I do mine." He tugged on my wrist, yanking me to my feet. "The air in this damn place is making you delirious."

I had no choice but to stagger behind him in a daze, my head spinning as deliriously as he'd claimed. As we entered the hall, he didn't shield me with his body this time. Side by side, we wandered the empty, breathtaking corridors until he shoved me through a doorway and I had to shield my eyes with my hand, blinded.

When my vision gradually cleared, I was convinced we'd entered another realm. One of luxurious sunlight painting a landscape of emerald green, surrounded by stone walls and positively *brimming* with roses. At least thousands, bloomed from vines and shrubs, spanning every shape and color imaginable. The moment I inhaled, I realized it was open to the air. Beautiful, crisp, fresh air. Up above, a blue sky melded with the scenic landscape, and I nearly forgot all of Dmitri's grim tale.

"Is this your apology?" I blurted as Dublin pushed past me.

"Whatever on Earth for?" He shot me a weird look even as he snatched a fresh rose from a nearby bush and held it out for my inspection. "It's merely somewhere we can talk in private." He glanced warily at the structure we exited from —a wall of gray stone. A castle?

"Talk about what?" I asked, struggling to stay focused.

"So, perhaps Dmitri wasn't entirely lying." He stared dead ahead, and I could only guess at how hard it had been for him to admit even that. "There's more to the Grayne's history than I told you. Superstitious drivel, but if you want to hear it…"

"Tell me." I crossed my arms, approached a worn stone bench and sat, still marveling at the wild space. It reminded me of some fairytale castle's crumbling courtyard, abandoned by a monarch who no longer craved the sun. I cradled a nearby bloom between my fingertips, surprised by the petal's softness. As Dublin neared, I whispered, "Tell me about Mero."

After the snippets painted by Dmitri and Raphael, I needed to hear the rest from him.

He came to my side, threading his fingers through my hair while snatching my rose away. "His name was Abrahaim." In a hollow contrast, his voice echoed cold and detached while his fingers casually parted my curls, easing a rose behind my ear. "Descended from Spanish Moors, he worked as a hired missionary in the heart of Andalusia, Spain. The stories he used to tell…" Something pained flitted across his expression too quickly to name. "He used to boast of sneaking into the Alhambra palace, stealing trinkets from the royal apartments. Of charming his quarry with myths of the crusades. A master thief. I met him as nothing more than a wandering vagrant."

He turned on his heel and approached a shrub containing a soft, pink variety of blossoms. He fingered one, manipulating the delicate petals with ruthless intent.

"By then, I had escaped Ireland, stealing away on an English ship. To skirt the British occupation." He shrugged as though referring to a minor inconvenience—not a defining event in a country's history. "I had no plan. No goals. I merely deigned to explore wherever work or curiosity took me. It just so happened that, in Spain, I decided to try my hand as a hired mercenary working for a merchant who traded along the coast. There, he caught wind of a series of vessels returning from some new, mythical land. The Americas.

"Rumors ran rampant of the riches the vessel might contain, ripe for the taking. At his behest, I snuck onto a ship—one whose name you won't find in the history books, mind you—in search of unspeakable treasure." He looked away, gazing into the past. "And I was nearly gutted by Abrahaim, who worked for a rival merchant. After some rather heated back and forth, we decided we were too evenly matched to kill each other within a reasonable amount of time. So we would split the treasure between us, our masters none the wiser." His faint smile fell flat. "Instead, we found a creature far beyond our understanding."

"Raphael," I supplied as he went silent.

He returned, pressing a new conquest against my palm—another rose. "Yes, Raphael," he admitted. "Starved after months at sea, he attacked us both. To this day, I still don't know his true origins. The man is, shall we say, obsessive regarding his past. Even the dates in the history books have been tweaked by him. I suspect your sister must have come close to the truth, for him to grow irritated enough to notice her."

He sighed. "But in those early days, believe it or not, he was but a scared young man tormented by a curse he didn't understand. One he'd inadvertently passed on to Abrahaim and me. But as *we* realized the new limits of our power, his curse became our gift. Our *revelation.* Anything we wanted or desired was ours with nothing more than a flash of fangs. I struggled at first, if you can believe that."

He laughed, fingering his cross. Slow, his steps carried him away from me again, to yet another rose bush. "The constraints of my religion weighed heavily on me. I was a damned, hell-bound creature. But in a way, I grew to accept that doom. I embodied it. Raphael and Abrahaim may have enjoyed their newfound control, but I relished in it. And under my command, we consolidated it, conquering cities from the shadows, building influence through contracts as we discovered creatures more varied than even the creators of the Bible imagined."

Awe painted his tone as he snapped the stem of another rose —a beautiful, creamy white.

"A triumvirate of allies, we were unmatched. If only you knew. Your little history books. Your legends and myths. If only you knew how much of it was a lie." He laughed bitterly, twisting his blossom between his fingers. "But then…the years marched on, unending, taking their toll on each of us in different ways. Raphael grew more reclusive, content to control his reality through proxies on puppet strings. Abrahaim on the other hand, became pensive, racked with more guilt with every additional life ruined. And I…"

He turned to me, but I doubted he even saw me. His eyes were wide, consumed by the past.

"I grew numb. Detached. It was as though I could only ever feel anything through violence. Through sowing fear.

Crushing souls." He formed a fist, crushing the rose into nothing. "Destroying lives. The more they bled, and agonized and screamed, the more intoxicating the power became. There is something terrible and addicting in sowing chaos… But every drug presents the danger of a relapse. When its high breaks and you fall from the glorious height. Increasingly I felt it, that *guilt*. A woman desired money to save her ailing father. In return, I consigned her to years of servitude, whoring herself, no different than hundreds before her. But in those days, I'd see her pain and, for a second, I'd feel it. *Guilt*."

He gritted his teeth against it, and I knew deep down that if he could have purged that emotion from his soul entirely, he would have.

"It became too frequent, too much. In yet another instance, I desired the soul of a succubus, and in the process, her daughter was harmed."

Saskia, I realized.

"As if conjured by heaven's mercy, Abrahaim was there to convince me that there was another way. We could control our impulses, he claimed. Leave that life behind. He made it sound beautiful. I will give him that." His mouth contorted into a painful imitation of a smile. "We took new names to reflect our rebirth—mine a reminder of where my was soul bound, while his was a simple phrase, chanted during the crusades his ancestors fought within. *Memento Mori*. Remember death. From it, he took the name Mero. Then he told me of a witch he knew, powerful enough to create a totem to keep him grounded. Help him remember the humanity we both had so eagerly shed."

"Your necklace," I whispered, eyeing the silver totem hanging from his throat. The one I found in the crypt took on a darker meaning. Not a backup of Dublin's, but something far more meaningful…

"Yes." He bowed his head, stroking his fingers along his cross. "Mero had one as well."

"How?" I whispered. "Doesn't yours…help you somehow?"

He nodded. "It's more than just enchanted by petty magic. It contains my blood. When you wore it, I could sense you even while halfway across the world. And while I wear it, I can control the urge to feed."

I swallowed hard as my thoughts spun, replaying all of the times he'd forsaken the necklace around me. Namely the night he returned when, by his own admission, he nearly killed me.

"We both know how hunger can affect you," Yulia had told him during a hazy conversation I barely remembered. *"I should have talked you out of ever giving up that stupid amulet in the first place…"*

"Mero never relied on his totem the same way," Dublin continued. "He spoke of a future. Of a life beyond this curse we'd been stricken with. The fool even mused of children born mortal. The only price would be his soul. His eternity. While he could never die, his seed would grow, and spread, and prosper. It was his dream. But Raphael was not pleased."

He turned, starting to pace. I doubted he was even speaking to me anymore. No, this tale ripped from his soul unabated was for his benefit alone.

"He considered it a betrayal, and in my selfish, callous addiction, I let myself believe it. Gratitude toward my old friend for showing me the light of redemption became hate. How dare he believe that we could change? How dare he threaten the world we had spent countless years creating?" He demanded the question of no one, his face upturned skyward. "Blinded with rage, I hunted him down, finding him in the Americas. I killed his lover, slitting her throat right before his eyes. He would see reason then—or so I convinced myself. He would surely realize it. Chasing happiness, and mortality and pointless joy was futile. We were Gods among men, how dare he forsake that?

"But I quickly realized that there are no gods. No Heaven. No Hell. Just pain and redemption. And as I watched Mero mourn for a woman whose life was but a speck of dust in the stream of time, I realized that my grip on power was just as futile as his lust for freedom. Neither path would lead to salvation. Just destruction."

He turned to me, running his finger across my throat. "In his grief, my old friend found a mortal to corrupt to his will."

"James," I whispered. My mysterious ancestor.

"Yes. I'm sure Mero spun his aim as some grand crusade against evil, but that was merely a lie. He wanted a bloodline to poison. A fertile bit of soil within which to plant his revenge. Yet I didn't want to fight that war with him. Call me a coward, but I alas, I was tired…"

He bowed his head, his eyes downcast. "So I went to Raphael. I traded my time in exchange for his avoidance of the Grayne. I let Mero plot in obscurity, telling myself that his promises of revenge were nothing more than fantasies. And I still believe that." He turned to me again, an eyebrow raised. "Do you want to know why? Because if my affections were the result of some twisted curse, I imagine I'd be easily wooed by a creature like your sister. I'd succumb with no resistance, hypnotized. But you…"

Step by step, he advanced on me and there was no escape. "I resist you, and you tempt me further. There is no mindless surrender. You claw your way through me like poison. There is no ease with you. I'm tormented. In lust, you torment. In pain, you torment. In happiness even…you torment me."

He trailed his lips across my forehead, lingering there. "I am the soul at your discretion. No curse could inspire that. You claimed Saskia told you I thought of your sister? How could I not? Let's say she is missing. That Mero has her. That he is using her as a pawn to lure you to him, knowing you would never abandon her. Killing her without your knowledge would easily solve the threat she poses to you. And yet…" He sighed and withdrew. "I know you would never forgive me if I took her life. So I haven't. He knows as much. I am sure of it. He knows exactly how to win this game."

My breath caught. I couldn't avoid asking, "Do you know where she is?"

"I suspect she's in hiding," he said. "And not only from me."

"Oh?" Fear gnawed at my stomach. I'd been able to ignore it until now—but as if conjured by his mere mentioning, weeks of pain descended. My sister. God, I wanted to face her. Demand my own answers. See her face.

Did she ever love me?

"Well, you'd think she could send me a letter, or a phone call, or even a goddamn homing pigeon just to let me know that she was still alive."

"Would that change anything if she had?"

"It would certainly make it easier to hate her," I blurted. Only he could do this to me—drag out the truths I wasn't even aware of myself. I eyed the rose in my grasp, ripped a petal from the beautiful mass, and watched it dance in the still air. "As it stands, she can't even bother to send me so much as a postcard."

Something in his silence made me look up, but for once, he didn't seem willing to meet my gaze.

"You wouldn't keep her from me," I insisted. Why did I sound so damn terrified? Georgie's abandoning me was one thing. But if he had purposefully led me to believe…

"Here." He reached into his pocket. "I found this in your crypt. I suspect it had been there for at least a few weeks before then."

I froze as he shoved something into my hand. It was small, soft. A crumpled piece of paper. Written on it was a simple message scrawled in painfully familiar handwriting.

Elles. I wish I could smile in that scrunched-up way I used to back in the days I could easily charm you after stealing one of your biscuits. I understand that this is different. I'm trying to find my own way to answer your questions. But remember what Mother always said—above all, blood remains. Remember that and you will always be able to find me. — Georgie.

God, it was the exact thing she'd say at a time like this. Clueless, mocking, and coy. Heat burned behind my eyes, impossible to fight back.

"Where…" The answer came to me before the words finished leaving my throat. The urn. Telltale signs of dust coated the edges of the paper.

He'd stolen it, perhaps that very day I'd mentioned our hiding place.

Teeth bared, I whirled on him, "I should kill you for this. Were there more?"

"No," he admitted. "But if there were, I would have burned them."

A scream of frustration left me hollow. When that wasn't enough, I found myself pacing in a circle, tearing my hands through my hair. It still wasn't enough. I had to hit him, swiping my nails at his flawless features. "I hate you!"

"You should," he agreed, not flinching so much as an eyebrow in the face of my assault. Without even leaving a mark, my fingers glanced harmlessly off his flesh. "Because if she proves to be a threat to you, I'll do far worse than that."

The veracity of the promise drained me of rage entirely. I just felt numb, watching the hint of a monster lurk beneath his callous façade. "You had no right—"

"I don't?" In a motion so effortless that I felt it rather than saw it, he snatched up my wrist, yanking me so close that my lips met the skin of his throat. Against my scalp, he murmured, "I don't have a right to be concerned when your sister consorts with a band of cultists who want you dead? I don't have a right?"

My skin stung beneath the venom in his tone. I'd never heard him quite this cold—passionless and passionate at the same time.

"Do you have any idea—" Within seconds, he had me backed against the stone wall enclosing the garden. When I dared to meet them, his eyes were midnight, flashing with rage. "Do you have any idea what I've done—what I had to bargain—to even bring you here? *Time*! More than you can ever imagine!"

He was shouting. Smoldering with rage, he alone made the sun seem powerless, and the world became gray with shadow.

"Do you have any idea what I'd do to anyone who threatened you? I won't apologize for any of it. So do not expect me to. And do you want to know why?" His mouth was against my hair, his words a low, mocking hum.

"I should never forgive you for this." I'd felt compelled to say it. To mean it, even as the words broke off in a gasp when his lips met the side of my throat. "Never... Not even if you beg."

"I never beg." The promise taunted me as he sank to his knees. In front of me. Right there in broad daylight. Swift fingers wrenched up the hem of my dress. His head darted beneath it, and then...

Slow, deliberate pulses of his thumb nudged my legs apart and a moan ripped from my throat, echoing on the secluded silence. I squeezed my eyes shut, throwing my head back against the stone. Neither action helped reduce the insanity of what was happening.

"Stop!" I wanted to cling to my anger. I tried to.

But a brush of his touch against my skin disrupted my senses. Perhaps he had been right all along? I was delirious.

"I believe we have concluded this discussion," he murmured against my inner thigh. "I promise to avail myself to your rage at a later time. But now... You were beyond me for days. I believe I am due some kind of recompense."

Recompense?

"But Georgie is your ideal," I hissed even as my body remained rigid, at his mercy. "And it's not like you're my type, either."

As my thoughts scattered, they turned to what my pride considered his worst offense, in addition to lying and scheming. Insulting my apparent appeal.

"*You're* too bold." As if to prove it, what felt like his lips grazed the side of my hip, making my train of thought sputter and nearly derail. "Too cold. Mean. C-Cocky—"

"Those sound like defining attributes to me." As he spoke, he did something with his hands that stole my breath. Soft, dangerous fingertips. Rough, sinful heat.

I found myself gasping for air. "You're too blond," I breathed. "I prefer brunettes—"

"Like that man you dined with?"

I heard the question as if he'd spoken to me through a tube.

"What was his name again?"

"Hmph?" My brain was too busy detaching from my skull to keep up, floating.

"Gabriel something," he recalled. Muscle and nerves melted. The vibrations of his voice dangerously enhanced the slow, steady pressure building between my legs.

I wanted to correct him. But then his lips slid lower, too low, and I panicked, desperate for ammunition.

"Oh, him… He was charming. A gentleman. The usual list of everything you aren't—"

He went too low. My back bowed, nails scraping against the stone on either side of me for any hint of stability. In response, he laughed, really laughed, and it was sin. Evil. Devastating. My spine turned to putty. Rudderless, I had to brace one hand against his skull, fisting my fingers through his hair.

"The man shrouds himself in an unusual amount of mystic," he admitted. "I do suspect he has ties to the mob. Or that he's secretly a crossdresser given his rather feminine aesthetic. I daresay you dodged a bullet."

"You actually stalked him?" Alarm countered pleasure. Mr. Lanic may have been a money-hungry grifter, but mere greed didn't warrant the wrath of Dublin Helos.

"I nearly killed him. Or just maimed, perhaps." His mouth withdrew just enough to make it easier to breathe again. "Alas, a sudden intrusion into my private sanctum by a madwoman made me rethink that plan."

Had I been? A madwoman?

Cool hands brushed my neck before I could decide, seizing the collar of my dress. When my eyes opened, I found Dublin on his feet again. With little care, he tugged on the silk in his grasp, tearing it right down the middle. He was intent on guiding my arms from the sleeves so that the material could fall at my feet. I barely registered then that I was naked in broad daylight. That he was quickly removing my panties as well. That his touch became more possessive by the second.

Hungrier.

But then he entered me in a single thrust and the world fell away. Hate disappeared. All that remained was selfish, desperate, grappling need. I lunged against him, seeking only one thing. He gave it to me. He took it from me— screams, moans, repeated whimpers of his name.

Guided by his corrupting touch, I floated to heaven and crashed to Earth while the sky darkened above me.

*P*eace could be more insidious than poison, stealing into a breathless silence with no warning. No escape. I would never be able to erase this moment or deny the emotions sowed with every breath spent lying naked beneath the stars—even if the person holding me in his arms contained a million secrets unwilling to be shared.

I was content.

Though I should have been worried that, any minute, someone might intrude upon our hidden space and find us. Dublin didn't seem concerned by the prospect, either. His only movement was to rake his fingers through my hair and guide me to face him.

"Drink." His bleeding wrist found my mouth before I even had the chance to question.

I obeyed, lapping obediently at my "meal" while my stomach churned for more. When I finally came up for air, he was already on his feet, still brazenly naked. His skin gleamed silver in the moonlight, enhancing the muscles rippling in his back as he retrieved our clothing from near the bench.

After observing the ruined state of my dress, he tossed me his shirt instead. "Put it on."

The soft fabric smelled like him. Like ice. Like winter.

"I still don't forgive you for lying about Georgie." I felt the need to tell him that even as he approached me and crouched to slip my shoes on.

Without a word, he took my hand and led the way into the dark until we exited from the door we'd entered through.

The corridors remained empty, though I swore the shadows flickered, betraying unseen figures lurking in our wake. Spectators, I suspected, spying in silence as the powerful Cael paraded his little mortal prize right past their noses. If Dublin sensed them as well, his expression didn't reveal as much. Serving as my stone-faced guide, he steered me through the hostile elegance. It was only as we entered the chilling interior of the bedroom that he spoke again.

"What would it take, should I be inclined to return to your good graces?" he wondered as I crossed to the bed.

I looked over my shoulder and found him watching me, stroking his chin in serious contemplation. As our gazes met, his tongue flicked between his lips and I choked. Something told me he enjoyed my anger far more than he should have—namely the possibilities that said "redemption" might present to *his* benefit.

It was surprisingly easy to come up with something nonetheless. "You could let me string you up by your toes and heed my every command and even then…I'd only consider it."

"We can add that as leverage," he decided. Suddenly serious, he averted his gaze and withdrew something from his pocket. Whatever it was, he kept it concealed between his fingers. "I propose another bargain—Raphael insists that no mortal knows the location of his precious little sanctum, and I do believe we have overstayed our welcome." He grimaced and opened his hand, revealing the small vial. A dark liquid glinted within as he held it up to the firelight, a deeper scarlet than even his blood. "Getting you out of here without catching his notice will require some drastic measures."

I smoothed my fingers over the front of his borrowed shirt, drawing it tighter around myself. "Like what?"

"Smuggling," Dmitri prompted, uninvited.

I spun around and found him near the door, leaning against the gilded frame. Just for how long had he been there, watching? His smug grin revealed no answer. "Raphael will not willingly allow you to leave. Especially not now." His gaze drifted down to my belly. "Not when you present an untapped well of time belonging to his most favorite of toys. So we must slow your heartbeat, and then act quickly before he and his spies notice the silence." He pointedly tapped his earlobe as if for emphasis. "The drug will help, but it is not infallible. Luckily, *I* mentioned how convenient it might be if we could disguise you beneath enchanted fabric designed to suppress the stench of your charming mortality. Not even Raphael would be able to track us in time."

"Enough games. Is she here?" Dublin demanded, turning to him.

Dmitri shrugged. "I think I heard someone screaming in French near the grand foyer. You must be such a lax master for her to rage so indignantly at being summoned. I, on the other hand, always kept her *disciplined—*"

"And you remember your boundary," Dublin warned in a tone so biting that I flinched. "You so much as look at her. Touch her. Think of her and I swear I will cut you down where you stand."

"Hmph." Dmitri pursed his lips, but the bravado was purely for show. The pointed glance he shot Dublin's fingers revealed just how seriously he took the threat. "I suppose. But we really should be hurrying this mad scheme along. Time is of the essence. Especially if you still plan to hunt down that devious little witch."

"Eleanor," Dublin returned his attention to me and captured my chin in his free hand. "I need you to drink this." He nodded to the vial in his grasp. "It's a mild sedative, but it will render you unconscious. Just long enough for me to get you somewhere safe. It won't harm you," he insisted. "And this way, I can arrange our...*escape* may be too dramatic a word. Let's call it, fashionable departure."

Warily, I took the flask. One inhale of the liquid contained within and I forgot my doubt. It smelled like him—spice, ice and winter. After a hesitant sip revealed nothing alarming, I downed it entirely. Before I'd even finished swallowing the last drop, the flask fell from my grip.

I staggered, too sluggish to catch it. My eyelids were heavy as well, my body weighed down.

And before I knew it, I fell into oblivion.

Reality reasserted its presence with the aid of a million unnerving sounds. Wood creaking. Fabric swishing. A man pointedly clearing his throat.

"The drug should have worn off an hour ago," he remarked, sounding somewhere between bored and concerned. "So either you're ignoring my attempts to wake you or you're really in mortal peril and require some lifesaving remedy. Either way, your lover will threaten to kill me if you don't show signs of life soon."

Ice fluttered across my cheek. A finger?

"I can hear your pulse racing," its owner taunted. "Do hurry. I would hate for you to miss the show."

I peeled my eyes open. As I blinked, my vision quickly adjusted, focusing on the beautiful creature watching me from a seated position nearby. Dmitri, his eyes flickering with mischief. Propped on his lap was a newspaper he was pretending to read while the two other occupants of the room argued nearby.

One of them I instantly recognized, his voice a growl. Dublin. He was standing near a wood-paneled wall at the back of a small, modestly decorated sitting room.

"I don't want to fight with you," he warned. Even in anger he seemed to be trying his best to refute the figure standing opposite him without shouting.

"You had no right!" the woman hissed, her musical accent beautiful even while shaking with rage. "How dare you even —" She broke off and flashed a strained but friendly smile in my direction. "Oh, hello, Eleanor. I'm glad you're awake." A heartbeat later, she rounded on Dublin again. "How dare you?" Raw pain sucked away some of the youth conveyed by her features. She looked old, aged overnight in a demure gray dress devoid of her usual flair. Her hair hung loosely around her face, swinging through the air as her hand lashed out and collided with Dublin's jaw. "You had *no* right. And I don't even get the courtesy of a full explanation—"

"I'm trying to explain now," Dublin insisted. "If you would just listen—"

"Listen?" Yulia threw her head back and cackled. "What? Are you going to exert your ownership of me again?" Her tone was ice. "I have always trusted you with my life. You have never given me a reason not to. But if you ever yank me around like this again, you will no longer have a loyal servant to do your bidding. Goodbye, *Eleanor*." With one last genuine smile in my direction, she stormed off through a nearby doorway.

"What happened?" I struggled to pull myself upright, staring after her.

"I happened," Dmitri mused without looking up from the current page of his paper. "Dearest Yuliana seems to be unwilling to let bygones be bygones. Even if her beloved new master puts his boot to her backside."

"Don't."

I shivered at the warning lacing Dublin's tone and my gaze flickered to him. He was Mr. Contractor once again, reinforcing his ownership over a soul in his possession.

"Remember what I told you?"

"Yes," Dmitri sighed, rustling his paper. His bright-teal suit diminished his attempts at seeming modest, however. As did his ever-present smirk. "No looking. No touching. No thinking—"

"And don't you dare say her name, either—" Dublin broke off, finally seeming to notice me. He took a step toward me, his hand outstretched. "How do you feel?"

"Fine," I croaked, still staring after Yulia. I sensed that her anger had something to do with the snippets of conversation I remembered before I'd drunk the drugged liquid. *Smuggling,* Dmitri had said.

I glanced down, noticing my surroundings for the first time. No longer were we in Raphael's lair. There were windows, for one, revealing a view of emerald trees and blue sky. The décor lacked any serpentine accents, instead consisting of dark, muted colors and simplistic furniture. I lay outstretched on a leather couch matching the style of the chair Dmitri was occupying.

And from here, furious footsteps were audible, storming deeper within the structure.

"Is she all right—"

"She's fine," Dublin snapped.

"She's upset. Is it because you made her help you take me from Raphael's?"

"No," Dublin admitted. "It's a bit more complicated than that."

"Complicated?" Dmitri folded up his paper and flashed a beautiful, chilling smile. "No, my dear. It wasn't making her 'escort' you with her poor, old master. It was *ordering* her to, utilizing the power of her contract. Even if she wanted to—which she very much did—she couldn't resist a direct command. All to ensure that dear Eleanor Gray remained safe and sound. I suppose that's the only reason why she hasn't snuck a curse into your suit jacket yet," he added, stroking the collar of his flamboyant jacket. "Nasty stuff. I know firsthand how devious her little brain can be—"

"Enough." Teeth bared, Dublin shot him a withering glance. "Do I need to remind you again of your boundary?"

Dmitri visibly shrank into his chair. "I will remain on my absolute best behavior." He returned to the depths of his newspaper, but I didn't miss the devious tilt to his mouth.

"She'll be fine," Dublin insisted before changing the subject. "Now. What did you learn?"

Dmitri rolled up his paper and set it aside entirely. "Despite my unwilling accomplice, we were able to make some headway to my connections," he murmured. "You probably don't want to know the details. Something involving a cursed negligee… Regardless, we did discover one kernel of information."

Dublin's eyes flashed and narrowed. With just a few lethal nuances in his expression, he made impatience into an art form. "And?"

"Our quarry lies in Leon, not far from here," Dmitri admitted. "It's a fitting hiding place, the rural wilds of France. Rumor has it she's made her home amongst the witches who still dwell there. Though it could be an elaborate ruse and she could be living under a bridge in some city in the States. You know how she loved her mind games."

My head was spinning. *Witches. Quarry. France.*

"Who are you talking about?"

The two men shared a look.

"Answers, my dear," Dmitri finally said. "As to your… condition." He nodded toward my stomach. "From the very witch who may have set it into motion, so to speak."

Answers. I looked to Dublin and he said nothing. His jaw was clenched, his eyes thoughtful.

Licking my lips, I asked, "How do we find her?"

"Well, we hunt her down," Dmitri said wryly.

Dublin, however, didn't seem convinced. He paced, his eyes focused on a section of the wall. "How accurate is this information?" he demanded of Dmitri.

The vampire shrugged. "You'd have to ask dearest Yuliana of that. I'm sure you won't trust *my* assurances—"

"It's true." Yulia appeared in the doorway of the room, her arms crossed. I'd never seen her so cold, her eyes frozen over, devoid of emotion. "I made sure of it. But I can recognize embellishment as well. There is every possibility we're being misled. After all, to stay undetected for centuries, I'm sure Adara has taken the proper precautions."

Dublin nodded once and met her gaze. "Thank you."

Yulia said nothing, but she didn't storm off again, either.

"So." Dmitri clapped his hands once and rose gallantly to his feet. "When do we leave? An adventure, how exciting—"

"Who said anything about you coming?" Dublin shot him a look that made even his cheerful façade crack a bit.

"Ah, but remember my price, Dublin." He fingered the white pocket square accenting his breast. "My assistance has not come cheaply. Think of it as a loan I expect to be repaid in full. Besides." He shrugged. "You don't even like witches, apart from the person whose name I am forbidden to mention. Especially *her*—"

"Fine," Dublin snapped. "We'll leave in the morning."

Dmitri beamed. "Oh, excellent!"

Yulia crossed her arms, her gaze fixed on the wall—coincidentally avoiding both men in the process. "Am I still under your command, *master*?" she inquired coldly.

"I would like you to stay," Dublin admitted. "As my friend—"

She stormed from the room. Dmitri snickered, fiddling with his paper once more—until a glowering stare from Dublin made him lurch to his feet.

"I suppose I will excuse myself as well," he simpered while exiting the room.

I sat there awkwardly, drawing my knees to my chest. "You've royally pissed her off," I remarked. I racked my brain, but I doubted I'd ever seen her frown, let alone furious.

"For good reason," he admitted. "I've never invoked her contract against her before now." He sighed and drew himself up to his full height, his jaw set in determination. "But she won't stay angry for long."

"What is her past with Dmitri?" I wondered. Though did I really want to know? On the surface, the other vampire seemed more mischievous than vicious. But even I knew that appearances could be deceiving.

In his own way, the vampire seemed more than matched with Dublin in the potential for sowing chaos and pain.

"He owned her," Dublin said, phrasing the words as carefully as he could. "Once. It was not a mutual partnership, if you can't already tell."

I nodded, hunched over my limbs. My shoes were off, and a thin blanket crumpled at the end of the couch made me suspect that someone originally draped me beneath it. "What did he do to her?"

"He abused her skills for his own gain and warped her mind just as viciously as Mero's poison did yours."

I cringed. Even now, that crippling, whispering doubt still snuck into the silence when I least expected it. *You're worthless, Eleanor.* A part of me feared it would never completely cease—and Dmitri seemed more than capable of such manipulation. I could still picture the dazed girl he'd brought to the opera, fully under his sway.

"That's horrible," I rasped.

"Neither of them will ever harm you again," Dublin swore. He was beside me in an instant, brushing his fingers along my hand, including the one sporting his ring.

"Tell me." I curled my fingers around his and marveled at the sight of my slim ones, intertwined with his larger, albeit more graceful appendages. "Tell me what happened between them."

"She was devoted to him," he said. "Wholly. Perhaps he thought she loved him? Either way, he enjoyed testing her, pushing her skills to their very limits. He would have her dress in clothing designed to tempt men and women alike and watch her struggle to ward them off. He would pit her against other witches with her skill and punish her should she fail." He frowned at the memory and I felt my heart lurch. Any cruelty that could arouse even Dublin's pity had to be unimaginable. "One night, he went too far and I intervened."

"And then you offered her a contract?"

He frowned. "Let's say I made Dmitri an offer he couldn't refuse."

"And she's been with you ever since?" I spoke softly, lost in thought as I tried to imagine just how old Yulia might be. She looked no older than I was on the surface, but there was no mistaking the ageless wisdom glinting in her gaze. "All this time and you've kept her away from him, I'm assuming?"

Dublin said nothing, though he didn't have to. I could already guess that part of the tale. *Yes.*

"And she's upset because you made her face him now," I suspected. But no, it was more than that. "You *forced* her to—"

"I had to." He didn't sound even remotely apologetic. Guilty, yes, but his eyes burned as determinedly as ever.

It was a harrowing reminder: He was more than willing to sacrifice even the trust of his few friends in order to get what he wanted. Which, in this case, seemed even more obscure than usual: the location of someone who might or might not be found there anyway.

"But she will forgive me," he said, sounding more than confident of that. "She's strong enough to face him, or I would never allow him in her orbit. I suspect her unpleasant reaction is merely her fear. He controlled her for so long, I wonder if she doubts that she can withstand him, even now?" He inclined his head, mulling over the prospect. "She's known all along that she would have to face him eventually. That he still holds some part of her soul she can never erase. Running from him could stave off the inevitable for only so long."

The wistful, deepening note in his voice warned me that he wasn't solely speaking of Yulia and Dmitri anymore.

"That's remarkably astute," I admitted. "For a man who is keeping the poor, innocent woman in his protection away from her only sister."

He flinched and dismissed the comparison with a shrug of his shoulder. His voice low, he countered, "Dmitri would never pose the risk of *killing* Yulia."

Fair enough. I swallowed hard, tearing my gaze away.

"Why go through all this trouble anyway?" I wondered, returning to our previous, safer, topic.

He sighed. "As Dmitri said, we needed information. A way to reverse—" He broke off, forming a fist with the hand he withdrew from me. "Just trust that my reasons are more than valid."

Rather than press the issue any further, I settled deeper into the leather cushions beneath me and watched the breathtaking scenery from the nearest window. "Where are we?"

Somewhere far more beautiful than the grim interior of a vampire lair, at least. Silvery clouds streaked with violet painted the edges of the navy sky. The sight reminded me of Dublin in a way: dark except for a few barely imperceptible dashes of color. Beautiful. Frightening. Navigable only with courage and ample skill.

"Somewhere safe," he replied, his back to me. "Somewhere safe…in the rural of France."

"Ah," I croaked, somehow not surprised. Apparently, Dublin had a knack for amassing reclusive properties—as well as for transporting an unconscious woman across the globe.

At a glance, this house appeared smaller than the last, yet the plain décor seemed cozier than even his lavish high-rises and manors.

"A tour?" I requested, extending my hand.

He took it, helping me to my feet. Whatever drug he had given me had little aftereffects, thankfully. I felt steady as I fell into step beside him.

The foyer was small, the walls inside reflecting the simplistic design of the sitting room. Hardwood and soft gray cast a neutral elegance. I was instantly endeared.

"Your room is at the top of the stairs," Dublin told me, nodding to a grand oak staircase straight ahead.

"And mine?" Dmitri wondered.

I jumped, turning to find him standing uncomfortably close behind me. His eyes sparkled, his lips quirking as he folded his arms over his chest.

"There's a shed out back," Dublin replied without missing a beat. He continued forward, leaving the foyer to show me the rest of the house.

There was a dining room, a modest kitchen, and a parlor-slash-library. Overall, it was a smaller dwelling, as suspected, but an air of security tainted the atmosphere, impossible to ignore. Something told me that Dublin had more of his shadowy agents already positioned at various stations. Watching.

And waiting.

Yet…

I couldn't name what else was lingering in the air, taunting me as I followed Dublin up the stairs next. An inexplicable unease deepened the shadows stretching across the hallway. For some reason, I found myself holding my breath as he approached a closed door and palmed the doorknob.

"You can sleep in here," he explained, pushing the door open.

Tension crept into my muscles, holding them rigid as I peered into the space beyond, wary of what I might find. Then…

I laughed, my eyes widened in shock. "Interesting color choice, Mr. Helos."

The furniture was white. The bed, the wardrobe, the curtains, the sheets. Even the fur rug spread over the hardwood floors was a pale, delicate shade.

For all their brooding seriousness, apparently some vampires still retained a sense of humor.

"I thought you hated the color?"

"On you," he admitted, but something in his gaze made me doubt that assertion. "I suppose it will do for décor."

I grinned wickedly. "I should redecorate Gray Manor in the color scheme. White lace everywhere."

He grimaced and I nearly clapped my hands in glee.

"Can you imagine?" I asked. "My room will resemble a biblical virgin's paradise. I shall order doilies and I'm sure I could find a cradle that—" I broke off, confused by the careless admission. Cancer had been a pathetic denial to cling to—I could admit that now—but the inverse of that claim terrified me far more. Even acknowledging it to myself was a struggle. God, I couldn't even look at Dublin.

"I'm sure that could be arranged." His finger slipped under my chin, lifting it despite my attempts. He frowned, brushing his thumb across my lower lip. "Though there are other rooms to choose from if this one doesn't satisfy you."

"No." Pushing past him, I approached the bed and ran my fingers over the delicate duvet. "This is perfect. Though"—I bit my lip—"it's just that this bed is so very large…"

"Oh?" His gaze was awaiting mine when I looked over, swallowing me whole, body and soul. "It might cause a bit of inconvenience on my part, but I think I can find a solution to that."

Heat sweltered in my blood. The hand I braced against the bed involuntarily clenched, seizing a fistful of soft fabric. At the same time, he reached for the door handle, shoving it back.

In retrospect, the bed wasn't all that big. His body had to curve around mine just to fit. Neither he nor I were prone to hugs. So the arm he allowed to fall across my hip was merely there by necessity. The cool fingers that brushed my belly were accidental.

The shiver that racked my body was entirely from his chill alone.

Nothing else.

Regardless, I slept, unplagued by nightmares, his taste on my tongue.

And I knew, even as I drifted off, that my mother's iron-grip on Gray Manor's interior would most definitely come to an end.

"Oh dear." Dmitri's narrowed eyes flickered along the length of my body as I descended the stairs the next morning. "This will simply not do. You are dressed all wrong."

"How so?" I fingered the hem of my skirt. It was a sensible cut, exquisitely detailed though relatively plain. "What's wrong with it?"

"Yes," Yulia pitched in from the doorway, addressing him for the first time. Cold, her gaze slithered over his face as dispassionately as Raphael's. "How so?"

Dmitri scoffed, but I didn't miss the step he took in my direction, widening the space between him and the person he was expressly forbidden from speaking to. There wasn't far for him to go, considering we were in the foyer, marshaled together, a motley crew of four.

"Do either of you understand adventuring attire?" He gestured to his lime-green slacks and his white button-down. On his head, of all things, perched a straw hat. Tutting in exasperation, he turned to the figure waiting for me at the base of the staircase. "Dublin, will you stand for this?"

The vampire in question seemed to be far beyond giving a damn about clothing. Distant eyes flickered between awareness and emptiness. He'd been that way ever since I'd woken up. Locked within himself, venturing from the depths of his psyche only for seconds at a time.

Why?

I wasn't brave enough to question it.

"It's fine," he muttered without looking my way. "Let's get moving before you bring the whole damn village down on us."

He left the drawing room. A second later, the front door slammed against what felt like the inner wall of the foyer.

"Well then." After smoothing his shirt, Dmitri followed him.

I fell into step in his wake, sensing Yulia behind me. Together, we packed into one car driven by Dublin, who said nothing during the terse hours-long trip through fields and forest.

The forested, beautiful landscape felt like a different realm from the city I was used to. Another world entirely. Breathtaking, yes. But also unsettling. Dread came to life in my stomach, twisting. Twinging. I had to flatten my palm beneath my rib cage to ease the discomfort.

Despite all the bargains and deals Dublin had made for my safety, I knew without a doubt that we were far from Raphael's territory. Could the old vampire's influence stretch this far? Something told me it didn't. Close-set foliage grazed the sides of the car as we drove through cramped roads, the sounds echoing almost like whispers.

No one can save you here…

"It will be a long trek," Dmitri promised as we crested the ridge of a hillside cut deep within a dense cluster of trees. "These crones hide themselves well among these hills. Though I'm sure you're prepared for any booby traps." He looked at Dublin, who didn't answer.

Eventually, the car came to a stop, seemingly in the middle of nowhere. As in Dublin didn't park, the engine just stalled, jarring me forward so violently that I had to brace myself against the front seat.

"Stay here." Dublin exited the vehicle, swiftly followed by Yulia and Dmitri.

Apparently, his command only applied to me.

With anxious glances at their surroundings, the trio continued up the road, led by Dublin. Only after two paces forward, they too abruptly stopped. Heart in my throat, I leaned forward and peered through the windshield to see why. At first, I saw nothing. Just swaying branches dripping with shadows and foliage. It was only on my second search that I saw her.

She stood, flanked by two sprawling trees, their gnarled branches twisted in her direction as if shielding her from sight. She was thin and fair. Hair so pale that it rivaled the hue of Dublin's skin fell down her shoulders in wild, unbrushed waves. Given the color, I expected her age to be reflected in her face, but she looked even younger than I was. Just a girl standing alone in the woods, confronted by two vampires.

Dublin said something. His posture was neutral, his stance open. From this angle, I could only see his lips moving, deaf to whatever words were passing between him and the woman.

But I didn't need to hear to notice the marked shift in tone when she shook her head and pointed to the car. To me.

Shivers racked my spine. The scrape of branches against the car's roof became more pronounced. Less like whispers and more like distinct words. *You...*

You. You. You.

The wind picked up, tossing scattered raindrops across the windshield. What little daylight there was dissipated, leaving an eerie glow that drenched the landscape in indigo darkness. Only Dublin had any definition anymore, his hair shining like burnished gold.

All the while, the woman beyond the trees just stared, her finger still pointing.

And that whispering within my skull grew louder, transformed into a faint, childlike murmur. *You. You. You must come alone…*

My hand was on the handle of the door. Before I realized, I'd pushed it open. Wind and rain lashed at my skin, trying in vain to slow my progress. My flats sank into the damp earth as I stepped out onto the path. It was freezing. The thin fabric of my blouse felt glued to my skin in seconds, sliced through by a bone-numbing chill.

The noise caused by the burgeoning storm should have been deafening: swaying trees, echoing thunder. But all I heard was silence broken by a low, distant hum. Thump… thump…thump…

And a woman's voice. "Only she can go any farther."

She stood on an incline and in reality barely came to Dublin's waist in height. Her hair hung down to her waist, mingling with the pale fabric of her thin shift. Grubby, bare toes melded with the earth and underbrush. Her delicate, small features formed no expression as her eyes cut in my direction.

"Just her," she repeated, her thin voice easily overpowering the growled hiss of the man before her. "Only she can come any farther."

"Then we're done here." Dublin's voice slammed into the eerie stillness like a wrecking ball. Anger flashed through his gaze as he snatched for my wrist, pulling me after him.

Hauled to the car, I found myself shoved into the back seat and immediately flanked by Yulia and Dmitri. The door slammed and Dublin appeared behind the wheel a heartbeat later. When he wrenched the car into reverse, it roared to life amid the squeal of skidding tires, jolting down the hillside. I looked back, and through the screen of green and swaying branches, I still saw the woman standing unmoving. Just watching.

Waiting.

You will come alone. The whispered promise haunted me, even as the dense forest gave way to lush, open fields and a gray sky. *Or she will come to you.*

~

The moment we returned to the cottage, Dublin pressed a cell phone against his ear and snarled commands into the receiver. From the general gist, I sensed a narrative along the lines of: *get the goddamn plane ready,* and *leaving as soon as we can.*

"Well, that was disappointing," Dmitri remarked on a sigh. He forlornly removed his straw hat, but even he seemed unusually on edge. "But I agree that a retreat is in our best interests. One never meets alone with witches, or so the saying goes." He cleared his throat, glancing in Yulia's direction. Then he promptly turned away. "Well, Dublin, I shall assist you in making the arrangements. As always, I do believe my jet will suffice perfectly..."

He simpered after Dublin.

"Eleanor," Yulia called to me with a strained smile. "In the meantime, we can catch up."

"Sure." I nodded, lowering my voice as she came to my side. "And then *you* can tell me what's really going on."

She faltered and shot a nervous glance at Dublin. Thankfully, he was too busy issuing rapid-fire commands like a general to notice my attempts at subterfuge.

"As you wish. Come."

I was hot on her heels as she entered the drawing room.

"Sit," she called before disappearing through a doorway that I assumed led into the kitchen.

I sat, wringing my fingers. When she finally returned, she had a tray containing steaming tea in two cups.

"It's a long story," she warned as she settled onto a chair across from me. Her gaze cut to the doorway and she shuffled closer as Dublin's shouting reached glass-shattering decibels.

"I think we have the time," I said.

She nodded. "I do believe you're right. Though perhaps I should apologize? I haven't been the best company as of late."

"I understand," I admitted.

"Do you?" She laughed softly, shaking her head. "Even I don't. It is strange how you can convince yourself for years that you can overcome any obstacle. But the second something unexpected arises…" She snapped her fingers. "You crumble."

"You don't have to talk about this," I said.

"In a way it ties to your own dilemma," she said, tilting her head thoughtfully. "They claim that there once was a witch who fell in love with a vampire, though he loved another. Even so, she was foolish enough, selfish enough, to give him whatever he wished…"

"And what was that?" I croaked, sensing her pause was my cue to ask.

Her gaze turned wistful, "A child with his lover. A *natural* child. It sounds pretty melodramatic," she admitted. "But love and devotion can be poisonous to your senses. While *that* witch perverted nature in her lust, I know of another who tried to kill one of the most powerful vampires in history by enchanting one of his tailored suits. Merely because her master commanded her to…"

Something in her pained tone made me suspect this other witch wasn't some distant figure from her memory.

"You?" I whispered, hazarding a guess.

She nodded and averted her eyes to her teacup.

Which meant that the powerful vampire she tried to kill could only be…

"Dublin?" I asked out loud.

Her lips twisted into a tormented grimace. "Dublin. Looking back, I realize now that he—Dmitri—" She hunched over as if saying his name physically hurt her. "I know now that he was just trying to test me. He'd grown bored of me then, I think. Whether I succeeded or not didn't matter to him. Just the fact that he could manipulate me into trying… I knew it was suicide, but Dublin…" She trailed off, her lips thoughtfully pursed. "Dublin didn't kill me. I can only assume that he knew taking me from Dmitri's control would punish him more. Be careful with him—" She reached out, grasping my hand in hers. "He may seem silly and harmless, but some fear him more than Raphael, or even Dublin. He likes to collect rare, talented creatures you see. Beautiful humans. Talented witches…" Her eyes roved down to where the table obscured the view of my stomach. "Anything or anyone gifted and unique. Don't trust him. Alas, the past is in the past, isn't it?"

She sighed and sipped from her tea. "Back to the topic at hand, the former witch's name was Adara. She was rumored to be remarkably gifted. I never knew her, but we all heard of the twisted magic she worked in the service of Mero. When he took a human bride, she corrupted the very gift he despised to sow a new life: a mortal life."

She stared off, her voice soft in awe. "But in return, she forever denied herself the possibility of death, as did Mero. Damned for eternity, they will never die, and trust me when I tell you that is not a fate anyone would desire. Even Raphael, as far gone in madness as he is, would shy away from such a bargain. The years change you with every passing decade. You become further adrift in a sea of numbness, losing contact with anything that may ground you."

She stirred her tea rapidly, shaking her head. "Such is the price for daring to pervert nature beyond its bounds." Her eyes met mine again, brimming with sadness. "But it is a price some men may pay, even in a reckless impulse, to save another."

While taking a sip of my tea, I nearly choked. Dublin didn't exactly tout the effects of vampirism, but to never die? And to think, the most reckless thing I'd ever done was sell my soul out of spite.

"And?" My throat felt painfully dry. I woodenly sipped more tea, but that only worsened the discomfort, not all of it physical. Shadows lingered on the horizon. An unshakeable chill prickled the back of my neck, patiently insistent. *Don't be so daft, Ellie. You know what she's hinting at. What he's done.*

"It's not that complicated, really." Yulia lowered her gaze to her tea, continuing to stir it. "Dublin wants to find her because he—"

"Tomorrow." Dublin himself appeared at the doorway and shot Yulia a pointed look, thus ending the impromptu teatime. "We'll leave then." This clearly wasn't his ideal choice; he wanted to go now.

Quest for answers aside, I couldn't shake the tense, suffocating pressure building on the air. Like a noose, it cinched my throat, tightening with every inch the remaining daylight retreated beneath the horizon.

While Dublin disappeared again, I retreated to my room and attempted to sleep. Attempted being the keyword. A storm crept in the moment I crawled beneath the sheets. Lightning flashed, illuminating the windows and casting the shadowed furniture into stark relief.

In a way, the chaos felt comforting. I couldn't hear the whispers. Nothing but nature raging…

Dmitri's private, climate-controlled jet felt ten times smaller with Dublin *and* Yulia on board. When we finally landed, I gulped at the fresh air, as relieved as the sole survivor of a grueling war. One fought with verbal jabs and biting sarcasm.

At the tarmac, Yulia went her own way in silence. Not long after, Dmitri retreated as well, slipping into a golden limo conveniently waiting nearby.

Dublin had also come prepared. Parked not far from the plane was a car I recognized as his. He drove silently, and we re-entered the city just as the midafternoon sun reached its peak. Of all places, we passed the park near the cathedral and I couldn't resist.

"Could we take a walk? For a second?" I couldn't suppress the longing in my voice. A walk. In peace. Among the sunlight and fresh air, devoid of shadow and secrets.

Dublin's grip tightened over the steering wheel.

So I pulled out all stops and resorted to one weapon I sensed even the devil was susceptible to—shameless begging. "Please?"

Sighing, he relented and pulled over to the side of the road. "Five minutes."

As we exited the car for the cultivated landscape of the park, I tilted my face into the sun, practically skipping beside him. For five glorious minutes, none of the danger surrounding us mattered. Just this. His presence. The easy silence between us, my hand in his.

I could pretend—for the briefest moment—that I was as carefree as I imagined Georgie used to be. Cherished, and wanted, and reckless in her happiness.

That was the terrifying, unnatural part of it all—I *wanted* happiness.

"The tumor," I began, eyeing a glorious array of flowers dotting the field around us. "If it can't be removed, then… We need to agree upon some course of action."

Dublin stiffened, his jaw clenched as if to bite back a phrase I could guess as clearly as my own thoughts—*Not this again. Please. I thought you were making progress.*

But he didn't mention as much out loud.

Not even as I came to a stop and hesitantly placed my hand against my belly. I felt nothing. Just flesh, and warmth, and skin. I closed my eyes, attempting to acknowledge some deep-down impulse for the first time.

I didn't feel any magical maternal impulse, strong enough to erase days of dread and terror.

But I no longer felt that terror as strongly as before.

"If it was a girl, would that bother you?" I slowly peeled my eyes open to gauge his reaction.

He cocked his chin, his gaze shielded behind an impenetrable stare. "Yes," he grated. "Yes, it would." Gradually, his mouth twitched, lifting at the corner. Softly. Higher. A genuine smile, though cautious in width. "Another Eleanor Gray? The world is not ready for such a creature."

"A boy would just conspire with you," I pointed out smugly. "But a girl? She and I can plot all sorts of mischief and you will be none the wiser."

"As long as it's healthy… As long as *you* are healthy, I would take any specimen imaginable." He looked so tired again. An ageless man, approaching my side, his hand outstretched for me.

I curled my fingers around his, marveling at the sensation of him. No fighting. No hating.

Tilting my head back, I eyed the sky, allowing him to steer me along in peaceful, beautiful silence.

But how reality loved to deny me. Within minutes, our haven was invaded and nothing could reclaim those cherished minutes.

"Eleanor." Dublin tensed, yanking me against him.

I looked around, expecting assassins to lunge from the trees. Instead, I noticed a young girl dancing across the expansive lawn paces away.

Dressed in a flowing white frock, she was prancing with more energy than I ever could, darting around flower beds. Her features were delicate, her dark curls spilling down her shoulders. But her eyes…

They fixated on me as she approached and I shivered. A deep brown, they were as ageless as Raphael's.

"I hear you've been looking for me," she accused, wrinkling her nose at Dublin. Just beyond his reach, she stopped, her hands on her hips. A small strip of blue velvet encircled her throat, supporting a small silver charm that swayed against her pale skin. "Why? Do you think you can kill me, Cael? Torture me until I surrender to your bidding?" She giggled into a hand tipped with hot-pink fingernails. "Have you not learned your lesson after all these years? Maybe you will during the many more you have left to your debt? He's been gloating, you do realize. He will never cease to own you."

"Adara," Dublin said tonelessly. Her name? Clearly, there was no love lost between them. He eyed her coldly, his eyes narrowed in disgust. "A rather unimaginative disguise, I must say."

"You should try it sometime," the girl countered, sticking out her tongue. She fingered the neckline of her dress. The white material formed a tight-fitting bodice that flared out over her waist—though at second glance it was *mostly* white. Three small scarlet drops stained the very center of the bodice. "Young ones are surprisingly nimble. I may keep this form for good—"

"Why show yourself now?" Dublin demanded. "I do admit your stunt in France was impressive."

She giggled. "Those old biddies do love to give a good scare. And I've always loved a good game of hide-and-seek. Don't you?" She twirled in a circle, eyeing the skirt of her dress as it billowed around her. "And you *play* with ruthless intent. So much so that you miss the most obvious moves your opponent may make." Skidding to a stop, she met my gaze and winked. "So wonderful to meet you again, Eleanor. Oh, do you not recognize me?" She raised her arms, indicating her dress. "I do appreciate your very generous *donation* my dear girl." Her voice deepened well beyond the range of a child's. Into a man's, one brimming with suave charm and undeniably familiar…

I recoiled in horror, just as my gaze fell over the small splash of color on her chest once more. The three splotches uncomfortably resembled three droplets of blood. Like the ones I'd bled during my "meeting" with Gabriel Lanic.

"I so do love this as a fashion statement," Adara chirped, sounding young once again.

In the flickering daylight, the nuances of her "dress" stood out to me more clearly. A slight design distorted the surface —one eerily similar to what might adorn the tablecloth of an exclusive restaurant.

"So, before you act upon that devious thought lurking in your brain, Cael, remember that *I already have her blood*." Her voice transformed again, expanding into the warning hiss of a grown woman. "I could kill her, as the young ones say, six ways from Sunday." She licked her finger and lowered it to the reddish stains.

Darkness. Suddenly, I was lying on my back, blinking up at the sky.

"Eleanor!" Someone was holding me in his arms, cradling my head above the ground. "What did you do to her?"

"She's fine," Adara insisted. "That was merely a warning. Do play nice with me. I don't want to hurt her—"

"So, what do you want?" Dublin demanded. "I'm sure that's the only reason you've chosen to show yourself now."

"What do I want?"

I looked over and found her stroking her chin, her gaze thoughtful.

"Maybe I want to see your face when I finally convey the bitter, cold truth I think you've known all along."

"Your curse," Dublin said coldly. "So tell me, what exactly did it entail?"

"What?" Adara shrugged her tiny shoulders. "You forget that this was never meant to be a punishment. At least not at first..." She smiled, teeth bared ferally. "It was a gift. Everything he wanted—life from death. There was a price to pay, of course. I'm sure you've already figured it out by now."

Dublin said nothing, his expression drawn tight.

"Oh, you *have*," Adara deduced. She cackled with glee, clapping her hands. "That's the whole bit of irony, I suppose —just as Mero intended. You see, the only way the curse would have ever triggered in the first place was if you tried to do something naughty, Dublin. Something, you swore you would never ever do."

My mind spun with her words. Something in her mischievous tone made me recall something Dmitri said the day he barged into the manor in Italy. *For all your loathing of the act, you must have feared for her life, I suspect. I'd heard Raphael tried feeding from her. That could... But that wouldn't explain why she didn't die. No. Though if you did try to turn her...*

"You tried to turn her," Adara said. She lifted her skirt and twirled in a circle while Dublin watched on, as frozen as ever. "I've heard the rumors: Raphael bit her, didn't he? I'm sure the bastard knew about the agreement you forged with Mero. He would stay in the shadows, averting a nasty war with Raphael. As long as you...what? Go on, say it."

When Dublin remained silent, she sighed.

"As long as you stayed away from the Gray bloodline. Why? Perhaps he owed it to his loyal servant, James? Or perhaps he knew all along." She giggled mischievously. "He knew that one day, you wouldn't be able to. That you who so cherished your restraint wouldn't be able to hide behind that silly necklace any longer. You defiled the charming Eleanor Gray—but in doing so, you triggered the so-called curse. A fate that Mero had always intended for himself. That kind of magic requires a price, you see. A blood price. His blood, or in this case yours. As the new life grows, that price must continue to be paid, or both will die."

"Blood," I croaked, the only word I seemed capable of saying at first. My mind grappled with the insanity of her words, piecing the morbid puzzle together. "That's why I could drink…"

"Yes," Adara said, as though it was as trivial a matter as a buzzing fly. "You need blood, but only to sustain the life growing within you—but that is not the true price paid."

"Keep talking in riddles, and I'll reconsider this conversation," Dublin warned.

Adara giggled, but I didn't miss the slight step backward she took. "Careful, darling. I truly won't hesitate to kill her." She fingered the front of her dress again, inching toward the reddish stains. "Alas, the true price is that…well, you've lost. You've forfeited her already, and you did it—here's the funny part—to *save* her. Funneling all that time to Raphael. And the cruel bastard gave up just enough to drive that point home, didn't he? Ten years, was it?" She eyed me, her lips bared in a hellish grin. "Ten years to spend with her. Ten years with your delicate, mortal child. Ten years before Raphael gets to yank your leash and call you to heel. Have you told her? No, you haven't. Because I doubt even you can admit it to yourself."

She stepped forward, her hands folded sweetly before her. "Your precious Dublin tried to circumvent nature when he attempted to turn you. In return, he gave up his mortality, and he doomed you to a life that he will—at best—enjoy ten years of before you age and wither and die. Your beautiful little daughter will only know him as a shadow flickering along the edges of her life before it fades entirely. Raphael may allow you to see her every now and again, but only so that he can use her to milk you for more, and more, and more, and more. So why have you sought me out? To save you? I cannot do that."

"Then we're done here." Dublin grabbed my wrist and pulled me to my feet. Using his body as a shield, he tried his best to shelter me from view.

"No!" Adara admonished, wagging a small finger as she sidestepped his attempts. "I'm not ready to let you go running away just yet, either…" Her grin turned feral. "As a courtesy for my visit, I would like to request a reward."

"What the hell do you want?"

"Eleanor, of course. Now you have to let me play with her!" She lunged forward, snatching my wrist, and took off, pulling me beyond his reach.

The fact that he even released me at all betrayed just how seriously he took her threat. *I don't want to hurt her.*

"Come on, silly girl!" She cackled maniacally, tugging me along. "Keep up!" Halfway across the park, she released me and collapsed, giggling into a heap. From the rumpled cloud of her dress, she eyed me and sighed. "You poor, pathetic little fool. If you at least showed some intelligence, I might be tempted to pity you."

I tensed, somehow knowing not to let the insult slip unchallenged. She reminded me of a cat in a sense, testing with claws drawn, every bit as mercurial as Tinkles. "How am I a fool?"

She fingered her necklace, twisting the tiny charm between her thumb and her forefinger. "Because you cower, and whimper, and *whine*," she spat. "You don't *play* the game. Like a good little pawn, you huddle in silence and let Dublin growl over you like some kind of a wild beast. It's disgusting!" She raised her arms in exasperation and kicked her legs into the air. "The worst part? You know he doesn't truly want you. It's the curse, you see. It's *Mero* who truly owns him. Everything he's done for you has been a mere delusion."

I swallowed. "You're wrong."

Or she was right and it was the truth…

"You don't even sound convincing!" She threw her head back and cackled. "Oh, the look on your face. You know it too, don't you? The little lie you let yourself believe."

That I could have a future. Happiness. Dublin.

A life beyond the grim existence that I spent years telling myself awaited me.

"I should just kill you now," Adara remarked, her tone flat. Bored. "With his life sold to Raphael, ten years of forced, dutiful contact with dear 'Dublin' would be pitiful to endure, even for me—"

"No." I shook my head, gritting my teeth. Those horrible voices lingered, whispering and taunting. This time, I *made* myself banish them for good the only way I could: by countering them out loud. "No! You know what? I'm done! I'm tired of denying myself. Why *shouldn't* I demand my happiness?"

I glared at the sky as if expecting an answer. "Why shouldn't I want to believe that Dublin Helos could want me? He's handsome. He's more beautiful than anyone I could ever dream of. Why can't I want him?" I started to pace as rage built within me. I wasn't just arguing with the voices in my head anymore—but my mother. My family. Old friends. Society. My sister. "Why can't I dream, for once, of a future with someone who loves me? That I deserve that future? No, you are wrong. I do deserve it. I want it, and I'm tired of everyone acting like I can't have it. Who cares if Dublin even wants me or not? I want him!" And I slammed my foot to prove it, as if twenty-six years of suppressed temper tantrums chose that second to explode from me at once. "So sorry, Miss…" My mind buzzed, so incensed that I couldn't remember her name until a heartbeat later. "Call me whatever you want. I refuse to continue to believe that I am worthless anymore."

Adara eyed me with no expression. Then she sighed. "Men." She rolled her eyes, even as her voice betrayed a wistful, almost pained note. "Sometimes they forget that *they* are the true pawns. I mock you when I am the one who loved a man so much that I stained my soul black for him, even though he loved another. And where am I now?" She shrugged. "And where is he…"

Slowly, she stood, dusting off her dress. "You should go back," she said, nodding to the vampire waiting in the distance. "Tell him that I cannot help you. He knows what must be done."

"What?" I croaked. Even though I didn't know Dublin's true reason for seeking her out, a deep-seated impulse made me press for whatever answers I could. "What must be done?"

"He must face his punishment like a good boy and own up to the pain he's caused. He can no longer run from it. He knows as much. I think our dear Cael is merely afraid of what he will learn: the truth." She eyed me with a sigh, and for once, she looked more childlike than anything. Helpless. "No matter how hard he fights, you are destined to die eventually. Such a fate is both his redemption and his doom. Goodbye, Eleanor Gray."

She turned and skipped toward the trees, vanishing beneath them.

And I watched her go, frozen in place until Dublin lifted me in his arms. He hurried to the car, and in his haste, the world blurred, reduced to a smattering of color and shadow.

When viewed in the grim, overcast daylight, Gray Manor felt less like my old childhood home and more like a diving board extended above an unknown depth. Every inch we traversed would merely hasten the inevitable fall.

Yet a part of me knew deep down in my soul that we were bound to it. Even as the danger of the Grayne, and Mero, and Raphael, and only God knew who else loomed overhead…

Somehow, Gray Manor seemed destined to be where it all would end.

Dublin's expression all but cemented that. He silently parked the car, his eyes a tormented silver—but above all, *resigned.* Whatever the witch had told him had sowed an air of surrender so alarming that I squirmed in the face of it.

It was the same expression he had been wearing the day before he'd vanished all those weeks ago.

Hopeless, vengeful, and cold.

Adara's words resonated in my mind, a foreboding declaration. *"He doomed you to a life that he will—at best—enjoy ten years of before you age and wither and die."*

His heavy sigh drew my attention, but he merely exited the car without saying a word. I remained seated as he crossed to my end of the car, but his hand extended before me was my only command to obey him.

I did, entering that drafty, unwelcoming home in his wake. I knew that its dull, dreary walls would never feel the same again.

The old Eleanor would have succumbed to the silence, allowing him to brood, and plot, and drift further from me by the second.

But I couldn't.

"Talk to me," I demanded as he started across the vacant foyer. "Please. Tell me."

"What?" He turned and I sucked in a startled breath. Shadows enhanced the contours of his face, making him appear hollow.

He was before me in an instant, cupping my cheek in his palm. His mouth lacked its usual frown. All things considered, he looked more neutral than upset, but I could sense the tension lurking in his muscles. The dread.

Adara's words had cemented something in him, making his posture rigid with resolve.

I could have danced around the topic, changing the subject to something trivial. Instead, I steeled myself against the discomfort and forced myself to meet it head-on.

"How much time did you barter for me? In exchange for Raphael's protection?"

His narrowed eyes scanned my face with ruthless intent. "I'm not sure you truly want to know the answer to that."

"Please," I whispered. Though he was right.

"How much?" He stepped up to me, lowering his mouth against my ear. "Enough." His hand twitched, hovering between us. Uncharacteristic hesitation kept the fingers suspended until, finally, they settled over my belly, remaining in spite of how I flinched. "Enough to ensure that neither Raphael or Mero—or anyone—will ever harm you."

"Why?"

"What else was I supposed to do?" His lips grazed my jaw in an almost apologetic caress. "I tried to protect you on my own. I failed. Should I just sit back and let him…"

"What if *I* sold myself to Raphael?" I countered thickly. "How would you feel?"

He laughed as if too stunned by the idea to take it seriously. Then his eyes narrowed into slits and I had enough sense to shudder. "I would kill you with my bare hands. Nothing would be worth anything he could offer. *Nothing.*"

Letting me go, he started across the foyer.

But I chased after him. "There is something you're not telling me—"

"If I had turned you, would you have hated me?" He waited until I'd reached him and then flicked the curls back from my face, his expression unreadable. Regardless, I sensed he required an answer. The truth. "Would you have despised the creature you would have become? Something your sister had been conditioned to despise?"

"I..." Didn't know. Mainly because that girl felt like a stranger now, someone I barely even understood. Fearful, doubtful, so determined to deny herself happiness that she'd preferred to await death instead. It had been easier that way; I could admit it now. No hope. No fear of the unknown.

No joy of what might come.

"That day after Raphael..." He began. "I knew the second your eyes reopened, still bright with mortality, that something had changed. That, in my impulse, I'd broken some boundary that could never be repaired."

And I sensed he wasn't speaking of me any longer.

He brushed his lips across my forehead, lingering as if to impart his next confession into my very soul. "Your sister knew. She wouldn't even let me do the one thing that I thought might save your life unless I agreed to leave you in exchange."

I flinched, recalling the strange tension that had grown between Georgie and me.

"I tried to find Adara," Dublin continued. "If I had, I could have demanded she fix it. I knew Mero was waiting for me —that he would use any pawn he could to lure me to him. Every waking second, I could hear him hissing in my ear. Reminding me of his goddamn curse. And when I returned, I knew, even as all logic warned me to deny it. He was right.

"How much one could crave what life could offer, beyond this tormented existence. In a way, perhaps I'd always consoled myself with the belief that ultimately…I could always end it. What did I have left to cherish?" He gripped me tighter, pulling me against him.

I remained still, letting him hold me.

"Perhaps I would have surrendered it anyway," he murmured. "Had I known. The ability to die. To follow you…" He pulled back, turning across the foyer. "Get some sleep. I'll make you something to eat. Should I prepare the baklava?"

"Yes," I whispered hoarsely, letting him retreat alone.

Something told me that now was not the time to argue. He needed silence.

And I needed to allow him that reprieve no matter how my heart twisted in agony.

Obediently, I went to my room and crawled beneath my blankets, but sleep wouldn't come. Doubt, that terrible thing, crept into my thoughts, but it felt different than before. Less disembodied and formless.

More desperate: a warning plea that dragged me into the hall and through the rest of the house.

Move…move. Move!

"Dublin?" I called for him to no response as I crept down the staircase in nothing more than a thin nightgown. "Dublin?"

I kept going, exiting the servant's wing on bare feet. My breath escaped me in pants as I raced down the walkway in the moonlight, driven faster. Faster. Eventually, I sprinted more than walked. Then ran. The wind nipped at my hair, turning it into a cape that fanned my shoulders as I wound up breathless before a structure that had never seemed more imposing.

My hand shook as I pushed the door open. Something wouldn't let me turn around. It was as if a hook had caught the center of my rib cage, tugging me forward ruthlessly.

A slave to the impulse, I descended the steps, passing the angel. I shivered, venturing deeper. Deeper still.

Then farther within the mausoleum than I'd ever been, in a section so distant that even Georgie and I had never explored it. Near the final chamber, barely concealed behind another hunched angelic statue lurked a doorway.

I hadn't known it even existed: a wide chamber containing a single stone sarcophagus, cut into the heart of the crypt itself.

A man was lounging outstretched on the stone lid. He glowed as if bathed in moonlight—though I couldn't make out any windows or entrances. Nonetheless, I had no trouble seeing him in excruciating detail.

Rich, dark skin set him apart from the colorless backdrop. Closely cropped black hair enhanced his stern features, no less beautiful than Dublin or Raphael's. In contrast to their formal dress, he was wearing a plain gray shirt and jeans that seemed insulting in comparison to the regal tilt to his chin.

I knew his name instantly, even without an introduction. *Mero.*

"And now," he declared in a voice that reverberated like thunder, "we may begin. Did you really think I'd let you confront me without allowing dear Eleanor to hear the truth as well?"

He was speaking to someone I didn't realize was standing nearby until I turned, spotting him there. Dublin. Confusion mingled with the fear goading my pulse into a surging rhythm. François had claimed the crypt was protected—a vampire could only enter invited.

Though Mero supposedly had invested in the Grays since our humble beginnings. In a sense, this land belonged to him over anyone else.

And he had presented Dublin with an invitation he couldn't refuse.

"And here I am," my Devil said, his arms outstretched. "You lured her here, and why? So that she can see how callously you toy with her family? Go on and reveal your final pawn."

"My pawn? I made it no secret that I held her." The man grinned in a stunning display of white teeth and stood. Gracile movements propelled him upright with the elegance of a dancer. "You merely chose to run and hide rather than face me, Cael. But alas, here you finally are. So, as you wish..." He brushed his hand across the lid of the sarcophagus behind him. The simple gesture seemed incapable of the strength required to knock the stone slab aside in a cloud of dust.

I stiffened in anticipation of a body—and there was one.

A woman lay slumped in the pit of the coffin, visible even from where I was standing. Tangled blond hair shielded her face, but her softly rising chest and the pink hue of her skin revealed that she was alive.

"Georgie?" I cried out, rushing to her. Cold, hard stone scraped my knees as I crouched and plunged my arm into the cavernous space in search of her hand. "Georgie?"

Her eyes were closed, her body unmoving. But her clothing... I swallowed hard, racked by confusion. The faint illumination in the chamber was just enough for me to make out her pink shirt and jeans. It was the same outfit she'd worn the day I screamed at her to leave.

"She is alive," Mero explained. "Despite her slumber, she'll suffer no lasting damage."

"Her letter," I croaked, stroking the hair from her face. I didn't even care that I was speaking to a creature even Dublin seemed to fear. Facing him, I demanded, "She tried to contact me. How?"

He smiled. Unlike with Raphael, emotion shaped his handsome features, giving them life. Definition. And in a way, the subtle nuances in his expression only served to enhance his imposing nature. "I woke her when it suited my needs," he said softly. "But you can rest assured that little she did was under her own will."

Including the bounty on my head? I tried to ask, but Dublin's voice sliced over mine, harsh and biting.

"And now what?" he demanded. "You want me to kill her? Slice her throat in front of her sister to prove once and for all what a damned, selfish creature I am? I know how your mind works."

"Is *that* why you have waited this long to face me?" Mero laughed as he turned to him. "I won't harm the girl. She knows nothing to be a danger to you, regardless. *Nor* will I harm your Eleanor. Why would I?" He raised a hand and slowly curled the fingers into a fist as if trapping my soul within them. "Killing her now would be a mercy to you."

"Don't touch her." Dublin lurched onto the tips of his toes, his teeth bared as Mero shifted his attention to me. But he didn't come closer, not even as the other vampire's hand settled over my scalp in dangerous reassurance.

"No. You would rage and attack me of course—but in the end, you would thank me. I would save you from it, this pain…" He stroked me once and withdrew his hand, placing the outstretched fingers over his heart. "This knowledge that there could have been so much more. No, Cael. I am afraid that what you truly fear will come to pass. I suspect you've already inferred as much."

He inclined his head, but Dublin said nothing.

Silence filled the chamber, unbearable in its all-encompassing weight.

"She *will* die," Mero finally declared. "As will your mortal child. But they will live before that day will come. Live and wither before your eyes to the point that even your blood will cease to have an effect. You can never turn them. Never chase them beyond the void." His voice softened, a lethal hiss as his gaze returned to his old friend's. "You will know what true love, and joy, and peace are, and then you will watch it slip away through your fingers, swallowed by time. And like me, you will not have the mercy or option of death. You know that now, don't you?"

Slowly, he advanced on Dublin's position, but his posture wasn't triumphant or mocking. Everything from the set of his shoulders to the tilt of his jaw conveyed only one emotion above all others.

Pity.

"In the end, you will come to know what true despair is, Cael," he murmured. "True madness. She will never be more beautiful to you than her next breath. You will grow to love her more by the second until you swear your soul can no longer contain it. And you will grow to hate her." He extended his fingers toward me in a fatherly gesture. "For her innocence. Her freedom. Her fragility. I pity you, my friend. Adara's magic turned out to be far crueler than I could have ever imagined."

He drifted toward the doorway and then looked back at me from the threshold, his eyes brimming with unshed tears. "She wasn't supposed to love you in return. That I did not foresee. And now that you have sold yourself to Raphael for more time than she could ever outlive, you will truly suffer."

He slipped from the room, but Dublin didn't follow.

And as if carried on an unseen wind, Mero's voice drifted back to us regardless.

"Know that I will be watching, old friend. Waiting. I will even leave the other Gray girl, for now… But I will return, merely to witness the moment you truly understand. There is no end to this life awaiting us. No end to the pain." A heavy sigh trailed the words as his voice softened, barely a whisper. "This beautiful, innocent creature you cherish will one day be an agonizing memory. And then we shall see in just how many ways I can extend your suffering…"

As if a spell had been broken, Dublin finally lurched into action. He raced through the doorway, a blur of motion. "Stay here," he hissed back to me.

I couldn't move even if I had the strength to.

My hand remained entwined with Georgie's, gripping her fingers though hers remained limp in response.

Despair, that bitter poison, lurked on the edges of my psyche, desperate to invade the second I allowed it to.

But I couldn't. Because if I surrendered to it now, even for a second, I would never rise from its depths again.

Eventually, footsteps approached, clattering over the stone.

"All is well, I hope?" a man called out. His voice sounded distorted, as if he spoke from outside of the structure, though I recognized his dry tone regardless. Dmitri. "If it really is how you say for the other one… My, my, he must have used quite the powerful drug on her delicate soul. Curing it could take some time—"

"It's all right, Eleanor," Dublin warned.

I hadn't even realized I was on my feet, hissing through my teeth as he approached the coffin.

"I can help her," Dublin insisted. But his eyes were averted away from me, his voice cold. In silence, he retreated and the sight of his back lingered even after my vision blurred with tears.

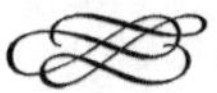

"You sold your soul to Raphael for more time than she could ever outlive."

Mero's return could have been a cruel nightmare, easily banished as I awoke in my bed to brilliant sunlight. The old Eleanor would have certainly taken that lifeline—ignorance.

Denial.

She would have pushed the terror to the back of her mind and merrily embraced her terminal cancer.

But I couldn't. Ten years had never seemed so daunting a timespan. Or so little.

And if Raphael's power could extend over Dublin the way his power had controlled Yulia, I didn't have to try hard to imagine what awaited us both as soon as my pathetic hold on his soul came to an end.

Moving as stiffly as an old woman, I stood, cradling my belly with the flat of my hand. Tears burned behind my eyes, but I refused to let them fall. Instead, I wandered the manor in a daze, finding no one in the upstairs hall.

Though I'd sensed his presence in my room throughout the night, it was as though Dublin were intentionally avoiding me now. My sole company was Dmitri, who was lurking within the main drawing room, reading a book as I wandered past.

"Morning," he groused, biting his lower lip. "Before you panic, your Dublin is nearby. In fact, he politely informed me that my services are no longer needed." He did his best to parrot Dublin's raspy baritone, but even then, his voice wasn't anywhere near deep enough. "Alas, I am waiting for my jet to be refueled…" He trailed off and looked up from his book, eyeing my face with a raised eyebrow. "What is it, my dear?"

"I need a favor." I crossed my arms, too exhausted to put effort to even attempt to intimidate him. So I improvised. "Deny me and I'll tell Dublin you tried to touch me in my sleep."

"Oh?" He set his book aside, his head cocked. "However can I help you?"

"Don't pretend like you don't already have a price in mind. Name it."

He smirked. "You misunderstand me, my dear. I know when exactly my services will be repaid. Everything I've done hasn't been for *you*." He eyed my stomach and reached out, boldly brushing his fingers against my abdomen. Even as I jerked beyond his reach, he kept his hand extended, chuckling. "It's been for *her*. My, what an interesting creature she will be. I would think of myself as her godfather of sorts. I am sure she will repay me more than enough for all of my exertions."

"What makes you think I wouldn't kill you before you could ever touch her?" Both hands shielded my stomach now.

His smile widened further. "Of course, my dear. I have no doubt that you could… Now, what did you want?"

"I need a distraction," I said hoarsely, choosing to overlook his assertion for now. "A very big distraction."

"Ah. You wish to lure the wolf from his lamb." His eyes narrowed, skeptical. "Ah, knowing his current mood, I suspect you plan to deceive him for good reason?"

"Can you do it or not?"

He frowned, betraying genuine unease for once. "There are antics I could perform that would draw him away from you. In fact, they all tend to carry an uncomfortably high risk of my death." He brushed his fingers along his throat.

And I bared mine in response, a dare in my tone. "Well, I suppose that's the risk you'll have to take, isn't it?"

"My my." A slow smile unfurled over his lips and he clapped his hands. "Oh, I do love this side of you! All right, you've convinced me. I can buy you an hour." He stood and approached the foyer. "But I will warn you that you should act quickly. And." He grinned and nodded to his discarded book. "I've already taken the liberty of mapping out your destination should you require it. Call it a hunch."

He wandered out of reach before I could demand an answer.

Not that I needed one.

This all felt like some twisted, unending game in which everyone *but* me had a clear view of the gameboard.

The only way to win was to give in to the one impulse that had never steered me wrong—stubborn childishness.

If I couldn't play on their terms, I would merely have to upend the entire damn table in defiance of it all.

~

I was in my room when I finally heard it: a door slamming below, betraying a figure racing through the manor so quickly that I barely scrambled down the stairs in time to catch him.

"Yulia," he muttered before taking off, an apology lurking in his gaze. "I'll be back as soon as I can."

I watched him go; then I spun on my heel and tore across the manor. Past the servant's quarters, the garage loomed empty, the old family Rolls stationed in its usual spot—

newly repaired, its backseat door fully intact. Banishing all doubt, I snatched the keys from their customary hook and climbed behind the steering wheel before I could talk myself out of the insane plan forming within my brain.

Driving was a terrifying, jerking excursion following Dmitri's scribbled directions, but eventually, I reached my destination unscathed.

A warehouse on the outskirts of the city, its brick façade containing a world of darkness within.

The entrance was unguarded, the door inexplicably unlocked. Perhaps such creatures felt no need to repel potential thieves; after all, they'd simply make for more fodder to sell.

I, for one, was through with having my soul bartered, however.

I barged into the structure with my head held high. A darkened hallway provided little by way of navigation. So I boldly marched from room to room until a furious Saskia appeared within the mouth of a doorway, dressed in a blood-red robe.

"What the hell are you—"

"Summon Raphael," I demanded, cutting her off mid-hiss. "*Now.* I wish to make a bargain."

~

I was afraid the ancient vampire would arrive far past my deadline, giving Dublin plenty of time to track me down—but a chill preceded his arrival before I could panic.

"Eleanor Gray." He stood alone at the back of the chamber Saskia had sequestered me in. Judging from the cavernous space, it was where that impromptu showcase had taken place, though now only two chairs positioned across from each other remained.

Raphael retained his regal aura, even at what I guessed was an unwelcome hour for him. His lifeless eyes honed in on me with interest. Today, in lieu of a cape, he was wearing a simple black suit with an unbuttoned ivory shirt underneath. Visible against the pale skin of his chest hung a silver pendant in the shape of a serpent. As he approached, its red eyes studied me, flickering like hellish flames.

"I was surprised to receive your request, I must admit. To what do I owe this visit?"

"I want to bargain," I confessed, meeting his gaze. "Via contract."

"Oh?" A cold smile twitched over his mouth, quickly suppressed in an instant. "In exchange for Dublin's, I suspect?" His laugh echoed, toneless and hollow. "You hope to trade your time for his. I'm sure I could find a use for you in some capacity."

"No," I admitted, my throat tight. "Not a trade, but a wager. The winner will take everything."

"Everything?" His eyebrow flickered, too frozen to rise fully.

But I had something so powerful and elusive that I knew better to squander it by wasting time: his interest.

"Dublin's time that you have in addition to *mine*. Every year I have left to live. That is what will be on the table."

"Oh?" Another smile twisted his lips, but there was no amusement within the expression. Just hunger. "On what wager?"

"The amount of time doesn't matter," I admitted. "I want us to bet it all on one simple outcome: How will Dublin react when you tell him?"

"With relief, I suspect," Raphael mused, clasping his fingers together. He drifted to the chair across from me and sat. I shivered, subjected to his chill despite the distance. "Pity for you, perhaps, but relief nonetheless. Do you truly think you mean that much to him?" He waited for a second and then sighed as if my silence alone contained my reply. "The man has spent years pining for his time. I am sorry, dear girl, but I believe the answer is too obvious to take advantage of your naivety."

"Even if I claim differently?" In response to the amused tilt of his chin, I lifted a folded slip of paper, previously hidden in my jacket until now. "My guess as to his reaction is on this paper. I'm assuming you'll think he'll leave in gratitude, and if you are correct, then you own us both."

He eyed me in silence. Just when I feared he may never speak, a pink tongue flitted across his lower lip. "And if you win?"

I inhaled raggedly. Even inside my head, the plot seemed insane. Madness.

Something reckless enough to befit the broken little lamb Dublin had described me as.

"If I win, then Dublin is free and you agree to never threaten me or…or our daughter."

"And how do I know that this isn't a planned arrangement?"

Despite everything, I had to laugh, and his eyes narrowed at the hysterical sound.

"Do you really think Dublin would let me meet with you alone, even as part of some harebrained scheme?"

Hence, I was here on a whim, trembling as the seconds ticked past, cutting my brief window of time shorter and shorter.

Raphael cocked his head as if catching a far-off sound. "Of course…" In a dazzling display, his smile widened. "Well, then we have a deal, my dear. And just in time, I suspect."

He turned to the door as a figure appeared there, his eyes blazing silver. They cut to me and he was beside me in an instant, shielding me with his towering frame.

"Eleanor—"

"It's okay," I told Dublin, bracing my hand over his forearm. Coiled muscle lurched beneath my fingertips, readying for battle. "Everything is okay. I've gotten your time back."

"In exchange for her own," Raphael murmured. His eyes danced, portraying something akin to glee. "Every year of her life, sacrificed for you. It is very touching." He brought a pale hand to his chest. "What say you, Dublin? Do you accept this freedom so graciously bestowed upon—"

"No!" In a blur of motion, Dublin whirled on me, his expression agonized. Gripping my shoulders, he yanked me from my chair and shook me so violently that my head jerked back and forth. "Tell me that you didn't—"

"It's too late," I whispered. "It's already done."

"No…" His hands skimmed my shoulders, caressing my throat. Encircling it…

Tightening.

Clenching.

Suffocating.

Gasping, I strained on the tips of my toes. Terror goaded my pulse into a frantic hammering—but whatever I was feeling was nothing compared to what his expression revealed. His eyes glowed, radiating pain and agonized intent. With every ounce of air to escape my lungs, something vital drained from his soul, rendering him hollow.

Lifeless.

Merciless.

And, as if from lightyears away, I heard Raphael…growl.

"Enough."

I broke away, sputtering, clutching my throat. Through watering, burning eyes, I watched Raphael's flicker in my direction. A crumpled piece of paper slipped from his fingers to the floor at his feet.

"Release her," he commanded, though Dublin had already let me go. "Such a foolish game," he hissed.

"But I've won," I declared hoarsely, still rubbing my throat. "Haven't I?"

Raphael said nothing, turning on his heel to leave the room. But his poised frame was trembling. For the first time, he no longer resembled that frozen, emotionless angel. He raged, every bit as vengeful as the serpent hanging from his throat.

Near the threshold of the room, his voice slithered back to reach us, a furious hiss. "You are freed. But trust, Cael, that when you falter. When your pathetic attempts at protection fail. When you require my mercy…I will be waiting. And you will come."

He left, and tension I didn't even know I'd been carrying within me snapped. I fell to the floor on my hands and knees, eyeing my reflection in the polished surface. Who was that wide-eyed woman with the stubborn tilt to her chin? Emotion constricted my chest, more suffocating than the hands that threatened to choke me only seconds earlier.

I wanted to laugh.

I wanted to cry.

I wanted to scream.

"I'm sorry." Dublin stood above me, staring down at his hands, his brow furrowed in agony. "Eleanor, I'm sorry—"

"Don't be." I managed to stand on quivering legs, but rather than comfort him, I crossed to the center of the floor and stooped for the page Raphael had discarded. On it was my scribbled answer. I traced every word as tears escaped down my cheeks, impossible to contain any longer.

Facing Dublin, I held the page out to him.

"I'm just glad that you were honest with me," I whispered. "My bet was that Raphael couldn't guess your reaction, and I was right."

He eyed the paper, scanning the words written on it. A simple phrase in retrospect.

What would Dublin do should I dare to throw my life away on a whim? If I dared to forsake everything he'd sacrificed? If I so much as dreamt of betraying my trust in him?

Nothing short of what I would deserve, I supposed.

He would kill me.

His eyes shot up to mine and I was in his arms within an instant. Our lips met and I tasted salt as my tears flavored the kiss. I was shaking, clinging to him with everything I had as the full weight of what I'd done crashed over me.

In the midst of the turmoil, I almost didn't hear the footsteps approaching. But the slow, callous clapping drew our notice. I stiffened as Dublin's grip shifted into a protective vise.

"Beautiful," Saskia said, her teeth bared in a snarl. Her features seemed grim without the aid of makeup, beneath the harsh, silvery lighting. "So beautiful. So pathetic. So pointless." She laughed, sweeping her gaze from me to Dublin. "I sensed her condition the second I touched her, and yet I didn't tell Raphael. Do you want to know why? No revenge that he nor I could plan would ever match the cruelty of *this*."

She gestured my way with a wave of her hand. "Your Mero is quite the sadistic bastard. She's broken, unable to be turned, but still doomed to die. I could taste her fate like sugar on my tongue." She licked her lips pointedly, her eyes glowing. "And yet you, dearest Cael... You will get to watch her grow old and haggard. You'll get to watch her die, knowing you can't ever slow the relentless march of time. And I will be there to witness every fucking second of it."

She turned on her heel, her laugh echoing throughout the chamber in her absence.

Even as Dublin led me from the warehouse entirely, it echoed.

I couldn't ignore it.

My stunt with Dmitri cost me nearly a full week of freedom. In the chaotic aftermath, Dublin shadowed my every movement. To be fair, it wasn't a particularly unbearable imprisonment.

I was allowed to leave the house at least, if only in the company of my new team of drivers. François had returned from wherever Dublin had held him all this time, looking none too worse for wear—but joining him in the garage was a figure I recognized the moment I spotted him across the foyer one morning.

He stood near the entryway, his hands folded before him, his eyes warily watching my approach. If I'd still felt any anger toward him for deceiving me, all of it faded the instant I saw his face.

"Harper!" I broke decorum—and Gray tradition—by crossing to him and throwing my arms around his shoulders. If I wasn't mistaken he squeezed me in return, just once before withdrawing to a respectful distance and inclining his head.

"At your service, Ms. Gray."

Dublin could be good for something apparently. In addition to Harper's return, he had also ensured that Mr. Tinkles was returned to his private suite and that a majority of the staff was quietly reinstated.

But overall, he was a corrupting presence.

Poor Gray Manor. My childhood home, once the pinnacle of emotionless, joyless living. For so long, the dust-covered walls had witnessed sex in only the most passionless form, as God intended.

But my Devil was so much more creative. By the fourth day, we'd corrupted at least three bedrooms. And the downstairs drawing room. *And* the alcove where the phone was kept in what had begun as a serious attempt to stock the pantry.

After that, Dublin retreated to the kitchen, and I—in an effort to return to normalcy—retreated to my room, ran a brush through my hair, and slipped into a robe.

Down the hall, I peered into a room where Yulia was dutifully keeping vigilance over a figure lying in the bed. "She's still sleeping," she said as I eyed Georgie's gently rising chest. "If she wakes up again, I'll let you know."

Whatever Mero had done to her had drained her body of all energy. Dublin claimed she would recover with time, but consciousness returned in ebbs and flows.

"I promise," Yulia insisted with a nod. She eyed my ensemble and winked. "I'm sure you're hungry, and I can smell something cooking."

When I approached the kitchen, sure enough, the scent of spices and cooking meat had my mouth watering. Even before I drew even with the figure busily at work behind the counter and realized one of two very important things.

The lesser item was that he was doing something incredible with his hands, manipulating a knife through various vegetables at once. The other realization was that he was stark, unashamedly naked.

I should have been appalled, I supposed. Yulia or my sister could intrude at any time, but Dublin was well aware of the limits of my manor and its occupants' positions.

As well as the fact that it was impossible to hear anything occurring in this section of the house from the wing containing my bedroom.

Pale daylight basted his skin, shimmering against the ivory so that he almost appeared silver. Muscle and limbs moved in tandem as he worked. So intent was he that he didn't even look up until I pulled up a stool to the counter and sat.

The moment I did, two gray eyes drifted up to notice me there. Almost instantly, he returned to his task of slicing up raw onions. Then the knife slipped, the blade slicing through the pad of his finger. The wound healed in an instant, even before my cry of shock left my chest.

"You make it hard to focus entirely on your welfare," he told me, his voice a dangerous rasp on the cool air. His eyes found me again, this time leisurely raking over my hastily tied robe.

Yulia, bless her soul, was a goddess. A devious, vengeful one who seemed to relish making Dublin Helos squirm. If only she knew.

"You don't like it?" I innocently fingered an exceptionally crafted collar formed entirely from lace. Ivory lace to be exact. The whole garment in general was composed of delicate lattice-like patterns that extended just above my ankles. Modest in theory, but certainly not in action.

Dublin observed the ensemble with a look that could only be considered aggravated. Carefully, he set the blade aside and wiped his hands on a nearby rag. Then…

His hand shot out, capturing the back of my skull and drawing me in. Cool lips met mine. Briefly. Softly.

Against them, I couldn't help but murmur, "This feels strange…"

Him in my home felt strange. Us interacting in this way felt strange. Strange as in natural. I didn't have to think. It took so much effort to hate him.

"It does," Dublin agreed, drawing back. "You know what else would feel strange?" Suddenly, his mouth was near my ear while one of his hands brushed the collar of my robe, nudging the panels apart. "Me...taking you against the counter, making you clutch it for balance while I..."

Dark scenarios dripped against my earlobe, each one more scandalous than the last.

"I agree," I forced myself to rasp as my cheeks caught fire. "If only I weren't so hungry..." My eyes were on the fangs glinting beneath his upper lip. "Then I might say no."

~

*A*nother presence in my room drew me awake.

Startled, I opened my eyes and fixated on a blurred figure nearby. "Georgie?"

No. Another woman was sitting on the edge of my bed, her skin the shade of caramel, her hair like spun gold coiling down her back. A plain black shirt and jeans disproved her potential as a maid or one of Dublin's henchmen.

I started to sit upright. "Who are—"

"So maybe you aren't entirely boring and worthless," she told me with a sigh while kicking her feet over the floor. "And maybe...you were right. Why can't you take your happiness? Why should *they* have all the fun?" She stood and languidly stretched her arms above her head. "And I must admit you were good to me, even if I *loathed* you at times." Eyeing me from over her shoulder, she stroked something encircling her throat: a light blue strip of velvet with a charm dangling from the center. "It was nothing personal, honestly. Something about that form just makes me despise all affection. As for Dublin, well... I couldn't resist rubbing it in his face, now could I?"

My breath caught. "Mr... Mr. T-Tinkles?"

"I did hate that name though," she hissed, crossing her arms. "Alas, I loved taunting Dublin right beneath his nose more. I can reward you for that. Or perhaps I merely want to pat myself on the back for guessing which sister he'd fall for?" She smirked. "Everyone was sure it would be the other one... But I grow bored of watching him agonize and brood. Besides, it's just not fair if he stays young forever while you age and wither. Eww." She shuddered, twirling to face me.

At a glance, she looked painfully young—younger than I was, even. Though who knew what her true form was, given her affinity for switching sexes as well as species on a whim?

"I've lived far too long for the words of a mortal to have any effect on me, but yours did for whatever reason. You said you deserved your happiness. *So fine.*" She waved toward the hand I had clutching my pillow. "I've enchanted your ring. As long as you wear it, you will never age. Only you have the power to remove it, should you decide that immortality is not to your tastes. And your daughter may have one as well when she comes of age, should you wish. The only caveat is that you cannot tell Dublin—*especially* about my feline form." She fingered her collar-like necklace, still smirking. "Should I need to utilize it again, I would hate for the fun to be ruined so soon. Besides, it will be so much more fun to watch him guess throughout the years. Just imagine ten years from now!" She giggled and skipped to the door. "But enjoy your happiness for however long it may last. And perhaps it's time, I find my own? Goodbye, Eleanor Gray."

I blinked and she had already vanished.

At the top of the grand staircase, I directed the movement of various pieces of furniture. It was a parade of everything from couches, to bed frames, to even a brand-new ivory piano imported from somewhere very expensive.

The frivolity would make my poor mother's head spin.

As would the breathtaking beauty of my sole, one-man "army" of movers.

"That goes in the drawing room," I declared, pointing to a pure-white chaise accompanied by matching armchairs. "Do be careful with it, slave. It's worth more than your yearly wages, I'm sure."

"And this?" the rather bold mover inquired, his gray eyes sparkling with mischief. In his arms was an ivory headboard, contrasting sharply with the ebony hue of his tailored suit. "Wherever does this go, mistress?"

My cheeks flamed. "Upstairs," I said with the air of a queen.

He approached me, mounting the first step. Then he paused, his gaze drifting to someone behind me.

I turned as well, spying a pale figure lurking near the end of the hall.

All thoughts of furniture forgotten, I rushed toward her. "Georgie?"

"I'm okay," she insisted, shrugging off the hand I'd placed on her shoulder. "I'll never get my strength back if you keep coddling me." Her mouth was flattened in determination, but the softness in her eyes robbed any resentment from her tone.

Forcing my arms down by my side, I followed her back into her room.

It'd been over a week since being rescued from under Mero's influence and she still slept for most of the day. Our interactions since had been few and far between. In fact, now might have been the first time she'd had enough energy to speak let alone leave the room on her own.

"It looks like things have changed," she whispered, eyeing me from head to toe. "It feels like I was out for years, not days—"

"I'm so sorry."

She dismissed me with a wave of her hand and sat on the edge of her bed, facing me. "I should be the one who is sorry." She bit her bottom lip, turning her gaze to the floor.

"Everything is still fuzzy, but…" She looked up, meeting my gaze with a sigh. "I remember leaving. I remember walking away, convinced that there was no way to save us. I know we were never close but… I shouldn't have lied to you."

"I wasn't exactly the easiest person to talk to," I admitted, inching closer to her. "I don't think I would have been able to understand, not then."

Her lips parted in a faint smile. "Well, apparently there is still much that I don't understand." Her gaze settled on my stomach, and I sensed that Yulia had attempted to catch her up on some events that had transpired in her absence. "I have been in contact with the Grayne though."

I stiffened. As far as Dublin would say, the faction was in chaos. There had been no further sign of Mero. No attacks. Perhaps he truly was lying in wait for my inevitable death.

Though, for now, my ring still sparkled on my finger, its promise elusive. Would I wear it for eternity, accepting Adara's gift?

"As far as I know, the entire cell has gone into hiding," Georgie explained. "I'm not sure why. But even if I decide not to run Dublin through with a stake"—she lifted her hand, scowling at the trembling fingers—"there is still evil being committed. Far beyond anything you realize. I can't sit back and let our family's legacy just…crumble."

"I know," I whispered, taking yet another step toward her. When I was close enough, I brushed my hand against her shoulder. She didn't flinch beyond my reach. "But we could always start our own legacy?"

She took my hand. "So...how are you planning to redecorate exactly?"

I laughed. "Well, I'm starting with a basic color scheme of white."

~

I left her room hours later and reentered the hall to find my "mover" carrying a piece of furniture down the hall. One I did not remember approving during my impulsive redecorating shopping spree.

My throat tightened as I observed the delicate contours making up the relatively simple square-shaped object. Once Dublin spotted my expression, he paused. His jaw clenched, his gaze wary.

"If you're not ready, I can—"

"No." I swallowed hard and approached him, my shoulders back. As I approached, I hesitantly trailed my fingers along the rim of the item, impressed by the quality of the wood. "It's beautiful," I croaked.

He had gone a step further. On top of the wooden frame was a small mattress draped in white.

"I've been thinking of names," I admitted without looking up. "What about Agatha?"

The silence that fell was deafening. My cheeks heated as the seconds passed until I finally mustered the strength to meet his gaze. His eyes were a stormy silver, a blond eyebrow raised.

"Agatha?" he echoed. "Absolutely not. No child of mine would ever be saddled with such a horrid name."

I narrowed my eyes. "Oh really? Then tell me, what name would please the big, bad Dublin Helos?"

He stroked his chin in genuine contemplation. "Something worthy. Like Drucilla. Or Mildred. Or Cornelia—"

"Cornelia?" I sputtered, my hands on my hips. "You think that is prettier than Agatha?"

"Immeasurably." He circled the cradle to stand before me.

Within a heartbeat, I was in his arms, his mouth near mine.

"Though, I suppose I am willing to negotiate," he told me. With every word, his lips brushed my cheek, sowing a million thrilling sensations I would never be able to fully decipher. "For a price…"

Hey there!

Thank you so much for reading! If you enjoyed the story, please leave a review and recommend the book to any friend you think would love this twisted world. You'd have my eternal gratitude. Even a short sentence goes a long way!

Then, come join the rest of us dark romance lovers in my Facebook Group where you can get snippets, sneak peeks of upcoming books and even help vote on aspects of future novels.

Come to the dark side:
https://www.facebook.com/groups/lanasbeautifulmonsters/

WANT MORE STUFF TO READ?
Join my newsletter and get a **free book**! Plus, you get to stay updated with any new releases, random giveaways and exclusive sneak peeks!
https://www.lanaskybooks.com/newsletter

Other Novels: https://lanaskybooks.com/

FREE BOOK - JOIN MY NEWSLETTER

DARK, TWISTED ROMANCE

Join my newsletter and get a **free book**! Plus, you get to stay updated with any new releases, random giveaways and exclusive sneak peeks!

https://www.lanaskybooks.com/newsletter

ABOUT THE AUTHOR

Lana Sky is a reclusive writer in the United States who spends most of her time daydreaming about complex male characters and parenting her Cockapoo Joey. She writes dark, twisted romance across several genres. Her titles include everything from mafia romance to vampires.

facebook.com/AuthorLanaSky

twitter.com/lanasky101

amazon.com/author/lanasky

pinterest.com/lanasky101

goodreads.com/lanasky

instagram.com/lanasky101

bookbub.com/authors/lana-sky

ALSO BY LANA SKY

For more titles by Lana Sky, please visit:
https://www.lanaskybooks.com

www.ingramcontent.com/pod-product-compliance
Lightning Source LLC
Chambersburg PA
CBHW071423190726
48292CB00001B/94